A COMFORTABLE CORNER

A COMFORTABLE CORNER

Vincent Virga

THE LIBRARY OF HOMOSEXUAL CONGRESS
NEW ORLEANS & NEW YORK

Published in the United States of America by
REBEL SATORI PRESS
www.rebelsatoripress.com

Cover illustration based on John Paradiso's Vintage Pansy collage,
property of Vincent Virga

ISBN: 978-1-60864-337-0

For J. with love and admiration
and for my Others
and
In memory of
Jackson Pollock
1912-1956

To Elisa Rolle, the godmother of this edition

There is nothing permanent except change.

HERACLITUS

And perhaps the way he saw everything was the right way, though there could be no right way but one's own.

HENRY GREEN
Blindness

. . . I keep circling this one small silly street in this one small town. . . I'm scared to leave it, that's what, as if I guess once away from it I'll be inside something empty, black, and endless. . .. So I keep circling madness!—but I love it, what I see below! And I just can't bring myself to give it up, it's that simple—just can't bring myself to give it up! Then I know I have to. It's a luxury I can't afford. Fuel is running low, almost gone, may be too late anyway, so—I pull the nose up, kick the rudder, bank, and head out into darkness all in terror! GOD, BUT IT TAKES EFFORT! JUST DON'T WANT TO DO IT!. . . But I do. Actually, odd thing, once I did, broke free, got into the dark, found I wasn't even scared . . . Or was I? Can't remember. . . Wonder where that town was . . . ?

ARTHUR KOPIT
Wings

VINCENT'S TREASURE CHEST

Eileen Myles

Vincent's *A Comfortable Corner* is skewed to please a certain audience: ex-Catholics, gays, New Yorkers and people involved or interested in the culture of publishing in the early eighties, anyone interested in the transformative powers of alcoholism and sobriety, the effects of alcoholism AND sobriety on the narrative of relationships, more specifically gay male ones, friendships between gay women and gay men, friendships period. I'm pretty much thinking I could make this entire introduction a list, a menu of sorts of what this gay recovery chronicle has also got. I think about pornography as writing that has a purpose, and I think when Vincent sat down to write this book, he meant to tell amidst the myriad of other things sailing around in its borders the story of someone getting better. Someone who in all likelihood should only be getting worse. A charming beautiful enormously talented gay male poet who seemed hellbent on dying and the story is told from the perspective of his long-suffering partner, Terence which (indulge me!) happens to be my brother's name and my father's name and my grandfather's name and by now it's my dog's middle name, Honey Terence Myles, she is. This *Corner* also a cat lover's book. There's a charming moment when in the midst of a flirtation with a conductor on metro north Terence discovers the woman suddenly occupying the seat next to him has a cat in a duffle bag on her lap and it's a white Persian, the same cat he Terrence has and hungrily as we do he absorbs the details of his cat's recent injury and it winds up providing the missing piece for the book Terence is almost putting to bed. He *needed* that cat and we do too. The moment the woman and her cat disrupt Terence's momentary sexual distraction becomes a rich private interspecies (and I mean man woman cat all of it in that gathering adjective) interaction that's profound in its commonality and even just a heartfelt illustration of how humans need to shift time, falling into another's situation, linking it to mine, ours and feeling the world is full of cats and satchels right next to my sex life and my writing life of course. *A Comfortable Corner* is a novel of great and small interactions. It's totally relational in that everyone suffers and then they turn to someone else and something else happens. It's a precise account because this is the world in 1982, its technology, its cultural references, its elitism, its unprotected sex, the shamelessness of mostly white privilege while we watch our characters fall vertically into gutters and deaths that could be anyone's. Or everyone's. Booze (as well as cats and sex) is the great levelling force in all these characters lives. I've never read another book that frankly talks about how the behaviors of those surrounding the chronic alcoholic are chronic too. I read *A Comfortable Corner* more than forty years ago. A friend handed it to me when I was trying to change my life. I bombed through its gleeful coziness and was delightedly puzzled that so much beautiful writing (and Vincent Virga is a beautiful writer – just go see for yourself – such passages! He *does* nature and bodies and cityscapes and food, he does everything in a lusty detailed rush in time) can also deliver a message because this is a book probably most of all for someone – well two someones, those interested in recovery and interested in a pitch perfect account of gay life and all the other surrounding lives I've mention in 1982 a moment just before everything happened and I'm thinking of AIDS and a lot of technology that's invisible now and an enormous reshuffling of who spent time with who and how and even what publishing was willing to do over the next ten years and then never again. There was a comfortable corner in publishing in 1982 and this fast and charming and heart wrenching novel came out as the roller coaster was just mounting the first big hill. Soon we will go down (and then on and on) but you shoulda been there and now you can and I love Vincent's vital message that *you* can get better too. I did.

O N E

Quickly, the sentence vaulted. Verbs grouped, enacting vivid maneuvers to coax two characters, men in their mid-thirties, into the narrator's pound net. Discovered in Neary's, a Dublin pub, these touring Americans squabbled. After sixteen years of wedlock, one wanted out; a separation would ensue. Distraught and frantic, Harold was to dump a half pint of Guinness into snide Geoff's corduroy-lap. Local citizens adept at overhearing milled around the odd-men Yanks while continuing their own rackety palaver. A barmaid delivered the healthy stout on cue. Bitchy dialogue was about to crescendo in Harold's histrionics, silencing every nosy, eye-bulging onlooker and forcing Harold, shamed and sobbing, to flee from the booze-sipping, broad-grinning, whispering collection down the alley into Grafton Street.

The telephone rang. Terence Strange, working author, paused. Suspended, his sentence collapsed, the words disbanded, and characters bolted as his active imagination stalled on hold.

Shit!

Checked, he picked up the receiver and grunted. The cat, curled by his elbow, stirred, stretched, and made off toward the kitchen.

"Terence! Have I disturbed your work?"

Using the voice perfected on children but soothing to all animals, Judith sounded tense but honestly concerned.

"No . . . it's OK."

Not really, damnit! Always so fucking civil.

"I thought you landed for elevenses."

"Is it eleven?"

Can't be. Would she lie?

He sighed. Outside, ample unattractive snow fell.

"It's eleven-ten, darling."

Cranky! Very moody lately. Needs a tumble.

What does *she want?*

"Will you come to dinner Saturday?"

His distraction became patrol-dog alertness.

No!

"Please, Terence! Don't say no without hearing me out."

"I'm hearing you out."

Hear her out.

While she hastily outlined her argument, he watched two large, winter-white rabbits scurry across the rear, snow-covered lawn, jump the stone retaining wall, and disappear into the area of the summer garden below. He sighed, remembering how rapacious cute furry bunnies could be, then recalled Judith's leg of spring lamb the previous Saturday. Most of Sunday had been lost counting caps of Brioschi; not that she could be indicted for his gross appetite.

"We're having Japanese. Misou soup, shrimp teriyaki, marinated vegetables, green tea ice cream. Nothing heavy. No thick brown gravy, darling."

"Hmmnnn . . ."

Terence was shamelessly partial to gravy. He had gorged himself, then feebly blamed the thick brown gravy.

"Hmmnnn . . ." he repeated, weakened by hunger and harpooned by the intention in Judith's patient silence. He eyed the accumulating snow. Could he get his car up their deathtrap of a drive?

"Gerald will bring the Jeep for you, darling."

He smiled, touched by her prescience. Although the tension was no longer evident, something made her words sound crisper than usual, neatly accentuating her acquired New England accent.

"And Gerald *promises* to behave himself."

Terence moaned theatrically. He had forgotten about Gerald's foolishness. Judith, fearing imminent disaster, hastily regrouped her strengths.

Damn!

"Gerald should mind his own business, Judith."

[2]

"He feels you and Christo *are* his business."

"Gerald is a silly romantic."

"So they tell me, darling. Too late, I may add."

She covered the receiver and snapped a command.

Jolted, Terence discovered her in her New York office. He was flustered by not knowing from the start; it altered specifics and made him uncomfortable as her business surroundings dropped clumsily into his mind like the painted flats of a stage set. He had missed his cue. He was relating to her disembodied voice as if it were projected from a visible low-hanging cloudbank, the second balcony of his workaday world. Andrew Desmond, the odious assistant, could be heard through her clamped fingers bitching the jacket design of a book on the spring list.

Monday to Friday, Judith Gunning was employed in New York City as a senior editor by Voyager Press; Saturdays, Sundays, and holidays she was, in Sharon, Connecticut, wife to Gerald and mother to two children: Deirdre, nine, and Gerald, Jr., eight. This was her schedule. Except for the occasional extended work-weekend, it had not varied the three years Terence had worked with her. What was today? Wednesday? A sense of fevered displacement swallowed his heart whole. Disconsolate, he tilted his head and stared at the white ceiling. There seemed nothing he could do to avoid this particular sorrow. A relentless, ulcerating grief lurked behind everything. A lapse of attention, an uncooperative household object, an unexpected physical sensation would swivel him into this state of confusion. After eleven years of living with Christopher and loving him utterly, all seemed of a piece. He applied the remedies strenuously.

Not appropriate. I'm alive and well and living in Amenia.

"Are you still there, Terence?"

"Yes, of course."

"There's someone I want you to meet."

He closed his eyes. Slowly, pulling in a practiced deep breath, he felt the anxiety dissolve, generating a rush of energy. He raised his eyebrows and commanded himself to take a bow.

"Please say yes, darling. Say you'll come to dinner so your favorite editor can get on with passing this *drek* manuscript for press."

"Who's your friend?"

"A famous neighbor, just signed to do a book for me. I invited him and *he* said yes without a peep. I think the two of you will *adore* one another."

"What does *that* mean?"

"It means, darling, that he's brilliant and charming and the shy, reclusive type. A 'member of the committee,' I'm assured, who—"

"Yes!" he interrupted, laughing. "Yes, all right."

She covered the receiver once again, braying, "What the fuck do you want *now*, Andrew?" then returned to Terence with an abrupt, "Go take your tea, darling. Talk to you later."

Instantly, he wanted a raincheck. Holding the dead receiver, he gazed dumbly out the window.

I can always change my mind. Or sing Isolde for the Met broadcast. Or pluck my eyes out with hot spoons.

He knew he would go. He wanted to be with Judith, to lounge with her and that back number Gerald in their comfortable mock-Tudor palace, to gobble their superb food, and even—he baldly admitted—to encounter her mysterious stranger. This solitude needed ending. He felt the suck of loneliness and expertly sidled away from self-pity.

Don't! Spare me. No larghetto. Thank you. Put some Mozart on the Victrola.

Judith's telephone performance, concluding without revealing the new leading man's identity, amused him. All publishing folk were histrionic, related to "picture people," with their deals and contracts and percentages, thriving on crises, using each book's production schedule to generate a dozen opening-night panics; but somehow Judith managed the *mishagas* stylishly. She rarely grew tiresome. Even when profoundly unhappy, her too-frequent condition, she cared how others felt most of the time. Gerald was another matter.

Gerald would make Saint Jude lose heart.

Terence never understood her not mulching Gerald. It was the second marriage for each; that might have something to do with it.

Why did I stay with Christopher through all the illness, all the madness! Because you loved him, Terence. Simple. Nothing is *that simple! Where have you been, Kukla? You stayed because you got plenty from him. You stayed because you could not leave. The disease would not allow you to go. And if you had somehow managed it what would you have done with your next alcoholic? Eighty-five per cent of us find another.*

Judith was no longer young, though forty-five was by adult reckoning not old. There were two children. Knowing little of children's emotional impact on parents, he graded them a superior reason, then jumped to more familiar commodities.

Children, like alcoholics, provoke complete retreat from rationality.

Their house was cluttered with treasures big-time museums unabashedly coveted: furniture, china, books, brasses, carpets, and Impressionist paintings ("Grandpa loved pretty colors.") That ridiculous manse alone, he reckoned, was reason enough. Twelve years before, while driving through England on their honeymoon, Judith and Gerald Gunning stopped in North Devon, at Cheriton Fitzpane. It was inevitably suggested by the courteous innkeeper that they visit Cheriton Barton, the historic house in the district. They meandered in its fateful direction. Gerald's startled reaction, his usual response to perfection, was, "I want it. I want it *now.*"

Judith later swore she quipped, "Ask your mother," intending no malice. "I said it as a joke," she insisted monotonously, voice rising.

"What a great idea!" Gerald said he said. "I will. She's been searching high and low for a wedding gift."

"She's already given us all that land, darling."

"And I know what for, precious."

When the current owner, the fourteenth to bear the title, grasped Gerald's intent to box and transport his home and heritage to two hundred acres of prime Connecticut land, he began to behave like an exasperated English character actor in one of the early talkies. Red-faced, sputtering and stammering, he politely excused himself; a servant showed the couple out.

"Gerald?" Judith whispered as they wandered in the maze with other bewildered American tourists. "Something tells me His Grace was not tickled by your New World notions."

"Fuck 'im."

Judith nodded, assuming the issue stashed away like the swiped Cheriton Barton primrose pressed in her dutifully kept journal. She was aware that her husband was childishly extravagant. She was not yet cognizant, however, of how the Gunning fortune was managed, or how he finagled to live on it as though it were his own bottomless kitty. She spun the happiest fancies. He did nothing to disenchant her. They never discussed finance, that was all. She had gone through school on a scholarship; she remembered the checks being there when promised. It was *obvious* that Gerald was lusciously rich. Logically, she was not perplexed by his petulant tenacity or his animal smarts; she considered them a sort of binding on the inherited bundles. In later years, whenever she related the saga over cocktails, Judith headlined and underscored a warning she would have done well to heed.

"But I was young, and he was the best lay I'd ever had."

Gerald had telephoned his indulgent mother, Veronica Gunning, who thought the idea of copying Cheriton Barton a charming and original one; she promised to get cracking and did. While she arranged for blueprints, the newlyweds were set adrift by her generosity and joyfully completed their four-month tour of Europe's three-star restaurants.

They sailed back to Gerald's home in the exclusive township of Sharon. That first address, a perfect red-brick early-American specimen ringed with enormous willow trees on an acre of manicured lawn, was Judith's urban-childhood dream of a home. Though meticulously redecorated while the "youngsters" were abroad, it was not viable to Vera; it was "soiled" by the presence of Melissa, the first Mrs. Gerald Gunning ("Is she walled up in the attic, darling?"). Judith brooded. As the second Mrs. Gerald Gunning, would she be allowed to decorate the second Cheriton Barton? Resigning from her moderately successful editorial career with a vanity press "to build a nest and reproduce," she

[6]

noisily studied interior decorating and became a favorite at the country club where she (a closet Jew) and Gerald had met while celebrating his cousin's (her Radcliffe roommate's) wedding. Gerald commenced scribbling ideas for an epic novel that would make them an independent fortune.

"I thought we *were* an independent fortune."

At this juncture, the egregious misconceptions were clumsily and painfully sorted. Eventually it dawned that Mother Vera held a headlock on the vast Gunning estate. Gerald managed on a "small" competence ("You call *that* small?"), and was dependent on the matriarch's sense of justice for most *divertissements*. Judith heeded this one. She vigilantly kept all her contacts in the publishing world against the unforeseen contingencies that she clearly foresaw.

One year later, they moved into the replica of Cheriton Barton, now an anniversary present. Gerald's Tudor delight was not an exact copy. The proportions were adjusted to spare three white birches in the grove, where the house was hidden like an immense stolen jewel. Judith quietly arranged the priceless antiques that Vera delivered by the truckload. Gerald devoted himself to the house's upkeep and to its grounds, The Park, as the hefty acreage was now smartly christened.

Deirdre, their first child, was named for Gerald's maternal grandmother, an ancient familial dreadnaught still hobbling around the earth. Gerald set about building "She-Baby" a stone playhouse modeled on a castle in one of Morgan Connelly's glorious children's books, a project which occupied him for a full year. Architecture had long been Gerald's passion. ("Oh?") He patiently drew and redrew complex plans for the fairy-tale structure he'd envisioned; completed, it seemed perched on a knoll miles away rather than within calling distance from the kitchen door; and the small stream he diverted for its moat sounded from the bedroom windows like an open garden hose. As soon as the castle's colors were raised, he was ready to construct for the newborn "He-Baby" a fort from another Connelly tale with similar precision (and similar expense) on the opposite side Of the house.

During the following years, other elaborate projects were successfully financed: an oval pond, an "enchanted" picnic dell, a more scenic driveway, a greenhouse for orchids, a cherry orchard, a formal Japanese garden, and a marble pool for *koi* in a heated "retreat." Each had effortlessly clipped chunks off his yearly stipend, or were made possible by a special grant from "Grandmama" Vera. (The procedures followed to receive funding were as complicated as any required by a corporate foundation or by the state and federal government.) Soon Gerald's priorities necessitated Judith's hustling for contributions "to keep this show on the road."

She telephoned every editor she knew in New York asking for freelance work, idly offering a touch of boredom as her excuse for ending the sybaritic existence in Illyria. Eager for good help, they were only too elated to send her at first their less interesting manuscripts, eventually trusting her with their big books to free themselves from the tedium of line editing for the more serious business of acquiring manuscripts over breakfast, lunch, drinks, and dinner. Judith Gunning became a renowned and treasured master with a blue pencil. It gave her visceral delight to organize blocks of text properly, to aggressively clip stray thoughts, tighten loose verbal constructions, and suggest more powerful or more appropriate adjectives. She had a finely tuned feeling for verbs, a precise ear for dialogue, and an innate sense of build and climax. Her cottage industry burgeoned. The money she made became essential to the Gunnings' survival. Permanent job offers proliferated. Delighted by her success, Gerald bought her an eight-cylinder faun Mercedes for Christmas.

"Much hubbier than repairing the burner, sweetpuss."

Disgruntled, Judith joined Voyager Press as a senior editor in the Trade Division. They were one of the largest publishing houses in America but she foresaw little difficulty holding her own. "Swimming with barracudas," she labeled her career, half in disgust and half in self-regard as her ability to survive and succeed in the "real" world became more and more evident. She possessed the requisite casual cunning to handle the intricate political maneuvering, as well as the temperament, the essential ferocious drive to ascend. But, most importantly, she had cultivated an unerring talent for scenting best-seller potential in a property or in a personality. Within seven months from her starting date, she took an apartment on Park Avenue and Seventy-fourth Street. Gerald immediately hired a housekeeper.

Always physically attractive, Judith became "interesting" as she neared forty, then graduated to "glamorous" as stardom tackled her. She heightened her *zaftig* qualities with a painter's eye for line and form and chiaroscuro. Her natural red hair was "adjusted" to titian one winter weekend. She frequented a Nautilus-equipped "spa" to keep herself "womanly"; she ate with a maniacal attention to caloric intake; she worked incessantly, reading voraciously "with the same attention that a nun pays while telling her beads," she boasted; and as suited her image, she dressed only in designer clothing.

As Gerald grew older, he became noticeably plump and appropriately gray at the short-sideburned temples. His patrician features softened, then settled, and his Republican attitudes hardened. In the classically unimaginative tradition, he assumed himself misunderstood, a man who never found himself, although Judith insisted he had been wise not to interrupt his habitual state of fugue: "The world's shelves are already overstocked with party favors." Rejecting the Freudian scheme for a more sacramental idea of nature, he developed a passion for the writings of Mary Baker Eddy. He learned to accept with a stoic grace Vera's impregnable health, and to play the role of eternal suppliant with patient good humor and endless good sense. At this point, Terence stumbled over him.

"I thought I could change him," Judith had told Christopher one lazy, hot Sunday while they boated on the skating pond. Though she was Terence's editor at Voyager, it was Christopher she most comfortably confided in at regular intervals over cocktails. "I thought I could gather his dormant forces and *shape* them, such as they are, darling, develop his *talents*, you know, *invent* him, so to speak. I thought I could do for him what Terence has so brilliantly done for you. "

"And what did you say to *that?*" Terence queried Christopher later, dressing for dinner.

"I *said* it seemed reasonable to me."

Terence had been neither pleased nor surprised. Changes were occurring that would alter everything. Christopher still sensed nothing.

"I would have died without you," Christopher added with a sodden half smile.

Now, years later, solemnly watching snow collect on the top of the stone retaining wall, Terence mulled over the conditions of his solitary life. He hastily reminded himself how it had developed. He tended to forget the route. He tended to treat his life like a sentence vaulting at someone else's command. He tended to discover himself arrived without recalling having booked a seat.

I tend to tend.

Cut adrift from Christopher after eleven years of married life, he thought: He would have died without me. He was dying with me all the while.

Opening his notebook, he wrote hurriedly: "The rocks in her head fit the holes in his. Like C and me. It is impossible to fathom love relationships. Most of the time it's hard enough to swim with one's own. Who can reckon where *wants* end and muckle-mouthed addiction begins? Like trying to discern sea from sky at pale-silver dusk. *Please* stuff it re J and G. Live and let live."

———

Christopher More awoke alone, frightened, and despairing.

Parched, he fantasized drowning in an icy sea. Recurrent failures provoked quixotic thoughts on death's opacity and stillness.

> *No path, abysses, death is not so still!*
> *You wished it, left the path by your own will.*
> *Now remain cool and clear, 0 stranger;*
> *For you are lost if you believe in danger.*

There was no reason to continue this messy charade. Why not finish it *now* while he still retained his looks, while a decent-sized crowd could be corralled with a few good friends to say a few kind words? Terence would manage it beautifully; he would boss everybody and dress the set superbly.

Christopher declared himself fated for an early quietus. It was a curse like lycanthropy. His grandfather had disappeared into a rolling cask at about the age he was now. His father was decidedly checking out, taking a little longer but dropping through the same ferret hole. Christopher strained to recall their recent meeting. He could remember nothing specific.

Wasn't it last night? What did I wear?

Reaching for the bedside water glass, he saw scrawled on a pad the name of a restaurant where they had met for dinner: a ritzy Italian dive. He had worn his gray tweeds. Had they eaten? He had resolved not to drink but he knew by the absence of knowing that he had. He drank because he could not stop. Every attempt led to this scabrous reality. His head thundered with a Bergian vengeance. His brain craved oxygen. He loathed failure. He loathed Christopher More.

Oxygen. Dreams and fantasy, the oxygen of the heart I cannot stop. Why torture myself? Kid myself? Christ!

His father, an emotional reef, surfaced in his thoughts. Self-pity shifted from his own consistent weakness to the loss of his father who, at each monthly meeting, seemed craggier, more eroded, and further vacated by life. He loved his father. Besides Terence, he loved no one else. The man had formed him. The man had inculcated what was most valuable; he had nurtured the art, the need to verbalize life. He had encouraged and enforced the discovery of style as the true subject of composition; joy in words was the key. He had informed a worship for wordplay and awakened the inherited lust for the perfect Manhattan's perfect peace. It was now, lately, called a disease. Christopher thought that cunning.

Some say love is a disease.

His father was the quickest, wittiest, best-read man he would ever know. Could anyone make words on a page burst into bloom so wonderfully? Did anyone view human foibles so compassionately? What did the loss of Christopher matter when measured against the loss of a William More? And, he was undeniably lost. Lost in the same descent, in a place farther along on the road to hell as himself. It was their fate. It was a family curse, a family tradition. Terence was right to fold his tent and move on. This was an absurd and disgusting way to spend one's days. But there was nothing to be done.

I've tried, God knows.

Aimlessly, he slid a shaking hand under his many pillows. There he found a folded piece of white paper.

Hate mail from the tooth fairy?

To his astonishment, he recognized his own sonnet, one of the earliest, written in the dizziest, most succulent first weeks of his passion for Terence, written when they were still in graduate school. It had been recklessly torn from an old notebook and tucked away like a totemic square of wedding cake. To bring sweet dreams by bribing the bitch goddess? It had not worked.

She cannot be had like a salted tear, for a tattered amorous ditty.

He was flailed by fearful dreams of destruction and death. He never awakened in the morning; he *fled* into the conscious state, heart pounding from the climb, glancing backward, feeling himself crumble into grains of caustic salt.

Salt Not sugar, mind. Preserve remorse.

The loss of Terence was a constant anguish.

"Double pain is easier to bear/Than simple pain. Do you accept my dare?" I never said it would be easy. Now *he's fatootsed!*

His loneliness was insufferable. The shame was considerable but of least importance; shame had become an inventive way of life. He was totally alone. There was no money. (The last of the loathsome books by other people had been dumped at the Strand.) The drinking alleviated feelings of abandonment but immediately, or so it always seemed, *immediately* revoked its gift of omnipotence, and exacerbated what it cured by taking the useless remnants of himself from his own poor company, leaving him truly desolate.

He could not work. Not the real work he knew his best verse to be. If he could stop, he would stop for his work. For seconds, as night's terrors dispersed, before the day's convened, there was an inanimate calm ("Hour of the Wolf, deathtime, toots!") when he remembered a life not controlled by booze. He yearned for it again. Now, momentarily at peace, he read his sonnet to Terence aloud:

"Crouched sitting—sibling penitents—we two
Upon the stair, above the cold, beneath
The light and music in the room, re-knew
The consequence of drawing common breath;
So much so and so simply, undenied
And so on to the next and next resolve
That we—not you, not I, but I beside
Myself as you, as one times one, told love
Stories about the stairs, about the snow
And how the nights' symphonic hush of time
Plays silences from no machine we know
Whose harmonies make our joy-blind eyes rhyme.
And so absolved we did forgive the night
Self-trusting then the dark; now next: the light.

"Not bad for a lovesick ingenue. Once upon a time the world was sweeter than we knew. . . . I'll use it. Angelo will never know."

He smiled He must talk to Terence. If they could talk together, really talk together without Terence doing his Rumpelstiltskin impersonation, everything could be resolved. Obviously Terence did not understand. Christopher was trying hard. It was not his fault. Right now he needed all the help he could get from his friend.

Go make tea. Skip the liebestod.

He gulped the brown dregs in the glass on the desk. There was money: a fistful of crumpled bills and the rent check. As usual, his father had come across.

Terence rose from his desk and walked into the kitchen to light the fire under the copper kettle. On the spotless wooden counter, the dark blue tea canister was beside the empty teapot. Irish breakfast tea first in the morning, lapsang souchong at eleven and three, Earl Grey after dinner, and chamomile at bedtime. He did not fret that tannic acid dyed his stomach mud brown; he classified it a baroque worry. The tea ceremonies gave the aromatic semblance of a structure that curtailed encompassing chaos.

Tea. My life is tea. Measured out in teaspoons. Days linked by rings around empty teacups. Gadzooks!

The kitchen was a large, usually bright room. Even today, with a flaking gothic sky, he did not feel the need for electric light. (Christopher never understood this proclivity to survive even when rich without blazing bulbs in every corner.) Terence loved the kitchen. Cabinet-filled, with a vast bay window, it offered the length of Oblong Valley. This glorious view was the single most important factor in his decision to buy the place. The seclusion, the apple orchard, the walnut tree, the seven-story ancient Dutch elm the size of the house—now a constant worry with its vulnerability to insect-bearing blight—the ten acres of forest land, the price, all had persuaded; but the romantic perspective convinced them. They made the necessary repairs and did one piece of minor surgery: The living room's rear window was replaced by a sliding glass door that gave access to a small field of unweeded lawn as well as brightening the room immeasurably. Terence set his desk there before the carpenter had finished sealing the frame.

The kettle boiled. He warmed the teapot and carefully measured the fragrant leaves.

They first viewed the house on a snowy November day. Judith spotted the for-sale sign while racing to the station in Dover Plains. She dispatched Gerald to nose around, and it was he who called them in Manhattan with the cheerful news that the long march was ending victoriously. There had never been a true campaign, only a convenient excuse for lovely rides on autumnal weekends with the desired house a reason powerful enough to galvanize them into enjoying the foliage or visiting historic covered bridges or raiding country stores stocked with apple cider, homemade preserves, and warm plaid woolen shirts for Christopher's "rough trade" look. Gerald referred to that period of their joint lives as the "questful days," as though all demons would be exorcised when both their homes were safely secured.

The telephone rang again. Carrying the teapot to the round oak table by the window, he stood for several moments struggling against fear, reassuring himself it was no longer appropriate. He could manage most things now. It was human to feel these disturbances, but he must not let them rule him. These were the ways of withdrawal. He panicked when anxiety prickled, as though he were set ablaze.

"Blame it on them fuckin' nuns," he muttered, reaching for the phone.

Christopher's voice was rough with sleep and sounded harshly in the dazzling stillness of the kitchen. Terence was swept by a surge of sadness, which he methodically squashed before it betrayed him and swelled into crippling grief or gnawing self-pity. Every emotion could miraculously metamorphose into rancid blubber; every emotion had to be scrutinized. It was wearying, but less wearing on the sympathetic nervous system than the disease's despair.

"How's it going up there?"

"Fine, Chris. I'm fine. This one is easier than the last."

"They're supposed to get more difficult."

"So they tell me."

He thought of Judith and automatically felt sorry that Christopher was not to be with them for Japanese Saturday. The silent image of him drunk and unruly at the table, wailing opera arias to a bemused mysterious stranger, stilled regrets at once.

"My stuff isn't moving, T."

"It will. It always does."

If you stop drinking long enough.

He almost quoted: "Verse is more difficult; the finer calibration," but he clammed shut. He no longer believed it was the reason, thank Christ.

He drinks because he drinks.

"Yes, I'm sure you're right, T. You always are."

"Not always. How are you feeling, Chris?"

Damn! None of my fucking business. Mouth always flapping!

Annoyed, he shook his head. He had not intended to ask. It

was a habit, a reflex action not yet replaced by one less conducive to stirring the shit.

"Fucking awful! I'm not in my right body somehow."

"I'm sorry, Chris."

"No you're not, either. How are you?"

"I'm OK."

"Don't you get lonely up there? Or have you got someone with you?"

Terence laughed.

"I don't see what's so funny. I wouldn't blame you."

"Nor I you."

"Nobody would want me."

"Oh?"

Since when? Six-two, blurbed in the mags the sexiest poet around. Nobody want you? Right! Uh-huh!

"Well, that is not *completely* true, T. Star fuckers would want me but I'm not interested in them anymore. *You* won't have any trouble. You still look the same as when I first balled you eleven years ago. I look like shit."

Terence gulped hot tea. Sorrow was stitching his throat closed and the pressure blew out what felt like the inner tubing of his heart. It flattened. Instinctively, he sat down.

I could always not answer the phone. Or pull the plug out of the wall Or hide under the bed Or—

"Yup, Terry-luv, you still look as young as when we met, still look like rosy fucking-fingered dawn."

"I've got my cracks and crevices."

Anxiety and anger aren't exactly moisturizing creams, fella.

Terence said nothing more. Noticing his cigarettes on the table, he lit one, his first of the day. The nicotine made him lightheaded. Violently, he stubbed it out, literally pounding it to death.

"Nobody ever calls me, T., now that *you're* gone. I feel as if I've got the heartbreak-of-psoriasis."

"No one cares, Chris."

None of our friends cares. They're sick of it. Sick of you falling headlong into the soup. Sick of me being sick of you.

"What are you doing for sex?" Christopher asked nonchalantly.

"Taking care of it myself."

"All you need is a lover and you'll be fine. A woman would solve everything."

Terence laughed again, familiar with this ploy.

"I like men. Men stimulate my imagination. I don't want a lover. I love you."

"Then why aren't we together?"

"You know why."

"I'm not drinking."

"I don't want to pay for it. I don't want to watch you die."

Simple enough. Clear. Lucid.

"Bullshit!"

"I don't want to talk about any of this. You know why I'm not with you."

He felt the abyss scissoring through his diaphragm. If he toppled in, he knew he would start howling. Glancing out the window, he eyed a single cardinal hovering among the laurel branches.

Alone. Like me. Shit! Avoid cheap metaphor.

The abyss sutured closed. Saved, he sighed. His heart inflated. It wobbled. Christopher was waiting. There was a lifeless silence between them.

"What are you doing today, Chris?"

None of your business!

"Having lunch with Judith."

"Give her my love."

"I might."

"Good-bye, Chris. I love you."

"No you don't, and it's a sin to tell a lie."

"I'm sorry you feel that way."

Christopher hung up. For the second time that morning, Terence frowned at a useless contraption held aloft in his fist.

"I don't have to answer the goddamn thing!" he explained to the cardinal. The bird, joined by its mate, flew away, oblivious to the distress of the human standing behind the thermal glass. He watched the two birds perch on a common, bare branch.

"Avoid cheap metaphor," he repeated aloud, smiling. Immediately, he dialed Thomas S. at work. While he waited for Mister Steiner, he was stabilized. The deflating leak was contained. There were few program friends with last names he knew.

"Thomas! It's Terence."

"Terence! How good to hear your voice. You OK?"

"Yes. I'm fine."

Thomas chuckled. Often at meetings, Terence recounted that no matter the extent of his disturbance, no matter the crazed estate of his mind, when asked how he felt, his denial mechanically answered "Fine!" It took years for him to realize that he had not been imparting information but reassuring himself, convincing *himself* that despite the chaos of his life, everything was under control.

"Fine?"

Terence laughed, steadied.

"Really, I'm OK. Christopher just called."

"How'd it go?"

"Well enough, I guess. I got angry but we didn't fight. I said: I love you.' He said: 'No you don't.' I made a neutral noise: 'I'm sorry you feel that way.' It defused the bomb. That's one of the best things I've learned. How's Robin?"

"He is *truly* fine."

"How long is it now?"

"Over sixty days."

"Thomas, has everyone stopped drinking but Chris?"

"He hasn't hit his bottom."

"Well, I've certainly hit mine."

Have I?

"You going to meetings?"

"On and off."

"A lot of people are still drinking, Terence. Watch out for self-pity. I can hear it oozing into your voice."

"I know. I love you, Thomas."

"We all miss you."

"Give Robin my love."

[18]

"Anything else you wanted to talk about?"

"No. I just wanted to clear my head. My heart was tumbling like a knotted sock in a dryer. How are you?"

"I'm doing well enough. Sobriety is a tricky time. We think all of our problems will go away once they stop drinking. Well, t'ain't so. His drinking didn't cause my problems. I did. Still do. Tricky time. Lots of meetings for both of us."

"You sound all right."

"I am. You take care, Terence. I love you, too." Relaxed, he sipped tepid tea and made a resolve to attend a meeting. It was Wednesday. He remembered the meeting in Sharon was Wednesday. Was that why he forgot what day it was?

T W O

Christopher tried willing himself back to sleep. He knew he would not, could not, but the attempt was soothing, something like sweated labor. He lay in dread of another convulsion; the last had sent him spastically hobbling to heave up the tea brewed before the call to Terence. He roasted with guilt for slamming down the phone. He no longer understood Terence. He reckoned himself abandoned and possibly afraid.

I will show you fear in a handful of dust.

After a calm interval, he raised himself to a sitting position. His limbs were shaking and the world beyond his physical discomfort was out of reach. An excruciating ache pulsed in a conga line down the muscles of his tense neck and meanly corseted his rib cage. He was back on the rock pile.

"Just one," he told himself, rising cautiously.

Just one slurp to ease the pain.

Slowly, with assistance from walls and sundry pieces of furniture, he made his tortuous way to the kitchen. The day before, he had laid in a quart of Jameson's by cashing a check from a book review. After one long belt, he stashed it for morning exigencies in the cabinet above the refrigerator. Now, leaning against the cool, purring surface, he rested.

How's the cat? Miss the bugger.

He reached for his loving bottle. It was not there. Panicked, he crashed through the neatly arranged glasses, knocking them like shattering bowling pins onto the dusty fridge. The whiskey was gone. He tried, but could remember nothing of it from the night before. The void was too familiar. He deduced he must have polished off the spirits sometime during the past fifteen hours,

Powerful thirsty!

Turning, he checked for the garbage. There was none. When Terence was snooping around, Christopher stuffed the empties in the trash and flung it down the hall incinerator, preserving the fragile peace by preventing Terence from tallying the dead soldiers. He had obviously killed this bottle and dumped the incriminating evidence. Force of habit? Attack of the Harriet Craigs? Need for a stroll? Or was he trying to keep the spiraling count from his own weak heart? It was not to be considered. He needed a drink.

He coughed. A wave of tidal nausea crumpled his body. Collapsing against the refrigerator, he pulled in long, quivering breaths. As soon as he could walk, he stumbled back to bed.

Do it, Iago.

Christopher knew what had to be done. Fumbling with the telephone dial, he managed.

"I can't dial it, Operator. I'm blind."

She connected him with the liquor store on Irving Place. After ordering a pint of blackberry brandy, he asked that the delivery boy step into the deli to pick up a coffee, regular, then *The New York Times* and *Gentlemen's Quarterly*.

Thanatos in Eros drag.

Judith sided with Andrew: The jacket for Lydia Berman's gothic was a mess. Frowning, she buzzed for him. His nasal voice immediately blasted over the intercom like a possessed announcer imitating Roz Russell on a news station. "Yes, ma'am."

"Please come in, Drew."

"Pronto, Your Majesty!"

She scrutinized the jacket proof, turning it upside down. Nothing helped. She would *shlep* down to Marvin's Art Department and explain why it did not do what must be done. She dreaded his firecracker flareups and ugly tantrums, convinced that a mean-mouthed nature was the truth behind his touted "artistic temperament." Why had she not seen the final sketch for this fuchsia fauvist atrocity? She glanced up. Andrew saluted

[21]

from the doorway.

"You rang?"

He wore green wool trousers so tight she could not imagine how he sat without doing damage. Perfectly coifed, he flashed more jewelry than she, and a more expensive scent; but the getup miraculously skirted the trashy. Brash, yes; vulgar, no. She smiled, pleased as usual to see him.

Judith readily admitted to the curious that Andrew Desmond was frequently difficult, snarly, and very often disrespectful; but he was a first-rate editorial assistant and, in the crunch, a reliable friend. He happened to be the only male behind a typewriter in the company. She felt no small triumph there, considering him part of her ongoing Diana-Prince fight against the unjust homophobia that haunted the hallowed hetero halls of Voyager Press. It seemed easier to battle than the more subtle but equally insidious misogyny that she swore was on the rise since they entered the conglomerate arena. She was the recognized champion of equal rights. (She also fought to raise the awful wages—"You can neither *eat* nor wear psychological perks!"—and to promote from within the organization.) She adored having the flamboyantly gay Andrew "manning" the phones. The two were a team. They were in this together.

"Andrew! What *are* we to do?"

Poor Lydia Berman. Miss Thing indeed!

"Well, seeing as how the opus *sucks,* we've got to give Miss Thing a decent jacket."

"I'll call Marvin."

"I already have."

"Why didn't we see the sketches? The jacket we ran in the catalogue was better and *that* was shit!"

"Marvin says we saw."

"*I* never saw a goddamn thing! Did you?"

"Of course not! Would *I* approve that *chozzerai?* I dropped into his cage while you were dishing with Strange. Trudy dug out the drawings. They were *not* initialed."

"So what happens now?"

"He's getting us Bella—*if* she's available. She did Miss Thing's

[22]

last, which I thought was OK."

"Me too."

The phone rang.

"I'll get it, Drew. Have you finished the letter—"

"I'm working on it! Jeese, give a girl a break!"

It was Christopher on the line verifying their luncheon date. He was sipping hot coffee and said he was feeling just dandy, "absolutely bingo, toots."

After washing the tea things, Terence went in search of his cat. Instead of returning directly to his desk, he crossed to the heavy swinging door that led to the dining room and sauntered around the oval pine table, through to the foyer at the front door. A few more steps gave an unobstructed view of the comfortable living room with his unoccupied desk at the far end. Whiting, the superstar cat, was not on the first floor. The wet snow made a patchwork on the windows. Winter's deep silence insulated the house from life's potshots, he hoped. He loved the place. At moments like this, he did not mind the solitude. The rooms seemed filled with friends.

Over the mantel hung the Hans Namuth portrait of Jackson Pollock sitting on the running board of an old flivver. Throughout the house, the walls were graced by works of other masters. Signed Ansel Adams and Cartier-Bresson prints hung with Atget, Paul Strand, and Aaron Siskind in the living room. Jacob Riis's smoking newsboys faced Berenice Abbott's smoking James Joyce in the dining room opposite George Platt Lynes's and Duane Michels's nude males. Elsewhere were two Nadars (Bernhardt and Balzac), two Hurrells (Cooper and Power), a Weston landscape, several of the FSA group (Evans, Vachon, Lange, and Lee), a W. Eugene Smith, a Robert Frank, and a Joel Meyerowitz seascape, the only image in color. They hadn't bought a photograph in years ("We have enough. Give others a chance."). They had taken to buying a friend's Painterly Realist work.

"Where are you, puss?"

He climbed the stairs that landed opposite the front door. The two guest rooms and the library/exercise room were closed. His bedroom door was open. The cat was not there. Pausing to make up the double bed, he diligently placed his pillow in the center and returned to the kitchen. Since the attic door was closed, there was only one other place worth hiding.

When alone, he always locked the rear kitchen door. It led to the downstairs bathroom, the cellar with the laundry room, the back entrance, and to a tiny aerie reached by a twisting narrow staircase. Added to the farmhouse, one presumed, to accommodate a family helper or a grown child, it had been converted by Christopher into his working corner. The kitchen door was ajar.

At the center of Christopher's large oak desk, the cat was curled asleep on a long blue pad. He did not awaken when Terence approached. His white silken fur sparkled like the snow drifted against the window.

A color photo of Christopher More, Lucite-framed and hung behind the desk, mesmerized him. The two-dimensional image was so precise, an attitude so adeptly captured that Terence stretched to stroke it tenderly; Those deep-set gray eyes, that slightly aquiline nose too broad at the base to be called delicate yet not a distraction from those high, sharp cheekbones, that mouth with its thin, sweetly crinkled upper lip and unabashedly voluptuous lower, that silver-gray-blond hair, all the elements cast in a long oval face to imprint extraordinary beauty.

"I look movie-star gorgeous!" Christopher had laughed, studying the print.

"You *are* movie-star gorgeous, bimbo!"

Bloated now. Swollen. Thirty pounds overweight.

Terence plunked himself down on the pillow-strewn sofa opposite. The picture was taken for an article in *Newsweek* on young American poets. Christopher More, newly published, the youngest and a shining bright beauty to boot, had generated a good deal of interest in the press. It was unfortunate that all the people who read the many articles he adorned did not read serious verse; but the splash won him a dozen reading engagements around the country, engagements that would have procreated if his reputation for heavy drinking and no-shows had not closed that exhausting but lucrative avenue. He loathed readings. He said their loss was a blessing in witch drag. Terence, exasperated, had yelled and complained, shrieking damning incantations like a berserk warlock. Now it seemed a long time ago.

Five years? I'm in the program nearly three.

Terence loved the room. It exuded a comfort that enveloped and sealed him in the past. It had vivid colors: lots of orange and blue. The white walls were dressed with pictures of themselves, of people they admired (their *lares* and *penates),* with ads and posters for their books, and two dozen postcards from myriad friends who zigzagged the globe and frequently thought of them: "The legendary couple" in Gerald's words, words that made them laugh while others nodded in acknowledgment and recognition; so, secretly, had they.

Hundreds of books, paper and clothbound, were randomly piled on sturdy oak shelves, spilling over to every available surface. Books were not corralled into Christopher's study, they filled the house; but here they gave the impression of a cache, here they were spine-snapped and enthusiastically notated. A four-inch color television for afternoon soaps doubled as a paperweight for a sheaf of fan letters, each to be dutifully and often affectionately answered by hand in black ink on gray Tiffany note paper.

Familiar cracks opened below the pressured region of the heart. Scooping up the startled cat, Terence fled to the living room, slamming the kitchen door hard and savagely turning the lock.

There had never been any discussion about the custody of the cat. Not that Christopher was unfeeling toward Whiting, but Persians required constant grooming and this one demanded particular attentions: Puss ate only one brand of liver catfood which Christopher construed as an elitist act. Terence made space for the cat in every situation but lovemaking. He felt uneasy at night if the cat was not curled on his pillow. When he left the Gramercy Park apartment, Whiting was under one arm.

We've been through a lot, this cat and I. He's been a good friend.

Originally, Omar Khayyam, the cat's registered name, was bought by Andrew as a Christmas gift for the Gunnings. Fabulous Felines provided a pedigree report as well as detailed dietary instructions advocating braised chicken livers, sautéed kidneys, and poached whitefish. The outrageously expensive kitten, costing nearly a month's wages, had not been warmly welcomed by the adults. It shed on the furniture. ("He, Gerald, the sweetie is a boy!") It nibbled the luxurious greenery. It hair-balled on antique lace. It climbed Renaissance tapestries. It converted groined fireplaces into litterboxes; the rooms reeked when fires were lit. But worst of all, it caught invading mice and stashed them under Persian carpets rather than eat the smelly things. Its first (and last) spring cleaning was a debacle. As rugs were raised and remains disinterred—each corpse having stained both pricey parquet *and* priceless weave—Omar Khayyam was bowled soggily into the spring rains.

Andrew fortuitously arrived three days later for a country weekend. His pitiful present was in dire need of a home.

"How could you leave Omar outside like that?" Andrew demanded of Gerald.

"It's useless. I can't spare the house room."

"Useless? He's beautiful! Isn't that enough?"

"No! Cats must earn their keep. It's a sorry slob!"

The children squirmed and whimpered. Gerald banished them to their rooms. He railed against sentimentality. He quoted Darwin. Judith sat with narrowed eyes, silently smoking cigarettes.

There remained only the gentlemanly thing to do. Andrew reclaimed Omar Khayyam and carted him to the Upper East Side, to a New York City apartment more perilous for the cat than a feral life in the park would have been.

Andrew kept a large yellow dog. The dense canine was a bad-breathed Llasa apso coyly named Commonweal, or Wealy. Though generally ignored by his owner, he was useful as a conversational gambit with other lonely men perambulating the curbs at night and desperate for quick, anonymous sex. In return, Andrew fed Wealy well, sent him for grooming weekly ("One mustn't make a poor impression or one is left to the Ugmoes."), and occasionally administered the traditional pat on the head.

The luxury-item feline was another matter. He did nothing. In return, his litter was changed by the cleaning lady when the stench caused her to gag and not before. His food was gobbled by Wealy. Tangled, he went brushless. Fleas and ticks infested, ears became a mite haven from the dog's country jaunts. Trapped in a Murphy bed over a Memorial Day weekend, sandwiched between a shutter and a window for one very hot August weekend, he was a wreck in no time.

Terence met the poor traumatised Omar Khayyam at the dinner party given by Andrew and Judith to celebrate the publication of his fourth novel, the first with Judith and Voyager Press. She had wrangled to get him accepted by the house and was guiding the independent publicists Terence had hired, but she was unable to offer her own apartment for the affair because the painters were at work. Voyager Press would not spring for a place; the "specialized" novel showed no promise to them. Andrew, passionate about the book, offered his small but "comfy" home. He was thrilled to host a classy affair catered by Voyager Press for the ravishing Strange, the renowned Christo More, and a few select intelligent types. The evening went well. Omar spent it curled on Terence's sheltering lap.

"This cat is tied up in knots," he whispered to Christopher. "He needs a loving home."

"That animal has a demented world view."

Toward the shank of the evening, Andrew, drunk on gin rickeys, bellowed an interminable toast.

"And," he concluded, "if *ever* there is *anything* I can do for you or to you—"

"Give the kid your fucking cat!" Christopher, equally drunk, loudly heckled.

Andrew over enthusiastically complied. To everyone's relief, Terence politely accepted.

"What will we call him?" Terence wondered that night in bed as he worried cat knots loose.

"Whiting . . . after the fish . . . and John . . ." Christopher dozed.

"All right," Terence informed the purring cat. "Whiting will do nicely for now."

Dominic Perrugio perched. From the last pew of Saint Mary Magdalen's he watched a widow-weeded crone, an octogenarian friend of his mother, light a candle at the statue of Saint Jude Thaddeus, the patron saint of hopeless cases. He wondered if the impossibilities facing her were as impossible as his were, had become, were evidently soon to be if Father Jerome's prediction was an accurate one.

Old fool. Senile. No other explanation. He knew the score.

The priest refused him absolution. Dominic had lapsed for two decades, true, but for the past four years, though casual in his devotions, he confessed regularly. As he approached forty-seven, he daily became more atavistic. The Church was a retreat. It gave him solace and offered comfort the way it used to when he served as an altar boy for Jerome a long, long time ago. There were days when he had no other place to go if trouble forced him from the house.

"Well," he reasoned aloud, "he can't keep me from coming and sitting here. Senile bastard."

Of course, he would not mention it to anyone. Who could he tell? With his mother in California there was no one to talk to, not that he could have told her this.

Jerome would never have dared if Mama were here. It would kill her.

He sobbed. The priest had pulverized and discarded him as though he were trash. The pietistic diatribe ignited, word by piercing word, inflaming his lungs; his heart, seemed ulcerated and puffed. Familiar terrors were revitalized by the priest's hatred for his "kind."

No hope here now.

There never had been hope in the Roman Catholic Church. It was an illusion. A cult of the dead with life beginning ever after. The longest-playing, most successful, cast of millions show on earth. A circus to keep the poor distracted. Why had there never been Jesus Christ bubble gum cards? He grinned. Who needed it?

He had more illusions in his head than he knew what to do with.

Billy says the Church is retrograde and lobbies against civil liberties. It ignores the separation between Church and State. It should pay taxes. He's right. Always right. Good riddance, Jesus baby. I have more than illusions.

There were many good years. He would be lying if he denied the long stretch of happiness; more happiness than most get in their lifetimes, he had in the first ten years. Now he was denied absolution because he wanted him dead. Doesn't everyone at some extreme of rage wish the person they love most in the world to die? He had not meant it.

Yes. Yes, I did I mean it. Still do.

There had been good years. But the last few had been so bad that nothing else mattered. He always forgot about the good years, the best years.

Ten? That many? More. Be fair.

There were vacations in England and France and Italy. There was love. Ten years of love. More. Twenty. He had not started hating until when? When had he crossed the invisible line? Not until recently, he reckoned, around 1970, when it got out of hand. He was a cook and a maid and a nurse and a skiv with a mop and a scrubbing brush.

A wop with a mop for a cock.

The sex was over. There had always been wonderful sex, the best he had ever known because he had never had it with love before. They had done everything all of the time. Every day sometimes twice a day for years and years. How many years? Now nothing. Nothing. It was like living with a zombie. It was not always that way. He reminded himself of the good sex because he wanted to be decent. He wanted to hate fairly.

Like sitting reading after the sun goes down. It wasn't always this dark. I used to be able to see the page. Can't see it now. Maybe there never was a page.

No. He knew the love was real once upon a time. He would be insane to deny the good things they shared. He recalled happiness, pulling pleasant memories from his past the way a magician pulls bright scarves from a seemingly empty hat.

He catalogued the good times. The list would never equal the collection of grievances but it was interesting to see how long he could continue. To his astonishment, he discovered that the good times were more than he had time to count. If he did not stop, he would never get home in time to cook dinner.

Bake the bluefish. His favorite. Maybe he won't do it too much tonight. Maybe. . .

Rising, he sidestepped into the center aisle. Genuflecting, he crossed himself and whispered, "Fuck you, Father Jerome."

———

"Lunch was a certified disaster."

"I don't want to know, Judith!"

It's none of my business.

"I *know,* darling, but it was beyond-belief ghastly. He is so *angry* with you. It was *horrible!"*

Was he drunk? He must have been.

Terence closed his eyes. His calm was wrinkling; it was already puckered around the edges.

"He *arrived* drunk. I'm furious! Very annoyed!"

"Judith! I *really* don't want to know! Please let's change the subject or let's hang up."

"He says his new collection is ready. Is that possible? He must be lying. I am terribly upset!"

"Judith, it is *not* your fault. It doesn't matter *who* was with him. *You* are not responsible for any of it."

Why do people —

"But darling, he went caroming out of the restaurant into the traffic! I don't know *where* he is!"

There was silence.

"Judith! Here I sit snowbound hours from Manhattan, unable to do *anything* about it! Why are you telling me this? *I* don't blame you. *Why* are you unloading your guilt on me? It is *not* your fault. Any of it! *None of it!"*

There was a deeper silence.

"Terence, you *must* be right. I feel better, darling! I *was* blaming myself. Isn't that silly?"

"No. . . no, it isn't," he sighed, fed up. "We all do it. We think if we said the magic words or chose a quieter place or planned lunch for yesterday—Jesus, Judith, Christopher's drinking has nothing to do with any of us. We haven't that kind of power over him! He drinks because he's happy. He drinks because he's sad. He drinks because the sun is shining. He drinks because there's rain. He drinks when he writes. He drinks when he doesn't. *He drinks because he has to,* damnit, and we've got to leave him alone to figure that one out for himself! It's called compulsive drinking. It's a disease. *And* it's contagious. *We* become ill! It uses our anger and our guilt and our fear to victimize us. We've got to stop trying to intercept him, to save him: all we're doing is interrupting for a moment the progress of the disease. We're all *tsimmis* freaks!"

"Yes, darling, I *think* I understand. I always feel spiritually naked without a splash of anxiety."

"Well, an alcoholic in your life will allow you all the anxiety you need to feel comfortable. Not to mention *guilt!*"

They both laughed.

"I must go, darling. Miss Thing is here to see me."

"Who?"

Judith giggled like a naughty child. "Lydia Berman. Andrew calls her Miss Thing and I've started doing it now. Her new one is just ghastly, but it will sell and sell. They always do, you know. *And* the reviews will be good! I don't know what would happen to this industry, darling, if intelligent people started reviewing books again. The barbarians are within the gates and all we can do is preserve our small portion of life. Go back to work, Terence Strange. We need you now more than ever. Gerald will pick you up at seven on Saturday. Gotta run. Thanks a bunch, darling."

He had oversimplified the whole thing. Talking to "civilians" was sometimes very difficult. How could he explain in five minutes what took him years to understand? "Allow you all the anxiety" bore invidious comparisons with est. The program was no hyped-up weekend cure. It necessitated change. It was a complex, demanding, annealing way of life. He sighed. He had done his witless best.

I should have said my symptoms of the disease are anxiety and fear and guilt. She'd never have understood that.

He called Thomas. "I'm like an emotional Electrolux," Terence laughed. "I suck up everybody's anxiety and pain. I *must* allow people the dignity of their own pain. I will. I'm getting there. I'm figuring it out. At least I see it now. . ."

———————————

Barbara "Bobbi" Edelston was Terence Strange's fastest friend. They had discovered one another in high school when he was placed one seat behind her in sophomore plane geometry class. The teacher, freshly minted, had been in the wrong profession, a mistake he rectified by retiring at the end of the term to sell used cars. While he stammered through the properties of points, lines, and planes at the front of the room terrorized by sadistic students, Bobbi and Terence at the back chatted about Dickens, their families, and distinguished many profound affinities. In other shared classes (and often in hallways) they passed notes to one another presaging the evolution of what was primarily an epistolary friendship juiced by an occasional visit and an infrequent telephone call.

After high school, he went to Yale; she joined the Navy ("I had to get out of that house!"). Stationed for five years near Washington, D.C., she settled in the area when an antigay witch-hunt forced her and her buddies to resign from the service. She remained deeply committed to her small group of friends, who lovingly functioned as an extended family. Living in rented suburban homes often miles from each other around the nation's capital, they merged each morning with the immense commuter population but remained at heart a community unto themselves.

"A gay ghetto," Christopher had called it. They banded together, fearful of being "read" and bounced from government jobs; or, if not directly employed in the civil service, fearful of being spotted and by association casting doubts on vulnerable friends. Professionals who shared homes had separate telephones with different numbers to prevent business associates from discovering they did not live alone. Checking in with one another daily, the group gathered frequently to introduce new mates, to entertain relatives with tours of Washington, to party, play cards, do the bars, or have dinner and watch Sunday football. Bobbi managed to retain some autonomy. A wry observer of her social "set," she preferred staying home alone in her comfortable "cave" draped in her four cats and reading seriously, or writing the verse she showed no one, or the long letters Terence cherished.

She shared his medium height but was not slim ("Fat, dear, I'm fat!"), and her short red hair was heavily streaked with gray. She had large round brown eyes, a generous nature, and a raucous sense of humor which Christopher found most enchanting. Her group considered her passion for books idiosyncratic, an unsocial weirdness; though admiring, most of them were wary of Terence but delighted by Christopher, whose riotous drinking was something with which they all could connect.

Drinking was precisely the subject that currently gripped Bobbi's mind. Her Saturday evening was cleared of chores and she planned to continue a letter begun the previous weekend. She expected no interruptions. A small party had been formed by her hairdresser, Stanley, to go dancing and boozing downtown at Pier 47. Stanley had no trouble collecting a group for his triweekly jaunts; Saturdays, of course, takers were numerous, but the midweek excursions were becoming too popular for Bobbi's comfort. Their friend Roger's grotesque death had left no discernible mark.

A *little month* . . .

Her doorbell rang. Exhaling menthol smoke, she glanced at the cats as if they were privy to something. The doorbell rang again. She could not pretend to be asleep; the lights were on and everyone knew her feelings about electric bills. What could she do? The bell rang again and the length of the call told her instantly who was waiting at the door. She should have known. Only Davey, Stanley's brother, would arrive without an invitation. She had him trained to telephone before visiting when the death of his lover, Roger, sent discipline skyward.

"He's pushing his luck," she muttered, trying to sound hard but not succeeding. She was Davey's anchor and she knew it.

The last few months were an agony for Davey. Roger's

hospitalization for alcoholism had not provided the hoped-for cure; he had begun drinking again as soon as he could manage to walk to the store. The gang had been supportive but then grew bored as Roger played hide-and-seek in the shadows of the valley of alcoholic death. Davey did nothing but complain. Everyone was disgusted with them both. Roger's recent demise had come as a surprise to no one but Davey, who had cradled him, dead, in his arms and who collapsed at every obsessive recounting of the gruesome details.

Bobbi shouted for Davey to wait a minute then hastily closed her writing pad and turned off the desk lamp. What could she say to help alleviate Davey's pain? Terence's latest letter offered several suggestions and she had resolved to try them *all* the next time the opportunity arose. Well, here it was, and all she wanted to do was write for a few hours to her dear friend before rereading a section of *Mawrdew Czgowchwz,* and then go to bed. She resolved to do her best.

Her anger at Stanley surfaced as she crossed the living room. The older brother had done nothing to help. He still told dumb hangover jokes in Davey's presence, but most infuriating of all, people still laughed at antics that had stopped being funny ten years before. These guys spent their lives in bars. The blaring music made conversation impossible and tables no longer existed, so there was no place to sit. They *stood* around eyeing one another and drinking themselves into a glazed stupor then called it a good time, cruising. Christ! She detested the bars. None of it made any sense.

Now there was Davey to contend with. He had called her the night Roger died and she had sped to his side. She contacted the police and washed Roger's face and brushed his hair because she felt it was the least she could do. (She also disposed of the gore-soaked sheets and cleaned the bathroom.) She had never liked Roger but in death he seemed desperately in need of the kindness she had always tried to give him in life. For a time he had been cast as archvillain ruining Davey's life, but with Terence's help she had overcome her unreasonable anger and had developed compassion for Davey and Roger, who were *both* victims of a disease. No, she had never liked Roger. He was a boring, pretentious drunk who probably would have been tiresome and pretentious sober. But, one must be decent at all times to people in trouble. What *could* she offer Davey? Perhaps Terence would come for a visit soon?

She sighed. Straightening her shoulders, she resigned herself to a very depressing evening. Perhaps he would leave before midnight? She almost had them trained. Now when people saw her reading or writing or listening to music they did not assume she was bored and had nothing else to do.

The trick is not to ask for too much.

Gerald, wearing bright orange earmuffs, honked precisely at seven. A morning blizzard had buried Saturday. A silver plow was attached to the front of the green Jeep and glimmered with reflections of the full moon.

"How's the new book coming, Terence?"

"Well enough, I guess."

"Good! I'm pleased to hear it. You're lucky you can work so quickly and efficiently. I envy you."

With Gerald, Terence shied away from the subject of his writing. He felt ashamed for not anguishing more in the great tradition. It was an old rehashed number. Christopher suffered and strained over every word all the time. Art was fashioned out of pain. He unequivocally declared that *that* was how it was for those in the know. It was one of the reasons he most commonly gave for drinking: His work made him need to do it, his work forced the necessity of it on him, and paradoxically ("All paradox is holy."), he could not work without it. Drinking irrigated the conflict and bade the creative spirit soar.

Bullshit! Alcohol is *the conflict. Cause, not effect.*

The snow crunched beneath the wheels. It sounded to Terence as if the Jeep were munching celery stalks.

"I work things out *exactly* in my head, Gerald. Most problems are solved before I start the actual writing with the actual pencil. It isn't as simple as it looks."

Maybe it looks as simple as it is? Is it?

"Oh, I know, Terry, I *know!*"

"I said that for my own ears, Gerald. To thine own ears be true? How are *you?*"

"Tops!"

"Tops? I'm not ready for this."

"I've completed new plans for my studio. I'll show them to you after dinner."

Terence lit a cigarette, exhaling a tumultuous white cloud to mask his sigh. For the three years he knew Gerald, detailed plans abounded to convert a corner of the unfinished attic into a studio. Discussion was the only pleasure greater than drawing ("Once a studio, always a painter?"). Terence pondered the Sisyphean labor. Zipping along in a green Jeep forced a certain perspective.

He should, be praised for climbing. . .

Although an extraordinarily gifted pianist, Gerald had decided to major in art history at Harvard. He graduated *cum laude*, but rather than take his doctorate, he returned home to pursue a career in music. The four-year layoff had drastically weakened his keyboard technique. After years of intensive private study with six hours of practice daily, he collapsed into an ironclad depression when he earned a rejection letter from Juilliard. With the help of an orthodox Freudian who sat behind a screen, Gerald "relaxed his watch upon the gates of Reason" and free associated himself to a resolution *of* the Oedipus complex. Along the way, he chose to become a "successful man of action" able to impose his wishes on reality, rather than an "artist" transforming his wishes into works of art.

He decided to become a psychiatrist, and to offer his life to the miracle of making the unconscious conscious, as well as to the joy of converting repeating into remembering. Proudly, he would defend the primacy of the Oedipal period. (His dream was membership in the New York Psychoanalytic Institute.) Enrolling in Harvard's program for graduates who experience a change in goal direction, he acquired the necessary scientific education to be accepted by Mount Sinai Medical School in New York City, where his mother had donated an operating theater in memory of her husband. At this renowned institution, the surgeons ruled with powers and prestige reminiscent of the ancient Pharaohs. Gerald responded directly to their Oedipally significant positions, and obsessed about joining their exclusively male club. For two years, his narcissism was placed on the line, creating a crisis that infantilized him: He started to cut classes and to hate the sight of sickness, of blood, and of the appalling ugliness of death. He resumed therapy, addressing his refusal to accept life realistically as a psychoanalyst. Reading Freud's *Moses and Monotheism*, he drew the logical conclusions: The goal of all successful men of action is to cut off other men's members. He decided upon the alternate route to commonplace unhappiness. Terminating therapy, he chose to become an artist eventually.

In the early sixties "when a buck was a buck," he opened Gallery Deirdre at Madison Avenue and Seventieth Street, touting it the most stimulating place since Stieglitz gave the world 291. Indulging his mother's fancy for Art Nouveau ("It reminds Vera of her youth when a buck was *really* a buck!"), he prowled Europe, disinterring parts of train stations from junkyards, rescuing hotel fixtures from wrecking balls, and plucking dusty *objets* from ateliers, shop basements, water closets. It was his perfect triumph: a glorious vindication of his latent ability to do something smart. The debut show received splashy coverage in every art forum. Nouveau was returned to an honored place on glossy calendars and collectors' shelves. Gallery Deirdre had been fixed on the map.

He then impetuously married a childhood friend, an amateur golfer, moved into the red-brick Colonial house in Sharon township, hired people to run the "shop"—the people to whom he eventually sold it when the search for amusing artifacts became too draining—and looked forward to a rich, productive life as a primary artist. Writing, he said. Most probably a novel.

"He is waiting for the Muse, *any* Muse to descend in a baroque trumpet fanfare and squat on his pretty face," Judith expounded years later, shocking company whenever Gerald publicly reflected on the state of his art. Gerald grinned his sheepish grin (the one perfected on Vera, but soothing to all women), colored, and laughed meekly, clumsily glossing over her chilling contempt. He remembered how his first wife admired his excellent watercolors; she had possessed taste in matters visual, but otherwise had been an imbecile. He accounted Judith visually illiterate.

At the present meal, Terence Strange noted that Morgan Connelly looked miserable from his flared nostrils down to his white knuckles, and horrified around his huge blue eyes and heavy black brows. Even his black curly hair and beard seemed startled by Judith's routine.

"When your sainted mother," she carried on, "has seventeen million cookies and enough Duncan Phyfe *chotchkas* to fill a barn like this, the urge to do anything but scour the neighborhood for that better grade of white truffle in January far overwhelms the creative you-know-what. Isn't that so, Poopsie?"

Terence was not smiling. Judith had scarfed down too many iced martinis and was in a fierce temper. Why were some people such nasty drunks? Christopher never turned mean. He quoted verse in half a dozen languages, sang opera arias, then promptly fell asleep. Next Judith would tell Morgan how Gerald spent thirty grand on filler so the house could be placed among the romantic birches. Judith was making it clear that they lived on her meager salary and that whatever it was, *it was not easy.*

Makes you not go back for second helpings.

"It's a very special house," her newest guest said to Gerald. "Mine's in a birch grove too but fortunately the trees were on a rise."

Morgan Connelly was a large man with a heavy body and a soft, husky voice. Physically, he was the opposite of the creatures in the intricately detailed, delicate drawings that had made him one of the most famous children's book illustrators and comic-strip artists in the world. He reminded Terence of an admired high school social studies teacher; he wore the same type of loose-fitting wool suit in a nondescript dark earth color, with a too-fat tie but an impeccably laundered crisp white shirt. Terence had dressed with especial care and now felt assembled, arranged, even though Judith wore a long satin skirt and Gerald a silk ascot of an apricot hue.

"Morgan is what people used to call a 'private person' before shrinks became so popular," Judith had informed when she called Terence that morning. "And he *loves* your books."

The evening did not open well. The children, excited by meeting Morgan Connelly, were reluctant to go to bed. Gerald, overly stem, annoyed Judith, who tended to indulge them on weekends, often with extravagant presents, Morgan Connelly being one of the biggest and one of the best. Morgan barely spoke. Gerald could not stop. Judith guzzled martinis like a fraternity teen swallowing goldfish. When the hot hors d'oeuvres appeared, she banished Gerald to the kitchen with guardianship over the soup. Terence, bored by the rerun of the Judith and Gerald Show, observed the interesting stranger.

And *he doesn't drink!*

A second vodka and tonic was refused. Morgan sat stiffly, munching a stuffed mushroom. Terence attempted conversation but Judith insisted on playing hostess: She constantly interrupted with some bit of inane business each time a rapport developed, forcing her two guests into a conspiratorial indifference to one another broken by shy smiles and brief sentences whenever she darted from the room to check on Gerald's progress. Morgan was pleased with Terence's forbearance, but disconcerted by the open way the younger man scrutinized him approvingly. He found the experience intimidating as Terence's oval, hazel eyes tracked and registered like intensely perceptive antennae.

When they convened for dinner, Terence turned charmingly loquacious through the soup course, then, satisfied he had done his bit ("a quick tap dance around the room"), he resumed watching and listening to Morgan Connelly who, among other tasty things, revealed himself as a sensual man for whom eating superb food was an erotic experience.

All in the flick of the tongue. . .

Judith and Gerald wrangled. Morgan resisted taking sides. He refused to posit advice or sprinkle suggestions on any subject. He gracefully box-stepped around the loaded dice. He assiduously ducked every wily toss to hook him into their situation-comedy format. And while backhanding the widest curve balls, he managed to display with some of his rebuttals an acerbic, telling wit. Terence was very impressed.

Full marks, fella.

After dinner, he sympathized in the oak-beamed parlor beside a blazing fire while the marrieds sparred in the kitchen, ostensibly over the bitterness of the green-tea ice cream. They sipped VSOP Napoleon brandy.

"This is not one of their better at-homes, Morgan. I'm sorry if it's been rotten for you. I'm used to a roundelay but this was low darts."

"Why do you return?" he whispered.

"Would you believe I like them? It isn't always this tacky. Judith is like me: She can't drink. But she gets schizy while I throw up. Luckily, neither of us does it very often!"

Morgan nodded but was unconvinced. Terence smiled and added very softly: "I am grateful to you. You dance beautifully. Great backbend."

Morgan laughed. He suddenly looked exhausted. "I've had a lot of practice. Their games remind me of my parents."

There was a long pause. Each shyly contemplated the other.

"I must be going, Terence."

"Can you drive me home? Gerald fetched me in his Jeep. I noticed you have one of your own."

"Can't live here in the winter without one."

"Do you live alone?"

There was a comfortable silence. Terence heard Christopher bemoaning this penchant for blunt, candid questions. Had the evening's conversation been amenable to anything but changing the subject, or had there been a third guest to act as a buffer between them and the householders, Terence would have ferreted out the major details of Morgan Connelly's life in no time flat. He was fascinated by other people (Christopher called it asshole sniffing); and he knew that most people enjoy talking about themselves. He would have worked to make a lasting impression on this man.

"Yes, Terence. I do now. My friend, Louis, died two years ago."

"Oh. I'm sorry "

How?

"You live with Christopher More?"

"I used to. We separated three months ago."

Morgan rose. Terence was astonished that Judith had not imparted all the messy details. Judith thrived on blood and guts.

Who the fuck doesn't?

"It must be a difficult time for you, Terence. It's much like a death, only harder."

"Harder?"

"I imagine so. There are always the doubts and fears in the middle of the night. With death are only regrets and resignations. Maybe not harder. Maybe just similar."

"Sometimes it's very bad. Much of the time it's not. I'm doing very well."

"I'm sure you are. I'd be delighted to drive you home. *If* we can leave *immediately!*"

They did not speak while Morgan expertly maneuvered the black Jeep down the steep, winding path from the house to the icy road below. Judith, guilt-ridden, had insisted they take some blueberry poundcake. While she wrapped the offerings, Gerald discussed his studio with the professionals.

"I wonder if he'll ever build the damn thing?"

"When I first met him three years ago, he was looking for a *simpatico* builder. He found one. Together they constructed a remarkable machine that mass-produces arrows complete with feathers. It was supposed to make them rich but nothing happened. The machine is in the woodshed. It really works."

"Arrows?"

They both laughed.

"I wish I could use it in one of my books. But who would believe it?"

"I admire your books, Terence."

"Thank you, Morgan. And I yours."

I'll never be as great as you. Never.

"Is your new novel like the others?"

"The same. Lots of pretty people suffering."

"Judith told me you're experimenting with new forms."

[41]

"She did? I am? What can that mean?"

They laughed again. Terence made a mental note to query her on this jacket flap copy.

"I'm doing what I always do, Morgan. Only *better*, I hope."

"You look different from your pictures, Terence."

Too beautiful! You and More ensemble *must be a sight.*

"I know. I photograph badly. I either look twelve and vapid, or fifty-eight and embalmed. I'm too self-conscious. I *want* to look air-brushed and it shows."

"How old are you?"

"Thirty-three. How old are you?"

"Forty-seven."

"Forty-seven's a nice age."

"Sure it is!" Morgan guffawed. "For *me*, not for you."

Terence smiled, embarrassed, then laughed at his own silliness. All his quip meant was that he liked older men. "Didn't you live with More for years?"

"Yes, years. Eleven . . . eleven years."

"A long time."

"And you?"

"Twenty-two years."

"A *very* long time."

"In our world, twenty-two minutes is a long time. Why have you separated?" he asked with a deep personal concern. Louis had always objected to his "grilling" people like this. If Terence objected, he would find a way to make it known. He seemed comfortable with questions.

"Lots of reasons, but one in particular. He has a drinking problem and I was making myself sick. I couldn't watch him die."

Terence was rattled by despair before the first sentence was completed. He stared straight ahead into the circle of yellow light speeding in front of them. Every time he told, it was as if he were exposing some dark, heinous secret, some private shame. He struggled with feelings of betrayal, reminding himself forcibly that alcoholism is a disease. If Christopher had diabetes or TB he would not harbor this guilt. It was the way people in the nineteenth century must have behaved when someone in the family suffered from mental illness. It was part of his denial. It was not a question of anyone's failure, but of his very own survival. The abyss cranked dosed, like a stage device. Terence noted the metaphor.

"I saw him twice at publishing parties. He was very drunk both times. I wondered if he had a problem. What a shame! He's so gifted."

"He's a wonderful man, Morgan. I love him very much."

Still love him. That answers that.

"It must have been hard going."

"Yes, but I didn't help. I made things worse. I thought I could save him. I made myself sick. I didn't know any better then. It's a long story."

"I'd like to hear it."

Terence touched Morgan's arm. The directness moved him. It was the value he expected from his friends in the program. Morgan smiled into his eyes.

Still loves him.

When they reached the house, Terence invited Morgan in for chamomile tea or a drink. The offer was politely refused. They shook hands. Terence watched the Jeep bounce away before he ascended the three stone steps and unlocked his front door. The cat snoozed on the foyer table.

THREE

Compared to the Gunnings', the Strange-More house was decidedly modest. Built in 1814, it was precisely what both had wanted. They furnished it in comfortable odds and ends that supplied a casual country-affair ambience. Originally intended as a weekend and summer retreat ("That little place just two hours from New York."), it quickly became a focal point of their entwined lives. Had it not been for their cultural pursuits in Manhattan, they would have surrendered their Gramercy Park apartment and retired to the country. Accustomed in the city to long stretches of isolation when Christopher was drinking heavily, they solidified their habits in Oblong Valley.

"All Christo needs for company is a flagon of Irish. All I needed was Christo."

They met on a stage at graduate school. It seemed to Terence as he pushed a cart through the maze of the Safeway that they had never left it. Physically they had, of course, but there was something childish about their symbiotic relationship and the way they conducted it.

A relationship? Finding someone to do what you want. Two babies playing house. A setup. Too much taking-care-of shit. Nurturing? So much resentment. So much negativism. Who knew?

He recalled what he had said at the last meeting Wednesday: "I allowed access to my most private territory. I opened the gate and let him in. I encouraged him to build a house there which I merrily inhabited, all the while accusing him of trespassing!"

For years their apartment and their country house looked as if students were in residence: scattered mounds of books, bookcases made out of books, sheafs of papers, piles of magazines, scads of notebooks, glossy pictures and newspaper clippings taped to every wall. Within reason, he had changed all of that. There were now miles of shelving and stacks of frames—a positive move, he thought. Christopher preferred it, too. Christopher approved of whatever he did and encouraged him to do whatever he fancied.

"What do you two *do* together after all these years?" a cartoon English friend asked Terence.

"He cooks. I clean," Terence quipped.

Everyone laughed.

Terence spotted Morgan Connelly near the frozen-food compartment. The man wore red plaid with great aplomb. The hunting jacket's collar was turned up and the matching cap's ear flaps were turned down. His stubby fingers were ink-stained. He required a few moments to remember Terence's name.

Minus ten points!

"Are you a good cook, Morgan?"

"I'm getting better. Louis always handled the fancy stuff."

"Did you clean?"

"Had to. Louis was with me on weekends only. Do now, too. I hate having others do what I should do for myself. I make the time. . . ."

"It's good to see you, Morgan."

"Yes, Terence, we must get together for that cup of tea one of these days. When I'm working on a book or sketching out a new series of strips, there just isn't anything else. I've started the book for our Judith. You understand."

Terence said he did but he honestly did not. No matter where his nose was there was never anything as interesting as Christopher's business. He understood the concepts of self-esteem and self-focus and lately had made great strides in working them, but he was easily distracted.

The longest journey is the one from the mind to the heart, Kukla.

———

Christopher More walked a frozen narrow path through the Rambles in Central Park. He was immersed in impressions from an enervating double-header with his analyst; and when offered an hour of stimulating intimacy with an attractive stranger, he sadly refused, not wishing to scatter the laboriously tessellated memories that he hoped would illumine his present sorrowful condition.

What is therapy but the art of the mosaicist? Mosaics go back five thousand years. Mesopotamia? Reflecting light. Mousa. A muse. Ah, so!

He ambled for an hour down the west side of the Park. He had begun with Reynall the previous winter on the suggestion of his father, who was kindly footing the bill. William More had grown concerned when his son continued drinking after the hospitalization. He suggested a Jungian therapist because he knew Christopher's aversion to Freud; he hoped the mystical elements would stimulate the process. He had been right. Terence had insisted that Jungians were sorcerers, not therapists, and what they opined would have no effect on the drinking, which he swore was a separate illness requiring its own specific cure. Christopher now conceded that Terence, too, had been right. There was usually something resembling reality in the *tabula rasa* truisms Terence endlessly cooked up. It was one of the most tedious things about him, one of the aspects of his personality that had not improved with age: He priggishly addressed life as if it were a black-and-white affair.

All things. Everything. No irony anywhere. No dialectics. Too bad.

An early conversation had spilled the beans. Discussing Aquinas with regard to good and evil one crisp autumn afternoon, Terence had expressed an understanding that evil existed *in direct proportion* to good on a scale of one hundred. It reduced Aquinas to a ludicrous algebraic formula of brilliant though wrongheaded lucidity. It had said it all. Life to him was quantities in terms of equations beginning with the endearing premise that goodness held the upper hand, was a well-meaning X with a fixed advantage over a wicked Y.

I never did say I loved him for his brains. *"Give me chastity and self-control. . . but not just* yet.*"*

Christopher had just been discussing Terence Strange with Dr. Reynall and was beginning to admit how much he loved Terence. Even anesthetized most of the time by alcohol, Christopher felt the loss as a stark trauma; it was constellated with the loss of his

[46]

mother, who had died when he was ten. As much as he loathed the synthesis, he accepted Reynall's ineluctable dreamwork inductions. That shimmering cone of past grief fit comfortably into some psychic design and acted as an abirritant. He was better for possessing it. He felt stronger. He could begin to forgive Terence for the devastation left behind because it was not all of his doing.

Ahead, through the bare trees, Christopher spied Tavern on the Green. He decided to take himself to lunch to celebrate the productive morning. His pocket was crammed with bills. Was there a better way to lighten the load? He was certain William would approve.

Coat checked, seated at a table to the rear of the Crystal Room, he ordered a double martini straight up while cursorily scanning the menu. Caviar blintzes and a bottle of Moet looked most attractive. He imagined Terence working his eyebrows over the prices; they were not that outrageous if one considered he had had no breakfast and would have no dinner.

It is *that outrageous. What the fuck! How often do you discover that your husband and your mother have the same taste in hats. . . the same basic shape of face?*

He sipped his cocktail and surveyed the environs. Many lovelies were scattered among the dowagers. He returned several discreet smiles, then focused his attention inward. Martinis were conducive to serious thought. He resolved to reject his childish predilection for the *démondé* Manhattan.

What if pater should feel traduced?

Images of his father abandoned, then abandoning to sail on a dark-brown sea of Manhattans returned him to his earlier meditation but with new impetus. He fought the impulse to telephone Reynall, and instead jotted notes on the filing card he always carried in his shirt pocket for wordplay.

The waiter delivered the chilled wine for his approved. He tasted and nodded, truly delighted. He dared for the moment to admit to happiness. He loved champagne. He adored having money. He adored being famous. He adored his beautiful lover about whom he wished to sing.

Freud was right, the old reprobate. We artists are venality incarnate. But only because we dare. Here's to the courage to serve gai sabre. *Here's to the gay science. Here's to the art of poetry. . .*

"You must make your own mayonnaise," Terence cautioned, "or it won't work."

"Why can't I use Hellmann's?"

"The sugar interrupts chemical interaction."

"Why?"

"Dominic, you ask more questions than *I* do!" he laughed. "Sugar fucks up everything."

"So I hear. Then what?"

"Mix in the ashes."

"How much? I have tons. Bill smokes three packs a day."

"Enough to make a thick paste. Apply liberally and let sit overnight."

"It *really* works?"

"Really! Guaranteed, Dom. I've used it a dozen times."

"I don't know how his glass got on my TV. I nearly died when I saw the stain."

"He lives there, too. He has the run of the house, hasn't he?"

"He's such a pig! You know what he did the other night?"

"I can imagine. I've been there, too, Dom. How are *you?*"

"I'm OK. Upset about the stain. Other than that OK."

"Uh-huh."

"I'm horny as hell but I'm always horny with the central heating."

"You need a break. I thought you were going to visit me."

"I can't leave Billy. He needs me, Terry. I look forward to our weekends. I keep hoping. . . ."

"I know, Dom, I know."

You keep expecting.

"You never can tell, Terry."

"And you want to be there."

"He may want my help."

"I know."

[48]

'Terry, why is this happening to us?"

"Why not us? Disease is never fair."

"Why don't I leave?"

"*I* stayed because I was trapped in the disease. I didn't know the way out. Then, when I learned the things the disease does not want me to know, I stayed because I still love Chris and it was the reason to go to meetings."

"I don't think I love him anymore."

"How can you tell what you feel? You're in such turmoil, *how* can you tell? Who can think? I started using my senses like an animal: I'd smell him when he walked in the door, I'd watch him to see if he was walking straight; I'd listen for the way the foot fell or the way the door was closed. . . . I could tell by the way the key was put in the lock whether or not he'd been drinking. Think? *Who could think?* We stop functioning like rational beings. We become obsessed! Just like they do! Obsession knows no time or place. It's a way of life. It's better than television!"

"You're right. I don't know what to do."

"Dom, why not try some meetings?"

"Maybe I will. You sure I can't use Hellmann's?"

In his kitchen, Morgan Connelly unpacked the groceries, carrying each item one at a time to its designated place. The frozen foods he stacked on a nearby wooden counter, planning to open the freezer once. At the supermarket checkout, he had bagged all the refrigerator goods together; they were the first to be resettled at home.

Potent images of Terence Strange, fiercely radiant, literally shining—burnished by the cold air—tantalized. Morgan had brutally suppressed the urge to touch.

Must think me a dolt staring like that. Such an old fool! Actually could not speak!

Settling himself in his studio, he worked for twenty minutes sketching a face of the young boy who was the central character in the new book. He had not resisted using Terence as the model; the evolved image would retain only the autumnal coloring and the mesmerizing eyes. Lines changed but they demanded a firm starting point.

He studied the completed sketch. It was a portrait of Terence Strange. Instantaneously, he imagined him naked and became sexually aroused. Reaching for a sharpened pencil, he distracted himself by altering the figure's high cheekbones and converting the slightly pointed nose to a snubbed one. He hated to surrender the full, plump lips. Instead, he enlarged the ears and transformed the styled unparted hair into a coarse, chopped tyke look. He added freckles. The remarkable lips remained. And the eyes, with their dark arched brows and thick double lashes.

Those I'll keep. I don't think he'll mind.

Desire assailed him. It seemed to swell his fingertips, hindering their dexterity. It seemed to sensitize the hairs on his body and make clothing constricting.

What am I up to?

He doodled three linked circles. He knew very well what he was up to. He had never approved of syzygistic relationships. He would unhesitatingly advise any friend to flee the cosmos before gravitating toward one. So why was he now aligning himself to avoid sighting Christopher More while welcoming the pull of Terence Strange?

"So why?" he asked aloud.

Why? *Menopause? A sudden moonstruck attraction for grief?*

He decided to drive to the city. He would buy a bag of books at Barnes & Noble, visit the Michelangelo show at the Morgan Library, see some friends, and definitely go to the Everard. He had not debauched himself in a dozen years, but he would go to ease this surging ache squeezing his heart and, by direct connection, his groin. He loathed the baths, but he feared the bar scene. He had never been comfortable cruising; too unwilling (and unable) to pose and pander to fashion, not to mention too off-centered looking, not to mention (now) too damn old! He had never had the courage to hit the streets; he had never learned the manners or the lingo. True, the apartment in New York was empty; he now had a decent bed for his catch.

With my luck, I'd end up a gay knock.

[50]

No, the tubs was the only place for him. It was all up front and, literally, out in the open. He knew he had a certain appeal.

Who knows? I might meet someone there.

He envied the young their sexual freedom. It was a futile gesture and only made him more agitated. He did not envy them their soulless sex; he would have used the liberty more creatively. Not for him the life of a uniformed dildo.

Staring at the drawing board, he thought of Terence Strange. He shook his head.

Poor Christopher More. What a waste!

Judith Gunning cut short her conversation with Cissy McGlone.

Lips, be still!

To continue on a rampage might encourage words to be regretted in the bath. Now, on reflection, she was proud of her performance: She had not raised her voice or uttered one unladylike obscenity, yet Cissy McGlone was made aware of her disappointment at the moment of impact. More than that she could not desire. If Cissy claimed not to understand the extent of her commitment to Judith ("to the death, honey") so be it. But maybe it was so.

Twenty-four is very young these days. . . they tell me.

Cissy had published three fine stories in *The New Yorker* but, evidently, was not inured to the way of the world.

The lay of the land, the rules of the game.

"There are things you just don't do," Judith quoted. "And *this* is one of them."

Narrowing her eyes, she clutched her desk. For eleven months she had wooed Cissy McGlone, certain that when the young woman was ready to sign with a book publisher, Voyager (and Judith Gunning, editor) would be her first choice. Judith had written a clever, witty congratulatory note when the first story appeared. When the second ran, she wrote a longer, wittier, cleverer note. The third merited a lunch and serious chatter about agents and the inevitability of a collection of stories, a *special* collection crammed with goodies to rival Elizabeth Bowen.

She could have told me then! The House in Paris, Eva Trout, The Heat of the Day, The Little Girls . . .

She could bear it alone no longer. Buzzing the intercom, she marshaled support. Andrew appeared, nibbling an Oreo.

"Close the door, Drew!"

He obeyed, grinning. He had just blitzed the vending machine to appease his boredom. The morning had lacked verve, but the fulmination pursing Judith's mouth told him he was in for a vivid afternoon.

"What's up?" he gagged, choking on the cookie in his haste to get down into the dirt.

"Emmaline just fucked me royally!"

"How?"

She trotted back to the beginning. He did not need carting back that far. Had not *he* typed those witty congratulatory notes? He told her to skip the diddlyshit and get to the fuck. Judith nodded, stirred by her own outrage and warming to the fever of his camaraderie.

"Late Friday " she began again, tightening her face, "Emmaline skidded in here for a chat. *Girl talk/"*

"What did the bitch want?"

"She told me how bare my fall list looked."

"She *didn't!"*

"She *did'"*

"The fucking *cow!"*

They nodded in agreement. Neither had a good word for Emmaline Claudia Finch, skinny senior editor and archrival of Judith Kohn Gunning.

"She wanted to commiserate with me. She claimed *others* were saying I'm slowing down and not pulling my weight."

Andrew, coloring puce, was too shocked to twitch.

"And I fell for it!" she pounced in skirling tones, reaching for a cigarette and tossing one to him. They lit from a shared match, then glared at one another in murderous rage at Emmaline Claudia Finch.

"How did you fall for it?"

"By telling her about Cissy McGlone."

"You *didn't!*"

"I *did!* And why shouldn't I, Andrew? She's supposed to be my colleague. Emmaline is supposed to be my *friend.*"

"No barracuda is a friend when fresh meat drops into the pool."

"I can't work this way, Drew," she whispered, verging on sobs, struck anew by the enormity of the betrayal. "She just *happened* to be in Sag Harbor last weekend and just *happens* to know Cissy McGlone's mother who lives in Sag Harbor on weekends, and she just *happened* to drop in for a visit when guess who just *happens* to be visiting Mother in Sag Harbor last weekend?"

"I cannot stand it!" he shrieked, leaping to his feet.

"It gets *better!* Cissy has a novel she's been scratching away at for two years. It's practically finished!"

"The sly puss," Andrew interjected, exhaling vehemently and bulging his eyes.

"My words *exactly!*" she hissed, stalking the room."

"'Can *I* have your novel?' Emmaline sweetly coos. 'But of course, Mrs. Finch. Mrs. Gunning wants the stories, but we never discussed the novel.' 'Oh, Judith won't mind, dear. It's all in the family.' Could you not *die?*"

"You could *die!* But what do we do?" he demanded, heart braying with excitement.

"I laid it on the line with Cissy. I told her I was upset. I couldn't press it because I don't want Voyager to lose her, and we will if she scents discord here over her. I'm going to circulate a memo detailing my pursuit of Cissy McGlone and my disappointment over her novel going to another editor. I'll attach copies of our correspondence. Then we'll tell everyone, you and I, *how* Emmaline stabbed me in the back. It won't get me Cissy but it will make me feel better."

Andrew clucked. Judith's outrage had dulled into a stinging hurt. He wanted to hug her. Instead, he circled to her side of the desk, where she now leaned disconsolately.

"You are the best, sweetie," he said softly, taking her hand. "If they were all like you, this industry would be the way it should be."

"How's that, Drew, darling?"
"Fabulous."

"When are you returning?"
  "I am *not* coming back."
  "You must. I have no money."
  "You have no money?"
  "None. Not a fucking dime."
  "I left plenty."
  "It's gone. I need more."
  "You had plenty of money."
  "It's gone. You *must* give me more."
  "No!"
  "You must! What am I to do?"
  "Write some reviews. Get a job."
  "I have a job. I'm a poet."
  "I mean a job that pays the rent."
  "My art is my only job."
  "Your art? Your *art? Fuck your art!*"

Terence awoke gutted by horror. It was three months since that hateful confrontation, but it periodically recurred in dreams, chased by a quick montage of either Christopher's funeral or Christopher's near death behind the locked door of their apartment with a push-button telephone on the landing handy for summoning the ambulance. That reliable telephone was a pernicious vestige of Terence's indomitable belief in his power over his lover's salvation.

Romantic illusions never give up. They have no shame.

He sat up, turned on the light, and grunted in exasperation. The cat immediately responded with a chirrup. Standing on the pillow, it arched its back, then walked gingerly over the comforter to curl deftly on the bedspread over his lap.

At one of the first meetings, Terence grasped his enabling in their money situation. Christopher's work had been highly praised but had brought in little money. Terence was responsible for supplying the money. He had worked as a temporary typist, as a model, a waiter, a checkroom manager in Broadway theaters, and even for a time as a kitchen porter when they idyllically lived in London. Then, one summer, Christopher was awarded a Guggenheim and Terence wrote a novel—a period romance plotted with a busy beginning, a tortured middle, and a happy end. They referred to the book as *Glorious Technicolor, Wide-angled CinemaScope, and Stereophonic Sound.*

Most of his present readers were not cognizant of his pseudonymous existence. He had given himself an outrageous moniker—Titania Allgood—and the book a delectable four-word title from a Dowson poem.

The *echt*-ravishing Irish heroine, a shameless conflation of Clara Middleton, Undine Spragg, and Nancy Drew, was spun from Dublin slums into royal British beds, from deportation to Australia and flights across American Civil War battlefields to magical stardom on the New York stage. Mara's fuel was obsessive passion; her road map, a grueling search for the thespian lover who deflowered her in Chapter One. The tricky plot was bolted tight by dizzy notions of love and honor that Terence plundered but more than half believed. Originally intended as parody of the bodice-ripper genre, the book gradually transformed itself into lyrical romantic fiction by the absence of irony. Relying on meticulous research, he imposed convincing period details ("fret work") while ransacking his favorite literature, from *Tale of Genji* to *Giovanni's Room,* and his favorite movies, from *True Heart Susie* to *All That Heaven Allows* for effective MOs. He completed the manuscript in one season by working fourteen hours a day.

Christopher shipped it to his agent, who placed it within the month. It was promoted into *the* best-selling escapist fiction of its year, longer in fact: seventy-four weeks on the hardcover lists, with another eighty-eight as a paperback hit. It produced one of the first seven-figure reprint deals, and after much hoopla reached the silver screen ("Radio City Music Hall, where the fuck else?"), collecting four stars from *The Daily News* and eight Academy Awards, including three of the big ones. Terence saw it six times, delighting always when his very own fake name rolled in golden flaming glory up and off the world's most famous screen.

From his first reading of the book, Christopher's father had been impatient with all *Glorious Technicolor* jokes. He cited the work as a joyful achievement and talked of its incontestable merits. After a second reading, he wrote a long, appreciative letter, urging Terence to keep working; he invited him to address a class in creative writing. He conjectured that Terence had the makings of a first-rate novelist if he could find the courage to take the risks and think a trifle harder. Christopher was dumbfounded by this hearty approval of Terence's talent. When he discovered how important these encomiums were to Terence, he thanked his father, who responded with a rare flash of anger.

"Don't thank *me!*" he snapped. "I didn't bless him with his extravagant imagination or his stylish prose. Mark my humble words! Terence will someday surprise us *all!*"

"He'll never surprise me, pater."

"Them's dangerous thoughts, son. Don't let love blind you."

Being rich eliminated none of the growing conflicts about the drinking between Terence and Christopher, who merrily switched from rye to Irish whiskey when they moved into a brownstone floor-through apartment in Gramercy Park. Terence maintained control of the household money, doling it out for food, which was Christopher's single daily responsibility. "Earning my keep," he called it, shopping and cooking the main evening meal, making certain there were supplies for breakfast and lunch. Since they both claimed corners of the apartment for work—Christopher in the clattered, lamplit bedroom, Terence in the vast, sunny living room—they ate most of their meals at home. The money allocated for the household expenses also covered alcohol. Twenty dollars a day sufficed to feed them well and get Christopher soused. If he needed a few cents for steadying brandy, review copies of books would be sold at the Strand Bookstore.

Once Terence worked full-time at home, things became more strained. After the demands of a best seller ceased to distract him, he wrote another convoluted romance which was a success— nothing to equal the first, though it made another fortune. He began a third but spent continually more time and energy observing Christopher, whose erratic schedule was a constant source of friction. While Terence worked compulsively from seven to ten hours a day, Christopher barely managed three—and those only at the best of times. He would rise at one in the afternoon (Terence was up at eight), read for an hour, watch his favorite soap on TV, bathe, make a few phone calls ("the coiled serpent"), shop, make a few more phone calls, then, at four-thirty, mix a "smart cocktail" and sit down to write *perhaps,* or make a few more calls or read or fix Terence tea or answer a letter or stare at the walls humming Schubert lieder. At seven-thirty he prepared dinner, too drunk to invent anything but culinary concoctions.

"I'm *always* working," he snarled whenever Terence harangued that a little more effort was required. "Don't *ever* confuse what I do with what you do!" was his silencing retort before swinging into Yeats for an unrequested encore aimed at Terence's retreating back:

> *A line will take us hours maybe;*
> *Yet if it does not seem a moment's thought*
> *Our stitching and unstitching has been naught.*

As the publication of Terence's third book approached, Christopher's writing occupied less than an hour of his own day. He ceased reviewing and gave up all pretense of contributing money to the house; previously his efforts, had been minimal but constant.

Terence threatened, pleaded, and cajoled. He shouted and moaned and watered the whiskey as Christopher escalated the drinking. Each night by nine, Christopher was sunk into a quiet stupor; by ten, he was passed out over the din of the color television. This ground into the stultifying pattern of their lives. The drinking, a monotonous annoyance, progressed to a gloomy misery. Confined in the apartment, they clubbed one another with recriminations, keeping each other poised on the slicing edge of guilt. Both desperately wanted to call it *off* but were unable to function without the disease that manipulated them. Each cherished his pain as unique, unaware that each was dying a commonplace, squalid death.

Christopher had always drunk a great deal. In school it was a running gag at parties that someone would have to carry him home. He drank cold beer for breakfast and iced Manhattans for lunch when everyone else was having Cheerios or a liverwurst sandwich. He was always eager for a smart cocktail, and was undeniably the most glamorous and sophisticated teenager in his animated crowd.

"Drinks and ciggies, ciggies and drinks are my lovers," he chanted at college parties, adding thoughtfully, "and verse, of course. We must never forget *gai sabre*. Or men. But *mostly* smart cocktails. I'd *kill* for a smart cocktail!"

To Terence he was on first sighting a curious mixture of a very beige Gary Cooper, a very blond Tyrone Power, a very volatile Bette Davis, and a wily, magical Irene Dunne when all were young and flawless. He radiated the irresistible pizzazz of a wittily inspired polymath. He was frightening, exhilarating, and the most desirable man in the school. He was approachable to Terence because the anomalous drinking brought him down to human scale; Terence was certain the anarchic boozing would stop once they settled together into blissful domesticity. Love would do the trick: Love would turn the tide. Love would save the day.

One look and I had found my future at last
One look and I had found the world completely new
When love walked in with you.

The drinking never stopped. It increased tenfold. Love let him down hard. At first Christopher would nod off after dinner; later he would nod off *during* dinner. Often he would disrupt dinner parties; later there would be no dinner parties. Often he would walk out to the "local" for a nightcap; later he would stay out in the locals for the whole night.

Trickle becomes a flood. The time bomb explodes is more like it!

He *always* passed out before, during, or after dinner. He sped into the deep, dark night, returning bloody, battered, and bruised, unable to remember where he'd journeyed.

[58]

He swung from fire escapes screaming for deliverance. He jumped into strangers' cars at traffic lights. He called collect from two blocks away at four in the morning to announce his imminent arrival, then never showed up. He pounded on the door at all times of the day and night because he always lost his keys. He threw up everywhere. He shit and pissed in the closet, in the kitchen pots, in the bed. And once he managed to set his hair on fire while lighting a cigarette.

"You smell something burning?" he asked a berserk Terence, who was flying toward him waving an open towel.

Visits to reputable doctors and four recommended psy-chiatrists brought new complications labeled cross addiction, with rigors of their own.

"You drink because you're nervous. Take a placidyl."

"You drink because you're anxious. Take a dalmane."

"You drink because you can't sleep. Take a seconal. But don't *ever* take one with alcohol."

"This is the fabulous twentieth century! When in doubt, *pop a pill!*" Terence shrieked at a therapist, a specialist in alcoholic disturbances, one Sunday morning when the prescribed drug turned Christopher's brain into a carnival funhouse. The sympathetic doctor ("Compazine often gives a paradoxical reaction.") telephoned the correct antidote to a nearby drugstore. Christopher, propped-up, held-up twitching and jerking, babbled all the way, unable to shut up. Fortunately, the anodyne counteracted the poison instantly. To be safe, Christopher doubled the dose, took everything at once, and washed it down with an astounding amount of Irish whiskey.

Through all of this, every morning, Terence left the money for the day's shopping on the bureau beside the bed for his Christopher to find when he awoke in the early afternoon. Every evening, for nearly a decade, Terence was surprised and disappointed to discover his Christopher drunk.

I was always surprised. Talk about denial, Kukla! You and Christo where the only two people in New York who didn't accept he had a drinking problem.

Until the incident with the police, nothing changed, except for the worse. If anyone bothered to ask, Terence said things were fine. Everyone knew the truth, but no one contradicted. What was the point? The two fought constantly, screaming and yelling, occasionally stalling the battle by tumbling into bed for frantic, aggressive sex that was like a thunderstorm after a drought, or by one dramatically slamming into the night, or, this particular time, by a drunken Christopher belting Terence across the open mouth. Terence, crazed, never having been struck before, dialed the police and howled to be rescued. After calling, he paced, waiting, smoking cigarettes, sustaining his fury by reliving past wrongs, dredging up past injuries, determined to present to the law the visage of a person driven to extremes by a monster. He was to be triumphantly vindicated! At last Christopher would *see* what degradation drinking wrought.

Christopher had lunged into the bathroom and was running water from all taps. The doorbell rang. Terence flung it open, admitting two uniformed men who, eyeing Christopher freshly shaved, showered, and calmly lounging in the easy chair, attempted to remove the frenzied, demented Terence as the one in need of Bellevue.

"Is he like this all the time?" one policeman kindly inquired of Christopher.

"Yes, officer. And it's been getting worse."

"Can you manage him now, sir?"

"Yes, officer. Thank you, officers."

Speechless, Terence watched the policemen go. Christopher howled with glee, pointing fingers and kicking his feet. Terence walked silently into the bedroom. He cried until dawn, comforted by a penitent Christopher. He had known for years what the drinking was doing to Christopher; for the first time, Terence comprehended what it was doing to him.

The next day, Terence phoned a gay counseling service to find out about alcoholism. The concerned man directed him to a recovery program for people who live with problem drinkers. He went to find a way to make his Christopher stop drinking. He heard at the first meeting that he could not make Christopher stop drinking; he could only stop himself from driving *himself* insane by attempting the impossible. He heard that alcoholism was a family disease, and that he, Terence S., was its other victim.

> God grant me the serenity to
> Accept the things I cannot change
> Courage to change the things I can
> And wisdom to know the difference.

He heard people describe situations similar to his own. He realized he was not alone; they claimed he was not unique. His high drama was nothing but commonplace symptoms, they said. He heard the word "enabler," took in its meaning but not much else: The way he controlled the money was the only way. It was Christopher's choice to buy whiskey, he rationalized, failing to learn that when Christopher was drinking, he had no choice. It took years before he knew that he could not pay for the alcohol because it destroyed his own emotional sobriety and kept *him* ill. There were so many things the disease did not want him to know.

How can I claim to love the man when I'm supplying the embalming fluid? That's love? What if I hated him? I want him unconscious. I know where he is. Safe. Safe? This is love? Do I love enough to stop enabling to death?

Now, alone, at the center of a winter's lonely night, he lit a cigarette. It made him gag. He stubbed it out.

Why *do I smoke? I hate it. Why don't I stop?*

He counted the days of self-exile. Three months. He was a failure. Perhaps he should have stayed and found a viable solution. Things were much better. Why had he packed and retreated to this cold, empty house?

Because Christopher is now alcoholically insane. In the final stages. Bellowing into the phone all night. Violent rages. Who could sleep!? Work? Couldn't live there. . .going berserk again. Got to keep out of it

Quickly, adeptly, he retrieved his confidence. He tended to forget the bad things. He *knew* he was not routed, but at times of stress, at three forty-seven in the morning, he was apt to discard the logic and react emotionally again. He felt his withdrawal cravings. There had been no melodrama. He had quietly picked up and exited when Christopher refused to make basic changes.

"How can I?"

"Get a job."

"Who would hire me?"

"You have to do something. I can't—*won't*—keep giving you money."

"You've always given me money and I've given you other things."

"But we can't do this anymore. I'm making myself sick."

"I'm going to keep drinking whether you give me money or not. You've been giving it for years and it's never been a problem. Besides, I *earn* it."

"I don't want to support you. I'm not your father."

"He doesn't want to support me either."

"Support yourself."

"How?"

"I'll pay for everything but not the alcohol."

"Then get out."

He had gone. Under other circumstances, he would have proudly supported Christopher. Alcoholism perverted everything. It was insidious. It tells lies. Everything got twisted. Denial is a symptom. Love could be the greatest enemy.

So he had gone. Often he had trouble remembering the other issues. He pressed himself.

The rest of it. Deliver us from denial.

"The anguish, the rot, the corruption, the confusion, the rage, the pain. The mess of it all, the lie-riddled mess of our sad, diseased lives. The loneliness, the isolation, the desperation that devoured me, still devours him. I left because I could no longer stay. I left so one of us will survive the epidemic, one of us will regain his strength, one of us will continue loving. I left with hope. Christopher isn't dead yet. Without me around, he may surrender the defensive position and see how ill he is."

The rest of it. Deliver us from denial.

"You're throwing up!" he had screamed at the retching Christopher.

"No! I'm not!" Christopher had sputtered between gasps and

spasms of heavy vomiting.

Leave him alone. Stop being the enemy. Leave him alone. *Go to sleep.*

He kissed the cat then turned off the light. Instantly, he turned the light back on. Rising, he carried the ashtray and the cigarettes to the other side of the room. He dropped the butts into a wicker garbage container and after a thoughtful pause, threw in the rest of the pack, the matches, and the ashtray. Laughing, he retrieved the ashtray.

Clean up your own act, pal. Bet his father will pay the rent. Wonder if Dom ever goes to meetings?

FOUR

William More was annoyed with his son. He had given the rascal February's rent, which the poet irresponsibly squandered on "other things." Trying to air the problem with Dominic, William won little support.

"Leave him alone, Billy," Dominic angrily advised. "Let him handle his own problems. He's thirty-four. Stop sweeping up after him."

"Puritan horseshit!" William haughtily spat, and they were off on a furious tussle. "Everybody needs a little help sometime!" Twenty minutes later, Dominic was emotionally pulped, weeping and howling incoherently; William was totally bewildered, wondering what he had done to warrant such a scene.

"The Ladies' Auxiliary"—Christopher's name for Terence's group—things were on edge in the Perrugio-More household. William assumed Dominic was more docile and pliant than Terence and not nearly as bright, which gave him real comfort; as long as Dominic was kept away from further contamination, he would never decamp the way Terence had selfishly done. But then his own drinking—admittedly a problem—was not as serious as Christopher's. It never interfered with work or changed his plans, though lately there were fewer plans to change.

Every weekday for the last thirty years he arose at six-thirty, showered, shaved, ate breakfast (with Dominic for the past seventeen), and went to teach literature at Sacred Heart Academy, a Catholic women's college built in 1851 on the lush, sloping banks of the Hudson. He taught two American survey courses, one Shakespeare or Milton semester (his alternating "specialty acts"), and lately freshman English to keep alert, "in touch" with the radically changing students, and to focus his attention on their ever-diminishing language skills. He led the creative-writing seminar, restricted to ten honor students for whom Christopher would soon be speaking. William More was considered a devoted, respected teacher.

His wife, the mother of his only child, had died of leukemia when she was thirty-two, leaving him after ten years of happy marriage with a precocious boy to manage. Christopher had been Virginia's responsibility; they shared him but she led the way. Besides being monstrously intelligent, he was difficult in the extreme and by thirteen was flagrantly in pursuit of carnal shenanigans with mature men. This was a verity he imposed upon his flustered father.

"I want you to know what I'm up to, pater."

"Why? If you were interested in women would you seek my blessings?"

"If I were screwing women, pater, you might never have to bail me out of jail."

The original confrontation regarding Christopher's preference occurred in a direct, uncomplicated manner. William arrived home early from school, the sudden death of a colleague having gained him an unexpected half-day holiday. There he espied on an unmade bed his virile son entwined around the unnamed man who should have been reading the gas meter. Breathlessly, thinking himself unobserved, William stealthily let himself out. Although strenuously occupied, Christopher glimpsed his darting reflection in the bureau mirror. That same evening, while they sipped Manhattans, Christopher sounded out his father.

"What do you want me to say, Chris? You want to go see a psychiatrist?"

"No! What for? I'm happy enough *now*. I've completed the requisite integrations. It was hell at twelve being a faggot but it's great now."

"I did my best, Christopher."

"I know. I don't blame you. I like it this way. What do you think?"

"I think *I* need a shrink. I'm not taking this at all well." The recognition of William's own sexual preference had not been as easily managed. His sight of Christopher cavorting with that man had profoundly disrupted his own inner harmony ("Such as it was, doctor!"). It took eight months of intense biweekly sessions before he could admit to himself that his initial response had not been one of disgust or revulsion or even disbelief, but one of consummate longing. The incessantly recurring image was, to him, searingly erotic; in his nocturnal visions the graceful meter man was gleefully doing to him what he had watched being expertly done to Christopher.

The psychiatrist assured and comforted. It was normal, a natural response, in line with the progenitor-male-child sexual conflict. Seeing his son performing successfully had threatened his own fragile male ego on the most basic, the most primal libidinal level. And the trauma of being witness to a perversion was not to be discounted. William bought none of it. He changed his therapist; fired him in mid-concept. He knew what he had thrillingly experienced. It bore no resemblance to terror of ritualistic patricide. He had felt *lust* for the meter man.

When he candidly examined his life, he realized that women played a secondary role. The passionate friendships were with men; all the anguish and unhappiness resulted from male-bonded relationships. He married at nineteen because he loved Virginia, but also because his first fumbling attempts at coitus had impregnated her, idealistic William did the right thing ("The wedding was real classy. The rice was puffed, *that* swell!"). His life was a series of correct moves. He had landed in France on D-Day, and after winning the war had gone to Paris for tea with Gertrude Stein.

Virginia's wealthy parents made them comfortable while he finished school on the GI Bill; he took his Fordham doctorate *cum laude*. They continued to pay the bills until he landed the teaching job and even then helped in every way they could. Sacred Heart Academy was perfect in more ways than he ever suspected: It allowed the new parents to live in Manhattan, where Virginia was happiest, and it surrounded him with young women who never provoked the awakening.

"Like all the best people, I, too, slept through the fifties. Must say I was happy in my fashion."

Two times he had experienced sexual tremors, but no defenses were toppled. Once on the Jersey shore, where he had taken his family for a summer vacation, the young husband in a nearby cottage suggested a few of the men convene for a midnight swim. The glistening naked bodies frolicking in the moonlit surf aroused him to such a frenzy that he distractedly swam out too far and was nearly taken by the current. He vividly recalled strong hands and willing arms plucking him from the sea. He dismissed the incident as midsummer madness.

On another summer evening, while riding the Manhattan subway during the rush hour, his fatigued back was pressed against the chest of a young man who stood straddling a small blue duffelbag. The stranger's crotch innocuously rubbed his left buttock, then suddenly snuggled into the cleavage, propelled by the shaking of the train. The impudent bulge noticeably heated and hardened. Lust stung William More. Mortified, he violently forced his way from the train at the next stop. The point of intrusion was evident to him for days as though he had been scalded there. His heart had quickened mysteriously at each remembrance. More midsummer madness, he reasoned: propinquity and all that sweat.

"The intent of psychotherapy is self-discovery," he told himself, "not interior decoration."

William More practiced his beliefs. Once having acknowledged and accepted his sexuality, he was determined to meet his own meter man. Knowing nothing of the mating rituals, he decided to take the most sensible approach: He would discuss this serious business with an expert. Christopher at sixteen knew everything about loving men. The genius son was a freshman at New York University, was living in his own apartment on Cornelia Street in Greenwich Village, and was immediately invited to dinner. William practiced the opening words of his confession for days, but when the time came for delivery he was unable to broach the all-consuming subject. Christopher, who had long since become a private person regarding matters sexual, was gushing with news of his independent life; he had decided to transfer from his beloved New York to Harvard and could talk of nothing else.

The two spent the weekend in an alcoholic haze, each vying to produce the perfect Manhattan.

For two more *years*, William led a quiet, celibate existence. Concerned wives of colleagues regularly created dinner parties for him to meet their eligible female friends. Once or twice he was tempted to marry again, but warming thoughts of his meter man would remind him that a lonely life with a hopeful heart was better than a lonely life with a cold lie. How could he not share this part of himself, newly embraced after so much psychic laboring, not to mention the expense? The anxious wives persevered, each convinced that a good woman, with luck a loving woman, was the solution to his very evident, and evidently increasing, drinking problem. A wife would assuage his loneliness, they insisted wisely. And why else does a good man drink too much anyway?

He was traveling home from a drunken seventeenth-birthday dinner for his son when he met Dominic Perrugio. William had resisted taking a taxi, though Christopher vehemently argued he was in no condition to execute the change from the subway to the bus at 242nd Street; but the stubborn William was saving for a planned sabbatical and was loath to indulge himself in an expensive taxi ride on this side of the Atlantic. He had recently moved from the house of Christopher's childhood to a new high-rise apartment on Netherland Avenue in Riverdale. The bus, caught at Van Cortlandt Park, dropped him directly in front of his home.

On the subway platform at West Fourth Street in Manhattan, he had settled into a seat and promptly fallen asleep. A transit policeman woke him and assisted him into his train; he did not reach 242nd Street until four in the morning. On the bus he fell asleep again. He would have snored his way to the end of the line, eventually shelling out the taxi fare to backtrack, if the bus driver had not politely awakened him to ask where he was headed. William rudely stared up at the handsome Latin face—Italian?—and smiled into the large, brown eyes.

"What's your name, beauty?"

"Dominic Perrugio," the young man answered, blushing.

"Well, Dominic, my angel, you have beautiful eyes. My name is William More. Please take me directly home!"

"Where is home, Mr. More?"

The next day, a Saturday, Dominic Perrugio telephoned William More to make certain he had reached his bed safely. William remembered nothing of the trip, but was touched by the man's concern and intrigued by the deep, sweet voice. William invited him to brunch on Sunday.

The following afternoon, at one promptly, Dominic arrived with a huge bunch of daffodils, the Sunday *Times* and *News*, a large loaf of warm Italian bread, some pickled eggplants his father jarred, and a diffident smile that touched William as deeply as he could be touched. They spent the afternoon talking about their families and their jobs.

I don't know. A bus driver, thirty, a huge family, straight? Finished high school at night. Lovely. What's the point? Charming. Delicious-looking, strong hands, arms, legs, magnificent ass. Bright. Laughs at all my jokes. Warm as the sun. . . .

William cooked dinner. Dominic, to thank him, insisted they go to the movies.

A college professor? I like him. He's nice. Ever been to bed with a guy? Doubt it. Stay cool. Keep it clean.

They returned to William's after the film. They ate sandwiches and talked until midnight when Dominic rose, stretched with feline grace, and extended his hand. William looked startled, then disappointed. Dominic smiled.

"I had a really good time, Billy."

No one had called him Billy in twenty years. His lace-curtain Irish family always used William, sometimes Bill; there had been some friends when life was new who had dared. He laughed and told Dominic he rather liked being "Billy," although at thirty-eight he felt beyond the Billy stage except for certain moments in the middle of certain nights when he felt more goat than human.

"Next time it happens," Dominic said, voice low, hand squeezing firmer, "call me."

Stunned by Dominic's boldness, William had a surge of lust. Pummeled by pulsating terror, the feeling retreated like a finger from fire. He wanted to shout: Now, now, I want you *now!* But he could only laugh, suddenly redfaced, and say that he certainly would call.

"Will you be home or out driving your bus? Perhaps I should open the window and fly my undershorts at half-mast?"

Dominic blushed and forced a smile. He was hurt and flustered, which confused William terribly. The two stood in silence at the center of the book-lined living room until William found the courage to say he was sorry.

"You'll never know how much I've enjoyed today, Dominic."

"Can I see you next weekend?"

William looked into his visitor's pleasantly pleading eyes. There was no denying the affection in them nor the sensuality.

Is my discomfort over this intimacy discernible?

The college professor is scared shitless! A cherry?

"Yes, please, Dominic. I'd like that."

"I feel sort of stupid with you, Billy. Dumbolla! All these fucking books! If you don't want to see me again, I'll understand."

Maybe it's better?

"You're not stupid. Besides, you're much too attractive not to be my friend."

Absurd thing to say.

Dominic guffawed. Head thrown back, hands on hips, he blushed again.

"You don't fool around," he said, pleased.

"I don't know how."

The younger man studied the older intensely, scrutinizing the expression on his nervous face as if to make certain he was not misunderstanding, as if to hear with his perceptive eyes.

"Call me Saturday, Dominic, yes? We can spend the weekend together."

"Can I stay over?"

"Call me Saturday."

When left alone, William More went berserk. He prowled the apartment drinking Manhattans from a brandy snifter. What was he doing fooling around with a thirty-year-old careerist bus driver? What could come of it?

I want a lover, someone I can make a life with, not some humpy Italian type *who only wants to nuzzle a bit.*

The idea, the mesmerizing fancy of them naked, entwined, in his very own bed, immersed in each other's maleness, quickened his pace. He had no experience, *none;* Dominic could remedy that, making available what was outside his curtained consciousness, acquainting him with the real business of life.

I might die without ever knowing how it feels. . . how it tastes. . .

The gentleness and tenderness he had witnessed in that enchanting smile, in those luminous eyes, erased all worry of unpleasantness, abolished all fretful notions of blackmail, burglary, ugliness. And the cleanliness of those teeth—

The telephone rang.

"Billy?"

"Who else?"

"Billy, this is Dom."

"Yes. I know."

"You recognize my voice already?"

William laughed, delighted.

"What's so funny?"

"You."

"That's OK."

"Where are you?"

"On the corner. I'm waiting for my bus. I'm just calling to tell you I had a really great time."

"Good. I did, too."

"You know, you're the first guy I ever spent time with that I ever wanted to see again. And nothing happened!"

"A lot happened, Dominic."

"Yeah. You're right. I guess a lot did happen. I been waiting all my life to meet someone like you, Billy." William gasped as though punched in the chest. Tears filled his eyes and he had difficulty speaking.

"Dominic! You hardly know me."

"I know you, Billy. I love you, Billy."

There was a long pause.

"Here's my bus, Billy. I gotta go. I'll call you next week. Take care of yourself."

He hung up. William More stood holding the phone. He was so shaken that when he finally managed to put the receiver into its cradle, he could not remember how to mix a Manhattan.

That night and the next day, he had difficulty concentrating. He could focus his attention only on Dominic's physical attributes. To William's astonishment, even his tardy sense of smell seemed overactivated. The one sensation more powerful than the excoriating lust swelling his groin to aching was a palpable doom that circled like a noose, threatening his most vulnerable professional life. Would the good Sisters want his resignation? How would they find out? Would he start to *look* queer?

He awakened sore with longing from a tormenting dream that had failed to deliver; and after frenziedly masturbating in the cold shower, he spent the morning drugged by the sensual tension in his limbs. Dominic Perrugio! The way he strutted when he walked, tightening the upper thighs—to keep them firm? To guard the treasure? His lithe, taut body, on closer inspection baroque in the fullness of its curves. Was there such a thing as delicately chunky? Thoughts flirted with erotic images like mating butterflies fluttering in midair carole. The way he laughed so unselfconsciously, head back, mouth open—eager for kissing? The easy way he sat *into* cushions with limbs left as they happened, akimbo.

Is he hairy? Is he hung? What a life! Good Lord! He must not be toyed with! He must be dismissed! *The last thing I need is an untutored lower-class bosky charmer. What would I do with him after the obvious things are done? And there have been other "guys." He told me so himself. Doubtless there will be others during and after me. Last thing I need entering my crucial forties is a case of the terminal hots.* "... *pillar of the world transformed/Into a strumpet's fool.*"

He was crude and vulgar and common and victim of frequent hysterical flushes whenever he contemplated the sweet thing's ass. He had never understood the fascination his heterosexual peers expressed over the female behind. All of that ostentatious turning in public places, twisting one's neck to gaze in rapture upon two lumps of bobbing flesh had always struck him as

[72]

nonsense. He had done his share because he believed he should but he had never comprehended what *exactly* he was supposed to be examining. Was it somehow connected to the canine preoccupation with sniffing one another?

Then, suddenly, inexplicably, the mystery solved itself. He could recall precisely the shimmering insightful moment when the one-syllable *ass* became freighted with profound reverberations. He was in the A&P. It was during a heat wave three summers past ("When else, Doc?"). A slim young man wearing cotton duck trousers, a slim young man not harnessed by underclothes, had come into focus pushing the cart ahead. From the small of the stranger's back to the tops of his thighs, two voluptuous mounds of prime virile meat swung together exquisitely, stretching the white fabric to glorious tautness recalling sails so perfumed that the winds were lovesick with them. William, caught in their wake, marveled at their dazzling perfections, their mystical syncopations, and hungered to touch on each side those pretty dimpled Cupids. After ten shameless minutes he swooned, crashing through a floor display of Del Monte peaches, which seemed belabored but appropriate to his fevered imagination. From that day, he considered himself an "ass man" and took comfort in having settled that matter once and for all.

I think I be transformed into a beast,/For I can nowhere find me like a man.

Ultimately, it was fear that forced his decision never to see Dominic Perrugio again. In just a few hours (eleven if he counted the movie), his new friend had become a person with a history (traditional, Italian-American working class), with admirable ambitions (to be foreman at the bus depot), and virtuous dreams (to settle down with the right person and make a good home). Add those to the dark curly hair, the Pompeian eyes, the white teeth, the high, round buttocks, the tender sensibilities, the intelligence, the grace, the sense of humor, the sweet disposition, the generosity, and Dominic became a formidable threat to William's potted notion of an erudite civilized WASP companion with whom he could enter the sophisticated salons revolving around Sacred Heart Academy without being found out. Would it not be evident to every sentient adult on this planet why William More was cohabiting with Dominic Perrugio?

I've got us married already! Couldn't we have a casual affair? A fling? Somehow. . . once it starts. . .

Could he pretend Dominic was a live-in houseboy or a refugee from the Big Brother program? What about the Fresh Air Fund? A needy nephew? No, everyone knew William was an only child. Could he not keep his two lives apart?

Who wants two lives? Difficult enough managing one stylishly.

Each time his thoughts strayed to the pleasures of Dominic's good-natured company, or to the feelings of affection that were crowding the shallow crevice of his hasty heart, his eyes glared over and he could not converse coherently. Fortunately, Monday held his lightest teaching schedule and only three students visited him for consultation in the departmental offices; but those unfortunate few found him too distracted to be of any constructive assistance in unraveling curriculum complications.

Too exhausted to cook, he dined at a local beanery where Goldy's hashbrowns were the favored item on an extensive menu. Home by seven, he was running a hot tub when the telephone rang. It was Dominic. Could he stop by on his way to work? William said yes, staunchly determined to have it out with the kid and send him packing. (William noticed again how at moments of emotional stress he assumed postures from forties' movies, a trait he shared with Christopher. In fact, he and his son had a great deal more in common than radical interests in booze and men.) He took the bath, which relaxed him, and finished a pitcher of Manhattans, which did not.

Dominic arrived at eight twenty-five. He was obviously nervous and had made a concerted effort to look his best: He wore carefully coordinated dark clothing free of wrinkles or creases, and his black-leather loafers gleamed. His hair was slicked down, waveless, forced to appear flat and straight: controlled. William's strained heart spread fanshaped at the sight of such buffing on his behalf; that *he* could instigate such behavior in one so lovely! The kid was far from flawless but he sure as hell was something else.

[74]

Dominic strolled the length of the room. Accepting a Bourbon and soda, he commenced to strut, refusing to sit, unable to settle. Within minutes, the air was heavily scented with his Old Spice after-shave lotion and cologne, a scent William usually despised but tonight thought curiously erotic. The guest prowled the living room. William watched, enthralled by the muscles undulating inside the tight clothing; he sat as captive as any cobra in the presence of an experienced mongoose.

"You think I'm a whore, right? Not good enough, *right?'*

"Dominic! What the hell makes you say that?"

"Because I told you I've been with a lot of guys. They don't mean *shit,* Billy. A guy's gotta get his rocks off. I could be faithful if I had a good reason. I *could* if I ever got the chance. You gonna give me the chance?"

"Dominic, we've got to talk."

"Billy, we've gotta fuck."

Shocked by this direct approach, William slurped another drink and rose to open a window. There was nothing he wanted more in this life than to lean against the kid, but he felt a great chasm between them and he could not see a way across. When he distressfully glanced again at Dominic, he glimpsed him building a bridge. Dominic was removing his shirt.

"It's hot in here, Billy. I don't wanna sweat up my new shirt."

William laughed nervously. He was pleased his young man was not wearing an undershirt.

"You've got a splendid body, Dominic."

I'd better sit down. The hairs on his chest and stomach look flossy. Those shoulders!

'"Thanks, Billy. It used to be better but all this sitting down on the job makes me a little flabby. I been doing isometrics all the time now."

He squeezed his firm pectoral muscles to emphasize the point. Consciously, he flexed and stretched, intently aware of the responsive twitchings around William's eyes and mouth.

"You look . . . *splendid* to me, Dominic."

"You look OK, too."

"I'm soft all over . . . almost."

"Too much booze."

"Yup, far too much."

I'll take care of that. . .

"You want to see something *really* splendid, Billy?"

It had been that outrageous and that simple.

"Sure," William said naively, standing, hoping for a display of tightened biceps.

Dominic quickly crossed to him, approaching at a canter. Stopping two feet away, he deftly dropped his trousers. He wore no underwear; nothing contained his proudest possession. Taking William's hot left hand, he joined the two.

"It's wonderful!" William whispered, clutching hard to keep from collapsing with joy and terror.

Suddenly, without warning, Dominic burst into tears. Moving closer, he rested his head on William's taller shoulder. Crying for several minutes, he paused briefly to retrieve William's transient left hand and return it to its original placement.

"I love you, Billy," he sighed, trying to appease his own sense of shame.

"I think I love you, too. I'm amazed."

"I'm sorry."

"Sorry for what? Certainly not for this!"

They kissed a wet, loving kiss while Dominic helped William undo his clothing. They backed onto the couch. After their first very successful sexual gropings, Dominic again burst into tears.

"What's wrong now, fool?"

"I was terrified you were gonna hate it and throw up. I'm so relieved you like it."

William laughed, pulling him into his arms.

I'm serious, Billy. I'm serious! It's happened! Cherries are scary people."

"How could I not love this?" William sighed contentedly, caressing the warm, strong back. "What time do you have to leave for work?"

"I don't."

"You don't!"

"Monday's my night off."

"But you said—"

"I know what I said. If I gave you a whole week to think, it never would've happened. It *had* to happen, Billy!"

He rolled over, pulling in deep breaths, desperate not to cry again. He would find a million ways to make up for this deception; and that cheap seduction con, waving his cock around, was not what he had wanted. But he believed attack was the most feasible approach.

"For someone who feels stupid with me, you do pretty well."

"Are you angry?"

"No."

"Disappointed in me?"

A whore's tricks?

"No."

"Can I stay the night?"

"Just try to get away."

Their daily schedules, though reversed, worked for them. Dominic reached William's apartment at six-twenty every morning, allowing him time to shower before joining William in bed after the alarm sounded. They spent a satisfying twenty minutes together (William preferred sex in the morning, while Dominic, slow to awaken, preferred sex in the evening, although he was eager at any hour). When William showered (frequently joined briefly by his playful lover), Dominic made William's breakfast. After William left for work, Dominic cleaned the apartment and did the laundry before going to his parents' home for dinner and sleep. Returning in the evening for more sex, he would breakfast with William, eating whatever his lover prepared for his own dinner.

"Stuffed cabbage for your breakfast, Dom?"

"I can eat *anything* for breakfast. My stomach wakes up real fast. I can't figure why my tool takes so long."

After six weeks of this routine, William suggested one rainy morning that Dominic sleep where he was rather than trekking wet miles home.

"I'll need clean clothes," was the hesitant response. "You can wear my socks. Your balls won't fall off if you wear the same drawers twice. Or you can go without underwear for one day. You've been known to do that before. In fact, why don't you stop by your folks' place later and pack a big suitcase. . . ?"

There was no response. Dominic had turned his back and was facing the wall.

"Are you crying, fool?"

"I've been praying you would ask me to stay."

"Remember Saint Theresa's answered prayers?" William moved toward Dominic and pulled him close.

"I love you, fool. I want you to live with me."

"What about your friends?"

"What about them?"

Dominic shrugged. They had never discussed them, but William's concerns had not vanished and Dominic had considered everything. It did not require too much smarts to figure it out.

"The few I have will love you as I do."

"That sounds like a greeting card."

"You want I should send out announcements?"

"No. Just don't ask me to go out to a movie when your friends come to dinner," he laughed, adding, "I promise I won't embarrass you, Billy. And I promise I'll go!"

"You mustn't feel that way!"

"You'd be surprised how I feel."

"Dominic! You are the most important person in my life, you could never embarrass me, fool. I love you. I want to live with you."

"I want to live with you, too. I know I'll make you real happy, Billy. You'll see."

"I know you will. You and your tool are doing a great job, baby. It's my making you happy that's got me worried."

"Don't worry, Billy. You're everything I've always wanted."

They kissed to seal the bargain. That afternoon, Dominic moved his belongings into his lover's apartment. The following week, Mr. and Mrs. Perrugio invited William more to dinner. Dominic was the youngest of seven children and the last to leave home. The parents were anxious he make a good impression on the college professor who was making their little boy so happy.

They made William feel comfortable in their home. The dinner was a huge success. The food was exceptional and William's decent Italian (a college requirement) had delighted the family. When they suggested the meal be repeated the next Sunday, William, to Dominic's joy, readily accepted the invitation. Sunday dinner with the Perrugios became a pleasant ritual that continued for eleven years, until Tony Perrugio died and Angelina went to live with their eldest son, Anthony, in California. At one moment during that first afternoon, while Dominic was in the kitchen helping his mother, Tony had smiled at William and said softly:

"Mama and I were worried about Dominic. We were worried he'd never settle down and make himself a good home of his own. How long you been teaching college, Billy?"

William never knew how much the Perrugios comprehended of his relationship with their son. He never talked about it with Dominic because there seemed no reason, the rest of the large family accepted the fact that they lived together, invited him to all the gatherings, and in time, all of the nephews and nieces called him Uncle Bill. Of all the transitions that had to be made, the one involving the Perrugios was the smoothest.

Talk about denial . . .

At school, William continued to function as a bachelor. He attended all the school's events and faculty parties on his own. Never accustomed to entertaining at home, he forced himself to extend himself to his closest friends and arranged for them to meet Dominic. Several of the male faculty members, given the opportunity, shared similar secrets and introduced the two to other couples. By the time Dominic was promoted to a daytime supervisory position, they had cultivated an active social life and were delighted by his change to a normal working schedule.

It took Dominic years to feel comfortable with William's friends. In the beginning, he occupied himself in the kitchen or with refilling drinks or emptying ashtrays because he felt all the people were "brains" and he was outclassed "damaged goods, seconds," until three incidents changed his sense of himself.

The first involved William's closest friend at Sacred Heart Academy. Michael Jeffrey-Porter, a published novelist, squarely

[79]

handsome, worldly wise, and nastily witty, lived in Manhattan with a lover in California who taught philosophy at Berkeley; the two men shared their vacations in New York or California or abroad. One evening, at a crowded party to mark the start of the Christmas break, Michael sat with Dominic in a quiet corner talking about gardens, about love, about William, about movies, about anything that came their way. Before leaving, he kissed Dominic and thanked him for making what could have been another dreary Yuletide fuss into a delightful evening. Two days later, a note arrived inviting them to dinner. Dominic flapped with happiness all the while William teased, obviously proud but not surprised.

The second incident involved Michael's lover, Stefan, an Austrian beauty who, during that same Christmas vacation, announced Dominic *the* most desirable man in New York and pursued him mightily. The night of the dinner party, he groped Dominic twice, pinched his rear at every opportunity, and cornering him in the kitchen, offered a special evening with an extra-special treat.

"I've got my own extra-special treat, *thanks!*" Dominic muttered angrily.

"I'll bet mine you do!" Stefan leered drunkenly.

Then, at another party, Stefan sat beside him and slid a large hand down the back of a startled Dominic's trousers, tweaking the hairs that warmed his coccyx. Dominic leaped two feet, causing Stefan to toss his drink into another's lap. Dominic spent the rest of the evening attached to William, who was saddened by the fate of earthly lovers. How long would Dominic's infatuation last?

"*He's* a philosophy professor?" Dominic snorted. "He's a *Pig!*"

"I see, William," Michael sadly stated, "that my husband is determined to bed yours. He displays excellent taste."

The next time they met that particular visit (and every subsequent one), Stefan was docile. He made no attempts to touch Dominic, but talked about his past, his work, his love for Michael, and his envy over William's having *captured* as captivating a faun as Dominic Perrugio. For months afterward, Dominic received postcards of paintings by Rothko or Pollock or de Kooning postmarked Berkeley but always without message or signature.

The third incident involved Christopher. Nothing had tormented Dominic more than the inevitable prospect of meeting William's legendary son.

Several months after they began sharing the apartment, William received a sheaf of poems that were soon to be published by the university as one of a series of monographs devoted to the best younger poets in America. Dominic tried unsuccessfully to read them; to him they were indecipherable. He was so ashamed of his ignorance that he cried secretly for days, fighting an overwhelming black depression with every iota of his considerable strength until one morning, after a sexual combat that nearly split William in half, he broke into uncontrollable sobs that terrified the still-gasping William, who clutched at him to comfort, refusing to leave the house without an explanation.

The answers came in broken bits smothered by more sobs and a harrowing quantity of hot tears. By the time the story was completed, William was furious with himself for having been insensate to his lover's needs. They had lived together long enough for him to know better. He was aware that Dominic had perused Christopher's poems, which proved difficult for *him*, a full professor of English literature! Why had he not been able to avoid all this grief? Why was he so full of his own meager self for having reproduced successfully?

He lifted Dominic and cradled him in his arms. The tears had ceased; the spasms were still rampaging. He was frightened. He had never seen such an outburst before. He felt profound respect for a being capable of such pain. He felt compassion for one forced to bear the weight of it. Gently pushing his hand between the clamped legs, he tenderly clasped Dominic's genitals. William knew this gave his lover a sense of surrendering himself in trust; it gave a feeling of security: These most vulnerable parts were respected as the center of a universe.

Dominic sighed, relaxing, comforted. William kissed his wet cheek, stroking his back. The sobs increased. More tears flowed. They were not violent and soon ceased. "You'll be late for work,

Billy. I'm sorry."

'I'm not going to work. I'm staying here with you."

"You have to go to work! *I* have to go to work."

"I *want* to stay with you. Besides, after the job you did on me before, who could walk?"

They laughed. Concern darkened Dominic's eyes. More obstreperous grief threatened.

"Did I really hurt you, Billy?"

"No! No! I was only joking," he lied. "We have a lot to talk about, fool."

Dominic nodded, nuzzling his head against William's shoulder. He spoke in a whisper.

"I've been really unhappy. I've *never* been so unhappy. It's been *awful*, Billy."

"I think it's time you met our Christopher."

"He'll hate me!" he cried in a voice barely audible.

"Did Michael or Stefan hate you?"

Dominic shrugged. He worked to phrase a reply. Did William really think a famous writer would admire his father for being a queer with an ignorant wop for a lover? Sometimes Dominic did not understand William at all. How could he be so stupid? How could he not know the way children feel about their parents?

"Christopher is one of us."

Dominic lifted his head and gaped.

"How do you know for sure?"

William related the meter man tale.

"If anything," he concluded, "he'll be jealous."

Jealous of me? He's crazy!

Lovingly he was fondled, and he stretched his hard legs apart and arched his strong back, displaying his particular masculine grace. He laughed as his body firmed and tensed, loving his own beauty for the pleasure it gave to William. Then his mood shifted: "Do you love me because of that?" he asked solemnly.

"You mean are you a sex toy?"

"Yes . . . would you love me if I were small and ugly?"

"Aren't you?"

"Be serious, William. Would you? Please, be serious."

"Of course I would! I loved you before you let me hold you, before I knew what *gifts* your loving me would pour over my parched life. It's not as if I selected you from a row in a butcher's shop window, for Christ's sake! If you shriveled up tomorrow— God forbid!—I'd continue to love you. I love *you,* fool. This is *nice,* but not enough to build a marriage on."

Dominic laughed, for the moment convinced.

"I get confused, Billy. Then I get scared."

"Make me some coffee, fool. Then bring me Christopher's poems and the three dictionaries. We'll need all the help we can get. *And* paper and pencils."

I'll have to explain sprung rhythm, solipsism. . . he's up to it. Am I? I hurt. Never understand masochism.

"I'm too stupid, Billy."

"Dom, do you care?"

"Of course I care!"

"It won't make you less a person, you know."

"It won't?"

"No."

"I'd like to try."

"Then try we will! You must never keep things from me like this. That makes us lesser persons. Give me a kiss, Dominic."

"Anytime, fool."

The intricate schematics of Christopher's poems quickly heightened an awareness of vocabulary, syntax, and references; but rather than giving Dominic familiar pleasures, they left him disoriented and menaced by the complex mind capable of devising such labyrinthine puzzles. William encouraged him to read other poets; there was an exhilarating sense of discovery. He enjoyed reading aloud. After dinner, the two would snuggle on the couch. He was self-conscious, but William's happiness eased him past the frightening shadows of self-doubt. They both looked forward to the reading; it satisfied unspoken romantic longings for both.

The telephone call inviting Christopher to dine did not simplify matters. After the acceptance, William attempted a little groundwork: "I've a roommate."

[83]

Dominic groaned, threw up his hands, and started cursing in Italian about the big crock of the Virgin Mary with all the saints as corks.

"A roommate?" Christopher echoed. "Anyone I know?"

"No."

"Who is she?"

"*He!* Dominic, Dominic Perrugio. He's a wonderful guy. You'll like him. He's a great friend."

Dominic groaned again. William swallowed an entire Manhattan. Dominic left the room, unable to bear any more.

"Good, pater. We need all the friends we can get. Should I bring anything?"

"A *roommate?*" Dominic howled from the bedroom when the conversation between father and son ended.

"That's what you are, sweetie."

"Cut the 'sweetie,' Billy. Why would *you* have a bus driver for a roommate?"

"That's for me to know and for him to find out."

"I don't like it, Billy."

"Relax, love, and give us a kiss."

The hours before Christopher arrived, Dominic was unable to relax, unable to speak. He had a whole Manhattan and was sipping a second when they were introduced. The boy's mind distressed but the body was more immediately disconcerting. Six feet of Irish beauty, the boy owned massive hair blindingly blond with the face a hero's face. It was all too much. First the one thing, then the other, and two Manhattans when one (or a sip!) would have been a killer.

Turning, stomach is turning. . .

What would happen if he threw up on the newly shampooed rug like some overexcited mongrel puppy? These two pedigrees would not even blink. They would scoop him up and shake him under a cold faucet. He fled to the kitchen to soak his hands in ice water. He was gone twenty minutes. When he re-entered the living room, his two men were finishing the second pitcher of Manhattans.

"I consider myself a *victim* of musical comedies," Christopher was ranting, to his father's glee.

Dominic busied himself with the table while they discussed the poems. William had magnificent dishes and glasswear and silver, wedding booty from Virginia's rich relatives (all of whom disappeared after her death). Dominic loved to arrange the table like something from a magazine. He had made no obvious changes in the apartment, but had filled it with fresh flowers, his one extravagance for Billy, and kept everything in its place, dusted and clean, so that every corner gained a subtle grace. He had uncovered a cache of antique Waterford crystal bowls; each was in use for this important occasion. To his dismay, he spotted Christopher using one for an ashtray.

He decanted the Chianti and called them both to the table. He had taken a Bromo and was feeling better, but it was several moments before he realized, with a gush of relief, that the duo was blind drunk on Manhattans and would neither notice nor care if he were a babbling troll. He became angry as soon as the relief dissolved. All of his work—-the marketing, the preparation, the cooking of his mother's lasagna—had been for nothing. He was appalled at their behavior. How could they be so damn inconsiderate? How could they do this to him? He wanted to hurl cheesy wedges at them both. He wanted to pour boiling sauce up their drunken Irish assholes. *He wanted* to—in midrampage, to his shuddering horror, William started kissing his hand!

"Dominic," he was slurring, "is the *best!*"

Christopher stared at them, squinting and swaying slightly.

"Pater! You two are lovers!"

"Right!' William shouted, nodding and closing his eyes.

Dominic felt faint.

If I fall off the chair, will anyone notice?

"Pater! Since when are you . . . I mean, *when* did you *join* the Lavender Brigade! Why didn't you *tell me?* "

"I couldn't figure out *how."*

The effort required to aspirate toppled him forward.

Dominic caught his shoulder before his face hit the full plate.

It's all my fault. All of it. Too much for him, his son, and me. I couldn't hold my own.

[85]

"I *love* Dominic!" William shouted, uprighting himself.

Queasy and lightheaded, Dominic was grinning hysterically while Christopher, seemingly sobered, studied him like some unrecognizable condiment. A radiant smile kiboshed the scrutiny.

"I think I'm jealous, pater. I'm awfully glad you've found someone so *attractive* to love. Sweet Jesus! What a hoot! He's much humpier than my meter man!"

Father and son howled with drunken abandon. Dominic blushed the deepest red and resumed the private litany of what he wished to do with steaming bits of the lasagna. He hated them but he felt off the hook.

"This calls for a toast!" Christopher demanded, hoisting his glass. "To my father *and* my new stepfather. May they live in perfect love and harmony till death them does part."

Dominic clinked his glass and sipped the wine. He sat back and waited for the conversation to begin. The other two drained their glasses and eagerly poured more. They poked at the food, grunting compliments, then sped back to the booze in the living room and to the talk, the raucous histories, the "poop" they had not brought with them to the dinner table. Within the hour, both were unconscious on he couch.

"Some fucking dinner party!" Dominic mumbled, scouring the pots, torn between disappointment and relief.

There were other adjustments as their two lives merged and Dominic's became William's. Dominic loved television; William would not own a set. Dominic read more but there were times when television was a necessity. Deciding the apartment was too small for the three of them, they bought a house in Riverdale. It supplied not only a TV room, but also a study for William and a garden for Dominic. They acquired a mongrel dog and a tiger cat.

Dominic was amazed to discover how similar their tastes were when decorating the house, and how William always deferred to his judgment. He assumed it was because William did not care. It was years before Dominic ceased commenting on the differences in their educations, but he never relinquished the gratitude that colored his satisfaction whenever they made love.

William introduced him to the opera, the theater, and classical music. Dominic loved dressing up; he happily went to anything once—subsequent visits depended on his enjoyment which, when high, was ebulliently high. Dominic took William to old movies in revival houses and introduced him to bowling, bocci, and baseball games.

They happily watched Christopher set up a life with Terence Strange. Dominic enjoyed the active friendship that evolved free of aggravation up until now.

"Leave him alone, Billy!" Dominic repeated, sighing. "Easy for you to say. He's not *your* flesh and blood."

"I care about him, too!"

"Sure. Sure you do."

"I do! You *know* I do!"

"You'll never understand."

"I understand *plenty!* He's a *drunk* like you."

"You understand *nothing!* It's your usual condition, fool."

Dominic sputtered with rage.

How long can this go on?

FIVE

Thursday morning, at eleven sharp, Judith called Terence to "*kvell.*" Morgan Connelly had just delivered a sensational book proposal.

"It is *gorgeous!*"

"Are you surprised?"

"Of course not! He's the most talented and the sweetest man I know."

"You mean he didn't mention dinner?"

"Ugh! Terence, you are a wretch! We're all entitled to slips, you know, and if *you* don't, who the fuck does?"

"*Touché,*" he said, routed, adding after a pause, "I'm not ready for this conversation, Judith. Why don't you go attack a manuscript with a sharpened blue pencil?"

"Forgive me, darling, even though you started it! That sounded *exactly* like Deirdre. Gerald wants to build a swimming pool. I may have to kill him. Who else would have me?"

"Not me, Judith. I have enough with my own unruly self."

"Christopher was in this morning."

"Oh?"

Uh-oh!!

"He stopped by for a book he's reviewing for the *Times.* They sent him a copy but he lost it."

"Probably at the Strand."

"That's what I thought. Luckily, it's one of ours, so I gave him another copy."

Why are people so fucking "helpful"?

"He wanted to take me to lunch. I said no, thank you, darling. Last week's lunch will last me a lifetime. To use your charming expression: He fell headlong into the soup. It was *not* amusing."

"You told me."

Pacing the kitchen, he circled the dozing cat. Terence knew Christopher could not get up at this early hour. He must have stayed up the entire night.

How? Where? With whom?

"He looks ghastly, Terence."

None of my business. OK. Turmoil inappropriate. OK. Sad.

"There's nothing I can do about it, Judith."

"I shouldn't talk to you about him. I'm sorry, darling."

"People don't save other people, Judith."

"I know, darling, I know."

He continued circling. The cat, now alert, eyed him warily.

"Are you absolutely certain about that, Terence?"

He laughed. "Trust me, Judith. You'll have to do it for yourself."

"I trust *you*, darling. It's myself I have serious doubts about."

"Well, that's a start. Join the club! Next you'll be discovering that what you need emotionally and what you want are fairly well aligned with what you have. That one's a pisser."

After hanging up, he called Thomas S., who was not at his desk. He called Jerry H., who was not answering his phone (were they together?). He phoned Lucille B., who was having a very bad morning and was grateful to hear his voice. Lucille's husband, a cab driver, was drinking again after two weeks in the hospital for detoxification. "I could punch him in the face, Terence."

"I know. But he's not doing anything *to you*. He's doing it to himself."

"I keep feeling he's doing it *to me!* And, if I punch him, that will give him an excuse to drink. Which is the only reason I *don't* punch him."

"He doesn't need an excuse, Lucille. He's a sick man. It has nothing to do with you. If I can remember that, I can control my anger. I can't control Christopher, but I can control myself. It's hard to be angry with someone who's sick, or punish someone who's sick."

"But he's sick because of his own doing. If he was a diabetic eating sugar, I'd be furious with him, too."

"When he's drinking, he can't control it. A diabetic has no

[89]

compulsion to eat sugar. A diabetic has no denial to contend with: A coma is not a normal state. It's normal *for* an alcoholic to be drunk. He has to go against his entire nature to stop. He'll only do that when his life becomes unmanageable. You know all this, Lucille! I forget all the time, too. The disease does not want me to remember. It's *normal* for me to be angry and frightened and guilty when I'm caught in the dynamics of the disease. Once I start, I can't stop, like him. The disease tunes me to its frequency."

"Yes, I know. I think I'm depressed but I'm really angry. I lie to myself! I'm never this bitchy with him when I'm depressed. I'm angry but I think I'm not supposed to be."

"Why not? When you're angry, you are angry. Nothing wrong with feeling angry. It's *being* angry that's the problem. It's no longer a feeling; it's a state of being. If we feel it, we can manage it; if we *are* it, we're controlled by it."

"Yes. I understand."

"It's human to feel. It's what we do with those feelings that matters. Denying my feelings is exactly what got me into the mess in the first place; the disease thrives on it. It's one of the requirements for a really good alcoholic relationship!"

They both laughed.

"I know when I'm angry I'm right back in it, Terence. He's all I think about. But how can he make himself sick all over again like this?"

"Lucille, how can *you* make yourself sick all over again like this?"

There was a deep silence.

"I never thought of it that way before, Terence!"

He had never thought of it that way either until at a meeting in Greenwich Village, a gay men's meeting at Saint Vincent's Hospital, when he finished agonizing over Christopher's drinking and finally formed the question: How can he keep doing this to himself? Joe R. raised his hand to ask, "How can I keep doing this to myself? When I feel crazed over his actions, it's because I can't let go of his problem in the same way he can't let go of his alcohol. I won't put down *his* cross."

"Lucille," Terence continued, "we know it's important for

him to fight with you and for you to fight with him if you're both to stay sick. We *know* that's the dynamics of this disease, right? Fight and fester! Right?"

"Right!"

"If we can hold onto that basic truth, it's easier not to hook into the crazies. You want to scream? Pick up the phone and scream with me. I'm not a toxic situation for you. Of course you're angry. He's killing himself and *you can't make him stop.* It's essential for me to feel that anger. And the fear. In the beginning, I confused suppressing my feelings with letting go of them. I was ca-razed! I gave a dinner party because Christopher's behavior didn't affect *me* anymore! Ho-ho! He passed out on the bathroom floor before the last person arrived. I was fine, perfectly calm, but for some reason I spent the entire evening crawling over his dead body to run cold water over my head or sticking my head between my legs because I was on the verge of fainting—literally fainting! But I was terrific! I was working the program, I thought. I was using the slogans as corks! That taught me. Before I can let go of an emotion or a feeling, I have to pick it up, name it, know it, *then* control it. If it's anger, guilt, or fear, or anxiety, I think myself through the disease-dynamics routine. If I stay in the *now* and relate all my emotional distress to the present alcoholism, my life is manageable. Keep it simple, I say over and over. I can change my behavior only in the present. The disease concept gives me something concrete to work with. It *always* works for me. I go through it all the time. I am teaching myself how to control myself. I'm training myself to respond to Christopher instead of reacting like a reflex to the disease. I'm learning how to suffer with, not because of, the person I love."

"Yes, Terence. He's a sick man. It's a compulsion *inside him* that makes him drink. I forget that. I'm so used to thinking of him as a weak bastard. I *see* he's sick. I can't get over me making myself sick. I'm suffering from a compulsion, too!"

"I was! Still am, but much of the time I can manage myself now. Most of the time I can control myself. I do it just for today. The idea that I won't be losing myself in someone else ever again scares me silly ; so, I have to do it just for today. It's hard changing

[91]

me. I want to change someone else instead. It seems a lot easier."

Lucille guffawed. The tension had vanished from her voice. She said with a sigh, "Terence, there is so much to learn. I don't think I'll ever be good at this."

"Uh-huh. That's just what the disease wants us to think. Why bother? We're no good. If we were any good, we would have solved these problems long ago. If we were any good, *they* wouldn't have a drinking problem! I have to shout sometimes to drown out that negative voice in me. I'm afraid of staying the way I am, and I'm afraid of changing. I'm just beginning to see that I'm plain afraid of *everything!* Lucille, how old are you?"

"Forty-two."

"How long have you been in the program?"

"Six months."

"OK. You're six months old. You've got forty-two years of attitudes to unlearn. You're doing damn well for a six-month-old girl."

He remembered her tears of grief at her first meeting. It was at Smither's on Thursday nights, the Henry Hudson Group. She said things he understood with an immediacy that identified her extreme condition as similar to his own rage. They talked during the break in the meeting, and over tea afterward. When calm, she was a wise woman able to communicate her feelings with extraordinary lucidity. He remembered her tears of relief when she realized she was not alone with her problem of living with a drunk.

"What are you doing after we hang up, Lucille?"

"Fixing lunch. He may not want to eat but I've got to eat something. You know, if I don't start yelling at him for drinking the beer, he'll eat."

"And *you'll* eat in peace."

"Right! And we'll eat together in peace. We haven't done that in years."

"Sounds good to me."

"And you know something else? He *knows* he shouldn't be drinking that beer. He doesn't need *me* to tell him! The doctors told him and he said to me yesterday that if he doesn't stop he'll die.

God! I forgot about that until just now! It's like you say, Terence: There are things this disease doesn't want us to remember. It's really true. It's like: 'You're throwing up.' He knows. I was fixing the sandwiches in the kitchen before when he came in for another beer. He looked at me so defiantly. I smiled at him and went on with my work just like he wasn't doing anything wrong."

She laughed, adding parenthetically, "Terence, ever since you said at a meeting that you use your own name to talk sense to yourself, I've been doing it, too! Sometimes I say, 'So I say to myself, *Terence!*'"

They both laughed, loving one another intensely.

"So I said, Lucille, it's not *wrong;* it's sick. Sick is not wrong. And guess what?"

"What?"

"He stood in front of the refrigerator holding the can of beer, practically waving it at me, and I asked him if he wanted mayo on the ham! So he put the damn can back in the refrigerator and said he'd wait for lunch and no, he wanted mustard. Just like that! Gee, I'm glad you called. The disease really confused me. I was sitting here getting ca-razed again wondering if he was gonna have that can of beer with lunch. I can't stop him. I know I can't stop him! But, I was starting to think that if I don't react, he won't drink. That's insane. I won't accept how powerless I am, I guess. If he *does* drink, I'll think I did something wrong. I still think I can control what he does. Isn't that something? I think I'll go to a meeting this afternoon. I've got better things to do with my life than sit here and worry myself sick. Gee, I'm glad you called me, Terence. How are you?"

"Better for having talked to you. I'm convinced that the only way I can stop doing something is by finding something else to do instead. I'm doing some creative replacements. Like talking to you, Lucille. I love you."

"I love you, too. So I say to myself, *Terence —* "

He hung up feeling quite happy. Lucille was working hard. And so was he, for the most part. For the *best* part.

[93]

Gerald sawed the plywood precisely as marked. The electric hand machine was perfect for the job; he had been right to choose the smaller model rather than the larger one proposed by Mr. Brooke at the local Sears. He lifted the board from the sawhorse and set it into place against the exposed beams. At this rate, he would have half the walls up by the time Judith arrived tomorrow. He did not want to hammer while she was in the house; she claimed the noise gave her a migraine. He paused to drink a glass of water.

Two days before, on Tuesday, he started the low-carbohydrate diet advised by his physician, and began jogging in the deepest privacy of his own acreage. Now, while he worked, he consciously stretched his body and regularly halted whatever he was doing to suck in his stomach severely while slowly counting to twenty.

At four o'clock he stopped working. The children returned from school at five; he needed a full hour of quiet before their appearance. He was resolved to send them to boarding schools in the autumn and he wanted to be a good father for the few months that remained. Such concentrated effort, such strict attention to their needs in the evenings required at least one hour's preparation.

Retreating to his rooms, he stripped off his work clothes. Taking a deep breath to contract his abdominal muscles, he marched front and center *of* the full-length mirror to do calisthenics: deep knee bends, sit-ups, push-ups, and basic isometrics from head to feet. His image profoundly distressed him. There was no denying the facts, the *ugly* fat facts, and he released his stomach muscles to stampede the facts home.

Where is the tone of yesterdecade? Tone? Nothing above or below middle C. Gone down the tubes. Down the scale? Up the scale! Stop!

Three times a day he stood glowering here, asking these far from inspirational questions. Would Mary Baker Eddy approve? She knew a healthy body was a well-tuned body. Poised, he commenced.

Suddenly and inexplicably this concern for physical fitness had sprung to torment him. Tuesday he had dropped his pajama bottoms and, feeling like a guilty schoolboy, peered at his naked reflection for signs of change. Alas, a schoolboy he was no longer.

The early-morning sunlight had been brutally unkind. He looked like a hairy pudding. Even his penis looked bizarre: a tiny pale purple rhododendron dangling on a bloated ocher stem, dead or at least dying. At that very moment, he charted his course. Sitting at the writing table, he made notes. The notion of a swimming pool buoyed his resolve.

Thomas Beacon had pestered him for years to join his advertising firm. He insisted that Gerald would be perfect as a liaison man on a free-lance basis. Gerald had never admitted his disdain for the advertising racket, but he managed to keep Thom Beacon from grasping the true reason for the constant rebuff. Years expanded the firm, but the come-on never changed; at social functions, whenever they met, Thom would prod "Gerry," who would politely decline to tackle the big-fish clients Thom name-dropped to entice. Monday morning, after breakfast, he had called Thomas Beacon at the New York office and had set a time to meet him the next day. He had then followed up with a doctor's appointment.

The meeting with Beacon had gone extremely well. Thom had been enthusiastic over Gerry's change of heart, taking him on a tour of the "playground" and handshakes with the rest of the "kids." It was all sophomorically jocular, not at all intimidating. The offices were impressively spacious, all done up as an aesthetic statement with "softer spaces," walnut walls, indoor trees, and Steinberg prints. Telephones "bripped" civilly. Copying machines reduced material to sixty-four percent its original size. Gerald was pleased with Beacon's efficient operation. The other two partners joined them for a Yale Club lunch, where accounts were discussed and Gerry invited to choose whichever two he fancied from a list of five. He chose the products used in his own home; there seemed something eminently sensible in that approach.

I'm to liaise. How extraordinary.

Friday evening as he sat in the car waiting for Judith's train, he concentrated on tensing his stomach and temple muscles to prevent himself from panicking. He had decided not to tell Judith of his plans with Thom Beacon, at least not until he was certain they would pan out. Then, he figured, he would work two or

[95]

three days a week and spend the nights in the city with her.

The train arrived. He watched Judith alight from the bar car with Thom Beacon and a neighbor whose name he could never remember. He knew the chap was in construction. The three walked along the platform together. She waved to him. He raised a brow, clenched his teeth, and started counting slowly to twenty. The three paused on the platform for final good-byes. Thom Beacon and the chap waved to Gerald. Gerald nodded. Judith looked puzzled as she approached the car.

Gerald's heart began to pound. He instructed himself in his most severe manner, in words muffled by the sound of numbers snapping by ascending toward twenty. No questions about the birth-control pills he had seen in her toilet case the previous Sunday. *He was not to mention them.* She violently opposed the pill, was forever preaching for the IUD, against the carcinogenic inevitability of flooding the female body with ersatz hormones. She insisted he share responsibility and he had complied, becoming an expert on the condom by browsing at the back of certain girlie magazines.

He lowered his brow, unclenched his teeth, and whispered: "twenty." Pushing forward his jaw and locking it hard, he resumed the count.

What the hell is going on?

Not ten minutes before Thomas Beacon had sat beside her on the five thirty-two from Grand Central, Judith Gunning reckoned she was happy. Her books were doing well: She had not one but two best sellers; Morgan Connelly's proposal had been cheered (or as close to a cheer as is allowed) at the Editorial Board meeting that very morning; and Miss Thing's atrocity had been made a featured alternate by the Literary Guild (not so much a surprise as a relief). She loved her work and was decidedly grateful for the arrangement she had with Gerald; it made the new, delicious complication possible.

"I'm a fortunate woman," were her precise words as she settled herself into her seat, covertly glancing to check her hair in the dirty window's reflection. The new short cut from Couture Trim, squeezed in after lunch ("Sally is a magician!"), suited her strong nose. She had had her doubts, but Andrew (bless him!) had been adamant: "It's perfect, toots! Very *Executive Suite!'*

The affair with Richard was progressing nicely. He was the first man she had become sexually involved with since her marriage, but she was annoyed at how guilty she became whenever Richard's smiling presence bobbed into her thoughts. It was not sex that had snared her—he was not nearly as good a lover as Gerald; it was the energy with which Richard did everything, and the conviction he held she would never meet a stronger, healthier male. He was certainly the most successful, but she never confused those disparate issues. In fact, when she perceived his belief that power informed maleness, she was touched and charmed despite her wiser self remembering the childish canard equating size with potency.

I'm having an affair with him because I'm having an affair with him. I'd like to leave it at *that*, Andrew."

He was a senior partner in what Judith thought one of the oldest most prestigious law firms in America ("The world, Judith, the *world!'* he had softly corrected; she had nodded, chastised); and he was currently engaged in the corporate rituals involving Voyager Press and its absorption into a mammoth conglomerate, which were tiresome for the editors. They were forced to attend endless business meetings, briefings, and slide shows intended to introduce them to the new management and, at the same time, impress the hell out of them by showing the strength of the new team they were joining.

"Joined? *I* haven't been asked to *join* anything!" Andrew snarled at one of the circulating memos. "What exactly is 'input' supposed to mean?"

Judith was certain the impressive consultant had noticed her at the interminable meeting organized to discuss how They were not going to interfere with Us, how Voyager policy would not be changed; but when he called two hours later, she pretended surprise ("Just as frilly ladies do in a novel by Miss Thing!"), which made her a tad annoyed and ultimately provoked her into accepting his dinner invitation to set some items straight.

Whose *items? Terence is right. Romantic notions die hard.*

Richard infuriated her with his asinine theories about women ("equal but inferior"); there were no female partners in his firm ("They claim the curse. . . ."), and no amount of rational discussion could alter his agreement with this policy.

"He puts me on a pedestal above the madding crowd, Drew."

"He puts you where he doesn't have to deal with you!"

He was obsessed with seeming a paragon of masculinity: He moved his limbs at right angles, wore only dark colors, swallowed his voice (lowering it an octave so Andrew said it sounded as if it had hair on it), and strapped his wrist-watch with its face above his palm where he cupped his unfiltered cigarettes like a hero in a World War II movie. He opened all doors for her, lit her filtered cigarettes, ordered her meals, walked on the curbside ("I mean, who's about to fling a pot of shit out a window on Fifty-seventh Street?"), and never failed to make her laugh by teasing himself about his need for these anachronistic trappings of manhood. That was the intoxicating twist.

"He touches my heart, Andrew. He's honest, and silly, and sweet, and—"

"—stupid, and sexy, and—"

"My heart, *Drew!* Do you know about hearts?"

"I'm not interested in fucking a heart."

Then there were the children. Judith was vulnerable on the subject of children. Her own were nearing the rapids of adolescence and she dreaded any part of it; this guilt seared the deepest of the many currently ruling her emotional life. Richard had five children. After two drinks, he talked of nothing else. She could talk and he would listen to stories of her own. She proselytized for their daughters' rights; he concurred but hoped they would never stoop to claim them. He encouraged her to chatter, a diversion she adored. He helped her stop berating herself. She would fantasize, remaking their joint lives the way one remodels houses one visits. He helped her pinpoint her guilts and gave her something to occupy her hands.

The image of the grinning woman in the window of the five

thirty-two from Grand Central was herself: successful, respected, with a house in Connecticut, a *pied-á-terre* in the highest-powered city on earth, a perfect nuclear family, a rich-and-famous (sort of) lover. Then Thomas Beacon bent into view and asked if the seat beside her was taken. Why had she not lied and said yes? But she was feeling good and thus gracious. How was she to know? Why Gerald was *now* deciding to change the order of things was bewildering. He had an exasperating ability to divine when to cut up rough.

Experience taught her to keep mum about this conversation with Thom. If Gerald instigated talk about the job, she would be encouraging, yet not overly enthusiastic. It only made his regressions into accidie more devastating. *Advertising? God help us! At least the gallery was worthwhile. He should regain control there and leave lower Madison Avenue to the likes of Thom. Maybe when he mentions it, I'll counter with the gallery and try to get him...*

"Yes, Thom, I could use a drink."

You don't suppose he'll want to stay with me in town? Who'll take care of the children? We can't afford boarding school. How much is Choate? Meet the right people. I don't imagine he'll make much money. He would have made a perfect psychoanalyst: It's an approved and lucrative situation for not getting involved with other people. Could Richard's little woman really be as happy as he says? She sounds retarded. What are two silly men doing in my life? Three if I count Thom. Four if I count what's his face here? I think he's in construction. Does he do pools? Williams? McOurgle? Marlowe? Shakespeare?

She spotted the car the second she stepped down from the train. She had intended to divorce herself from Thom but he refused to be shaken. It did not matter. She knew Gerald would assume male complicity as a guarantee of secrecy; and Thom had said he really should not be telling her but he knew how happy she would be for them all, and on and on. Yet Gerald was looking ferocious behind the wheel. His face was all contorted into a hideous muscular spasm. Is that what he called a cheery grin? She waved. He raised a brow and scowled, holding the squeeze for the length of time she needed to say good night to Thom and Harry Noonan. She studied Gerald as she approached the car.

He was staring straight ahead, jutting his jaw and dilating his nostrils.

What the hell is going on?

Christopher woke not knowing where he was. He knew he was spread-eagled on his stomach in a bed, but that was the extent of the information available to him without his prying open his crusted eyes. Birds made their deafening noises recklessly; and at a great distance from his supine body, cars made theirs. Was he in the country? There was a faint food odor but none was cooking, thank God! He thought of a cracked egg cradled: The slightest movement would spill him out of himself all over wherever he was. He peeked. His face was turned toward a draped window. He could read daytime by the ribbon of light along the blue carpet.

His internal situation was noticeably precarious. His guts were holding steady but were eager to churn and expel soured contents over the pretty pink sheets. His mouth needed a strong cleanser. A cold wetness seeped from his bowels. The fluid, draining over his cowering testicles, rattled him with terrifying visions. How long had he been hemorrhaging? Had he become incontinent already? There were other things fated to give out before the bowels, or so promised the barnstorming prophets of alcoholic doom.

Dispatching his left hand to investigate, he discovered his nakedness. The hesitantly prodding fingers slowly reappeared from beneath the covers smeared with a quantity of viscous, whitish liquid that was definitely not blood or diarrhea, although bits of feces were evident. Certain the digits were coated with a deadly pus, he turned his head in flight from the compulsion to sniff. On the neighboring pillow he found a dark, tousled head resting. He returned his own to its original position, sliding his soiled fingers out of sight while he tried to reconnoiter.

Where am I? Who is this person in my bed? You'd think he might have the decency to go home! Where did I expect to be?

The neighboring presence stirred. Christopher lay still. The body wriggled itself on top of his own and after whimpered maneuverings inserted its male self into his anus. With a sigh of relief, Christopher identified the wet; but before he could shift himself into a position more advantageous to his fluttering guest's pleasure, the visitor groaned, spasmed, shuddered, paused, detached, rolled off, and spoke:

"Was that good for you, Mr. More?"

"Was *what* good for me?"

"That knightgiggle."

Christopher turned his head to examine the deficient person in bed with him. The kid—for the being could not claim more than fourteen years—was staring with the bugeyed intensity of an ardent fan.

"You call that squirt a knightgiggle?"

Once, a long while ago, he had written a piece of giddy juvenilia inspired by Terence, who in deepest sleep produced a series of cadent giggles; when queried upon awakening, he thanked Christopher for fucking him exquisitely in his dreams. A sweet "ditty" in waltz time resulted. His piece, entitled "Knightgiggle," was recently included in a popular gay anthology, and the title was stenciled on T-shirts as a gesture of gay pride.

"I've been doing my best, sir."

"Sir"? Who is this twit?

"Your *best*, lamb pie?"

"Yes, sir. I'm sorry, but I'm exhausted. That was the eighth wad in twelve hours and I haven't slept very much. I just wanted to make you happy."

Christopher groaned. No wonder he thought his bowels had opened. This brain-damaged infant had used him for a sperm dump all the night long.

"Eight times?"

"Yes, Mr. More. Just like in your poem."

"I don't remember doing arithmetic in my poem."

"No, sir. You just say 'times out of mind.'" Christopher rolled onto his back. Having successfully completed this action, his mood brightened. He looked closer at the dark youth and saw a fledgling beauty if he squinted.

Jaw's nice. Unfortunate nose.

[101]

"How old are you?"

"Seventeen, sir."

"Stop calling me 'sir.' "

I hate jittery faunlets.

"How did I get here? You're much too young for me."

"You asked me to bring you."

"Where are we?"

"My parents' house."

"Oh, my sweet Jesus!"

"They aren't here. They're in Florida."

"Well, good for *them!*"

The thin boy squirmed from the bed, crossed to a desk, and with downcast eyes returned carrying a book discreetly held to shield his privates.

Suddenly he feels shy. Sweet, Cute ass.

The book was a copy of Christopher's latest poems. With a shy grin, the boy extended the slim volume to the reclining author.

"Want my autograph?"

"I have it. See for yourself."

Christopher opened the book and saw upside down a scrawled inscription that right side up barely resembled his handwriting: "Get me out of here. Take me home and fuck me gently."

He had finally done it. He shocked himself. What if this young person really had parents attached, a burly father loitering in the back of the auditorium anxious to see what the famous writer had writ? What if. . . ?

"You were very drunk. I was disappointed with the reading and a lot of people were asking for their money back. I figured if you at least signed my copy . . . it's a first edition . . ."

"So I wrote *this?*" he interrupted, staring in disbelief.

"And I did!" the boy chirped proudly.

"I have always leaned heavily upon the kindness of strangers," Christopher mused, "but why did I pick *you*, a beardless babe?"

"I don't think I like you."

"You had a good time. You won't have to jerk off now for at least two hours."

"You aren't very nice."

A sick fuck on a death trip!

"No, I'm not. I'm not a nice person. I'm really not."

"Here, I bought you this when I went out before."

He pulled a white paper bag from under the bed. It smelled peculiar.

"What is it?"

"A Big Mac."

"Good! I can use it as a Kotex."

The boy laughed, shocked.

"That's better," Christopher smiled. "Now get rid of that gunge and come here. Let me hold you."

Warily, the boy inched over. Christopher held him closely, breathed in "tot pong," and suddenly felt like crying. He remembered he was somewhere in the Dakotas. He flew there. When?

"What's your name?"

"Alexander. Alexander Devlin."

"Tell me, Alexander Devlin, what day is this?"

"Friday."

"The time?"

"After five."

He sat up. The exertion made him violently queasy. The boy led him to the bathroom. After dry-heaving to the brink of insensibility, he bathed and shaved, borrowing the elder Devlin's equipment. He smelled bacon cooking. Pretending not to notice, he opened the window wide, welcoming the frigid air. In his trouser pocket he found the receipt of an airline ticket. Delighted, he rushed to the phone and called the information office to ask when his return flight departed. A patient woman informed him that he had cashed in the ticket upon arrival Thursday afternoon.

Where am I? Ask! No. Don't want to know. Find out soon enough.

He remembered none of it. Had the school—was it a school?—paid him for the reading? He searched his clothing; $6.72. What had he done with the money from the plane ticket? If the audience was howling for a refund, would the school—why did he insist it was a school?— expect him to return the fee before letting him go home? Where was his briefcase? How could he have slept while Alexander Devlin plugged him eight times? That, perhaps, was the scariest thing of all. Lately, when he passed out, it was a kind of death.

In the breakfast nook in a bright yellow kitchen, he found a newspaper neatly folded beside a plate containing two perfectly fried eggs and eight crisp pieces of bacon.

One for each knightgiggle? Cute! Sweet!

Every muscle from throat to pelvis twisted at the sight and the smell of the food. The water sipped in the bathroom sloshed dangerously in his stomach. Lifting the paper, he pretended to peruse the headlines while studying the logo.

Lansing, Michigan? Why'd I think it was the Dakotas? I'd kill for a view of the Park right now.

"There's a story of you on page thirty, Mr. More."

The boy's modulated tone bristled with mischief. It was a little too lilting, a little too arch for your run-of-the-mill newspaper piece on a poetry reading. It was similar to a toady rugrat asking an unsuspecting waif, "Would you like a Hawaiian Punch?"

"I loathe reading about myself in small town wipes. Is there a picture?"

"No."

"It can wait until I come upon it."

"Eat your eggs before they get cold. I'm taking a shower."

"Good for you, Alexander. I approve of pretty boys keeping their crevices clean. Be prepared, that's my motto."

Alexander blushed, pleased. Christopher smiled his justly famous smile and added in his softest voice, "Thank you, Alexander Devlin. You've been damn good for me."

"It was no big deal. Besides, I think you're a great poet."

Starfucker! Bet I'm the first stellar nookie you've corralled so far. Jesus! Wudya expect? Yuth!

"Thanks, kid."'

The instant Alexander left the room, Christopher sprang from the table, taking the food with him, and headed for the back door. Outside, mounds of clean snow, more snow in one place than he had ever seen, covered the earth to the far horizon. Houses dotted the area with vast snowy spaces between them; he assumed himself stranded in some exclusive suburb. A quick flip of the wrist sent the two eggs sailing through the air; they landed with a plop on the shoveled walk. The bacon pieces scattered in the gentle breeze, marking the snow like dog turds where they fell. Returning to the table, he sipped cold milk and munched dry toast until he heard water running upstairs. Stealthily, he ransacked the Devlin premises for something adult to drink.

Nothing! Not even goddamned cooking sherry! Haven't these hicks heard of Julia Child?

Sitting down again, he opened the paper to page thirty.

"Stricken Poet Christopher More Disappears After Aborted 'Reading,'" he read the headline aloud. He scanned the first paragraph for flattering adjectives, then slid down to the last.

They returned the fucking money!

He felt desperate, verging on histrionic. He was tempted to clip out the article and mail it to Terence with a short note: "You don't know me but it might be in your interest to study this and congratulate yourself for pulling out when you did. Signed, A Quaker meetinghouse."

Fuck, shit, piss!

"Are you ready?"

Alexander stood in the doorway. He was wearing an overcoat and earmuffs.

"Where are we going?"

"I have to go into town and I thought I'd drop you at the U."

"What for?"

"They must be worried about you."

"Let 'em worry!"

"We've *gotta* go!" he whined repulsively. "I'm expected at my aunt's for dinner by six."

"OK! OK!"

Can't depend on a kid for shit.

"I'll warm up the car."

Moving toward the back door, Alexander was startled by the urgency with which Christopher called his name. "Aren't you going to kiss me good-bye?".

The boy shrugged, suddenly looking prepubescent. He

approached the table and, grinning foolishly, lowered his flushed face to be kissed as he might to a maiden uncle. Devilishly, Christopher sucked sloppily at the boy's mouth, all the while trying to think how to prevent him from going out the back door and slipping on the eggs. *Why didn't I fling them under the fridge?*

Alexander responded to the messy kissing like a crazed guppy unfed for a month. When Christopher tried to stand, planning to lead the boy into the living room far away from the back door, he felt the quick stinging in his shoulders and chest that signaled the onset of his chronic alcoholic eczema. If he didn't get a drink in a hurry, the shakes and maybe worse would start.

This will have to be fast babe.

Sitting again, he fumbled with the woolen layers of Alexander's clothing, locating with little difficulty the object of his search. Completely overwrought, the boy required minor manipulations; bellowing stentoriously at his penultimate moment, he gave Christopher the first happiness he had known in weeks.

"What about you?" the boy sputtered, breathless.

"I'm OK, Alexander. Thank you. Your pleasure was mine."

"You *sure?*

"Yes, I'm sure. That happens to you sometimes when you get older."

"You won't get blueball or something?".

"Only if I don't wear a scarf. Would you get my wrap?"

"You didn't have one."

"I didn't have a coat? In this weather?"

"I guess you left it somewhere."

"Yes, I guess I did."

With my whole mind.

His boy, assembled once again, shuffled toward the back door.

"Wait! Can't we go out the front? I feel like a dirty old man sneaking out the back way."

"We're not *sneaking!* This way's closer to the car."

"Alexander Devlin! Stars never condescend to the existence of back doors. I'd forgotten that houses come equipped with secondary exits. Is your home on fire?"

"You're silly!" he said, laughing. "You're silly and absolutely beautiful and *everything*. . . the way great poets ought to be."

Christopher nodded, accepting the eloquent tribute, believing it, wanting more, sidestepping in the direction of the front door.

Fifteen minutes later, he jumped out of the car and waved to the rear of the white Corvette. He had asked to be dropped at a decent hotel; he chose the one with a tavern attached. The Howdy-Do Lounge was entering its "Happy Hour: All Drinks One Buck" when Christopher moseyed into its cowboy ambience where comfort was enshrined in shimmering quarts tiered and spotlit behind the endless walnut bar that curved like a welcoming smile. A man in a blue plaid shirt invited him to buy a raffle ticket.

"Winner gets half a dozen drinks on the house, sonny. It's for a good cause."

Christopher dropped a Susan B. Anthony dollar into a pretzel basket, then thrust his arm into the proffered flour sack filled with billiard balls. He pulled out the black one.

"Eight has been happening for me," he explained to the laughing people gathered around. He paused to shake hands and introduce himself, to exchange a few cheerful words with the smiling strangers. Not wanting to appear to be in dire straits, he paused, vibrating with desperate longing but refusing to leap for the bar as though newly sprung from the state pen after serving fifty years for molesting little boys.

He won the lottery. Six Irish whiskeys on the house. He had to make do with Paddy's. For all their pretensions to class (they had a blond doxy playing a silver cocktail organ on a dais), they didn't stock Jameson's. Those six free drinks added to his $5.72 were certain to get him through the night.

━━━━━

"Terence? It's Bill More. Is Chris with you?"

"No, Bill, he isn't. Why?"

"I was supposed to have lunch with him today and he didn't show. I came to the apartment but he isn't here. The super let me in. I thought maybe he was with you."

"No. He isn't with me."

"Oh. I was hoping he'd be with you."

"I have no idea where he is. Sorry."

Fear is not appropriate.

"I'm worried about him. The last time we spoke he didn't sound terribly well. It's not like him to miss a luncheon, especially when I told him it was on me."

He forced a laugh.

He's not well. He's horribly ill. Skip it.

"How's Dominic?"

"Great! I've given him membership in a gym for his birthday. He's taking it very seriously. He's been only a few times but I can feel the difference already."

They both laughed warmly together. It helped them relax with one another. William was slurring a little. Terence tried not to hear it.

Nothing to do with me.

"Where are you standing now, Bill?"

"In the kitchen."

"Go into the bedroom and look for his *New Yorker* desk calendar."

"OK. Hold on."

Terence heard the phone placed on the wooden tabletop, and the footsteps on the hardwood floor. In his mind, he watched Bill walk down the long book-lined corridor from the kitchen to the bedroom and search the messy desk. The extension telephone was lifted.

"Terry?"

"Yes, Bill."

"No calendar."

"Then don't worry. He went visiting. Or perhaps a reading. A new paperback edition usually brings a few. Could be delayed by a storm. He never goes anywhere without that calendar."

Memory shot.

There was silence. Terence felt William's discomfort, but he corrected himself and called the feelings his own. He had no idea what William was feeling. If Christopher packed, it was a planned excursion. To worry about him would be tantamount to saying he could not take care of himself. It was humiliating for the other person, he reasoned.

"You seem pretty calm, Terence."

"Bill, I've been living with this sort of thing for the past five years. He'll appear the same way he disappeared."

What if he's hurt somewhere?"

"If he's hurt, what good will it do us to get crazed?"

"I'm worried sick."

"He can take care of himself."

"Should I call the police?"

"First call Bernice. One of the young women in her agency keeps track of our readings for our bios and their cut."

"Where's the number?"

"In the blue book under the phone. See it?"

"Yes. I'll call her."

"Cunningham. Bernice Cunningham."

"Sorry to have bothered you, Terence."

Do I detect irony? Sorry you feel that way.

"No bother. Best to Dominic."

Sitting quietly, Terence stared out the window. The sky was opalescent. He waited for the Furies to descend, and was pleased the only visitor was the agile cat ascending with an easy leap, displaying an entertaining panache. Still calm after five minutes, Terence carried the purring cat into the living room. They snuggled on the couch until Terence decided to build them a fire. He was not surprised when the telephone clanged. As the blaze caught, he answered.

"Terence Strange?"

"Uh-huh."

"Hold the line, please. I have Bernice Cunningham for you."

There were several loud clicks, like someone snapping bubble gum.

'Terence? Bernice here. Bill More just rang. He said you were worried."

"No. *He* was worried. What's up?"

None of my business. Too late. Next time.

"Christopher has vanished, the sod! The Poet's League rang in a snit as if I personally pried open his lips and poured the firewater down his gullet. Lansing refunded the patrons' dough and Christopher absconded with some *child*. He is going to get himself impounded one of these days."

"Child? That's not his style. He's not attracted to children. He likes big and hairy *men*."

"Terence, you are neither."

"Bernice, how do you know?"

They both laughed.

"Terence, I can do *nothing*."

"Welcome to the club."

"Unless he calls."

"Then what?"

"*Then* I'll wire him money. Or shouldn't I do that?"

"Do you owe him any money?"

"No. But I can't leave him out there in the tundra. Do you want me to abandon him out there in the toolies?"

"Perhaps if he found himself stranded—"

"I'll get him a plane ticket. But he'll owe me! I'll deduct it from his royalties."

Why are people so fucking helpful?

"Do whatever you want, Bernice."

"How's the new one progressing?"

"Not too well. I'm having trouble with it. I'm thinking of becoming a temp typist again."

"When you receive the royalty check I've just posted, my sweet, you'll quickly change your mind. You deserve a vacation, Terence. Why not investigate Wala Wala or Fiji or someplace *hot?*"

"I have work to do."

"You know what I think?"

Spare me.

I think that someone as rich and famous and as *gorgeous* as you, my dear Terence, would not be alone for long unless he wants to be. *I* think you're waiting for Christopher to come crawling to you. Why else would you station yourself up there in that snow palace?"

"And I think you're wrong, Bernice."

What do I want? Everything every way and *my way. Won't do.*

"You love him, Terence. Two people who love each other the way that you two love each other must live *together.* You can work things out *together.* A lot of people drink, Terence."

"Thank you, Fannie Hurst."

"That bad?"

"I have to go slave for you."

"Terence?"

"Yes?"

"Are you angry with me?"

"No."

I did not *leave to teach him a lesson. I left so I could get well. For now. I left for now. For today. Only for today. He was psychotic from the booze. I don't want that chaos in my life now. Today. Only for today.*

"I don't want you to be angry with me, Terence."

"Why should it matter? You still get your ten percent."

There was a murky silence.

"Bernice, you aren't laughing."

"Well, Terence, that wasn't very funny."

"No, I guess it wasn't. Anxiety fucks up your comic sensibility."

"Don't be anxious. He'll be fine."

"Did it ever occur to you that maybe, just *maybe,* I'm anxious for myself?"

"No, my sweet. You're Gibraltar."

How could he be angry? For years he had worked to give people that impression. Terence the competent one, the stoic, the healthy one. Christopher the lush; Terence the courageous. Christopher the sinner; Terence the carved saint. Christopher the irresponsible; Terence the mature. It was all part of his denial, like being "fine."

"I will be OK, Bernice."

"Good for you, Scarlett."

She cackled expansively. "Oh, Terence, lest I overlook business: Some gay magazine on the West Coast wants you to do an article—short!—on the gay sensibility."

"I don't believe there is such a thing. It's a fiction, like woman's intuition."

"They'll pay a grand for five hundred words."

"I'll do it. I'll find something to say: I know! I'll explain why it doesn't exist in my economy. If they don't like it, they can sit on it. You think they'll go for that?"

"Is a pig's ass pork?"

Terence guffawed. The cat, curled on his lap, fled the up-heaval.

"They want an interview, too."

"Notice how you saved the zinger for the end? Is the grand contingent upon the uplifting chatter?"

"No. They seem awfully *nice.*"

"They seem awfully rich."

"That, too, yes."

"West Coast buddies! God love 'em. Where would we be without them? I always love touring out there."

"They know how to handle royalty. What say you, Strange?"

She always pronounced his name perfectly, poised exquisitely above Strong. It was her English background, although his Scottish name had Old French roots.

"Will they come here?"

"I'll find out. Must run. There are two calls holding. I'm always here for you, my sweet. And for Chris."

"I know. I know."

He tried to work but could not force the pencil. Usually the books formed quickly in his head, plot first, usually from a single idea and from two characters colliding. Then it evolved to the end.

"Novels don't *end,*" Christopher insisted. "They merely stop."

"Our lives stop. My novels end. Begin, middle, and end. Tell pater I'm thinking as hard as I can, thank you."

After the third potboiler, he wended his way deep into the morass of self-pity and illness before joining the program. Then, after a time, he wrote a small novel about the world, "the real world, as far as I dare go into it, my world such as it is." Written in longhand on legal-size yellow pads with a specific lead pencil, the manuscript was held secure in a beautiful holder from the Freer Gallery in Washington, D.C., a Christmas gift from Bobbi.

"You're the gay Françoise Sagan," Christopher applauded after reading the final draft. "You lack her *élan* but the book is damn good. Let me help."

"No. It's mine."

"It needs a poet's soul."

"Mine will have to do."

"Please yourself."

Terence did just that. The book, published by Voyager Press, earned good reviews and sold surprisingly well. The reading public was "ready" for a work that did not use homosexuality as a plot device or to explain villainy. It was neither explained nor defended. The characters, successful adults, moved together for a time, anguished quietly, and behaved childishly before ending it one way or another. All of the characters were victims of their romantic illusions.

After he signed the book contract with Judith Gunning, Terence flew to visit his parents in Arizona, where they lived nine months of the year. His father, a retired pediatrician, suffered from emphysema, making the damp Long Island summers shorter, soon perhaps an impossible place for him to be. His mother, an interior decorator, had successfully transported her career, thriving on the spacious desert. Terence went to prepare them for the new book, to be published without the pseudonym. He had never discussed the depth of his relationship with Christopher. He knew they felt uncomfortable with the reckless drinking; he allowed that to open a breach between them all rather than face the other issues.

There was not much of a discussion. They confessed thoughts on the subject of his sexual preference but decided it was none of their business. They were eager to read the new book and were delighted he was seriously applying his gifts, no longer relying on conventions to do most of his thinking for him. Both were particularly loving for the duration of the visit, and each managed to take him aside and assure him of their individual support. However, they both agreed brother George would be a problem.

"He's so damnably straight," his father interjected.

"You mean dumb, James," his mother corrected. "I often wonder where he came from. I love him dearly, but he's a real moax."

George Strange was forty, the proud father of six (five girls), and a gym instructor as well as assistant principal of a private school outside Albany, New York. While Terence was slender and delicately built, resembling both parents, George was and always had been heavy, broad, and "big boned." George admitted early on to little interest in a life of the mind ("Never met a brain that wasn't an asshole!"); he expanded into administrative work merely to supplement earnings on the teaching staff.

"I wonder what he'll think of my book?"

"It'll probably kill him, son."

"Who's going to tell him?"

"You are, of course, son.".

"I'll write him a letter."

"That might be best," his mother agreed thoughtfully.

"I could dispatch Chris. He's crazy about Chris. They could go into a bar and get drunk together."

"I think he'll be pleased, son."

"Don't get carried away, James," his mother cautioned, smiling. Then, frowning, she asked: "How is Chris?"

"Fine."

"Still drinking so heavily?"

"Yes. That's not so fine."

"It's dreadful! Terry, have you ever heard of organizations for people who live with alcoholics?"

I love it when they behave like two storybook parents.

"I've been going to one for over six months."

"It's all so frightening. We've been reading about alcoholism everywhere lately. Suddenly it's in all the papers. Now, James, about your son George."

George seemed to take it very well. He called Terence when he received the letter. It was OK with him—what Terry put in the letter—and he always thought Chris a helluva good guy. And about the new book? If Terry thought he could handle the shit that was bound to come down after writing such a book, if he was *sure* he knew what he was doing, then it was OK with George. But he hoped Terry was damn sure he could survive all the shit.

He called Arizona the same night. He used the same words, but added it was too bad he could never allow Little George to visit his uncle alone in the city.

"If Chris were straight, would you worry about the girls? When you thought he was, *did* you worry about the girls?" his father questioned, voice rising.

"No. Of course not, Pop. It's not the same thing. Queers—"

"George!" his father shouted. "Don't you ever use that despicable word again."

"Listen, Pop, I'm sorry, but that's the way it is. I work with boys. I know about these things."

"I spent my life with kids, you *moax!*"

"It's a different world today, Pop. They're out dancing in the streets wearing makeup and looking for converts."

"*Converts?* You think they're some kind of *sect?*"

"Pop, believe me, I know about these things."

"What has all this got to do with your brother?"

"They can't help themselves, Pop."

"If your mother weren't standing here waiting to talk to you and Gloria, I'd slam down this phone."

"Aw, come on, Pop!"

"James, slam the phone down, James. You'll feel better for it, and I can always call Gloria tomorrow. I'll answer when they call back. Give him time. He'll come around. He loves Terry as much as we do. . . ."

"Aw, Pop, will you listen to me?"

"George, I am hanging up. When you call back, your mother will answer. Good-bye."

He hung up and sighed. Rising from the chair, he allowed his wife to take his place. The telephone rang. He left the room.

It never ends, the problems with the children. One keeps hoping, but it never ends.

They never told Terence about George's true reaction. There

never seemed any cause. They prayed the world would be a different place by the time Little George grew up and started asking to stay with his Uncle Terence and his Uncle Chris.

What else can we do?

Terence's second novel published by Voyager followed the same winding path into the much-tracked cave of the heart and firmly established him as a talent unto himself. It was a national best seller and was nominated for the National Book Award. He marked his progress in building a life to his own specifications by the writing of his two serious books and by constant attendance at meetings.

His home meeting was the one that met at eight on Wednesday nights in Saint Vincent's Hospital. When he called the gay counseling service, he had expected a gay meeting. He was convinced only gay people would understand. That concerned man directed him to Saint Vincent's. He arrived at seven fifty-five.

The large room was crowded with people of all ages. They were happily chatting with one another, kissing in greeting, and waving across the rows of separate wooden seats. It looked like a gathering of carefree friends waiting for a screening of a favorite Fred and Ginger movie. He never expected such varied men and women. He never expected laughter. He asked a young woman if he was in the right room.

"Yes, this is it! Your first meeting?"

He nodded, terrified by the boisterous crowd. If they were so happy, they could not be living with an alcoholic, he reasoned, eager to flee.

"Welcome. You've come to the right place."

He had serious doubts. What could they know of his suffering?

"At *my* first meeting," the woman continued, "I couldn't figure it out either."

He nodded.

"It's because here we're not alone anymore. You're with friends who really understand what you're going through and know all your secrets and love you because their secrets are the same. It's scary, but it's such a relief. My husband's been sober two years but I need my meetings more than ever. These rooms are my salvation."

Her husband?

"Oh, I'm sorry. My name is Carol."

"Mine's Terence."

He did not hear much of the welcome the chairperson read. Terence scanned the group and felt both frightened and furious that he had been reduced to this: a self-help group? It was all Christopher's fault; everything wrong with their lives was Christopher's fault. If Christopher would stop drinking, theirs would be the perfect relationship. Everyone said so. It was *that* obvious.

The chairperson continued reading: "We who live with the problem of alcoholism understand as perhaps few others can. We, too, were lonely and frustrated, but here we discover that no situation is really hopeless and that it is possible to find contentment, and even happiness, whether the alcoholic is still drinking or not. We urge you to try our program. It will show you how to find solutions. . . ."

Whether the alcoholic is still drinking or not? Who can be happy when he's killing us both? Solutions? Give me solutions. Teach me how to make him stop.

A woman was the speaker. Her name was Caroline and she was going to speak about courage.

Courage? What the hell has courage to do with his drinking?

They went around the room introducing themselves by first names only. Suddenly everyone was very serious, but, people still smiled at one another and mouthed silent hellos to the latecomers, who nodded in return as they weaved among the seats to reach an empty one.

Caroline told her story. A qualification, she called it. She had never spoken before, she announced; she said she was terrified. She knew she had to speak because only by sharing her experience would she be able to change. Many people murmured encouragement. After the initial shock when Terence heard her mention her *husband*—obviously the switchboard had been in error about this meeting—he settled in and listened carefully, always intrigued by a narrative.

Caroline met her husband at school, just as Terence had met Christopher. Gregory was a produced playwright who made little money; Caroline paid the bills, bought his food, bought the booze. She told a story that was not precisely his, but similar enough to make him very uncomfortable. Caroline and Terence shared a very tight corner. They had not only screamed into the same European sunsets, but also concocted similar home remedies to control the drinking: hiding it, pouring it down the drain, watering it, mixing weaker drinks, making themselves ill by drinking the stuff themselves, shifting the dinner hour, lecturing, lying, crying, cajoling, begging, threatening, punishing, rewarding, scolding, cursing, nagging, silence. Their drinking careers were identical.

Faced with the same problem, he responded the same way she responded. They even had similar vocabularies for their hatred and their rage. He found himself laughing with the others as she told of following Gregory from bar to bar and waiting outside all night in a blizzard to make certain he got home safely. He was driven home by a friend when the bars closed. She walked. He went to work the next day. She caught pneumonia. When she blamed him he told her: I never asked you to make like the little match girl.

"He was right," she said. "But I was the long-suffering martyr."

For the first time, he saw how insane it all was. The things they both had done in the name of reason were patently insane. She explained that alcohol made people irrational and their situations irrational; by trying to manage irrationality, she had become irrational. She spoke of guilt, of her making Gregory guilty, thinking that would make him stop. She quit that when she learned guilt was a weapon of the disease. She said she had believed herself responsible for his drinking, and unwittingly had helped him to continue. She talked about learning how to examine her motives.

"Everything was inevitable until I learned in the program *how to get well* We went around and around and around. . . ."

Terence was shaking. He was so frightened by what she was exposing in himself that he wanted to run out of the room. Then her words ceased to make sense. He tried to follow, but he could not grasp whole sentences. Phrases jammed in his head, echoing and fragmenting into gibberish. One impression emerged.

We're all the same in our illness. We're only unique in our health.

Caroline's voice pierced the dense fog: "It takes great courage to seek help, to stop denying his problems. We deny as strongly as they deny. Once you stop denying, you have to do something about it."

He had never thought of himself as courageous. He was a coward. If he had any courage, would he be putting up with Christopher's madness? Why did he stay with him?

I stay because I can't leave. Takes courage to stay. Do I love him? I can leave. I can always leave.

He had forgotten he could leave. He was so caught up by the insanity of the situation that he forgot he could leave.

Choices. There are choices. I have choices.

"I hope for the courage to live my own life without this disease to blame for my own fears and my own failures, without this disease to hide behind."

A disease? *What is a disease? Something with symptoms, with a beginning, a middle, and an end.*

When they opened the meeting to the other people, there was an enthusiastic response. Hands were raised and common experiences shared. Everyone agreed with Caroline. They, too, thought they were helping but learned at meetings that they were making matters worse. Courage was trying a different route. Courage was admitting that the disease exacerbated their own problems, twisted them to its own shape, and only when they solved their own problems would they be free of the disease. "Money," "anger," "rage," and "self-pity" were key words for most of them.

Terence felt inundated but at the same time strangely calm, as if a flood were lifting him to freedom. He recognized the calm of reason. He had not felt it for years. Again and again, he was stunned to discover himself one of so many with the same problems and the same feelings and the same sense of failure.

We're all the same with this illness. Like rats in a maze.

During the break in the meeting, Carol approached while he was sipping a cup of tea.

"Well, what do you think, Terence?"

"I'm confused."

"Good! When I admitted I was confused, I stopped feeling I had all the answers. You thought we'd sit around and teach you how to make her stop."

He nodded. She laughed.

"I want him to stop drinking," he said, oversensitive to the pronoun.

"I know what you want. It's what we all want when we first come into these rooms. Some people have been coming for years and it's *still* all they want. There are other things to want from life, Terence. In any case, you can't make him stop!" she insisted, switching pronouns without a blink. "You can only get yourself well. Two sick people can't solve a problem. We come for them. We stay for us. You have to learn to detach. You're holding on to the disease for dear life and you're dying. You have to learn to detach with love. It's a hateful business, painful as hell, but we have to do it or *we* are doomed. It all sounds so stupid. Go to some beginners' meetings. Here's a phone list. Use it. Coming for coffee?"

He said no. He was eager to get home to Christopher.

Home to Christopher. Home to Christopher.

After the break, the meeting was directed to newcomers.

Did he have any questions? Yes, he had questions. He loved Christopher. How could he stand by *detaching* and watch him die? He wanted to help. A man named Thomas S. responded:

"Because there is nothing else we can do, Terence. We detach from the disease, not from the person. We detach to look at our situation, to see what's going on. We go blind from our anger. I'm sure you've tried everything that Caroline tried. I know *I* did, and *nothing worked.* He kept on drinking and I got sicker. I thought it was my *duty* to make him stop. I learned here that I'm not responsible for another person's disease, that my primary duty is to my own recovery. Then *perhaps* I can aid in the alcoholic's recovery: As we get better, the situation at home improves. Most doctors and psychiatrists are arrogantly ignorant of the disease. They see it as the effect of other problems; here we see it as the cause. We know how it works here. We come together to share that information. We assess damages most professional 'healers' don't know exist. Then we share ways, practical ways, to get well. It's an action program. We don't ask *why* did the illness happen. We ask *how* can we stop it from continuing. Try beginners' meetings. Use the telephone to keep in touch with us. If you call one of us, you are trying to solve the problem; if you take it to Chris, you want *him* to make it all better, you want him to make you happy. No one can make us happy but ourselves. We love you, Terence. We need you. Keep coming back."

"Detach? What's this *detach?*' he pondered on the walk home. Christopher was the one attached. It was all mush. A program? They sounded programmed: spouting preprogrammed jargon, slogans, praying to a "Higher Power." Caroline had said she had no personal God; the group's collected will was her "H.P." He could buy that notion—it was vaguely Jungian—but he had no time for bijou jingles.

Easy Does It. Live and Let Live. One Day at a Time. Give me a break! Christopher's dying and they offer me hit tunes?

He was living with a hopeless drunk and they told him to have hope, to be grateful they were still alive and had time to learn the steps and work the program. He needed tough *advice*, not loons comparing notes on what assholes they had been before they saw the light. He would never go back. Simplicity patterns were not for him.

A disease? More like Simone Weil's evil: gloomy, monotonous, barren, and boring. Won't go back.

He did *go* back. After nights fierce with fighting Christopher, and bleak nights crying over his passed-out body, and desperate nights, long sleepless nights waiting for him to be home alive, nights livid with rages steeped in terror, and nights promising only more of the same, he went back. If those people were crazy, they were crazy as he was crazy and he needed comfort from his own kind. He was desolate, vacant, and worthless, yet they welcomed him. No one asked him to justify anything. And when a woman wept because she had thrown a glass of brandy in her husband's unconscious face, Terence wept with her; that very evening, before leaving home, he had done the same to Christopher. On the way to the meeting, he had despised himself and damned himself to hell. Thomas, beside him, held his hand. Thomas whispered that he had done it, too.

"Welcome to the human race, Terence."

Months later, after countless meetings, when he lifted the pencil to begin the first of his small novels, to write in his own voice, he was paralyzed by fear. Christopher had been totally supportive and called his father with the good news. His only question was why had Terence not done it sooner?

He watched himself change. It was not the way he had imagined it would be. He wanted to resemble a flower opening rapidly on time-lapse film: a symmetrical, graceful experience, effortless and natural. But it happened in spurts, clumsily and painfully, full of unpleasant regressions and unruly behavior.

In my heart there is a kind of fighting. . . .

First the angry voices had to be stilled so rational discourse could commence; then that "irritating retard" his unconscious had to be taken into account and treated with infinite patience, requiring every change be explained over and over and over: It refused to take direct orders, and had a life of its own intercepted by means of the most cunning scrutiny. Then the conscious mind had to be convinced there was something it could not handle on its own, for his heart soon came to accept the group as a power greater than himself. He typed Nietzsche on a card and taped it to his notebook:

"Consciousness is the last and the latest development of the organic and hence also what is most unfinished and unstrung. Consciousness gives rise to countless errors that lead an animal or man to perish sooner than necessary, 'exceeding destiny,' as Homer puts it. If the conserving association of the instincts were not so very much more powerful, and if it did not serve on the whole as a regulator, humanity would have to

perish of its misjudgments and its fantasies with open eyes, of its lack of thoroughness and its credulity—in short, of its consciousness. Rather, without the former, humanity would long have disappeared."

It became a battle for survival, a battle for himself against himself. He learned that change occurred in small ways: a pot not washed compulsively, a shirt bought for himself, a play gone to alone, a shattered glass not swept up, Christopher's body left where it fell.

"When I want to yell, alarm bells go off. A sane voice in my head tells me to shut up, not to step into the disease's arena. I know. I *know*. I now know what I'm doing. My instincts warn me when I'm heading for an attack of the crazies. I walk away and go brush my teeth. I talk to my anger. I tell it that it's no longer wanted on the voyage. I can control it *today*. And that's all I have to do: control it today! I remind myself that it's a symptom of the disease and I do not want to be drunk on anger. Or anxiety. I refuse to pick up the first anxiety. I picture rows of anxieties like glasses on a shelf. No, thank you. Not today, I say. Instead of screaming, I nod and clench my jaws until I can get to a phone. I don't want the grief that I get when I scream. He passes out and I'm in a rage all night while he snores and then I'm hung over with the loss of all self-esteem. If I don't react, the disease doesn't take me. The idea is to stop being the avenging angel, the enemy, my own as well as his. When he seems to be provoking, I remind myself that it's the bottle talking, not Christopher. I remind myself that not screaming is doing something! The key for me is accepting alcoholism as a disease, a physical, mental, and spiritual disease. Once I accepted the disease concept, I could feel compassion for him and for myself. Once I felt compassion, gained the heart view of him, my anger was manageable. Once my anger was manageable, I was a sentient being again. It's damn hard for me not to yell, and I have to remind my yelling self all the time. I'm conditioned to thinking of it as a weakness, a loss of self-control, that I forget. After ten years of being one with the disease, I slip back into its comfortable grasp. It's a disease, I say over and over, reminding myself that I am not the cure. I remind myself that alcoholism *lies*. I come to these meetings to raise my reality quotient. This program is not solipsistic. It's a sanctuary where I rest and heal and discover my true relation to my others. I'm biologically attached to other human beings. I need other people as much as I need air and water. Alcoholism is a disease of isolation. In these rooms, I reclaimed my life."

Now, years since that first qualification, he sat in his snow palace watching cloud patches scudding overhead.

I love to lose myself for a good while
Like animals in forests and the sea.
To sit and think on some abandoned isle,
And lure myself back home from far away,
Seducing myself to come back to me.

He was marvelously calm. Neither the call from William More nor the one from Bernice had upset him. Why?

Can it be? Have I finally put down Christopher's cross? Must be. I am fine. My *life is fine. Terence, you know you can't save him and you no longer need to try. He'll find his own way. How could I have believed his destiny was in my hands?*

The telephone rang. It was Angelo Santangelo, Christopher's editor at Paine & Berg. Terence smiled when he recognized the voice.

La principessa di gelo. The final test? Three strikes and I'm out of the game? Watch it! Shades of Claude Steiner.

"Terence?"

"Who else?"

"Is Christopher with you?"

"No, Angelo, he is not. He and I aren't living together for now."

"Where is he?"

"I haven't a clue. He and I aren't living together for now."

Same inflection. Doesn't notice.

"His manuscript is due today. He promised he would bring it to me today. If he doesn't deliver it today, we won't be able to publish it in the fall. It's in the catalogue for October, Terence. Where is it? Does it exist?"

[124]

"I don't know. He's been publishing poems here and there. I saw one in *The New Yorker* a few weeks ago. I'm sure it exists."

Watch it! Old song. No excuses.

"Don't be so sure! Christopher More is famous for his flights of fancy. A few poems scattered around in magazines don't make a book, and that one a few weeks ago was just OK. It needed work. I know he's hiding from me. When I called Bernice just now, she said he's lost. Lost! I *know* he's hiding from *me*, Terence! I don't understand why I bother. . . ."

"Don't you?"

Pathetic. Who else but a drunk could deal with you day in and day out?

He started humming "Night and Day" up in his sinus cavity. Angelo continued undaunted.

"No, Terence, to be honest, I don't understand why I bother. I told him so the last time he called. Last Thursday. It was right after lunch. I had an upset stomach for the rest of the day. I went out to Sag Harbor on Friday and had a lousy weekend, too."

"Gee."

Hysterical queen!

"I told him he can't behave this way anymore. And I mean it, Terence. I mean it this time."

"Maybe you should let him go elsewhere. There have been offers."

"After all the work I've invested in him? Not to mention the money! When he's dead—which could be any minute— he'll be solid backlist, and our insurance will return the cash he owes us tenfold. I'm not worried about that! It's his attitude. He owes me some respect. I've taught him a lot, Terence. I want to know where he's hiding."

"How much money could he owe you? You gave him a thousand-dollar advance on his new book."

Prestige house? Shmucks! *Your place isn't even air conditioned. Air cooled. Lovely in the summer. Free ice cream* por los peones *while you're off in your fucking* dacha.

"We gave him what he deserves, Terence. He'd only drink it away. We want him to be able to write. We don't make any money

[125]

on his books. You, of all people, know that!"

"Uh-huh."

End this conversation, puh-lease! *Soon he'll be shrieking at you.*

"We'll just have to cancel the contract."

"That might be a good idea."

Scare Christo with that one. Not me, gelo.

Christopher's first volume of poems with Paine & Berg had been two years late. The announcement appeared in four consecutive catalogues. Angelo had procrastinated due to overwork and constant hypochondriacal illness, then had informed Christopher that his own obsessive concern for "just that word" was the *sole* cause for the delay, the poet was convulsed with guilt and fear and rage; the smallest manipulations were required by the prestigious editor to put that one over. Angelo was acknowledged an eccentric genius in the industry. Terence had long since ceased to believe that was a good enough excuse for such "psychotic passive-aggressive carryings-on, bub."

"Just how *long* does he think he can hide from me?"

Terence wanted to make strange noises, clutch his throat, and fall to the floor. It was too, *too* absurd! The whine in the man's voice was like fingernails on a blackboard.

"He's very ill, Angelo."

Give it a try. He can get behind "ill."

"You're telling *me?*" There was mirthless, maniacal laughter. "You think he has a book?"

"I don't know, Angelo."

Need it for your fabulous list? You guys are too ritzy for lists. You need it for your life.

"He won't get away with this, Terence. He'll be sorry."

"When he remembers you exist, he's sorry already. Good-bye, Angelo. Please remember that until further notice, Christopher More doesn't live here anymore. And I'm not Sue's Answerphone."

"You should have thrown him out long ago. He's a bum. He's a *genius,* but he's a bum!"

"Thanks for the words of wisdom, Angelo."

Terence sat quietly after hanging up. He decided it was

unfortunate that James M. Cain never wrote about the publishing milieu. Angelo was just like a brunette Phyllis Dietrichson ("He'd wear that platinum wig if he could!"), with tortoiseshell glasses and a pipe and a Sears, Roebuck college degree. Maybe he, Terence Strange, working author, would someday have a stomach strong enough to make use of it all.

Ach! It's the same everywhere. Who do I fuck to get out of this picture?

The telephone rang. It was Morgan Connelly. He wanted to know how Terence was doing. He wanted to tell him his book proposal was accepted. They talked for twenty minutes and made tentative plans to meet for tea or a drink or maybe dinner with a movie. They would get together for something. It was only a matter of good time.

S I X

Christopher stared at the hotel ceiling, tracing with burning eyes the filigreed plaster; it resembled the antimacassars lace-curtain Irish pinned on the backs of chairs. His stomach convulsions ceased after slurped gulps of whiskey from the half-empty glass by his bed. He impelled himself to concentrate on the dulcet voice of the radio announcer. He attempted visualizing a face, but the shudderings in his muscles shot slivers of terror up his rigid spine.

Too far. Gone too far. Again! *Terry warned extremes would. . . fibrillations. . .*

Perspiration congealed on his brow, forming a crystalline mask to be brushed away like sand. The exertion of raising an arm to a head dragged his stomach into his throat and instigated wrenching spasms of nausea. Reaching blindly for the glass, he knocked it to the floor. The shattering deafened. Gagging, he bolted upright and turned himself out of the bed. Lunging for the bathroom, he stomped on the serrated bottom of the glass, securing it to his left foot, while severing the vein beneath the ankle. He howled. Suddenly convulsed by dry heaving, he toppled into a nearby chair. He closed his eyes. Tears welled. The warm blood oozed between his toes.

Afraid to look but too curious not to, Christopher glanced at his wet foot. The shard was inserted into his heel. It overflowed with caught blood.

"Looks like the remains of Cinderella's Wedgie," he quipped aloud, trying to laugh, but the cold pain slithering up his stiffening leg was not amusing.

Good Lord! What a way to go! In Lansing, Michigan! A flower beneath the foot Terry, Terry. . .

Reaching down, he grasped the glass crown and eased it out

of his flesh. The pain was negligible. The sight of the bright blood cascading from the puncture wound like so much strawberry syrup shocked and fascinated. It dripped to form a veritable puddle on the wooden floor. He stared at the remains of the glass in his hand: a jagged base now transformed into a chalice of blood, his very own precious blood which he respectfully placed under the chair.

Must do something.

Hopping into the bathroom, he grabbed a towel and wrapped it tightly around the wounded foot. The row of towels, in its pristine whiteness, offered comfort which he eagerly snatched. They reminded him of the brown washcloth that his father kept in the bathroom for childhood's bloody emergencies; brown to prevent him seeing his blood seep into the fabric; brown to avoid instigating further panic. His father had been very clever about certain things. His mother may have had something to do with it, too.

He sat on the toilet. Casually bringing the damaged extremity into view, he frowned at the blood now clearly visible through the several layers of twisted toweling.

Primal fear. Men see blood only by mishap. Women familiar with blood. She'd be upset but not amazed blood is so red. Viscous, too. Smells. Now what?

Staring at the tiled walls, he sighed, then quietly began to sing:

> *I was a stranger in the city*
> *All alone was I, not with people I knew*
> *I was no stranger to self-pity*
> *What to do, What to do, What to dooooooooooooooooooo?*

Rising, he unwound the soggy towel, scooped it up, and dumped it into the tub. Talking to a smaller one, he gently folded it over and around his foot before hopping to the phone. He dialed 0.

"Operator, is there a doctor in residence?"

"No, sir. Is there anything wrong?"

Wrong? *Of course not! It's Take a Doctor Dancing Day!*

[129]

"I've had a *minor* accident. Will you call me a cab like a dear? *No!* Wait! Just a sec, hold on, please."

Skipping to the trousers that lay in a heap with the rest of his clothing, he searched the pockets. Discovering them empty, he returned to the phone.

"Cancel the cab, operator. Thanks."

"Are you OK, sir?"

"Yes, I'm nifty. Thanks."

There was only one sensible thing to do. He would hitchhike to the nearest hospital, wherever that was. It had to *be*. Lansing was a big town. There were probably several *huge* ones.

All the bored students attempting suicide, and the logging accidents.

Crossing back to the bathroom, he tried to lift his foot, into the sink to wash it before taking it outside, but the entire leg had stiffened and he could barely raise it into the toilet bowl which, to his relief, did not contain sapphire-blue disinfectant. After three flushings, the bloody water cleared. His submerged extremity appeared grossly swollen but he assumed it an optical illusion. He watched his blood depart from him like wispy smoke clouding the numbing, improvised bath. Flushing again, he lugged the heel over the rim and held it suspended, aghast at the melodramatic way it had bloated itself. The blood continued to course, gather, and plop into the toilet.

This is getting muy *serious, toots.*

Hopping hurriedly to the piled clothing, he disentangled the essentials. Yanking them onto his naked body, he groaned with pain as the hurt leg was gingerly maneuvered down the trouser channel, then yelped as pubic hair was caught in the recalcitrant zipper. Before he reached the door, the unlaced cordovan was wet with blood; by the time he reached the elevator, it was making squishing sounds. He refused to inspect if he were leaving an incriminating trail on the dull maroon carpet.

Surprised not feeling faint. Lost a gallon by now. We've thirteen pints. Artery gives a sixteen-minute checkout. Must be a vein.

He glanced at the elevator's tiled floor, but only for a second to gauge whether the puddle forming would make a blue-haired lady in a flowered hat shriek should there be such a creature waiting to ascend from the lobby. Hobbling adeptly across the deserted foyer, he tossed a jaunty greeting to the young male desk clerk, who nodded and smiled an overly warm response.

Not now, fella. Thanks. Maybe later.

Luckily the carpet was royal blue. The sunlit sidewalk instantly revealed the crescent-shaped insignia he had embossed since leaving the room. Unable to decide whether a nimble leap into the rushing traffic (with a wiggling thumb thrust high above his head), or a hop to a sidestreet would be wiser, he careened into the Howdy-Do Lounge for advice. Greeted affectionately by several unknown faces, he attempted a cheery wave but managed an unenthusiastic fillip.

"Chris, my boy, what's got you down?" a fiftyish, good-looking brunette asked with honest concern on her heavily made-up face. She was settled at the bar and invitingly patted the adjacent empty stool.

"Josie," he said, her name reclaimed as if from a dream, "I need help. I've cut my foot."

With a dancer's agility, she bounded to his quivering side. Her solicitous questions while she guided him to a chair brought tears to his eyes, and he clung to her, suddenly faint from the strain of facing impending death alone. He began to shake uncontrollably. The rash pricked his shoulders. He tried to speak but could only sob. She ordered the bartender to sit with him while she went to get her car.

"Be right back, hon. Don't leave him, Buddy."

She was gone. Josie was gone but Buddy brought a double whiskey and some peanuts. For a few wonderful moments, the alcohol calmed him. He and Buddy grinned at one another until a third man with a high, thin voice joined them at the table.

"Where you bleeding from, Chris?"

"My foot. I stepped on glass."

"Josie's a real good driver, son," Buddy said softly. "You'll be OK,"

"This place looks like a slaughterhouse," the third man observed cheerfully. "Sure you didn't hit an artery?"

"I think I'd be dead by now if I did, Sammy."

Sammy? Yes, Sammy. Drinks Harvey Wallbangers.

The three men nodded and smiled. Christopher craved another double but knew one on the house was the limit.

If I'd lost a toe he'd give me a refill. Probably for only the whole fucking foot. He'd want to see it on the table.

Josie honked from the street. When Christopher tried to rise, he faltered, unable to locate his center of gravity with one leg gone: His left one was numb. He sat grinning in confusion until Josie honked a second call. Sammy watched, puzzled.

"You need help, Chris?"

"I reckon so, Sammy. Yes. Please."

The two men hoisted Christopher out of the chair. Sammy whistled in shrill amazement as he and Christopher made for the door.

"Sure is a mess in here, Buddy! Got sudsy ammonia?"

"Think this is the first blood this floor's ever seen? Help the boy to the car. Leave the housework to me."

Curbside, a relic of late fifties splendor shimmied, its red door flung wide. Josie sprawled the length of the leather front seat. With braceleted arm outstretched, her hand waved as though directing a flight pattern. Reaching the car, Christopher spied pages of newspaper spread on the floor, which made him feel queasy, unhousebroken, a mess. He squeezed his mind shut for a dizzy moment before tumbling inside the vibrating machine. The door slammed. As he turned to mumble thanks to Sammy, Josie floored the gas pedal, jetting them into the heavy traffic. Horns shrieked.

"Stuff it, friends!" she fearlessly shouted. "This is an emergency! Make way, shits!"

Christopher laughed, clutching padded dash.

"I'm OK, Josie."

"Sure you are, kid. Don't try to talk."

Christopher smiled. Closing his eyes, he was with Ida Lupino and they sped along in a '48 coupe. He heard in her husky tones that she lived for this type of action, and he always enjoyed a true pro who was around when people valued good crises. She lit cigarettes and passed one to him. He wanted to answer with something tough but accepted in silence, nodding and exhaling through nostrils as quickly as he could.

"How you doin', kid?"

"Holding my own."

"Hang in there, hon."

"You're a good woman, Josie."

"Sure, kid. I'm a brick. We're nearly there. Sit tight." Right on cue, a police car wailed in their wake. She skidded over and rolled down the window as the uniformed sunglassed law approached.

"Listen, I got a *bleeding* man in here! Will you lead us to emergency?"

"Sure, Josie!"

Star! She's a star! Even the cops want into her act!

"Oh, boys?" she called as an afterthought.

"Yes, Josie?"

"Turn on your siren!"

They roared off again, this time in real style.

"Glad it was those two," she laughed, lighting fresh cigarettes. "They come in handy sometimes."

At the hospital, she retained command, refusing to fill out the requisite forms until the doctor saved Christopher.

"He's been bleeding for too long, Sister. He'll go under before we remember his Social Security number."

The nurse led Christopher into an adjoining room. Josie followed but immediately retired when the doctor asked her politely to leave. Ten minutes and four stitches later, the doctor sought her in the waiting room.

"Any reason you can think of, miss, that he might have done it deliberately?"

"You kidding, doc?"

"No. I'm very serious."

"Do himself in by slicing a vein in his *foot?*"

You knucklehead!

"You'd be surprised. A lot of people do it that way. A vein's a vein." The doctor frowned, waiting.

"No, doc. Not Chris! He's a famous poet! He came out here to read his stuff at the college. This was just a crazy accident. He doesn't want to die. Honest! He's a good kid, doc. Come on! He's got a plane to catch."

"He's been drinking."

"Who hasn't?"

In the car driving back to the hotel, she related the conversation. She avoided eye contact even when handing him a lit cigarette.

"Your *foot?*" she laughed.

"Yeah . . . imagine that."

"Christopher?"

"No, Josie! I'd take a nose dive before hacking up my tender white feet."

Might fall hard for a shrimp queen one day.

"When are you going home?"

He told her the truth. She listened to the story in silence, smoking a cigarette, exhaling through her nose. When she spoke, she left the butt between her lips.

"What'are your plans?"

"I'll call my agent. She'll wire me money."

"Wire you money? That's what my husband said when he left to find work in Detroit ten years ago. He was like that."

"Like what?"

"Slow."

They both laughed.

"It was OK with me, don't get me wrong," she kept going, settling her face for a long story. "I knew we were finished. I'm not complaining, mind. We were too young. It was all sex and liquor; we had nothing else."

It sounded familiar. She had probably related the entire scenario the night before, but he knew she was eager to tell and he was eager to hear. His foot was throbbing, sending soreness up his inner thigh. Whatever tranquilizers the doctor had given had taken care of the other problems as well. He felt comfortable. Closing his eyes, he waited for her drama to draw him into itself.

"We should check you out of that hotel," she interrupted herself to say. "You can stay with me until the money arrives."

"Thanks, Josie. It won't take long."

[134]

"That's what my husband said!"

"I'll pay you for the room."

"Sure, kid! I ain't at the point where I'm takin' in boarders yet"

When she paid his bill, the desk clerk looked surprised and disappointed.

"He's my long-lost son," she explained with a smile. "If you're nice, I'll send him over on Saturday nights."

The young man blushed.

"I'd like that, Josie," Christopher said sincerely, smiling tenderly at the confused desk clerk, who turned away to blush again.

Josie studied Christopher for a moment, then shrugged. "Takes all kinds," she said, laughing.

On the way home, she stopped to buy some Bourbon. She picked up a fifth of Jameson's for Christopher.

———

"Giovanni Lorenzo Bernini, 1598 to 1680, and Carlo Fontana, 1634 to 1714," William More softly read from the catalog, anticipating the wonder illuminating Dominic's face hovering over the case. "Document signed, undated, concerning work on a staircase in Rome."

He was exactly right. Dominic's neck shaded the deepest color of primroses. William imagined his friend crashing in a swoon through the glass. The tension between them for the moment had abated.

Glad I came. Do this more often. Show him a good time when we get home.

"Bernini, Italian school, seventeenth century," he continued, resting his free hand on Dominic's broad back. *"Interior of Saint Peter's with the Wooden Model of Bernini's Baldachin,* pen and brown ink, brown wash, graphite." Stepping aside, he gave full access to the third-class relic. Swelling with Dominic's happiness, he grinned with satisfaction until every sensation was overriden by' obstreperous thirst.

"I'm off to the men's," he whispered. "Be right back."

Dominic nodded, taking the catalog. The euphemism for a quick nip annoyed him. This was the third "pee" in an hour. He wondered how much was left in the half pint Bill had stashed somewhere on his dapper person. Dominic sighed, returning his attention to the drawing. Enraptured, he hugged the expensive catalog, which he never would have bought for fourteen dollars; but, after checking the coats, he was presented with it by a chuckling William. Though grimacing, Dominic had been pleased. William squeezed his arm knowingly and led him into the first room of the exhibit.

Three months before, discovering the show in *The New Yorker*, William insisted they go "soon," as if he, Dominic, were the cause of their never going anywhere. *Soon* was another euphemism. Originally it tormented with a *mañana* that occasionally arrived; now it was a decided never. Determined, Dominic plotted, undaunted by William's predictably waning interest. Now he joyfully studied his meed. It was the exhibit's last weekend and here he was staring at Bernini's own signature.

Turning, he surveyed the second-floor room in triumph. That very morning he had flared into a termagant's rage when William announced his decision: Museum viewing on Saturdays was *de trop,* not to mention insane. If lunatics wished to shoulder through the unwashed and the untutored to ogle some Renaissance scribblings, *they* had his blessings; he would not, could not venture forth, and why had they not gone some *night?*

Why didn't I kill him?

He could not remember *why* he swallowed the rage, but he silently left their bed planning breakfast before taking off for the Morgan Library.

Why should I miss this because shithead is hung over?

He was furious. William never budged. They never left the house. He took a shower and dressed noisily, slamming doors and banging drawers shut. William pretended sleep ("Can't go. Can't face it. Can't move."). As Dominic tied his left shoe, the lace snapped. It was the end. He felt himself tottering on the brink of cantankerous tears. It was Saturday and they would not be together. Why did he have to travel downtown all alone? Why could they not be like other couples who go places together? He would not go. William asked him a question.

"What?" he snapped, split between anger and martyrdom.

"Where's my coffee?"

Must go. Day will be hell here. He won't go alone.

"I thought you wanted to sleep."

"Don't you want me to accompany you?"

"Of course, Billy, but—"

"You expect me to journey to that fashionable *faubourg* without a cup of coffee?"

"I'll make breakfast."

"No! Just coffee! I'll take you to lunch at a place near there I know."

No food! Would crush me.

"I'll get coffee."

Bastard! Plays hard to get.

The trains arrived with admirable speed, and the Morgan Library was not crowded. There were a dozen harried people with self-satisfied grins, procrastinators like himself, Dominic thought, buoyant on his own mnemonic joy.

Bernini 1971. Rome!

The signature stirred him well beyond telling. The disparity between his life for five weeks in Rome and his day-to-day existence now despondently converted the floridly blazoned name embellishing a contract's lower half into a necromantic talisman: He had known in Rome that his life with William More was a failure.

As soon as William had grasped Bernini's power over Dominic's imagination, he notated a street map and they converted the city into a Bernini exhibit. Methodically, ecstatically, they searched each district for its treasures. William playfully engineered the seduction. Dominic ignored the drinking as the city was scaled to a compact parcel easily studied, eminently comprehensible from the baroque's perspective. Dominic was enthralled. William never enjoyed his ebullient presence more. But all the while, Bernini revealed the joy missing from their life in New York; he clearly foretold the barren years ahead. Dominic had refused to know. Now, volition gone, it all seemed ineffably sad.

He reread the catalog notes. William had left out the best bits as always. In the top of the case, his single reflection was suddenly contiguous to William's fatuously grinning face. The eyes were already showing the alcohol. Things required seconds longer to register.

It's infuriating. Like a movie out of sync.

"I'm getting hungry, Dom."

Better eat soon. Don't fuck up.

"You should have eaten something before we left!"

"Why? I've been looking forward to introducing you to Mary Elizabeth's for months."

"Is it expensive?"

"No. I've told you no. *Not at all.*"

"Anyplace with you drunk is expensive. Drinks cost a fortune out. You've already spent fourteen dollars on the catalog."

William sighed, stung hard. The carapace of guilt pinched the blood from his heart. Without it, nothing made sense; only when he was at fault did he feel certain of himself.

He's off now. Too bad. Bernini was good while it lasted.

"I should have come alone like I wanted. Did you finish your bottle or have you saved some for the men's in Mary Elizabeth's?"

William walked to the next case.

God help me! You think I enjoy public toilets?

"You ruin *everything!*" Dominic stage-whispered. "I should have come alone."

They ate lunch in silence. They returned home directly. William took a nap while Dominic lemon-oiled the furniture. He read his catalog and proclaimed the day perfectly grand.

———

Terence, awake, replayed a night, a Tuesday, two hours after midnight. He had been awakened then by Christopher bounding around the room searching for shoes.

"You woke me!"

"Go back to sleep."

"It's after two. What are you doing?"

"Go back to sleep! First give me money."

"Why?"

"I need ciggies. Make it a five."

"Five dollars for cigarettes?"

"Make it a ten and I won't come back."

He refused to give him money. He would pay for everything, but not the alcohol. Christopher, enraged, careened into a closet and began to throw clothing toward the center of the room.

"Get out. Get out *now,* you piece of shit—get *out!*"

He had gone.

Terence went to stay with friends for three days before returning to the apartment to pack a suitcase and drive to the country with puss. He spent two days with the phone unplugged, then returned to his program friends, Reggie and Joyce, in the city. He was not able to be alone. He went to meetings. He projected terrors that never arrived. His withdrawal from Christopher seemed relatively easy, but he knew to expect no reaction for several days, even weeks, maybe months. Only when he communicated directly was there an inkling of the lurking chaos: Everything seemed to be given new names.

Christopher was too stunned by the action to do much. He carted a dozen art books to Strand and laid in supplies. He telephoned his few remaining friends at wee hours to discuss a sonnet sequence on the subject of revenge. He telegrammed everyone in his address book announcing the end of the world: "not with a bang but a gurgle." He prowled the streets finding comforting sex. He plotted revenge, invoking Amneris as role model, loudly humming her music for incentive.

The fact of Terence's betrayal, and he saw it as a betrayal, made him berserk. He had not been disgusting or abusive *ever.* He had not been outrageous *hardly.* He had done only what he had always done because that was the way he was, which Terence knew when they hitched up together.

Two stingers and I'm up on the piano singing "Fish Gotta Swim."

So why the big fuss now, if you please? Why this melodramatic slamming of doors? He, Christopher More, did only what he was driven to do, Moira. He was a poet. All poets, all *good* artists, drank a bit too much. Should he go down the list? He could understand if he beat Terence or was always too drunk to keep him well fucked.

Terence telephoned. Christopher apologized for everything before erupting into howls that Terence could not do this to him.

"I'm not doing anything *to you*, Chris. I'm doing this for *me!*"

"I am very angry with you, Terence," he would say calmly, flatly, before hanging up.

The definitive statement devastated Terence. Every conversation closed with it. Each time, Terence was unable to walk. At a meeting, a woman coincidentally spoke of her crippling fear of other people's anger. He identified this fear as his own. It did not go away, but he knew what it was and set about finding ways to control it. As an added bonus, he discovered that Christopher knew him better than he knew himself.

"It took me six months to leave," Terence wrote to Bobbi. "For six months I set up my support network. I remember a night one week before I left, right after his return from that reading in Mississippi; we made love. It was splendid, the way it can be when you've been apart for a few days. I remember thinking right after that I loved him more than any of my possessions, more than my library, more than the apartment. Even more than the cat! I didn't know then but I was saying good-bye to everything. One week later, I let go of him and was able to leave. No scenes, no blizzard, no bloodhounds nipping at my rear end. I just left quietly. For years, I had imagined it a million different ways but never the way it happened. I'm still amazed. No, no I'm not. Not really. I was ready to do it. That's it. I was ready. *I knew what I wanted.* Ambivalence is the torment at those of us who will be perfect. I want everything every way *and* my way. I'm Master of the double message: I love you/Who are you? Come in/Why are you in? Go home. Take off your clothes. I'm either lonely or feeling trapped. Never happy. God forbid I should be happy! I'm daring to find out what *I* want and trying to stop blaming others for not knowing. I'm daring to venture from that corner. I still want the option on everyone's love. In the immortal words of

Auden, *'I've often thought that I would like/To be the saddle of a bike.'* Don't ask."

Terence awake remembered a telegram from Christopher:

What to such as you anyhow such a poet as I? therefore
    leave my works,
And go lull yourself with what you can understand, and
    with piano tunes,
For I lull nobody, and you will never understand me.

He had replied with lines from the same Whitman poem:

> *Did you find what I sang erewhile so hard to follow?*
> *Why I was not singing erewhile for you to follow, to*
>   *understand — nor am I now. . .*

Terence awake examined his lot. He was solitary but not lonely. He hoped everything laid still for a while. He would be dandy if he kept to the low side of the street.

I'm hungry.

There was cold chicken in the refrigerator. He went downstairs clutching the cat. The house smelled of darkness, winter, and ghosts.

His hand moved slowly. Squeezing, he savored the thrilled quickenings of self. His body tensed, seized by adored response. Solicitously, he eased toward the slippery edge before halting precipitously, exhaling heavily, and basking in an undulating semi-orgasm. Kneading the hot center of this startling pleasure, keeping himself, confined, afloat, he let the giggly spasms crest, eddy, dissolve, before tightening his oiled fist and greedily approaching again. After ten languid minutes of easy, poignant climbing, pursuing, retreating, breaking the keenest swells to bathe in the effervescent ripples, an aching rigidity provoked him to lunge over the top. Through dilating space he tumbled into Eden: unadulterated joy. For some moments, he was calmed and loved, at peace.

———

Morgan sounded delighted when Judith called with another dinner invitation. She mentioned immediately that Terence Strange would be there. She asked if he would play taxi with his Jeep.

At seven, promptly, Morgan was at Terence's door. They drove in pleasant silence before Morgan switched on the radio for a weather report; the wind was rising and the massing dark clouds looked up to no good. Pachelbel's *Canon* arched over the thrumming of the engine. Terence smiled.

Great movie music. Just like love, this. Chris and I: friends first, then passionate friends, suddenly lovers, consorts. Slowly developing, resolving. . .

"This is my new book," he said quietly.

Things change or die.

"How do you mean?" Morgan asked distractedly.

Terence was scented wonderfully. He wore a light fragrance: *eau de fleurs d'orange.* Was it in his hair? Or had his slender fingers streaked an invisible course up the length of his long neck, dabbing the swell of his Adam's apple? He pared his nails on a curve paralleling the white crescent rising above the cuticles. His wrists were thin. Morgan imagined his own thumb and pinky circling that wrist with inches to spare.

"This new book is dream therapy for me," Terence was saying. "I've taken the way my life *should* have gone—if the gods were *really* in the know—and set it down. If everything can be resolved in art, why not in life, too?"

"I do something like that with all my books. I never thought of it as dream therapy."

"There's a 'primitive' tribe in New Guinea that incorporates their dreams into their waking lives. They control them. The two men in my book grow old together. Their love grows. It alters, becomes more complex, richer, but retains the same essence, has a through line, a basic structure that never changes. It's like this piece of music. Am I talking horseshit?"

"No."

He still loves him.

Terence rested his left hand on Morgan's right arm. Its response attenuated the silence. Then it leaped into the dark space between them.

"Did you and Louis love that way, Morgan?"

"Louis and I loved in our own way. I always had my work, he always had his."

"Was he in publishing?"

"No. He was a dentist."

Terence stared at him in disbelief.

"When I came up here, things changed between us. He'd join me on weekends."

"How long have you been here?"

"Twelve years."

"How could you stand it?"

"Ours wasn't a very physical relationship. It was always more important to me than it was to Louis. I managed. It was sometimes difficult. I have my work. . . ."

"One thing about Chris and me: We had a very sexual relationship. *Lots* of it. Of course when he was working intensely, there was less."

"The drinking didn't kill it?"

"No. Well, sometimes. It becomes a weapon. Hate makes you frigid. He never drank whiskey until cocktail time. We had the early afternoons. I worked at home. I was so needy I learned to persevere. He had a therapist once who swore he wasn't an alcoholic because he never drank in the mornings. Chris neglected to report that he slept until noon! Once I learned at meetings to accept what he could give me the way he could give it, I wasn't angry. I stopped rejecting him because he wasn't what I thought he *should* be. I was shoving him away, then complaining he wasn't around. I had to learn that for me the smell of whiskey was not as upsetting as sexual deprivation. I think sex is a problem for many people."

"It wasn't always not physical for us. It gradually happened. I think it happens to a lot of people, too. I didn't think it could happen to me. I certainly never planned it that way. But it did. There was too much else to let it ruin things. We were happy enough. We loved one another."

"Uh-huh."

Not to me. Never to me. I'll never let it happen to me.

Morgan glanced at him and smiled. He hand rested again on his sleeve. He had not noticed its arrival. The well-being it pressed home was deep green to the white outside world.

Dinner went well. The food, not surprisingly, was superb. Judith made a crock pot of veal and barley stew, following a recipe from a cookbook she was editing. She was in fine humor, full of terse quips yet responsive to everyone, free of the strain from overcompensating for Gerald, who was more relaxed and charming than he had been in years. Terence was reminded of their first visits together, before they felt comfortable enough to ease up on the etiquette: Never interrupt while someone is speaking, never contradict, never speak with your mouth full, never throw food—no, it had not come to that at the worst of times, and from the look of things tonight they might all be in for a Gunning rosy patch.

"I feel like a new man," Gerald said and laughed.

"I'll drink to that," Judith giggled.

"I figure I'll work two or three days liaising. If nothing else, I'll develop a greater appreciation for my free time. Maybe find the nerve to paint, or work on the great American you-know-what."

Judith admitted she was pleased and invoked a team of wild horses when describing Gerald's determination to join the ranks of daily commuters on the expressway; she wanted him to take the train. Flying was logistically awkward. The Mercedes would make it a bearable trip.

Everyone agreed he looked marvelous. It was conversation fodder for the rest of the evening, but Gerald grew reticent and deftly turned the subject to Morgan's planned home improvements.

"The outside has to be scraped and painted. There are layers of old paint suffocating it. The wood can't breathe, which is why the house is so cold."

Avoid cheap metaphor.

They commiserated over the projected disorder and distress. After dinner, opera records were played in the music room. Gerald confessed a hatred for Puccini. He was shouted down by the others, who found the cynicism appalling.

"Only a deeply troubled being could utter an unkind word against *Sour Angelica!*" Judith insisted, ignoring Gerald's musical arguments at the piano. "More coffee, anyone?"

"Surely Minnie can be taken seriously, Gerald?"

"Only by Mickey."

Morgan drove Terence home. He refused a cup of tea or a nightcap. He said good night with a short wave and a smile.

———

Barbara "Bobbi" Edelston's visit to Amenia proved a respite from the solitude permeating the snow palace.

"Hi ya!" she chirped over the phone, the way she did whenever she stole the opportunity. She was mired in a strict budget; her calls to him were her one great extravagance.

"I was at a meeting," he said.

"That's what I figured. I tried before."

"It was a good meeting."

"Was it? Good! I'm glad."

She lit a cigarette. She was a chain smoker; he could picture her balancing her blue phone between ear and shoulder while she struck the match and inhaled the menthol-cooled smoke. For the first time since quitting, he craved a cigarette.

"How are you, Toddy?"

She was the only person in his life who used his childhood name. Reverberations hurtled around his heart like brightly colored marbles.

"I am *fine,* now! The afternoon's interior was overcast and testy. Christo called from Lansing, Michigan, where he's *holed up,* to tell me how annoyed he is with my behavior. He's convinced himself that all our problems— *his* problems—are due to my temper! I know better, but I have to keep reminding myself. I would love to see you for-"

"No!" she snapped.

They both laughed.

"No!" she repeated. "I can't afford it. See? It gets easier to say no the more times you practice."

"What if I gave you the fare?"

There was a single-beat pause.

"OK. I'm not proud." She paused again, to improvise hastily, referring to the schedules she carried in her purse. "I can take Friday and Monday as sick days. I'll arrive. . . at ten-ten tomorrow night. How's that?"

"*That* is wonderful! How is everyone?"

"Great! Except for Davey. He's dug up a live one. The guy gets drunk and beats him up. It's happened *three times* so far. Last night I sat him down and told him again about the program. He says he can't go now because he's working the night shift in the lab, but as soon as he's able, he says he'll go. I don't believe him."

"There's nothing more for you to do."

"I know."

"We'll talk about it when you get here."

The trip from D.C. to Amenia was two hours longer than scheduled. She disembarked shivering and seething. The Amtrak delay was due to snow; the absence of heat on the Conrail train was caused by an electrical short-out. Terence turned the heat in the car to maximum and drove home as quickly as he dared. Bobbi huddled, sullenly smoking, encased in her black fake fur.

"I'll make some tea as soon as we arrive."

"Nothing *fragrant,* Toddy, please."

"Would you prefer coffee?"

"No. Tea will be dandy. What's a visit to you without tea? Tea with a drop of something to get it on its feet. I *must* have coffee in the morning, you know, or I won't wake up."

"I bought five pounds of French roast, Melita ground. Would I kidnap you and not lay in supplies? If only you'd fly."

"Hmmnnn. Birds fly."

"People fly, too, these days. It's approved white magic."

"Neat-o," she muttered under her breath.

He thought it wise to leave her to warming. The rest of the way they rode in amiable silence. Her fists slowly unclenched. She blew smoke rings, hooking them on the rearview mirror.

Blanketed and propped in front of a massive fire, she smiled. "I love this house. I'd sell my soul for a fireplace."

He asked about her work. That question led them into a quiet, easy talking, connecting the pieces of their separate lives, easing them over the strains of the sudden reunion.

She hated her job. She worked as a receptionist/secretary for a pencil manufacturing company. It paid the bills— *just*—and was not demanding, allowing her several hours every day to read. Her friends, "the guys," were all well: One had split with one; one was seeing another. Life progressed in familiar ways. She was still fairly content with most of the choices she had made. A new woman, Michele, had joined the group; she worked with Howard, who was one of Bobbi's favorite people. Michele was Bobbi's age and showed promise of becoming an intimate.

"She doesn't play dumb games. If she's got nothing to say, she keeps quiet. It's been years since anyone's appeared who's even interesting. I like her. She reads! *Books!* We talk about Kafka! She's been to Paris. You know how choosy I am. I want all or nothing."

"Compromise, anyone?"

"I'm all for compromise, dear. What is love *but* compromise? But not on the first date! Compromise comes later, when you know the structure's sound. I have my standards, Toddy."

They both prepared dinner, which they ate in front of the fire, sitting on the overstuffed cushions that Bobbi had sent as a housewarming gift. He cleared the dishes, tucking them into the dishwasher. Then they resumed talking together quietly with the cat settled between them. They paused only to refill coffee cups. At 3 A.M. she announced a halt.

"Can I have the purple room?"

"Need you ask?"

"A girl must be polite or she might not be invited back. I even brought my own towel."

"It's *your* room. You chose that color."

She hugged him tightly. "I love you, Toddy. You're such a

good friend. Who else would paint a room in his beautiful house such a hideous color just for me?"

"I'm glad you're here," he said, laughing, remembering the complications of her purple/brown period.

"I would have let you bring me sooner, but I needed to be certain you wanted me around."

He smiled. The night he phoned her to announce his leaving Christopher, she had remained silent. Two days later, he received a letter explaining. She would never take sides. She loved Chris. She hoped things would work out for them both. Now, pausing on the upstairs landing, her hand encircling the doorknob to her bedroom, she was phrasing a question. Terence waited expectantly.

"Will you go back if he stops drinking?"

"I don't know! Certainly not *because* he stops drinking. Booze would still be pulling the strings. I want to cut *all* those damn strings. I want to go back because *I* want to go back, *period*. I feel like the guy who went into the pet shop to buy a canary. 'It's for my friend and *must sing.*'" he says. He pays fifty bucks for one guaranteed to sing like Galli-Curci. He gives it to his friend and can that bird sing! Sensational! His friend loves the bird, but the guy notices the bird's left leg is all shriveled up. He tells his friend he'll take it back but his friend won't part with it. He goes back to complain anyway fifty bucks is fifty bucks. 'A gimp leg?' the shopowner moans. 'So what? Did you want a singer or a dancer?'"

They spent Friday in front of the fire. It was a cold, blowy day with high winds lifting the fallen snow, churning it into a dense swirl that dropped a veil over the house. He baked bread and planned a veal roast for dinner; she made a potful of chicken soup. Then, after tea at four, she decided to turn out a chocolate cake for a treat while he worked for a few hours. Impulsively, as she cleared the tea things, she hugged him.

"You look and sound so *good,* Toddy!"

"I feel, pardon the lingo, in a fine comfortable place emotionwise. Low uncomfortability."

"Plus," she laughed, knowing he loathed the construction,

"you're not doing so bad surroundingswise. The house is pure heaven!"

"As my friend Joyce wisely says, If you have to suffer, suffer comfortably!"

The telephone rang, supplying the perfect exit, leaving her laughing.

Judith insisted Terence bring Bobbi to Sunday dinner. He covered the mouthpiece to convey the invitation. Bobbi pulled a *moue.*

"If the prospect of a meal with Gerald Gunning and me doesn't set her toes tingling rapturously, darling, would the chance to meet Morgan Connelly do the trick?"

"Will Morgan Connelly definitely be there?"

Bobbi waved and grinned, opening her eyes widely and exhaling a hefty gust of smoke from nose and mouth. The' sight of a human with smoke coming out of her head struck Terence as most peculiar. He was pleased he no longer smoked.

"Just a sec, darling. Let me ask him."

"I think Morgan's with her," Terence whispered to Bobbi, who now stood expectantly by his side. "Unless she has him on the other line."

"Oh, I would *love* to meet that man."

"You'll like him."

"You *know* him?"

"Didn't I tell you?"

"No, Toddy, you did not tell me."

"Oh. Sorry. He's a neighbor. He's doing a book for Judith."

"Morgan says he'd be pleased to meet our Bobbi."

"He says he'd adore meeting you."

"That is *not* what I said, darling, but never mind."

"Tell Morgan I'll be there.

"She says she'll be there, Judith, toes tingling."

"Toes tingling?" Bobbi exclaimed, gagging on smoke. "Who said anything about my toes?"

"Judith did," Terence whispered.

"I *loathe* that bitch."

"OK, Judith. Sunday at four."

"Toes tingling! That's disgusting!"

"We'll expect him, Judith. Thanks. Bye!" Terence hung the phone back on the wall.

"*Who* are we expecting, Toddy?"

"Morgan. Sunday at four. He'll take us over in his Jeep."

Bobbi sighed, relieved. She had flared with alarm over the prospect of a visit from Gerald bearing expensive gifts: special preserves for their breakfast, a crock of frozen blanchette, hothouse tomatoes, something exotic that would give him an excuse to descend and sit for hours. She considered Gerald a pathetic nuisance. Judith she detested: "A killer" was her sharp verdict. Terence thought her harsh and regularly reprimanded her but with no noticeable results.

"Judith needs meetings," he said frequently. "Too bad Gerald doesn't drink. She could use my program."

"I hate groups," Bobbi responded. "But if it works for you, Toddy, I love it."

"It works for me. It fucks up your crazies. Freud was right."

She hesitated before asking what Freud had to do with living life one day at a time. She knew how Terence felt about Freud's theories and she wondered if he was trying to be ironic.

Christo is right. Toddy cannot iron.

She did not have to ask. After he set the dishwasher, he read her a page from his notebook: "I need a similar *other* to understand myself. We're social animals; we learn from one another. Freud said once we harnessed the healing force inherent in our empathetic responses, once we *saw* others successfully change behavior, then we would emulate in movement away from pain-provoking yet familiar, comfortable though destructive behavior. We must learn to *see* and *hear* our others, then use them as a route to ourselves. Therapists were not expected to become cabalistic high priests; they were intended to be liberators, educators, founders of a brave new world. Unfortunately, that priesthood attracts only anal-retentives so we're not much farther along on the yellow brick road. But Freud had the right idea. Jung revealed its wellspring: the collective unconscious. My group with its program for change, my meetings where I gather with my others,

[150]

teaches me how to take emotional chances. *We* are all healers. Insight alone won't induce change. Because I know *why* I do something does not mean I can stop doing it. When will people understand that? When will they stop talking about 'relationships' as if they will solve everything, as if they exist outside themselves? Relationships don't exist. There's only the verb: to relate. People talk about fixing their relationship as if it's a house or a car they own." Snapping the book shut, he added: "You'll like Morgan. He's a lovely man."

She nodded, accustomed to his *non sequiturs.* She knew the two of them would discuss his notes at another time. He was expeditiously returning to the subject of greatest interest to her.

"Tell me about him."

"Well. . . he's lovely. . .

"I see. OK. How old?"

"Forty-seven."

"I've seen pictures."

"He looks just like his pictures, only friendlier."

"Is he tall? I've never seen him standing with anyone I know and furniture can be misleading."

"He's taller than I am."

"Sorry, dearest. Except for the people in your books, most of us are."

He smiled. It amused him that she believed herself taller than he.

"I *am,* Toddy. You've always had problems with spatial relationships, which is why you nearly flunked geometry."

"Morgan loves my books."

"I'm not surprised."

"He's gay. He lives alone."

"That's nice. Maybe not."

"His lover died two years ago. He was a dentist."

She guffawed. "Toddy! You say that as if he were a gherkin pickle."

"I mean—"

"I *know* what you mean."

"A dentist? Imagine spending your life excavating in people's mouths."

"No one is asking you to, dear. We *all* can't be artists! I love my dentist. *He's* an artist."

He studied her face. "I am such a fool, Bobbi. I'll never learn!"

"I think you will! True romantics fight to the bitter end, and you are the fucking truest. You're the only person I know who cried over *The Well of Loneliness.*"

"Why did I tell you that?"

"You tell me everything, dear. That's what friends are for."

SEVEN

Friday night Christopher More partied with a lawyer named Gregory Hillthorpe, who gave him a lift home from Kennedy Airport, then convinced him to share his dinner, his drinks, and his Brooklyn bed. William More perused *The Anatomy of Melancholy* until 4 A.M. Dominic Perrugio watched *The Great Lie* on television for the third time, waiting for the part where Mary Astor and Bette Davis are locked together in desert combat. Judith Gunning and Andrew Desmond went to a performance of Martha Graham's company before catching the eleven-forty to Amenia. Gerald Gunning prayed for one hour after putting the children to bed, then drew plans for an indoor pool. Morgan Connelly read *Measure for Measure*, pausing over Claudio's first lines in Act III:

> *The miserable have no other medicine*
> *But only hope:*
> *I've hope to live, and am prepared to die.*

He quoted Rosalind's: *"Men have died and worms have eaten them but not for love."* He continued reading aloud.

Saturday morning at eleven, Terence's telephone did not ring. Christopher had called from Lansing on Friday night to relay that Bernice had come through and was flying him home. He catalogued some new ills and raved about Josie. Then, after promising to call from Kennedy, he hung up abruptly. He never called. Terence was determined not to call him.

During their years together, the telephone was a lifeline. Every day, when Terence was away from home—at first while working, then on tour—he called at noon to awaken Christopher. Now he knew those calls were for his own comfort, too, keeping him in touch, giving him the "fix" he needed to get through, afternoons away from the nest, away from the cave where he was safe and secure.

Terence could not concentrate. He walked into the kitchen to make tea. Normally he would have called Thomas S. or Carol W. or Joyce M. or Lucille B., but Bobbi was expected any second from the bathroom above; he could hear the toilet flushing.

He decided to make a cottage cheese salad for lunch. Eschewing the Cuisinart, he began shaving a carrot by hand to occupy himself. Dropping the peeler, he quickly crossed the room and picked up the phone. Christopher answered on the second ring.

"Chris! Hi!"

"Oh, hullo."

He was sleeping. What did I expect?

"I was wondering how you are."

"How should I be?"

"I don't know."

Asshole. Now what? Hang up.

"I was with a friend."

"A friend?"

"In Brooklyn."

A friend in Brooklyn?

"Brooklyn? Who do you know in Brooklyn?"

Wrong! Detective. Getting angry.

"A new friend. Just got home."

Terence was dizzy with anger for having called.

Hang up.

"I just wanted to make sure you were OK."

Why didn't you call? I know. Dynamics. Shut up.

"I'm OK, T."

Why shouldn't he be? You were hoping. . .

"The flight was OK?"

Hang up.

"Sure."

"Well. . . good-bye, Chris. I love you."

"How nice for you."

Click. Christopher hung up. Terence flushed puce. *What did you expect? A sobbed thank you? Got what you deserved for getting back into it. You know better. Made a mistake. It's OK. Made a mistake.*

He returned to the cutting board by the sink. Plugging in the Cuisinart, he cut the carrot in two seconds.

A friend in Brooklyn? Why not? When he's drinking, he's a world traveler. Round and round riding shotgun on a bottle.

Seven seconds more macerated the carrot. He caught a bubble of self-pity on the rise. Identified, it burst before body snatching. He stared at the pulped remains of the carrot.

Avoid cheap metaphor. Will you stop? One step forward, two back. What is this penchant for tossing out neatly packed psychic baggage? Worry is holding on. Why don't you listen, fuck-face? You do. You do. I know you do. Two forward, one *back.*

"Terence?" he called aloud. "*See* this grief! If you dialed not himself, this would not be. Got it? Let him alone. This is regression. Bore-ing!"

He poured the carrot juice into a glass and drank it. Then, lifting an unblemished green pepper that shone like the one in the Weston photograph over the counter, he carried it to his lips. The beauty in the contours calmed him. It graced the moment with a peace that segued into serenity.

"*A noir, E blanc, I rouge, U vert, O bleu: voyelles,*" Christopher whispered to rout terror, but the dream persisted, overwhelming even the tumescent pain in his head.

> *I, pourpres, sang craché, rire des lèvres belles*
> *Dans la colère ou les ivresses pénitentes;.*
> *I, purple, spit blood. . . penitent drunkenness.*

The dream, revivified, commanded his attention. Their hospital ward sailed center stage in full-dress regalia with thirty-year-old Charlie strapped at its helm in the narrow bed next to

Christopher.

Charlie. Charles van something. The dying Dutchman.

Terence's call had interrupted Charlie's unwelcome eternal return. Yet again, stomach convulsions ruptured esophagus varicose veins filling the stomach with blood; yet again a clot lodged in the windpipe. Christopher awoke with Charlie's strangled moans transformed into a metallic scream of the telephone. Although grateful for Terrence's incursion, Christopher was too dehydrated to talk.

I should have stayed in Brooklyn.

The stench of cirrhotic stupor (*"fetor hepaticus,* friend") seemed to fill the bedroom, causing him to gag. He sat up and reached for the glass of water on the desk. Draining the glass, he stumbled out to the kitchen, where within five minutes he drank three cans of diet Dr Pepper. The absence of sugar in the soft drink left his thirst unslaked. He groped for the Irish whiskey and swallowed two fingers straight from the bottle. Steadied, swinging the bottle by its neck, he headed back to bed where Charlie throned, waiting to be shooed back to hell. Christopher was strong enough to handle the brute.

The other men in the alcoholic ward had narcotically slumbered while Charlie spewed lumpy blood over the blankets, splattering the floor between their beds, before the clot cut off his air supply. Leather-strapped to avoid death by violent delirium tremens, Christopher was restrained from ringing for the night nurse. Frightened to near fainting, he was unable to shout. Charlie, also shackled, could not roll over. He was dead within seconds, but his body twitched involuntarily for what seemed a very long time.

The mephitic odors of the ward—black tarry stools, rancid sweat, floods of putrid vomit and urine—now tormented him as the visual hallucinations once had done: kamikaze books flying at him and spontaneously combusting; rapacious lines of verse like loose-vertebraed reptiles writhing free of their flaming containers to seek him out and strangle him. The pervasive stench merged with the night sounds like an invisible tide of fetid sighs and noisome sobs lapping around the bed, churned by screams and demented shrieks to which he unwittingly contributed frantic howls while in the clutch of demon-inhabited sleep. But not that night. He could not get to sleep that night, his first night in the ward.

The sights had banished sleep. The faces cobwebbed by angiomas, and the shriveled muscles on wasted limbs, and the swollen protuberant stomachs, and the imbecilic toothless grins, and the yellow carotinemic skin, and the withered fingers clutching atrophied testicles. He would never be like them. He would stop before that happened to him.

His brain, awake, not lulled into a falsely disinterested stupor by alcohol, hummed on ativan before plunging into the nightmarish insanities of withdrawal from its drug. Alcohol. He would stop before such deteriorations occurred in him. The hospitalization had been an accident, an overreaction on Terence's hysterical part. He was not like Charlie in the next bed, whose hospitalization for "abdominal pain and vomiting" was his *fifth* time inside this madhouse.

The next day arrived and the ward awoke without Charlie's evanescent corpse. A doctor visited Christopher. Young and earnest, the doctor gently reassured him that no one could have saved poor Charlie. Christopher was grateful for the doctor's words, instigated by the nurse who spotted his horror when she discovered the dead Charlie. The concern had cleverly become a lecture on the importance of Christopher's working to make the therapy "take."

Doc was right. I don't wake up. I come to.

Chills besieged Christopher in the quiet of his own bedroom. Warmed by more whiskey, he thought of summer's blessed heat. Sipping tequila sunrises rich in vitamin C, he would wear a white linen suit and nappy white bucks like the ones he owned in high school and once in Paris. Terence had kept them as white as August's tenting clouds. He intoned grandly, in his most tragic mode:

> *E, candeurs des vapeurs et des tentes,*
> *Lances des glaciers fiers, rois blances,*

frissons d'ombelles. . . .
E, whiteness of vapors and tents,
Lances of proud glaciers, white kings,
quivering of flowers. . . .

Why write another fucking line?

When Morgan arrived to pick them up, Terence was jolted by his grand appearance. In place of the casual coat, he wore an elegant suede one with a fluffy lamb's wool lining; instead of the hunting cap, a tan corduroy number perched jauntily on his head. His beard was carefully pruned and shaped. A vivid maroon turtleneck sweater brought out his "pinks," as Christopher would have said, meaning it heightened his colors and made him look very healthy, very alert, and very handsome. Bobbi was impressed.

"He's gorgeous!" she whispered as they moved around the rear of the Jeep. "Why didn't you *tell* me?"

Terence shrugged, flapping his hands aimlessly. He wondered why he had never seen it before. He always considered Morgan attractive, sexy even, in a rugged, furry sort of way. Well, he was wrong. The man was extraordinarily wonderful to look at, a fact made clearer as Terence settled himself into the back seat and Morgan leaned to assist, bringing his sweet-smelling face within kissing distance.

The operative word's been "round," when it should have been "firm." He isn't bubeleh*, he's a bruiser. I don't get it. Must be anxiety. Anxiety fucks up your synapse. I did* record that smile!

Not only was Morgan looking beautiful, but he was also charming enough to endear himself to a hostile alien. His laugh was killingly potent: the male Muse incarnate. It sent a frisson of guilty pleasure skidding up the knobs of Terence's spine. And the voice was mesmerizing: deep, warm, eager to make friends. It was expressing his delight in the progress he was making with the new book, the surprises it held for him, although he felt best when a project finally became a publisher's problem. He said this one had been difficult to get off the ground, then he effortlessly shifted the subject to Bobbi's job. The two chatted happily, laughing often, all the way to the overlit Gunning door.

Climbing out of the Jeep, Bobbi dropped her glove. Terence stooped to retrieve it.

"Thanks, Toddy. I love these gloves."

Terence grunted, remembering her delight when she undid the Christmas wrapping. Christopher had suggested gloves. Morgan turned in his snowy tracks.

"Toddy? Do your friends call you Toddy?"

"Only this very old friend."

"You prefer Terence?"

"I became Terence."

Morgan held his glance and smiled. Terence felt caressed.

I have never seen this man before! Wander if he drinks?

Stopping at the rear of the single-file formation that was trundling up the shoveled path, Terence gaped horrified at Morgan's back.

God in heaven! Is he one of them?

He remembered Morgan's refusing a second drink the night they met.

A closet boozer? A periodic? It would be just my luck. . .

Bobbi called for him to hurry. He rushed to her side.

"Why didn't you tell me?" she hissed in mock anger.

"Tell you what?"

She was sitting beside him. Could probably smell it.

"Toddy! You mean you don't *know?*"

He shrugged, feeling foolish and inept.

"I don't believe how dense you are!" she whispered, giggling like the quick schoolgirl who sat behind him catching theorems as they sped over his head.

By the time Terence regained his equilibrium, admitted his powerlessness over everyone, and shakily resumed following the slippery path to the house by placing one unsure foot firmly in front of the other, the door stood open, revealing Andrew Desmond posturing and nattering as official watchdog at the Gunning gate. Terence scowled, muttered a low but audible "yuk," and assumed he now understood what (and who) was going down in the great big world around him.

Jesus! I cannot believe this! Morgan and that air-brushed mimp? Minus ten points. . .

Morgan received both a hug and a demonstrative kiss when he crossed the threshold. Bobbi's arm was politely touched and convivial greetings nicely exchanged. Terence winced as his own right hand was vised. Using the gained leverage, Andrew pulled him forward.

"I'm just *devastated* about you and your divoon mate," he cooed softly, shaped brows converging over a purchased James Dean nose. "You two dreams are my *favorite* couple. I hope you make up and *suck* pronto!"

Terence acknowledged the condolences with a curt nod, all the while marveling at Andrew's fashionable costume, half in distaste and half in begrudged admiration for the tall well-honed body it displayed shamelessly. The dove-gray velour trousers were molded to reveal what Morgan had obviously trimmed his beard for; the mint-green silk shirt had several pearl buttons undone, exhibiting a hairless tanned chest with ostentatiously large nipples, and a gold cross with a thin chain—the current decorative item on the disco circuit Andrew relentlessly pursued.

"Dancing is my life," he had once confessed.

"What a life!" Christopher had rejoined in mimetic Stanwyck deadpan.

"Do you live in Brooklyn?" Terence now asked nastily.

"God, Bella, no! Is there *really* such a place?"

Judith laughed too loudly. She stood just beyond them at the center of the foyer beside a huge potted fern. She was dressed sveltely in a red-quilted taffeta evening skirt and matching top; on the gold collar in the form of the vulture of the goddess Nekhebet, she flashed enough precious gems to fill a commodious hatbox. Her gold bracelets were brothers to the ones adorning Andrew's thick tanned wrists.

Terence surrendered his three-year-old tweed overcoat. Immediately after kissing Judith and waving to Gerald, he made for the upstairs bathroom. Framed in the full-length mirror, he

[160]

studied his disgruntled self. The dark-blue cord trousers were expertly tailored but did not do for him what Andrew's did for him. Not that he wanted to look as if he were for rent! A sensual curve, no vulgar bulge, would be attractive, manly; it was not due to his not being equal to any male, which was a well-kept secret in those conservative straight legs.

I guess it rests with the underwear, or in, *tucked away where it belongs, fuck-face.*

His shirt, a blue and tan plaid from Saks, he loved. Opening the three top buttons, he tugged the collar apart. His neck looked scrawny and the dark hairs revealed, obscene. He felt careless, unfinished, as if his fly were unzipped. Sighing, he closed the shirt. His English cowhide boots he truly preferred to Andrew's red Gucci loafers, but that was not the point of this heart-to-heart.

My butch look. My only *look. I like these clothes. I wouldn't be comfortable in chic sissy.* And why not? *You have to go shopping.*

He looked tired and drawn, with unflattering circles under his large hazel eyes that in the harsh fluorescent light were as green as Andrew's shirt. Terence's hair desperately needed cutting and shaping. Andrew, with his closely cropped "blond" hair and fashionable facial growth, a Hitler moustache, looked newly risen from a gay magazine's centerfold: "The roach look," Christopher had sneered. To camouflage his urgent need for a stylist, Terence plunged nervous hands into his flat auburn hair and wiggled fingers frantically.

Now it looks like carrot greens, Kukla.

He noticed there were several new creases around his eyes, and that the old ones had deepened. He opened the medicine cabinet, found some moisturizing lotion, and applied it liberally. When he leaned close to his image, he spotted a siege of blemishes on his nose. He wondered if Andrew ever had a zit in his entire hedonistic life. Terence wanted to go home.

Anxiety fucks up your face.

Slouching toward downstairs against his saner judgment, he intruded upon Judith and Andrew baiting Gerald, and Bobbi talking intensely with Morgan. Terence's presence immediately tilted the construct, making him awkward and more ill at ease.

He settled alone on a vast egg-white sofa halfway between the two groupings.

"Anyone for seconds?" Judith yelled into the ever-louder chatter.

"Me!" Andrew yelled. "Art is long and life is short. As that old warthog reminds us on television, it took Martha Mitchell ten years to write *Gone with the Wind.*"

Judith sprayed the last of her martini into the middle distance. The other three laughed loudly. Gerald rose to fix the drinks.

"I think you mean *Margaret,* Andrew," he corrected haughtily, sending Terence into a knot of hysteria that had him rolling around the couch.

"In your hat, Margaret! Here's to Pansy O'Hara!" Andrew toasted.

Gerald smiled as if they were playing a friendly game of Scrabble. "Pansy?"

"Her original name, Gerald, before an editor made her change it."

"Here's to editors!" Andrew toasted again.

Terence zeroed in on the others as soon as he could see.

The evening was picking up. Not having had a first, he wanted something serious now. Fleetingly, he wondered why someone had not offered before; he could hear Christopher bellowing, "Don't I have a mouth on me?" Judith and Andrew were swilling martinis. Bobbi and Morgan nursed Campari and soda. Gerald sipped champagne. Terence sided with the big girls.

"I'll have a martini, Gerald, with two olives, please. Thank you."

Bobbi stared at him and frowned. He pretended to be out of her firing line, unwilling to face how poorly he drank. She had not intended to chastise; she was pondering why he wanted to be sick. In front of him on a low table was a block of pâté with a generous assortment of crackers. She glared at the spread pointedly, wishing him common sense, then returned to her conversation with Morgan Connelly.

Terence ate the pâté and studied Judith. Her getup was very severe, capped by hair elaborately coiled with tiny gold chains and an emerald tiara. There were more emeralds stuck in her earlobes and weighing down her hands.

Rocks as big as the damn ashtrays.

She looked superelegant, "drop dead" rich, but not the least attractive. He usually enjoyed seeing her in full drag. She had a sassy way of appearing to be comfortable though no one else had expended such energy to be decorative; she made it a loving gesture executed to give others pleasure. Tonight was different. The glaze of couture blazoned a warning; it achieved a silver-screen distance. The color was no accident—it was too heavy-handed. And Andrew fluttered about the open flamepit playing coy minion to her bitch goddess.

What the hell is going on? I've been here before.

The first time he and Christopher visited the Gunnings, Andrew was a houseguest. (Soon after, Gerald requested his visits be kept to a minimum.) That time, too, Andrew had played the resident fool. He flirted with both young men the entire weekend, even asked Terence who did what to whom and how frequently so when he dreamed of them he would not screw up the details.

"He was only joking, Terry. . . I think," Christopher had soothed.

"He must be a comfort to her. Undoubtedly gives great phone. Why else would she keep him?"

Andrew and Judith had collaborated like two monstrous imps to derange Gerald. They attempted to elicit support from Christopher and Terence, but one was too occupied with the Irish whiskey, and the other with being parent to the lover and rescuer to the husband. Christopher passed out before dinner reached the Chippendale. Terence monopolized Gerald's attention, wresting it from the other two, who savaged him without letup. It was that very night Gerald announced his plan to paint a portrait of Terrace as Hamlet. He had drawn the first plans for a studio on his napkin.

Tonight, Gerald looked ill. His tension level was so high that a nervous tic caused his upper lip to leap. Terence spotted the quirk as he lifted his martini from the Paul Revere silver tray. He forced a glance into the two panicked eyes and thanked them for the two olives.

Cut! Print! Basta!

Unable to say another word, he stared at the rare rose Persian carpet near his shifting feet. He traced the intricate blue-gold pattern. Pouring half the martini into his mouth, he swirled it around with his tongue. Christopher despised his drinking technique. He swallowed quickly in two uneven gulps. The heavy numbing taste of the cocktail delighted him. All reckonings of its *macho* potency were relegated to limp-wristed myth. With a flowering bravura, he drained the Steuben glass, pressed both olives against his palate, and decided that tonight he was a two-martini man. Instinctively, he attacked the pâté, longing for a huge hot eggroll to absorb the second "drinkey" Gerald was efficiently delivering.

Bobbi called his name. Startled, he dropped a clump of pâté. He watched it plummet to the highly polished floor between his spread-wide knees. In one swift movement, he scooped up the blob and slipped it under the carpet: a belated revenge for Gerald's abuse of his own most beloved puss. He had an urge to telephone Whiting and have a good laugh.

"Toddy!" Bobbi called again excitedly. "Morgan didn't know you wrote *Glorious Technicolor.*"

" *What?'* Andrew shrieked, sending half of Terence's raised glass dousing the couch. "You didn't know *he* is the divine Titania? I thought *every*body knew that?"

"Surprise, surprise," Terence sang, absently toasting the buried blob.

Bobbi narrowed her eyes. She considered the alternatives.

"You are a man of many talents," Morgan toasted, amused.

"Terry's *heaven!*" Andrew apostrophized, fortunately not approaching the man under discussion. "I'd move to Brooklyn for Terry."

Terence did not budge. He sat staring at the empty glass aloft in his fist. He debated whether to demand a third. "Actually, a second and a *half,*" he figured, eyeing the stain that curiously resembled Great Britain on the cushion by his right thigh. Gerald swooped, brandishing a crystal pitcher of the liquid mercury dissolving Terence's brain and making his head grow larger.

Drink me! Drink me!

"What fun!" Terence enthused as he slurped.

Suddenly his stomach mutinied. Gin-stunned neurons twanged. Cold sweat dripped and rolled. Fearing embarrassing upheavals, he speared the pâté's collar of fat and chewed as an offer of atonement.

Holy shit!

Judith announced dinner as if she were telling a funny story. She and Andrew shuffled into the dining room accompanied by Gerald's forced merriment. Terence stood, sat, and stood again. He felt decidedly, dreadfully unwell. Bobbi and Morgan seemed to belong to another dimension.

There was no seating plan. Judith and Andrew, drunk as skunks (Terence observed), held hands and howled, beside themselves (and each other) over some private trifle they refused to share with Gerald, who pleaded to be included. Bobbi sat beside Morgan discussing Terence's high school drama triumphs. Terence landed next to Gerald, determined to form a simple sentence that would occupy himself and distract Gerald from unfair life in general, Judith and Andrew in particular. Terence noticed that Gerald's tic had conquered the entire left side of his ashen face; Terence could not *not* look. He was horribly uncomfortable. For an instant, he wished Christopher would materialize, but cursorily dismissed that thought when he realized the evening was difficult enough without one of them wailing opera arias and falling into the soup.

Can *this be? Taxi!*

Judith and Andrew were not hungry for soup. They demanded vociferously that Gerald slice the standing rib roast *now*. Morgan and Bobbi were laughing together, separate, as though at a private table in a noisy restaurant. Gerald refused all nourishment. Terence insisted he taste the soup, but was too out of focus himself to swallow in a straight line. The leased serving maid replete with lacy cap delivered the meat.

One glance and Terence suffered a violent attack of visceral hysteria. The huge side of rare steer seemed to be breathing. He vaulted from the table and fled whimpering to the second floor, purposely avoiding two bathrooms on ground level to be securely hidden. After locking the door, he splashed water in all directions, then ran it forcefully over his wrists. Calmer, revolutions momentarily squashed, he sat on the sink to reconnoiter.

Oy!

He locked his head between his shaking legs. It helped. But not for long. The martinis and the clots of pâté reappeared in a rancid gush. He collapsed, hugging the flushing toilet bowl.

It's my damn white shoes! I am not Gerald's psychiatric nurse. Terence, he is old enough to take care of himself. I cannot drink martinis Only with hot eggrolls. Oy!

He stood. His reflection revolted. He looked as if someone *large* had sat on him. He first rinsed his mouth with Listerine, then scrubbed it twice with powdered dentifrice. In the medicine chest, he found an astringent which he liberally cottoned over his ravaged face. He applied more moisturizer, and was debating whether or not to take a bath when someone knocked on the door. There were only two raps, but they were urgently sounded.

I want to be pressed between the covers of a fat book.

"Who is it?" he sighed, opening the door. He forced a vaporish smile for Morgan, who looked endearingly distressed.

And rightly so, babe I am over the edge.

"I'm fine, Morgan. Thank you," he enunciated slowly and clearly, the way he would have if Morgan were deaf, or if he, Terence, were a nun.

What is this fine? Shit! Terence! Stop telling yourself lies, goddamnit!

"Morgan, I'm demented," he said firmly, not wanting to be patted on the head.

"Do you want to leave, Terence?"

Leave? I forgot I can leave. Why do I always forget I can leave?

"Leave?"

What about Gerald? He can leave too!

"Yes, Morgan," he said hesitantly, pleased by the absence of shame. "What a good idea! I'm not feeling too well. Get me out of here."

Short-circuit is mended.

Stepping forward, he rested his sweaty head on Morgan's shoulder. The man embraced him comfortingly.

"You'll be fine, Toddy. I'll get our coats."

Judith stood at the foot of the staircase trying to look like royalty awaiting the guillotine. Abject and arrogant, she extended her hand to receive graciously the news of their departure. Coolly smiling, she chaperoned them to the door and personally wrapped Terence in his coat while ordering Bobbi to put him to bed as soon as they got home.

I'm sorry, darling," she whispered in his ear as she tightly embraced him.

"Uh-huh," he responded noncommittally, though undeniably moved by the tears in her eyes.

In minutes, he was in the Jeep wrapped in a blanket. Bobbi, leaning from the back seat, rested her hand on his arm.

"I'm proud of you," she said.

"Why?" he asked, feeling great freedom as the vehicle rolled through the calm night.

"There was a time, and not too long ago, mind, when you would have force-fed Gerald and done nip-ups on the table to smooth things over."

Morgan laughed. Terence snorted, recognizing truth in her hyperbole. He had had a slip.

Slip? Slide? Retreat? Return? Rerun? A short one. I stopped it. Rather have not begun it, tut-tut. Should've stuck with these two. Undeniably a slip, klutz.

"Welcome to the human race," Thomas S. whispered in his mind.

Morgan paternally patted his knee, evincing a similar sentiment. "At least we are out of there."

"But you two were having a swell time!"

Bobbi hooted. She squeezed his shoulder and shook hard, exclaiming her disbelief. "Toddy! How could you? Andrew is *the* most hateful person. Chris is right: He's like a buffed nail! Judith is a silly cow, and poor Gerald . .

Terence shifty-eyed the driver, waiting for his rendition. What would the honorable gentleman say in defense of his aging

Ganymede?

"Andrew is a problem," Morgan offered, eyes straight ahead.

Even that much he gives reluctantly. A catamite always wins in the end. Jesus! Pun intended. . . I feel rotten!

"I'm not well," he sputtered fiercely, on the prowl for an argument.

"There is one other problem," Morgan noted.

"Whuzzat?" Bobbi instantly asked, cigarette midlight.

"I'm hungry."

"So am I!" she laughed, exhaling.

"Humpf!" Terence snorted. "There's cold veal in the fridge. And your soup. And your chocolate cake. There are eggs; there's cheese—Cheddar, morbier, chèvre, and Brie. There's a ton of peanut butter—*real,* not plastic gunge full of Crisco. Also, we've a frozen apple pie—Ms. Whoeey's. We've many ice creams, five strawberry fools, steaks, liverwurst, tuna, sardines. . .

"That will do nicely, Toddy."

". . . bacon—thick-slab, no nitrites; salami, cottage cheese—small curd; yogurt—plain and delicious, no sugar, black olives.."

"Can we make a fire, Toddy?"

"In the fireplace and without this dumb faggot, *yes!*"

"Feeling better, I see."

All three ate a healthy supper with Bobbi's soup as the main course. While the pie baked, suffusing the house with a redolent comfort, they sat on the cushions facing the fire, continuing a discussion of children. Morgan thought it unfortunate that gay couples did not have children to raise.

"It's hard to remain childish when the real item is in your life. One's priorities naturally change. One's values and attitudes are challenged daily. Most gay couples never alter the patterns of their lives from when they meet. They rarely grow old intelligently, and rarer still, together."

"They're out hunting for gods. When they see they've snagged a mere mortal, a frail human, they pack their baubles in a beaded bag and leave home. They hit the road to search some more for Mr. or Ms. Right. Like everyone, they're looking for someone to make them happy. I hate kids," Terence concluded. "They scare me."

"They are scary, Toddy."

"Kids aren't helping Gerald and Judith Gunning."

"All sick relationships are the same," Morgan smiled. "The healthy ones are dissimilar."

People are unique only in their health.

Terence offered pie á la mode.

"Speaking of kids, Toddy, you have the largest collection of weird ice creams I have ever seen. I always thought Chris liked that strangeness."

"So did I. Until I began missing them when he wasn't around. As with dozens of other things. I thought I cleaned for him. The house and apartment were spotless. Yet, now with him gone, I find Harriet Craig still supervises the housework!"

Why was Christopher made responsible for everything? Did it honestly make life less frightening?

Morgan left at two in the morning, promising to return the following day for lunch. The old friends curled against one another on the warm cushions. Terence selected Chopin *Études* for the stereo. They listened in silence to several before Bobbi spoke: "He is a wonderful man. Promise me one thing?"

"What? Promise you what?"

"Treat him well."

Gerald Gunning, speechless amid the clatter of Judith and Andrew, watched the three guests depart. He remained at the deserted table until the front door slammed, then he quietly excused himself to the bewildered maid, and retired to his dark room. He expected Judith to apologize. Falling asleep as the clocks in the house chimed midnight, he dreamed a thorough examination of conscience, desperate to locate where he lacked grace, convinced he could make amends if only he knew the cause of her displeasure.

Judith Gunning, distraught, furious with Andrew for provoking her into being rotten, and furious with Gerald for not making them stop, for taking it all evening before skulking off to his room to pout the minute her back was turned, and furious with Terence for making an ass of himself and ruining her evening, slept in a guest room rather than chance awakening her husband because if he failed to yell at her she would kill him, and if he dared she would shout him down and blacken both his piggy eyes. The men in her life were real losers.

Andrew Desmond dozed immediately. He was not delirious to be sleeping alone. He had planned to spend the night under the famous artist's roof: "Under the artist," he chuckled, but things occasionally backfired, flopped, were not upbeat. Was their brief encounter nearing its end? He doubted it. Terence Strange was a weak sister not worth frets. A fart in the wind. Thank God the next day was Monday. He *hated* these country weekends. They were always so exhausting and unsatisfying. All this *fuss* to be surrounded by *trees!* Humpy bodies swirling to drums and electric *anythings* were more his backdrop. There was the poetry in modem life. He thought of Christopher More. Should he call the beauty and offer condolences and try his luck? Andrew wished himself wet dreams. Was there any other kind worth praying for?

At four the same morning, Terence and Bobbi sat in his kitchen sipping hot milk, smoking cigarettes, and blearily eyeing each other across the table. Neither had been able to sleep. When he heard her flush the toilet, he intercepted her in the hallway and suggested the milk.

"I don't believe I said that," she fumed. "What was I thinking of?"

"Let's have some warm milk," he repeated.

"I hate milk. Do you have any Scotch?"

"I'll put it in the milk."

"I love milk."

He prepared the skim milk and counted out four white tablets.

"What the hell are they?"

"Dolomites. They help us sleep."

"Us? You and your other face?"

"Human beings, dear one."

"What the hell *are* they?"

"Calcium and magnesium: nature's little tranqs. They really will help you sleep."

She looked skeptical.

"Trust me, Bobbi."

She shrugged and swallowed the tablets with a hefty swig on the spiked milk.

"You still taking all those vitamins, Toddy?"

"Just A, E, C, a B complex, pantothenic acid for my sinus, dolomites, and liver tablets: desiccated liver, four of them."

"God! I don't know how you do it."

"I got into the habit when I bought them for Chris. Booze bums out your B's."

"You could sing that."

"I did. It was one of my most popular arias for years. Followed by a *cabaletta* on how expensive vitamins are."

She laughed.

"You really think he likes me, Bobbi?"

"Yes, dear. Trust *me*. Only a man who likes you would be interested in your performance as Papa Doolittle in the twelfth grade."

"Polite conversation?"

"No. Sorry! When you came downstairs after your first trip to the head, he stared as if he'd never seen you before. That ain't polite conversation. He gazed on you the way one looks at a shooting star, dear."

"Treat him well?"

"I know, it's awful. I'm so ashamed! It's pure Titania Allgood."

"And why should you be free of her? She's alive and well in all of us. She takes many *pretty* forms. Most commonly, she's Ms. Good incarnate. *I* thought being good meant pleasing other people. Brother's keeper and all that? I wanted to be Jane Wyman in *Lost Weekend*. If I were good enough, and strong enough, and wise enough, and loved hard enough, Christopher would stop

[171]

drinking. If Jane could do it, *I* should be able to do it! He drank long before he met me, yet it never dawned that the drinking had nothing to do with me: I didn't cause it, I could not control it, sure as hell never could cure it. But in the movies, in books, on television, noble Janes and Jacks save the people they love all the time! What was I doing wrong? I was as blameless as she, God knew!

"After some hideous evening, friends would ask why I didn't *make* Christopher stop: 'You're such a good influence on him' or 'Why don't you tell him how boring and ugly he is?' or 'You deserve better' or they would ask me to take him home as if he were my fault and then they would not invite either of us back. They wanted me to be Jane Wyman, too! I listened. I listened and felt guilty with them. I listened and was enraged at myself and Christopher for a decade. As far as I knew, it was my very own failure. I was a dud. *I'd* never be a star like Jane."

"I've seen people do those things to Davey."

"Sure! Why not? We're all sitting in the same corner, dying from the same illusions, and sharing the same box of popcorn."

"What happens?"

"We stopped going out. Like everyone else caught in an alcoholic marriage, we closed in on ourselves and the dis-, ease flourished. We became more and more obsessed with the drinking. It was the focus of our lives. It *was* our lives!"

"I think I meant for you to go slowly."

"Slower than *what?* It took me a year before I got into bed with Chris. If I were in a toilet with a glory hole, I'd first send a note to ask: Do you love me?"

Morgan had been given plenty of opportunities. Many pots of tea had been offered. Many pots of tea had been refused.

"He said he was working, Toddy."

"Right! True! He said he was working. I believe him! I'm relearning to believe what people tell me. After ten years of lying and denying, I'm beginning to trust people and myself again. Lies are the chains of an alcoholic marriage. Denial, like dolomites, is one of nature's tranqs. Why am I shouting? He could have called."

"Hmmnn," she hummed shrewdly. "If he's got any smarts,

and I'm positive he has *many,* Toddy, a full deck, he wouldn't get involved with someone who just broke up, ambivalently at best, dear, an eleven-year hitch. Nobody wants to deal with that kind of pain and that kind of madness when the break is final. What about when it's just bending a little? Worse pain, worse madness."

"Nobody but a pain freak?"

"You got it, friend. A healthy man would barricade his door. Unless he's a meanie. Morgan is not a creep."

"Hmmnn . . . I don't know."

"Trust me."

I will *treat* him well.

The next afternoon, the three sat assembled again before a new fire. The sky was cloudless, a perfect day for traveling. Bobbi rose to make everyone a drink; she wanted a toast to her safe, enjoyable, *warm* journey. She cracked ice in the kitchen. When she returned to her cushion, she found Terence missing.

Upstairs, he dialed the phone slowly, propping himself comfortably on the bed. The call was answered on the fourth ring. He requested his friend.

"Thomas? Terence. I just had the urge to call."

"Where are you?"

"Upstate."

"You OK?"

"Yes. I feel good. I'm with friends, not program people. One just dropped ice cubes into a glass."

Thomas laughed. It was precisely the response Terence needed. He laughed, too. Every time he mentioned at a meeting the panic aroused in him by the sound of ice cubes colliding in a glass, he got a loud laugh of recognition. He never had to explain those things to his friends in the program. They knew every haunted corner of his soul.

"I've met a man I like, Thomas. I feel a little afraid."

"Afraid of what?"

"I don't know yet."

"You'll find out soon enough. Don't project."

"Am I starting already?"

[173]

"Could be. What do you think?"

"I think I want to be standing at the edge of a spewing volcano smoking cigarettes."

———

By the Lincoln Center fountain, Christopher More drunkenly waved good-bye to his laughing father and the back of Dominic Perrugio. The three departed the Metropolitan Opera environs in different directions after a calamitous evening at *Dialogues of the Carmelites.* Had there been a third act, they would probably have been eighty-sixed before the end of it.

Well into the first act, father and son loudly discussed Poulenc. His argument had begun over dinner; its noisy sibilance outraged their orchestra-seat neighbors. Christopher loved the opera but hated the conductor; William abhorred both. Dominic, mortified, hissed and tutted like a lunatic virago until the plight of the doomed nuns brought home to him the consequences of being denied absolution, and his sobs and groans added a further annoyance.

More liberal drinking during the intermission inflamed all three. The Mores' wranglings and Perrugio's tearful invectives carried them through the second act. At the opera's climax, William snorted and mocked the rhythmical beheadings of the martyred nuns. Incensed and overwrought, Dominic beat him with the libretto and the program. Christopher boisterously approved. A furious neighbor sped up the aisle seeking management but never returned, having used the altercation as an excuse to escape Poulenc. When the gold curtain dropped, the three were carried by the dispersing crowd to the fountain, where they parted unceremoniously.

"Thank Terry for the tickets," Dominic called after Christopher.

He nodded and waved. The tickets had been a Christmas present. If the intended third party had not called to cancel, Christopher would have forgotten the performance; and if William had not called immediately afterward to invite him to lunch, the three would not have convened so merrily. Crossing Broadway, Christopher made a quick telephone call from a pay booth, then hailed a cab and ordered a ride to his current favorite address, a town house on Joralemon Street in Brooklyn.

EIGHT

"The iron gates are closing. I must stop."

"Oh?"

Watch it, bub.

"His doctor said so."

Doctor? What doctor? Who?

"What did he say?"

"He says I'll die if I don't."

"You've heard that before."

"It makes more sense the second time around. Like love."

Terence smiled. He missed Christopher times out of mind.

"What are you planning to do, Chris?"

I love you.

"Stop."

"How?"

Hold it.

"By cutting down."

"You've tried that before."

Watch it. No inventory.

"I know. This time it's different."

"Uh-huh."

Illness is a condition, not an act.

"I won't go to meetings or any shit like that."

"Uh-huh. OK."

It can be done alone.

"I just wanted you to know I'm going to stop. I must. The iron gates are closing."

The moment the conversation ended, Terence arranged his day: He zipped upstairs to clean the bedrooms, changing the linen and waxing every wooden surface including the floors. Expanding his blitz out into the hallway, he finished in the remote furry corners of the bathroom. After breaking for a late lunch, he pounced on the kitchen and the living room, which took him to tea time. Relaxed, and with several new ideas for his book, he settled into a hot, sudsy bath. The scented steam churned from the water forming dense clouds that resembled cotton bunting fluttering from the ceiling.

It was a year since Christopher last attempted to stop drinking. With the support of an endless cache of tofranin, he had tried in earnest, having just been sprung from a hospital, a sanitarium, a "leafy bin" for problem drinkers, where he had been carted after an attack of the DTs.

Terence afloat remembered that dismally bright March morning. He was awakened at dawn by Christopher's heated body shivering like a tongue of flame. Unconscious, it jerked and twitched, foaming at the mouth, emitting a high-pitched shriek, and perspiring gritty sweat: His entire body wept crystalline tears. Terence forced brandy down the throat, then called a local hospital. Waiting for the ambulance, he watched in cold terror as the star-white body sprang stone-hard into the air and balanced on its elbows like a fluttering kite of pain, all the while pissing a stinking arc that welcomed the medics.

They gave Christopher paraldehyde and removed him to the hospital before transferring him to be dried out, detoxed, and psychically reassembled; the alcoholic short-circuiting of his brain had shattered the sense of his own indestructibility. He was enrolled in group encounter sessions that used Transactional Analysis ("TA? I would have been better off on the BMT!"), fellowship meetings ("Simplistic shenanigans!"), and private counseling ("Wasn't private enough, honey; the counselor—a sweet guy—insisted on being there, too!"). After twenty-eight days, looking better than he had in years, he returned to the house in the country. He assured Terence that he had learned his sacred lesson. He swore he would never drink again. He began a series of poems to that effect; doodling in a new notebook, he considered writing a comic novel, *This Lush Life*.

For four idyllic days, he drank bottles of salt-free seltzer in a tall totemic Baccarat glass with hefty wedges of lemon, orange, and lime. On the fifth afternoon, he flamboyantly added a dash of orange bitters that splattered the ice cubes like drops of anemic blood.

"The bitters are fifty percent alcohol, Chris," Terence recited, reading the label.

"It's harmless. It tastes good."

"It's a diuretic."

"I've had diarrhea all my life. I'm used to it. The stuff tastes good. Relax. This amount of alcohol won't hurt me."

"Uh-huh."

The previous afternoon, when Christopher had nonchalantly dropped the bottle of orange bitters into the supermarket cart, Terence had stumbled along mute in petrified disbelief. At the check-out, he flared over the high price of peaches. In the car, he yelled about the cold weather, but—except for a brief exchange the next afternoon on the alcoholic content of bitters—he never directly referred to the drinking

The seventh day, Christopher took one glass of wine with dinner. The eighth, he finished half a bottle. The ninth, he had a cocktail, just one before dinner, and knocked off a whole bottle of wine. The tenth day, he was splayed out cold beside an empty fifth of Jameson's bought that day when they went shopping.

By the tenth exhausting day, Terence was a tense wreck, frightened and enraged, too anxious to write, torpid, pouting, and snarlingly unpleasant at every chance, but—except for a short yelp at the price of the Jameson's—he never referred to the drinking. He read murder mysteries instead of program literature; he made no telephone calls to any informed friend. He missed the meeting in Sharon because he was preoccupied. Agonized, he sat and dumbly waited for the end. Mesmerized, he counted drinks and clocked every sip. At the eleventh dusk, he held a teary wake over the snoring, comatose body.

When Christopher awoke, Terence let fly eleven days of accumulated rage. Christopher poured himself the last drink. When Terence refused to drive him to the store, he hitched. Debilitated, they mounted the drunk's carousel and would have ridden until one, or both, fell off dead if Lucille had not telephoned to say hello and to talk to Terence about a problem she was having with her anger. In three hours, Terence was driving to the city. During the conversation, he had remembered he could leave the house and break the spell; he could end the torment without ending Christopher's life. He needed to be in the city. He needed meetings every night to reassemble his mysteriously discarded equilibrium.

We *get trapped in the bottle.*

Terence afloat remembered the madness. Lifting his right leg, he extended his foot to turn the hot-water tap. The bath was cooling; serious rehash required wet, enveloping warmth. Grinning, he thought of Christopher's annoyance whenever he dexterously used toes to lift pencils or newspapers or small bits of dry catfood.

> *Not with my hand alone I write;*
> *My foot wants to participate*
> *Firm and free and bold my feet*
> *Run across the field — and sheet.*

He purposely trumpeted membership in the animal kingdom; Christopher considered only his hegemony in the pantheon.

> *We admitted we were powerless over alcohol*
> *that our lives had become unmanageable.*

The first step. The taproot of the program. He read it aloud from a plaque, a gift from Thomas that hung from the showerhead. He had been in the program two full years when Christopher resumed drinking, yet he had smoothly disengaged from rationality like an unfettered helium balloon. During the weeks that immediately followed this debacle, Terence had attended meetings every night and talked incessantly, obsessed with his penchant for collapsing under fire.

"I thought I'd taken care of *that!*" he angrily exclaimed. "I may have accepted I was powerless over alcohol but not over Christopher. Or I may have honestly detached with love, then swiftly attached 'lovingly' again! As I myself quote: *Reason pauses. I must continually remind myself of my own good. I'll always be. taking the first step."*

At the nub lurked denial. He could see it festering: Christopher's denial that he could not control the drinking; Terence's denial that he could not make Christopher stop. They were both prideful to the point of extinction.

"I fight myself. I teach myself. I conquer myself. It's an ongoing action. If I really live it, I won't have time to mind his business, or time to attempt controlling him, which I cannot do in any case. No one can control another human being. I'm not choosing not to control him. I'm *accepting* that I can't control him. Big of me, huh? This struggle to accept reality scares the shit out of me."

"A compulsion. A mental, physical, and spiritual compulsion. A compulsion to be overcome only from within. It's not some clever trope. It's reality, bub. A to-the-death war within the sealed confines of one's very own soul."

"Look at yourself! You're a mess! You can't control yourself. Why do you expect him to do what you can't do? Answer me, Terence! Stop making your sober corners such unpleasant places to visit."

He memorized a definition from his dictionary:

Disease: a particular destructive process in an organism, with specific cause and characteristic symptoms; specific illness.

Fuck Nietzsche. Keep it simple!
Drawing fresh hot water into the bath, he dumped in two caps of oil and recalled it all. His toes were puckering. He would drain the tub, but not until after the fun part, not until after he started to learn something.

The miracle had occurred the summer before in East Hampton on the south fork of Long Island. His parents had gone abroad for September and Terence insisted he and Christopher use the house. The Labor Day weekend would see the tanned backs of the marauding hordes, he assured; the white sand beach and the picturesque town would be almost deserted. He had been persuasive. Fortunately, the weather was late-summer perfect: in the high eighties during the long days and in the fifties at night. It rained three days but the rain was warm, its sound beautiful on the gabled roof and the sheltering pinnate leaves. The potato fields beside the house were being harvested; the loamy smell of the furrowed earth provoked delirious sighs from Terence and humoring nods from Christopher ("To come all this way merely to experience all this weather!").

The summer-warmed ocean was cooperatively clean of grasses and residue, and playfully grasping.

Terence spent whole days at the nearby beach, wading and swimming, sunning and reading Edith Wharton. He rode his bike on back roads for miles, browsed for hours in The Ladies' Village Improvement Society Bookstore, and made tentative inquiries into buying some property. Christopher rarely left the house. He shopped for dinner in Gristede's and replenished his supply of Jameson's. Drinking and reading until dawn, he slept until two, watched his soap opera, napped, cooked, napped, and dozed. Terence managed a relative passivity.

William More and Dominic Perrugio overbalanced the seesaw with their visit on the second weekend. Dominic joined Terence while Bill sat in the living room, occasionally venturing in the direction of the tree-shaded veranda, and consuming with his son a great wave of Manhattans. Terence observed Dominic closely: "We are the same person."

"I don't want *us* to ruin *our* visit," Terence stressed, pointing his chin at the duo zonked on the couch. "Come on! Let me show you the *gonza* elms in town."

They kept themselves happily occupied. Saturday night they went to the movies. On the way home, Terence offered information and pressed for more time together in the city. On Sunday night, Bill and Dominic cheerfully kissed Terence good-bye.

"Say farewell to my drunken son," Bill laughed, waving to the unconscious body on the couch. "He drinks too much. I worry about him."

"Uh-huh," Dominic said, smiling at Terence.

[181]

"Uh-huh," Terence answered.

Two sane people a meeting make.

Christopher was not sober for more than an hour a day. He went from wake-up tea to Jameson's. By four, he was napping. It seemed to take less to knock him out, less to get him high, but he consumed more and more.

It's progressive, they tell me. Now I see what they mean.

Terence said nothing. Every evening at dusk, before Christopher awoke for the second round, he rode to the deserted beach. Slipping off his bathing suit, he splashed naked in the surf and shouted a litany of instructions:

"Leave him alone! He *knows* there's something wrong. He won't have to look at it as long as you are there to distract him by carrying on. If you start yelling or pleading, *you'll be* ca-razed! You know it won't stop him; you're tried and failed, bub. I am powerless over *his* compulsions. Take care of my own. Illness is a condition, it is not an act. He is not doing anything to you. Leave him alone. Let him be. Anger is your sickness. Don't become sick again. God-damnit! Keep your mouth *shut!*"

At home, Terence struggled to remain patient and quiet. No matter what cunning ploy Christopher's illness used to frighten or anger him, he refused to react, to get into the fray. He was determined not to lose even a fraction of one September day.

One morning, Christopher threatened suicide: "I can't keep doing this to you," he moaned.

"You're not doing anything to *me.* If you killed yourself, *you'll* be dead. I'll miss you."

"You'll find someone else."

"Probably. Would you like some tea?"

"Make me a drink."

"I'm going to the beach."

One evening, Christopher belligerently insisted they go to a fancy restaurant for dinner. He did not want to cook: "This is my vacation, too, you know!" Terence had no intentions of leaving the house with someone who could barely crawl. He politely but firmly refused, saying honestly that he did not want to eat out: "I'll cook." Christopher bellowed obscene threats and to demonstrate his fury, shredded the nightshirt off his back. Terrified, Terence clutched the cat. He wanted to flatten Christopher for the inane excess, for being so drunkenly disgusting, but he sat fiercely determined: He would not react to such patent insanity. Silently, he chanted his anodyne.

"Did you bring pajamas?" he insouciantly inquired when the tantrum stomped to its close.

"No," the naked Christopher stated flatly. "What do you want for dinner?"

"How about the flounder I bought this afternoon?"

"OK. I'll take a bath and fix dinner."

"I'm going to the beach."

He bicycled to the shore. Sobbing with relief, he tumbled into the surf. He was exhilarated. He shouted instructions for ten minutes, swam for twenty more, put on his shorts, and bicycled home.

The next day, a Saturday, William More called. He and Dominic were visiting friends in Sag Harbor. Could they drive over for lunch? Terence wanted to say no, said yes, and instantly felt invaded. Furiously lashing out at the newly awakened Christopher, he savaged him for the drinking, threatened to leave him forever, then demonically stormed from the house and pedaled down the drive with the basic-black vengeance of the Wicked Witch of the West. A victim of his own vitriolic mayhem, he was breathless and horribly nauseated.

Too fucking easy! Always there to blame for everything! No more! No more!

He turned his bike and rode back to the house. Christopher sat at the kitchen table. The truce had obviously ended. He had no idea how it started or why it ended. Afraid, he winced when Terence reappeared, looking windblown and possessed.

"I'm sorry," Terence stammered. "I get frazzled and I scream about the drinking. If I get frightened or taken by surprise, I use it as an anchor!"

"It's OK."

"No! It's not! It's crazy! It doesn't make me feel better. It's a reflex action. It only makes things *worse!*"

[183]

"Yes," Christopher said softly, eyes brimming with tears. "It only makes things worse."

Terence crossed to him. Christopher pressed his head against Terence's chest.

"I'm sorry!" Christopher cried. "I've been so *bad!*"

"You aren't being bad. It isn't a question of good or bad. Illness is a condition, not an act, goddamnit!"

In the surf that dusk, Terence wept. Inside himself, at the still center, an adjustment had been made. It was slight but perceptible, like the shifting colors on the surface of the sea. He would never be the same in quite the old way again.

"I *want* to leave him alone!" he shouted. "I *can* leave him alone. I *will* leave him alone! I understand! For today, I *understand!*"

He kept in constant touch with his friends and went to meetings in East Hampton on Thursdays at eight. It was a small, loving group who listened and delivered crucial support. His new awareness was triumphantly present; attitudes were changing. There had been similar times when the concepts of the program breathed inside him, but now he had burrowed to the core. The illness was a third presence in the home. His salvation was clearly on the line. Reason raggedly coupled with feelings; messages were passing to and fro on an unsteady but clear signal.

I left to think, bub. To think, *not obsess. It's easier to end a relationship than to break an obsession.*

Dripping and steaming, Terence rose from the bath. Reaching for a gamboge towel, he began humming "Sempre Libera" from *Traviata.* He was hungry. An expensive loin lambchop was on the menu for dinner. The cat, asleep on the bath mat, awoke with a chirrup, stretched, and opened his mouth in a silent command before leaving the room at a trot to speed downstairs for reasons of his own.

"Oh, Lord, Chris! How will it all end? You always said you'd die early. You were wrong. There's still time for a long and a happy life."

People don't drink to commit suicide. They drink because they're suffering from a disease. Illness is a condition. It is not an act. *Death is never a viable option. Go out a window. Hack open an artery. Maybe then, in a deranged, impulsive sprint. He drinks to feel good, then perhaps not to feel bad. But not to die. He drinks because he drinks. Romantic notion for biographers: alcoholism as suicide. . . alcoholism as symptom. He couldn't write,* so he drank. *Real poetic. Booze as cheap metaphor for cheap, lazy minds. Avoid death by metaphor. Murder by metaphor. Metaphors put you where you die in this life. Poor Scott. Poor Delmore. Poor Faulkner. Poor Chris. In the great tradition of mendacity. . .*

"The iron gates are closing?" Christopher repeated to himself. "Wonder what I meant by that? Terrible!"

His hand still rested on the telephone, and his long sore body quivered from the presence of Terence's voice in the room. He closed his aching eyes. The stale smell of cigarette smoke was heavy and unpleasant. Terence was right; he should never smoke in the bedroom.

If we inhabited a Jane Austen novel, I'd be in Amenia. I would have traveled by coach yesterday to Judith and Gerald's, then ridden over this morning on a chestnut mare. We couldn't talk unless we were sitting together or strolling in the shrubbery. I'd grope him. We'd kiss I hate telephones. Telephones are blunt instruments.

He was relieved. Terence had not crushed him to confetti by doubting or confronting him with a bag of failed tries to stay *dry,* never mind sober.

"I'm no good," he sighed, luxuriating in the black-and-white big-screen truths. "He'll never forgive me. No good at all."

He thought of Beverly, Claire, Cleo, and Ida. Then he thought with a cherished sorrow of Terence. He had to admit he was better since finding God, although the whole scene was only a sketch of the truth. Things were not that bad! Terence always overreacted in the most prosaic manner possible.

Talk about kitchen-sink histrionics!

The hot news was that *he,* Christopher More Strange, was not paralyzed by the morning uglies. Was he finally on top of that crazy thing called booze?

Sing it out, Louise!

He rose and opened the window. The air was luscious, filled with the smells of spring. Spring! Easter morning! He would wake up and there would be flowers all over. He decided to ask his father for a new outfit. He would feel reborn in a white linen hat with a lavender band.

In his hand he held a crumpled letter from Josie. He had written a short note thanking her for taking him in; she answered with a shorter one suggesting he check out programs for alcoholics, and requesting a copy of his latest book. In the postscript she told him to send it COD.

I've been to see those people, Mary! I don't want another religion.

He planned to nestle back into sleep. A rest day was just what the doctor would have ordered had he existed. Christopher knew all about doctors and could conjure one at will. The routine, if not done to death, was good for milking a sympathetic response when he was feeling rocky. There was usually more feedback from Terence but better sweet reserve than an attack of the D-flats. Christopher knew he was not losing his touch; Terence was practicing saintly self-control.

Nothing as trying as trying.

He would spend the late afternoon at Mansfield Park, meet Angelo at a book party, then check into the Regency Cinema after sunset for sweet M-G-M dreams, a double bill of Harlow films. Dare he hope for 35mm shimmering glistening nitrate prints? A *true* silver screen?

He answered the phone before the first ring crescendoed. A young poet friend was having a small roundup at his loft in NoHo. Could Christopher come? He did not have to bring a thing but his famous gorgeous self. His spirits rose like a white kite taken by the promise-crammed airs of Mama Gotham. Sure! Why not? What time?

Party girl. T. is right. I'm a to-the-death party girl. A flapper and finale-hopper. Go anywhere for a bash. Splash some "dinner party pickup" — fuller's earth and witch hazel? — and I'm ready to fly! And why not? How could life be without a party going for it? A farewell fling. Cross my whorish heart, T. One cup of wine. Moderation. The new me. It's a goof. Never really tried to quit. Try tomorrow. Cry tomorrow? Stately plump Christy More with, a heartburn up his arse. I'll stop. Have to. Well, as well now as another. And yes I said yes I will yes. Fuck 'em.

———

"What did you say?" Morgan asked without hesitation.

"I said OK. It's all I can say."

They sat in Morgan's kitchen. It was a large pine-paneled room with chocolate-brown appliances. They had finished an excellent pot roast dinner and were now eating generous slices of carrot cake. Two large Saint Bernards dozed in one corner.

"You still love him?" The calm delivery revealed none of the inner tumult.

"Yes."

"You couldn't detach with love?"

"You've been doing your homework, Morgan."

"Just catching up on my reading."

Terence smiled, touched. He freely admitted his confusion. He could not live with Christopher. He was discovering he could live without him.

"He's living inside a bottle. He's incapable of sustaining a connection. I want a lover, a *whole* lover. He's too Sick to honor even the simplest agreements. I still want to try, but for now it's not possible. He's abusive. He *never* hit me; there are other kinds of abuse he's not even aware of when he's drunk, which is all the time now. There's no justice in our life together now. I'm tired of telling myself how well I'm doing in an impossible situation."

Morgan carried the dessert dishes to the sink for a quick rinse before adding them to the others already arranged in the dishwasher. The kitchen was immaculate. He had methodically prepared the dinner using a few utensils; a visitor who dropped into the room would never know two people had recently finished eating a full meal.

He cooks the way I do. If Chris doesn't dirty every fork and require that the walls be hosed down after, it isn't a good meal. I could live with this man.

"Terence, would you like to walk the dogs with me?"

[187]

It was a cold, clear night. The sky was crowded with very bright stars patterned around a full moon. Morgan identified the major constellations. They walked along a narrow path to a frozen pond, which they slowly circled. Both dogs lumbered behind.

"When Louis died, I went senseless. I was rocked numb. It took a long while, one entire spring, for me to start feeling again. I mistook numbness for grieving. I was wrong but the period of shock was a blessing. You may be going through that now. Changing is a kind of death."

"How did he die?"

Changing is a kind of death. I mourn for what I lose in myself.

"A heart attack. Quickly, very quickly. He was about to be released from the hospital for one when he had another. He'd been complaining of pains but they told him it was indigestion. He was born in Wichita, Kansas. His family took him home to bury him in the local cemetery with his kin. They didn't invite me. I hear that's common, but it wasn't decent of them. They even tried to contest the will. The funeral might have helped. Sometimes I'm angry; sometimes resigned. I miss him every day. I keep busy. I've done *two* ninety-minute films, three books, the syndicated daily, three television specials . . . not bad for two years' work! It's what I needed. Thank God for my staff in New York. And enlarging the studio keeps me hopping."

"Why enlarge now?"

"I need the space. Besides, there's always the chance one of the workmen will be beautiful."

"So famished for Hyperion's curls you'll rip your house apart?"

"I was. Till I met you."

They both laughed. It was like dialogue from one of Titania's books.

"It's a pity your characters never go into a sunset arm in arm. I'm partial to sunsets."

"The only thing that happens when you walk into a sunset is things get dark!"

"You said this one has a happy ending."

"Yup. They buy a town house, three stories circa 1850, east of

Madison in the sixties, make many changes in their lives.

"I don't take change well."

Hmmnn. Interesting.

"Neither do I. Dream therapy, remember? Bravely, they change like hell!" He took Morgan's arm. "They resolve basic animosities, but I'm not sure *how* yet. They agree to continue, to try *for today* to behave like mature adults together. Fast curtain. The end."

"They do the best they can."

"You got it."

"Let's have coffee."

Christopher More, penniless and beyond exhaustion, weaved his lone way up Ninth Avenue. Homeward bound after closing a new bar near the docks, he decided at Eighth Street not to step on any cracks in the sidewalk. The concerted effort required to stick to his plan was keeping him from settling into one of the comfortable-looking niches to his right. He knew he would never surrender to the temptation. Doorways were not his style.

Snatches of disturbing happenstance and conversation from the night before, from the book party and from the loft party, recurred in his weary brain's vast memory chamber, echoing as they had all the long while he traveled this night from one known haunt to another opening of another show. Like a song endlessly replaying itself on a jukebox ("in the whorehouse of the mind"), certain phrases and events burned hotter with each obsessive spin. That cuntbreath Irving Sombodorother had thrilled in revealing why Christopher's last two poems submitted to a usually fawning forum had been rejected. And Irving insisted he knew the dirt because the editor was an erstwhile lay who had no cause to lie over a Bloody Mary brunch. Besides, Irving insisted, Christopher deserved to know the truth because it might do him some good.

Beware of critics bearing good.

Christopher originally chalked the rejection to the length of the poems. In fact, he and his father had concluded it was the only plausible reason. They were too long, not to mention too dense or too whatever for the artsy rag that was quickly becoming the *TV Guide* of the erato set.

"Booze soaked." That toady shit had told him the editor called them booze soaked. The words scalded, and not all the alcohol he poured down his aching throat softened their lacerating power.

Fuck. Shit. Piss.

And Angelo had seduced him to the book party for that bimbo female novelist too sensitive to bring a sentence in under fifty words, had gotten him there merely to get the goods. He'd used the have-a-few-drinks and the meet-some-important-people ploys. Important people? Christo More was an important person, goddamnit! "You bring the poems?" Not even a hello. The poems, the poems, always the poems. Then at closing time, he had sidled over and offered to share a cab but once they hit the sidewalk and hailed one, he had grabbed the poems and sped off downtown leaving Christopher standing in the middle of the street.

Fuck. Shit. Piss.

Two men now approached him from behind. The taller gripped his arms; the shorter flashed a knife. They both demanded money. It took several seconds for him to comprehend what was happening. When he attempted to pull away, the taller threw him to the sidewalk; the agile companion stomped a booted heel into his groin. A monstrous pain contracted his stomach; convulsions instantly resulted. The knife zigzagged in front of his bleary eyes. The Steichen photograph of J. P. Morgan seated with his hand resting on a polished chair arm that reflects as a dagger appeared in his mind; the awe he felt on first viewing the picture merged with his current terror, and the pristine image was replaced by the actual grotesque reality.

"I have no money! Would I be *walking if I* had money?"

The knife dipped. The point nicked his arm. He screamed. A foot thudded against his side. He vomited a flood of reeking bile.

"Fuck, man! You puked on my pants."

Enraged, the soiled cuff poked his back twice before landing solidly on the right side of his head. Christopher rolled with the blow. Another caught him on the shoulder blade, pushing him into the garbage along the curb. Dog shit filled his mind. He moaned. Somewhere overhead, a window rattled open and a female screamed angry words. The two men kicked Christopher one time each before fleeing down the deserted avenue. He felt himself losing consciousness.

"Terry! You always said I'd end up in the gutter," he whispered, grappling not to slide away from himself. "No. No . . . I always said it. . .. poor me."

Morgan Connelly understood. From the light swell of tender feelings toward the younger man, he had reckoned the consequences, the dangers; but, with these exhilarating sensations evolving, taking air within, he, bemused, had rejected all notions of snuffing them. It had been decades. At first he could not identify the warmth of these particular pleasures. Then he readily named them the early stages of infatuation, and he frequently blushed a rosy mixture of consternation and delight.

Standing upstairs in the dimly lit Gunning hallway, comforting and briefly holding the distressed Terence, had raised his disheveled emotions to a new pitch. The trust expressed, the vulnerability displayed by that lithe movement into his arms, the grimace of pain twisting those beautifully fine features, and—no less important—the sweet scent of ruffled auburn hair, all catapulted his mind (and full lonely soul) to some aerie where rational thought withered and nothing sounded but his own thumping heart.

"I'm too old for this," he scolded, held fast by his own sense of wonder. "No!" he corrected. "Thank God!" He was gladdened by the rapid ascension of tenderness toward love.

He was enthralled by Terence Strange, and perceived him to be strong and courageous, intelligent, witty, whole, and very well-read; and he craved in the pit of his stomach to see him naked, to touch the camellia skin, to stroke the supple body, to fondle what was so modestly concealed. He imagined instigating maximum excitation. He was amused that his own predilections played a secondary role in these sexual fantasies. He experimented giving to Terence, curious what would arouse the greatest response, assuming unquestioningly there would be a response worth shouting about again and again. There was a sharp edge to the way Terence held one's glance, an intensity that boldly informed on sexual energy to be sparked if judiciously tapped.

As Morgan walked the dogs alone the next day, he reviewed his position. The young man was in a singularly emotional condition, recovering from a long siege with serious illness. He was highly volatile and not to be taken advantage of or used to appease the satyriasis of a sexually starved hermit.

Sexually starved? Yes. Take solace in just loving him for now. Just?

He quickened his stride as he circled the pond for the third time. The dogs, sensing turmoil, stayed within touching distance. He was determined not to force his attentions on the young man, not to press him for any declarations or insinuations. There would be no displays of affection. If anything developed—the possibility caused his heart to bounce like a Jeep topping a hill— if they reached an understanding, it would be one mutually acceptable on every point of entry. He would not allow himself to be used.

"I would allow *anything*," he corrected.

He would not allow himself to be used to alleviate someone's pain, to cover some wound like a psychic bandage doomed to be discarded. He must take care of himself, have compassion for himself. If Terence had suffering ahead, faced with dissolving bonds with Christopher More, given the bonds *were* dissolvable, he was willing to suffer *with* the young man but not because of him.

And what about Christopher More? He was the unknown quantity. Terence admitted his love. That could change but was not to be denied.

People can love more than one person at a time. I'm not possessive to the exclusion of reality. Some hearts are crowded continents.

He confessed to himself as he rounded the pond a fifth time that he was willing to be loved beside Christopher More, along with Christopher More, if Terence were capable of sustaining such a relationship. Morgan was not certain, but he must learn.

He knew it took time to chart someone's interior geography.

I know relatively little about Toddy. It did happen in his first book. More dream therapy?

He resolved to be patient. He would enjoy the easy companionship, allow his feelings to expand naturally, and sit on his hands. He would enjoy the journey and not worry about the destination.

"One day at a time," he said aloud, grinning as the wisdom of the phrase soaked him with peace.

The dogs broke free in pursuit of a chipmunk. He watched the small striped creature scurry safely away before he called the barking dogs to follow him home.

———

"He's calling for you, Terence."

"How badly hurt is he, Bill?"

The telephone had awakened him. He lay rigid with fear for a moment before reaching for a cigarette. There was none. He no longer smoked. Should he run downstairs and ferret for one? Were there any? He hated the telephone.

"Thank God, not *too* badly, Terence. A woman chased the scum away and called the police."

"He was lucky."

"Very! If you can call two cracked ribs, a minor concussion, bruises all over his body, and a knife wound in his writing arm *lucky*. He's sleeping comfortably."

"Good. I'll talk to him this afternoon."

"You're not coming *now?*"

"At five-thirty in the morning?"

Drunken asshole. Just what I need: Magnificent Obsession.

"He's asking for you, Terence."

"You just said he was asleep. You sound like you should be doing the same, Bill."

Oii! *Big mouth! Wanna go to the moon, Alice?*

"Don't *you* start telling *me* what I should or should not be doing, young man. You are in no position . . ."

A voice outside the hospital phone booth interrupted. There

was what sounded like a scuffle before the panting victor continued the conversation.

'Terence? Dominic."

"How are you?"

"Tired. I'm exhausted. Bill's drunk, crying a lot over Chris. He's crazy."

"Uh-huh. He sounded half a bubble off center. I'll come this afternoon."

You said, you'd call before. Now you're going?

"That'll be fine, Terry. Chris is sound asleep. How am I going to get Bill home? He won't leave."

"So let *him* stay. You go home."

There was silence.

"I never thought of that, Terry."

"You ever go to meetings, Dom?"

"No. They weren't doing much good. He'll never stop. He gets angry when I go. He won't give me any sex if I go, Terry. He can't do anything himself anymore but he still takes care of me once in a while. Unless I go to meetings. Then there's nothing."

"Better horny for now than crazy, Dom."

I'd kill for sex, Dom.

"Terry, when I'm horny I'm crazier, believe me. I don't know what to do."

"Of course not. We have to be taught. No one is prepared for what happens to him."

"Yeah, I know."

"Dom, please take care of yourself. How's the gym?" Dominic laughed, pleased. "Great! I'm beautiful! But what's the use?"

"It won't make him stop drinking, baby, but if it gives you pleasure to see all the other muscles bulge . . ."

They both chuckled.

"It's the only thing I really enjoy, Terry."

"I can't wait to see."

"You can have a private demonstration anytime."

The harmless flirtation, a game begun when first they met, ended the conversation.

Remember what you said to Bobbi! You've done all you can do. You can't manage people's lives, stage-manage people's lives. Love is not a crown of thorns. Love is not suffering. Love is not pain. Killer love. Suffering ain't love, bub. Suffering is shit. Go back to sleep. I dare you.

The next morning, after a deep sleep, Terence called Morgan. When Terence told of his plans to visit Christopher, Morgan offered to drive. Terence's mood brightened.

"We can lunch at my club, Terence."

"What club?"

"Princeton."

"Golly! A Princeton man."

"You prefer Yalies?"

"I'll take what I can get!"

Morgan laughed, charmed.

"Let's go to MOMA, Morgan, and walk through the Park, and have dinner at Le Cygne. I'll make the reservations."

"How about the ballet? I have a friend who can get us house seats."

"Which ballet?" he asked, perpetuating a joke begun days before.

"Is there another ballet?"

"Lord, I would love it! Unless it's a Robbins program."

"No Robbins. No drek. All Mr. B. I have the schedule in front of me. I clipped it from the *Times* just in case."

"When should we leave?"

"When can you visit Christopher?"

"Christopher? Oh, Christopher!"

The ride to town was delightful for both. The weather was a paradigm of late-winter lovely. The snow, dry and flaky, floated back to earth when disturbed. The enameled sky's hard blue distracted and seemed unnatural, like the pale-green sunsets at the end of Long Island. The clarity of the light alerted the travelers to life's wonderful contingencies. They laughed a lot. Stimulated by each other, they made nonstop talk. When they reached the West Village and turned their attention to parking the car, Terence had a twinge of guilt.

I've not given Chris a thought. How can I be enjoying this errand of mercy? Errand of mercy? Your ass!

Christopher More appeared suitably dejected. Settled in a large ward beside a full vase of white spider mums, he wore a cap of bandages but his torso was wrapped in clear plastic tape, exposing his bruises to air and eye. The right side of his face was puffed and ringed with rainbow hues like sloppily applied finger paints.

"You look good in Saran Wrap," Terence lied.

"This is where the bastards knifed me."

"And *this* is Morgan Connelly."

The two men nodded agreeably at each other, smiling and mumbling the appropriate exchanges and ignoring their surroundings momentarily. Terence's eyes nervously panned the room. Each bed contained a bare male torso wrapped in yards of transparent bandage. He imagined a traveling crane shot, then cut to the neighbor beyond the mound that was Christopher. The chap proudly displayed a scooped hole in the center of his chest; it looked to Terence like a corsage of pressed purple violence. Instantly, he felt stomped by nausea. He glanced away into some man's gaping shoulder wound that looked inhabited. Then he found a stomach that seemed hastily stapled shut. He was dizzy and lightheaded.

I'm going to faint! *I am!*

Rapidly, he executed a graceful bend from the waist. Swinging his head down between wobbly legs, he ordered his blood back into it. He groped for the laces on his shoes, either foot, both, pretending an adjustment was urgently required. Trying to draw deep breaths, he struggled not to topple into a deranged heap.

"Terence?" Morgan called.

"He's trying not to pass out," Christopher impatiently explained. "This happens every time he gets within farting distance of the wounded. Clara Barton he is *not,* poor flower!"

"I am tying my shoelaces," Terence weakly insisted, panic-stricken, gaining no relief from the creeping coldness, convinced he dared not unbend without instant disgrace.

"For Christ's sake, T.! Mr. Connelly, would you see to the baggage, please? Shall I ring for the oxygen man?"

Morgan rested his warm hand on Terence's damp neck. The

young man shuddered and moaned between clenched teeth: "Let's go outside, please, Morgan. Get some air. Stuffy. . ."

"*Stuffy?*' Christopher wailed. "We're *dying* in here and you find us *stuffy? I beg your* pardon, madam!"

"Not *you*, the room, shithead!" Terence hissed, rising, whiter than the flowers beside the bed.

"Please, Mr. Connelly, remove this dizzy carcass from my sight."

"Bastard!" Terence exploded. "Why are you all wrapped like leftovers? It's disgusting!"

"Because we are leftovers, you *amadan*. Leftovers from life."

Terence stared into Christopher's eyes, blinked, flushed, and laughed raucously, leaning over the bed.

"Darling!" Christopher whispered, grinning. "You're making a scene! Could always make you laugh, toots!"

"Chris?" Terence asked as soon as he was able. "This a gay knock?"

"In the middle of a gutter on Ninth Avenue? They were after my *gay pennies*, Terence. They were going to *Kill Me!* Kill as in dead, as in doornail. Look! They stilettoed me with one of Carmen Miranda's *heels!* If that concerned citizen had not screamed her tits off, I quake at the scenario."

"Have the doctors noticed anything else wrong with you?"

What is this? Terence, are you trying to be funny? I hope they like these jokes on the moon, Alice, 'cause that's where you're going.

"No. These damages satisfied their curiosity."

"Uh-huh." Terence shrugged. Christopher wanted to continue with how frightened he was when the marauding apes struck, but Morgan Connelly stood there looking bugeyed with concern for Terence. Christopher felt inhibited and angry, deprived of his best audience. Scrutinizing Morgan, he noted many attractions.

Could it be? No. Not T. And why not?

He glowered at Terence, who was inordinately pale again and visibly drooping. He seemed to be having trouble focusing his eyes.

"I'm sorry, Chris. I'm awful at bedsides."

"Unless you're taking off your pretty clothes."

All three men laughed. Christopher raised one eyebrow.

Why is he *laughing?*

"You'd better go now, Terence, before we have to requisition a bedpan for you. Call me?"

"Do you need anything? Who sent the flowers?"

"Bernice. No, I'm all moved in. I'm not bad . . . considering. . . ."

"Yes. OK. I'll call."

"Tonight?"

"No. Not tonight. We're going to the ballet."

The ballet? *I will cut you both into little bite-sized pieces.*

"Have a good time, you two kids."

"I wish you could join us," Morgan said, smiling.

Yeah, I'll bet! Me and the clap.

"Thanks, Mr. Connelly. I do, too."

"Maybe next time," Morgan consoled, reaching for Terence's dangling arm.

Bought a season's ticket, sport?

He watched the two walk the length of the long ward then turn left out of his purview. There was something so *obvious* in the older man's conciliatory manner, something so publicly *disgusting* like an ugly straight couple necking in the subway, something so *comfortable* in the way he leaned to whisper a tender word of encouragement, or was it a lewd suggestion at the sight of all those half-naked men in beds? Christopher wanted to fling his urine sample after them and howl *faggala!* Yet even more distressing was the cozy ease Terence had displayed as he accepted Morgan's arm for support.

"Off to the Registry, those two," Christopher muttered, sliding toward tears. "This is what I get for being bad. Bad, bad, B.A.D.: Busy Acting Dangerous. Yes, it's true. All men desire me—for I am such a comedian. They are definitely a *hot* item. Terence, I will kill you. I will stab you *to the heart.* Then I will kill myself! Leaves will swirl." He closed his smarting eyes and diligently plotted cruelties. *"Je me vengerai,"* he whispered, imagining himself buffing his nails.

Reaching the street, Terence sat on the shoveled steps. He took deep breaths and counted to ten. He was grateful to Morgan for having suggested the bathroom when they were halfway down the ward's narrow aisle flanked on both sides by the dead and dying encased in plastic for easy shipping. He felt the earth move. Was it the subway? He counted to ten again.

"That store sells ice cream." Morgan pointed. "Let's get some."

"Yes. Ice cream. Good! Right! Uh-huh."

The two made their way across the icy street. Once inside the tiny corner shop, Terence trashed himself for swooning, hated himself for reflecting in the plate glass like a larger version of the vanilla cone he clutched in his unsteady fist. He and Morgan stood in the window between racks of paperback books. Instinctively, Terence routed two by Miss Allgood, but was not up to a systematic search for the others. His hunched shoulders relaxed. The shivering became shuddering, then ceased. His colon stopped quivering and puckering like nervous lips. He lapped ice cream, pleasantly distracted.

"Even damaged, Christopher is extraordinary looking."

"Yes," Terence sighed, relieved to be talking about him. "Big hairy deal! So he's a looker! So are *you*, Morgan! And I'm no-blueberry muffin!"

"I mean—" Morgan laughed, amused by this sudden rush of energy. It had been very instructive watching those two interact. He was willing to share in the fallout.

"I *know* what you mean, Morgan. People used to follow him home like dogs in heat. Still do, more'n likely. And bone structure has a lot to do with it, too. What can I say?" Outside, snow began to drop behind their images. People, singly and in every possible grouping, scurried by on their way. The two men stood watching, silently nibbling ice cream.

"I'm sorry, Morgan. It's terrible seeing him like that. He looks horrible. It frightened me. And all those men . . ." There was a long pause. Morgan said nothing. "When I was growing up," Terence shared, "my family would go from Riverside Drive to East Hampton for the summer right after school closed. My father would commute on weekends. We should go spend a weekend on Long Island soon. It's fun in the winter, deserted and wonderful. The house is a shout from the beach."

"We will. I love the ocean."

"Me too. I wanted to buy a house on a dune but Chris can't work there; the sea makes him morose, he says. I know now that I didn't buy a house because the damp would ruin my books. Anyway, every summer the family would move there. Are you familiar with Cockney rhyming slang?"

"I've heard of it. I don't know any. Why?"

"In London, Cockney boys call their cocks Hamptons. Hampton Wick is rhyming slang for dick. *Really.*" They both laughed. "I bring it up, you should pardon the expression, because the beach near the house is a gay beach, full of men prowling the sands looking for other male bodies to do whatever they do that takes only two and a half seconds. As a tot-teen I'd watch them cruise. I never felt flattered when they approached me for a quickie. They all seemed so desperate, so bloated, and it didn't matter to them what I looked like as long as the part of me three feet above the ground functioned."

"Did you never go into the dunes?"

"Once. With an old family friend, a lawyer who had interested me for years. It was early in the morning, just past dawn. August. High summer. I was thirteen. Get the picture? I'm splashing in the surf nude. He waves and joins me. It started as a swimming lesson. He did his backstroke beneath my fledgling crawl. I loved it. Knew early on what I wanted. He never showed up again. What was the point of all this?"

"Wasn't the beach a temptation?"

"Yes and no. The *idea* excited me. I wanted them not only to take me, but to love me, too. It seemed degrading to reduce it to fucking like sand fleas. All those men . . . that's what started this. I don't know. There are so many people in this world. Maybe I've just been afraid."

"Afraid of what?"

"VD? Amebiasis? The clap? What a conversation to be having in an ice-cream parlor!"

"Some parlor! Let's go have lunch."

"I feel better. I'm starving."

"You Yalies are all alike. All you ever need is a little ice cream."

Terence began meeting Morgan every day. When the phone rang at eleven, the caller was Judith gossiping trade news, or Christopher reporting his hospital progress (calling collect, sober, and sounding fragile: voice limpid and warm), or Morgan offering a ride to the village for marketing or the library or some other pleasant break in the routine of their working lives. Several times after a short jaunt, he accepted lunch, stayed on for tea, then did not leave until after dinner; the two new friends sat close, talking all the while. But these long visits were not as frequent as either wished. Each had his work and feared distracting the other.

One afternoon during a visit, Judith called. She mentioned difficulties reaching Morgan.

"He's here with me."

"Oh! Isn't that *cozy*?"

"We're having tea. I made a soda bread. Do you want to talk to him?"

"No. Just tell him to call Annie MacGuire."

He knew the name belonged to the head of the Production Department at Voyager Press; no further explanation had been necessary. After dutifully delivering the message, he dismissed it from his mind.

Over the years, Morgan had gained the reputation for being difficult. In truth, he was a perfectionist who expected others to care as deeply about his work as he did. Exceptionally organized, meticulously neat, scrupulous about deadlines and details, he posed a threat to hands and heads less steady than his own. He also had the ability to make adjustments in emergencies that endeared him to his staff, who respected him and understood his demands as nothing beyond a truly professional standard. He was an artist and a craftsman, with little patience for those who attempted to be the one without the other.

Success had come quickly to him. While still an undergraduate at Princeton, he started his famous strip, *Spoiled Rotten*, in the school paper; by the time he graduated, he had won a Pulitzer Prize and was syndicated in 161 newspapers. An invitation from a book editor to illustrate a fairy tale of his choice developed into his first volume, *The Stone Flower,* that in its day won all the major awards for children's books and became an international best seller. He supervised the motion picture; encouraged by its great success, he animated his rich-kids strip for television, which led to lunch boxes, sweat shirts, toys, posters, peanut butter, and cookie endorsements, and a dozen other notions controlled by his lawyers but scrutinized for quality and accuracy of detail by a devoted tyrant on his staff named Rosalie Fagioli, who was chiefly responsible for his reputation as a demon.

He escaped the Korean War through the graces of a trick knee acquired playing football in high school. He often claimed in semiseriousness that he was offered the book contract because all the other talented young men were off fighting behind lines instead of drawing them.

"I was talented, sure, but there was a dearth of bright, promising talent on the market. I was in the right place at the right time."

"With the right amount of genius, Morgan," Terence added, moved several emotional yards by the modesty.

"True!" he admitted reluctantly. "I'm not denying my gifts. I guess I sometimes feel bewildered about being so successful. A therapist years ago said it was the reason I chose to live so far away from Louis: to punish myself. I never really believed that. I never really believed anything that guy told me! I don't think I'd do such a thing now, but I doubt if that simplistic reduction was accurate."

"Why did you move here?"

"It seemed like a good idea at the time. I needed the peace and quiet. I wanted big dogs. I had my reasons, Toddy."

Two days later, their publisher called again. Terence was alone, finishing a chapter. Andrew, sounding rushed, asked him to hold the line; another call had that very second come through "from a foreign shore, L.A., doll," but Judith wanted him to wait if he could because she would not be long with poor Miss Thing who was having a nervous breakdown. She, Judith, needed to discuss a literary luncheon where he, Terence, as a bestselling author was expected to lecture.

"I hear you've been seeing Morgan Connelly," Andrew's

voice cooed unexpectedly.

"Yes. Uh-huh."

"Uh-*huh!* Lucky you! The two of you so close together up there in man's country. Keeping warm and toasty together. He'll mend that tattered heart of yours in a hurry, don't you worry. Funny, when I first saw him, he reminded me of a Raggedy Ann doll. . . ."

Raggedy Andy, bunghole.

"But believe me, honey, he *ain't* stuffed with straw. You feel like you are afterward, but *woo-weeeeee!*"

"Andrew!" he commanded in his darkest tones.

"You mean you haven't *yet?*" Andrew gasped, clucking in horror like a chicken gone bonkers. "What *are* you waiting for, *sister?* 'O Promise Me' on the skin flute?"

"Andrew! Stop *now,* Andrew!"

"You can only wear white once, sister. Free *him* from those baggy pants and the frog turns into a king-sized prince!"

Terence could not speak. Rage literally erased his whole mind.

"The *first* time, Toddy, was *dee-voon.* And it keeps getting better! Honey, you can swing on it!"

Terence threw the phone down. Rigid with fury, he had not budged from the spot when the thing rang again. While it clanged, he stood beside it, breathing heavily. With a hard yank on the cord, he pulled the plug from the wall. The shrill sound continued upstairs in the bedroom, above his head on the other side of the house like an abandoned bird screeching in the highest branches of the elm tree.

He was stunned by the force of his rage, humiliated by its power to sweep him along. He grabbed for the tools to control it. How dare Desmond invade his newly burgeoning friendship, trampling upon his anticipation and hope, maliciously sullying its purity.

He can do what he wants. I don't have to react this way. I can't change him. Thank God! I'm not responsible for him!

He was furious with Morgan, furious with Judith and Bobbi, and furious with Christopher for being able to enjoy easy sex— "recreational sex," in his smart ass phrase—the way he, Terence

[203]

Strange, could not. *Would not,* he corrected, making himself even angrier.

Why do I care so much what Morgan Connelly does with his hands or his life or whatever else he has nothing better to do with than give whatever he gives to that dumb-shit fool who probably has a friend who lives in Brooklyn?

He paced the living room and tried to differentiate between being "shaken" and being "upset." He broke down the confusion to examine it one emotion at a time.

Manageable bits. I feel hurt. I feel traduced. I feel virtuous. I feel a damn fool. I feel lost. I feel lots of things, Kukla.

All the rising emotions deflated into sadness.

Self-pity? No. This is sadness, Toddy.

He dropped into the nearest chair. In under four seconds, he deduced that he had not connected the emotional dots of the past few weeks correctly. Somehow he had drawn the wrong conclusions. He had misconstrued Morgan's libidinal commitments. He had expected their friendship, their *simpatico* leanings ("Stances, please. We try not to lean."), their whatevers, to turn a rosy shade of passionate. As with all expectations, they left no room for the other person to demur.

Demur? Say no! Refuse. Make other plans. Say "Buss off, twit!"

Sexually, Morgan was preoccupied elsewhere. That's why nothing had happened between them. Terence was right all along. Yet again, he had missed the ferry to Paradise Island. He felt demolished. He was too obtuse to continue conversing even with himself on any serious matter of the heart because he obviously did not understand a blessed thing and obviously had never understood anything *ever.* Why else would he be sitting in a darkening corner of this snow palace attached to people by the telephone only?

Hold it, klutz. *You're near the edge.*

Thomas's presence interrupted, his voice as clear as if he were sitting in Terence's lap. He cautioned against absolute statements: a sliding pond into that old black magic called self-pity. As a bonus, he threw in warnings against asking questions that have no answers. Keep it simple. Perhaps Morgan had reasons?

Reasons that had nothing to do with Terence Strange?

I want to make Xerox copies of my *moral standards and pass them out to the world. I make the rules. Can't I change them?*

The telephone rang. Without pausing to plan a snappy rebuttal, Terence plugged the extension into its socket, narrowed his eyes, cleared his throat, and lifted the receiver. Expecting Andrew's unpleasantly nasal twang braying unctuous apologies, he opted to be magnanimous, not to mention detached.

It was Morgan Connelly.

"Right on cue!" he snapped, resentments rising fast.

To the moon, Alice! He has done nothing *to you. That's the problem! Shut up!*

"What do you mean, Toddy?"

Instantly, resentments were whacked over the head. Morgan rarely used his nickname. Each time he did, Terence felt caressed. The inflection he gave it, the way the tongue tapped the consonants caused his lungs to fill with stars.

"I was just trapped into a low-darts exchange with Andrew Mouth about you, Morgan."

"Oh? What about me?" he asked softly.

Terence imagined him lifting his bushy brows, then the corners of his lips in a sweet vulnerable smile. He could never be cruel to this man. "It was nothing serious, Morgan."

I could never be downright cruel to anyone. *Face it, Kukla, you're a nice person. Sit on it*

"What did he say?"

"He said when he first saw you, you reminded him of Raggedy Ann. He meant Andy, but I got the message. I really loathe that twerp. He is *not* your normal healthy gay. He is *very* warped."

"You sound upset."

"No. Not really," he lied badly. A quake *of* sorrow rattled him. He was not willing to risk explaining his pain to Morgan. No. That was not accurate. He did not want to justify his pain because Morgan was not responsible for it. He was angry at his very own self.

You got it!

What *could* he say? The old words came but he rejected them.

He did not trust himself to speak calmly and rationally; anger would shred self-control and he would zip into clumsy irony or bravely fight back snotty tears, which would make conversation awkward and were guaranteed to bring unsettling negative attention: A deeply felt "poor Toddy" from Morgan at this stage would push him shrieking over the edge. Besides—and this was more to the sharpened point—a panting confession would irrevocably damage the delicate balance, the secret harmonies, the fragile bond they had so gingerly, so fearfully constructed.

What if he doesn't find me sexy?

He said nothing. He hated himself for doing what he always did—churning up so much *tzimmes* that he could not think straight. Was admitting he did not know what to do thinking straight? What did he want? He suspected himself of lying on every front, and of lying from underneath where he could not see. Why, in a pinch, when the chips were down, when the cards were on the table, did he don psychic roller skates?

"Andrew is a problem, Terence."

"Yes, Morgan, Andrew is a problem."

Not my *problem! I hope you solve it soon.*

After some desultory chatter, the decision not to meet evolved and they disengaged one from the other by pressing down matching black buttons on their separate telephones.

Morgan stared at the frozen pond from his kitchen window, damning the results of hastily gratifying his needs, seeing clearly the inevitability of certain facts converging. He lived such a circumspect, discreet life. The irony of this one error having such painful repercussions was not lost upon him. How could he explain? Why should he explain? Why did he feel he owed an explanation? He smiled wryly. The answer to the last question was sufficient to instigate a search to find an answer to the first.

Will he ever forgive me?

Terence sat staring up Oblong Valley, damning the fact that he really did not understand what was going on.

I thought he liked me. He does. Wait and see?

The whole business was growing more complex than he wished it to be. It was beginning to curve like one of his novels but

[206]

he could not control the outcome. There was a comfort in knowing someone else was handling the plot. If he was not satisfied, he would not accept the part. First he had to wait and see what was being offered. Then he could decide. He had control over himself and his actions, theoretically. The rage was unacceptable, a recurrence of the "blackout" syndrome he experienced whenever crossed, whenever Christopher continued drinking even though ordered to stop. Whether or not he responded with rage before Christopher was not the point. He knew how it had become an insidious means to a deadly end; he knew how it operated by putting it in a context, *the* context where it had become the "normal" way to respond, the instrument of self-destruction.

What did he want? He wanted Morgan Connelly. He would make that clear, somehow. Then Morgan would make a choice.

He may not choose me. True. Too true. But perhaps he will choose you. Don't project. Leave this be for now. Call Thomas.

"You can swing on it?" he wondered aloud, marveling at the image.

NINE

Gerald and Judith Gunning met at the Four Seasons. They had arranged the date over Sunday brunch; this was his second work week and it was to be a celebratory repast. He could not remember when last they lunched together in town. Although not fond of the restaurant, he knew from Judith's gossip that it was currently *the* chic publishing haunt, and he wanted her to feel *au courant*. Now he wondered if she was ashamed to be *en famille* rather than with some superstar agent or some celebrated hack. They sipped iced Perrier in which delicate twists of lime floated. Each held an oversized menu.

"Are you still dieting?" she asked, lighting a True.

He answered he was and would not stop until his weight was down to where it belonged. He was wounded by the question; were his actions so unimportant to her that she could not retain from moment to moment what he did? He *told* her that morning when she called to confirm lunch that he was opening a membership in a health club for midday workouts; be planned to buy some home equipment and still toyed with the idea of an indoor pool, though Judith seemed obsessed with the problem of mildew. This was serious business. His person was lighter by nine pounds, seven ounces, and that was only a preview of coming attractions.

They ordered steak tartars and more Perrier. They agreed to ignore the desserts. Both were pleased with themselves and with the other, more so than was usual.

Gerald's first week had been like his college orientation experience. He now knew where things were kept. Everyone was pleasant, determined to explain the workings of the place; yet no one had revealed the style that differentiated Beacon & Dean from other advertising agencies. (It would take months for him to know that agencies did not have style, only unique creative responses to individual clients; it took him months because he lacked a point of reference.) Until Thom Beacon took him to lunch alone, he had no idea how he fit into the organizational structure. Thom had been disarmingly honest.

"We need a ladies' man like you, Gerry. You have a real way with them. I've watched you. You could tame a lioness, pal, and we've got a few lulus badly in need of taming. You're as good as a queer but a lot less neurotic. You fit in, too. You're a rare bird, Gerry. Know what I mean?"

Gerald was receiving a fuzzy picture but he smiled and nodded in agreement. He did not want to make trouble; all he wanted was a job. And he knew he was being flattered. Beacon continued: The two companies Gerald originally chose were accounts controlled by demanding strongwilled women who were disgruntled with the service.

"And rightly so, Gerry. I'll be honest. We've been careless. But the faggot lush was canned and we're counting on you to help pick up the pieces. You'll handle five as soon as you're ready. Plus Hubbard."

Isabel Glinn was a major problem. She was vice president in charge of advertising at Hubbard, Inc., one of the country's largest manufacturers of ready-to-wear casual clothing. Hubbard had recently launched an expensive designer line, collecting a Coty nomination for its first season. Ms. Glinn was not pleased with the way the campaign was managed. She was making accusatory noises and was threatening to take her account elsewhere. Gerald felt moderately secure with the assignment. He had a fondness for the nursery rhyme about the widow and the bare cupboard; he knew that boded well. Yet even with Thom overseeing and guiding him, his ignorance of the advertising game undermined any confidence in his own abilities. He vacillated between exhilaration and despair.

"You're being paid to liaise, Ger, *not* to make decisions. I'll do that part of it. Just wipe her sweet ass for us. We'll do the rest."

When he finally faced Ms. Glinn in her comfortably appointed office—china table lamps and many coordinated pastel colors—

he was delighted he had not requested another assignment. Ms. Glinn may have possessed a feral temperament but it was domiciled in the loveliest British body. The warmth of her laughter at his Cheriton Barton story, told with himself as innocent abroad, assured she would not be a problem much longer.

Thirtyish, he figured. She was a wraithlike stunner—her teeth glistening, her skin taut and pale, her ears flawless, tiny ears which she evidently favored, he surmised, because her pale-red hair was cut to reveal them flatteringly and her only jewelry, pearl earrings, decorated their plump lobes. Her small eyes were common lupine blue. Her profile, bearing, and accent were decidedly aristocratic; he knew all three could easily be acquired by a clever, ambitious woman, but her vowels were so nasally pinched that only a psychotic would make such sounds unless inured at birth to the distortion they imposed upon her words. He was certain she was the genuine imported article.

They discussed the problem head-on. Direct confronta-tion with heavy eye contact was part of Gerald's conquering technique. Along with a mellifluent vocal manner and an easy smile that never jumped his witticisms, his eyes were the prime mover in his charm mechanism. They convinced the uninitiated of an uncanny rapport with her, perhaps a rapport she alone had shared with him, *ever.* His true humility at the sight of his powerful effect on women toppled the most recalcitrant and the most sophisticated.

Isabel Glinn wavered for twenty minutes before capitulating. She decided with noticeable relief—changing agencies was such a tedious bore—that he, Gerald Gunning, was the man to solve her problems. He understood Hubbard's difficulties and, yes, the agency was very sound. Its track record was impeccable. They made a luncheon date for the following Wednesday.

Two hours later, to his unspeakable joy, while he and Judith lunched at the Four Seasons, Isabel Glinn moved by his table with a female companion. She greeted him by name.

"Who's *she?*"

"A client of mine."

"Wonderful-looking woman . . . so *slim!*'

"Yes. English."

"She looks English."

Stunning suit. Hubbard.

"We're having lunch next Wednesday."

"I'll bet you are! Watch it, hubby."

He grinned and raised his glass in a toast, seriously considering Ms. Glinn. How long would it take for him to maneuver her into his bed? Or himself into hers, which was far more practical? Before his marriage to Judith, he had been an unabashedly profligate cock about town. Lonely women in the art world were as thick as cumulus clouds. Desire stirred. Shifting the weight of his body in the chair, he spread his legs slightly to allow for a natural expansion along his inner left thigh; the movement was not yet necessary, but the prospect of getting an erection in this dressy dive amused him.

Judith raised her glass to return the toast. She felt wonderful. She had waged and won a ferocious battle that morning at an Editorial Board meeting, defeating a suggestion circulated by Joe Rosen, the director of publicity and a corporate vice president with a seat on the Board, to delete several scenes from a novel by one of her authors. Rosen, known as the Boob to his adversaries, found the scenes unacceptable because he worried what effect the violent, explicit sodomy depicted would have on his fourteen-year-old son, Stu. He had demanded them "excised for decency's sake." Rosen frequently succeeded in tampering with the "product," as he called the books, but Judith had refused to comply with his censorship and had rallied support to defeat him. She had also won the vote to maintain the book's working title, which made her victory over the Boob and his own very powerful contingent complete. Now she would have to make certain he did not sabotage the book by funneling its advertising budget to his own pet projects.

Looking across at Gerald, seemingly marvelously "together" (in Drew's hateful jargon), and undeniably attractive, Judith gave herself permission to end her affair with Richard. It would not be difficult. He would not require an explanation: His children were expected home from their sundry private schools for Easter vacation. And Gerald had assured her that he was content commuting for the time being; the dreaded invasion was postponed. She had nicely simulated disappointment. Now she willingly believed herself the happily married woman she wanted to be.

"To us!" Gerald waved his glass.

"To us, darling!"

The mildew was a stroke of genius.

———

Terence never forgot a face. His memory for names was problematical, but on the sights he was superb. Why was it now failing him? Was his visual retention on the blink? Had anxiety fucked up the ocular imprinting service? Was it all over?

He was certain he knew the young man seated at the kitchen table opposite, but if what Rudd Rooney said was true—and why would he lie?—he had never been out of California before, and in San Diego for the past three years. Since *he* had never been to San Diego, they had never met in California because his first visit was three years ago. Yet the sensation of familiarity—familiarity to the bewildering brink of intimacy—persisted. Where could he have met a beefcookie like this Rudd person?

They were drinking coffee. Rudd nervously handled his large cassette recorder squarely set between them. He had been sternly instructed to salvage the interview from the farcical misadventures that had ruined the trip East for him and for his boss, Mr. Kauffman, who, that moment, was laid up at their New York hotel with two impacted wisdom teeth.

"It's only the beginning of our troubles," Rudd said, puzzling why the machine would not rewind automatically.

"We can use mine," Terence offered, acutely aware of his guest's panic and feeling decidedly frazzled himself.

Rudd and his boss were booked on a return flight to California the next morning. If the scheduled interview with Terence Strange was not completed, they would miss their deadline—they were six days late as it was—and the magazine would be put to bed with a gaping hole in its center.

"Bad planning," Rudd charmingly confessed. "We're not too organized yet. We're sort of *new*, you know?"

Rudd Rooney was the assistant to the editor. He was twenty-three. This was his first independent assignment. He had gotten lost twice on his journey to Amenia and arrived seventy minutes late, too flustered and embarrassed to talk in paragraphs. Immediately apologizing for his inexperience, he stammered out phrases lionizing Terence, about how honored he was to meet him. Then he blushed purple and asked to use the bathroom.

Terence was equally disconcerted by the glorious sight of him: the quintessence of California beach-blanket stuff. He stood six-four, had thick-cropped black hair, a sturdy body squeezed into Mr. Kauffman's too-small winter sweater, a model-rough square face in the black Irish beauty mold, and a loudly golden embellishing tan. When Rudd scurried off to the toilet at a halfback trot, Terence checked his own reflection and was not displeased.

If I were easy, he'd be in danger.

Mr. Kauffman had fortuitously provided Rudd with a piece of legal-size yellow paper covered hastily with scrawled questions ranging from "What was your first sexual experience?" to "What writers influenced you the most?" Standard fare that strained no muscles. Rudd's style, shy and restrained, was immensely appealing. Once the machine was whirring, he lobbed the questions, occasionally made pertinent comments, then withdrew, leaving the tape to Terence, who always enjoyed talking about himself. As the tension drained from Rudd's forthright, upright, dark-brown eyes, Terence became warmly involved. They slid speedily down the list. A sense of exchange united them. Team spirit soared.

"Is it hard for two writers to live together?"

"No. It never bothered *us*. When I was living with Christopher—"

"Past tense?"

Did I say was?

"That's what I said, bub."

"You were together a long time. Eleven years, wasn't it?"

"We're still together. We're just not living in the same corner for a little while. . . ."

Rudd was sitting in late-morning sunlight. Snakelike, he shed the sweater, tousling his hair and baring two heavily muscled arms that erupted from a short-sleeved shirt the color of his eyes. He had a potent sensuality, unmistakably calculated but nonetheless effective in close quarters. Terence stared rudely, feeling oddly stirred.

"I could swear I know you," he had difficulty phrasing. Rudd smiled, sat up noticeably straighter, and with his large right hand snapped off the machine. The hand rested on the controls halfway between the two of them.

"I wondered if you recognised me. You really gave me a scan when I got here. Was that the *only* reason?"

Terence tilted his head and glanced out the window. He wanted to resume the interview. He wanted to end this gross impertinence. He wanted to place his own hand on top of Rudd's. The impulse to touch astonished.

"I never forget a face. How do I know you?"

Rudd had been the winner of a centerfold contest in *Guy,* a national monthly magazine that Terence bought regularly. He had been a favorite pinup, adorning the back of the Gramercy Park bedroom door for half a year before taking his honored place in the large manila envelope filled with other tonic stimulants.

"It was a pretty big deal," Rudd explained with lessening bravado as he moved through the cautionary tale. "I hoped it would make my acting career, but nothing *real* happened. A producer offered me a lead in one of his porn flicks. I said no. I was serious about acting. I studied. Nothing happened. I dated a lot. Everybody wanted a piece of the action. It was fun and *hot* for a while. I'd do it again. It's been three years since it ran."

Terence shook his head sympathetically. Rudd's narrative style was not smooth, but he communicated his disappointment and disillusionment with great boyish intensity and physical force. He caught Terence's eye and held hard.

"Things got pretty heavy for a while. I felt washed up, a has-been at twenty! Then one of my friends told me about est. It changed my life!"

I see. Change the subject.

"How did you get this job?"

"I answered an ad in a magazine. I could never have done anything like that before."

> *Life was not peaceful at the dime store,*
> *Life was not calm and serene. . . .*

"Well, how did you get into the contest?"

"My lover—we're not together anymore; it was nothing like you and Chris More, only nine months for us but it was very meaningful for me—he took some pictures with a Polaroid, nothing fancy, and sent them to *Guy*. Hey! Who's interviewing who?"

Enchantingly, he laughed a chimed laugh, then disarmingly blushed at a startled loss for the next sentence. A heady sense of communion stilled the warm, sunny room. Terence felt it wiggle through him and nuzzle behind his heart.

Why do they all have eyes like startled deer?

"Would you like some tea?"

Rudd reached across the table and touched his arm. Dazed, Terence was not certain how they managed the transition from his offer of a calming beverage to what directly followed but, evidently pursuing some interior logic, Rudd softened his voice and asked if Terence was "well endowed." Terence heard himself nervously respond in the affirmative rather than curtly instruct his visitor that it was too personal a question for a cassette interview. The tape was not turning. Rudd tightened his grip on Terence's stiffening arm.

"I've never tricked before," Terence stammered apologetically. He culled some phrases to stage a diversionary tactic, a short speech not condemning the practice, although for himself—

"So what's the big deal?"

Terence shrugged, not removing his now-paralyzed arm.

"I like you," Rudd said confidingly. "You're not like the others."

I don't believe he said that! I wouldn't even use that in one of my books. I didn't know people still. . .

"No, I swear it, Ter! I'd like to make it with you."

Make it? Get it on? Have it off? Do it?

"What do you say, Ter? I'm well endowed, too."

I know, *guy.*

"God has been good to us both, Rudd. I'm glad."

"How big is yours?"

"Big enough."

Terence was appalled by this inane dialogue, but he felt its adolescently erotic power churning his emotions as if talking were doing the deed.

I often confuse feeling with doing. The nuns equated thinking with doing. Interesting. . .

It was upsetting, whatever else it was or was not doing. He grinned crazily at the lab specimen opposite. No doubting it, the body was done to a turn: a faggot's true fantasy; he had the documented, glossy evidence in a bureau drawer somewhere safe. If this vision had a hump on its back or a clubfoot, would he feel less foolish, less unoriginal? He felt threatened. What about his reputation? He could imagine Rudd Rooney adding a brief postscript to the interview in the shape of a peter meter. The thought momentarily stopped his twirling heart.

My reputation? For what? Sanctity? Do I care? I care! *Why? Not now. I think I want him. I want to touch him. Do I want him* really? *Or do I just* think *I want him? What's the dif?*

He knew intellectually that having/sharing/doing sex with a person was not equivalent to taking the veil and devoting body/mind/soul to that selected fleshy edifice. But, for him, emotionally the connections between sex and love were like the one between hip and thigh. His heart was actually waltzing. His eyes were bulging. Tears of heated confusion threatened to disrupt everything further.

Rising from the table, stalling for time, he clumsily ambled into the living room. He had an erection. It mortified him. Since he never wore underwear in the house, his physical condition instantly impinged itself upon the observant Rudd, who laughed a low, guttural, chirrupy growl, like the cat would do upon sighting a delicious-looking robin. Conflict scissored through the functioning portion of Terence's mind. He paused in his wanderings to stare sightlessly out the living room's front window. He fingered a silvery-green furry begonia leaf. How could this nonsense be happening to him? He was terrified. He was indecently aroused. Thank God he bathed that morning.

I can never make decisions. It's one of my most grievous character defects. What's the big deal?

"Ter?"

I'm not being unfaithful to anyone. Unfaithful?

"Ter?"

Chris is right I should dress properly when guests are here. I'm probably staining my pants now.

"Terence?"

He turned to answer. He would give a *firm* refusal. He would not be nasty—why should he be nasty?—but he would be positively negative. A "thank you" would be nice. Just because this cartoon cutie chose to toss it, *he* did not have to catch it.

He gasped. Rudd, naked, heavenly hirsute, leaned against the mantel posing lasciviously. He was a wet dream's radiant factotum gloriously made manifest He was a sword-bearing angel of the gay God come to drag a sniveling Terence from the sanctimonious path into the sanctified bushes.

"Why do I scare you, Ter? I wouldn't hurt you. I'm not going to tell anyone about it or anything. I want you for myself. Let me hold you."

This approach was a wise one. Terence relaxed, allowing his sexual drive to make a right turn into his will. Any dissenting voices were ignored to death.

"Ter, you've got to go with it. Get in touch with your feelings. Reach out to your needs."

"Uh-huh."

"Flow with them, Ter," Rudd whispered, slowly approaching, arms extended, every muscle taut in superb delineation.

"You lift weights, Rudd?"

"Used to. Since I was eight. Now I do it sometimes for tone."

"Nice. Not musclebound. I *hate* knots."

Life is knots. Thanks, Dr. Laing.

"You've got a great body, Ter!" Rudd hummed, running his clever hands over particular areas of interest, squeezing the squeezable as if he were selecting loaves of Wonder Bread.

"Well, Rudd, I eat right, exercise, take . . ."

They kissed. Unbidden, Rudd pressed his hot tongue forward. Terence was zapped. He reddened from the explosion of lust in his chest and groin. He pulled away and shut his eyes, trying to regain control of himself. He could not find the steering wheel. The tongue had frizzed his nerve ends. He was shivering like a novice and violently excited. "Let's get to a bed, Ter. I want this to be great for you."

"Upstairs!"

No floor? The couch? Under the table?

In one outrageous gesture, Rudd Rooney lifted Terence Strange into his arms and effortlessly carried him up the stairs.

"Your Rhett routine is a knockout, Rudd."

"I always wanted to do this with someone."

Me, too. Yes, yes. . .

The serious kissing started at midclimb. Rudd's multifaceted experience helped him control Terence's histrionic passion. Rudd was overwhelmed by Terence's abandon and provoked into giving more than he usually carried into the arena. This sense of extension confused him.

"*Wow!*" he sighed immediately afterward. "I've never met a dude so in touch with his body before who didn't know it! You are dynamite!"

"Uh-huh." Terence was torn by a dozen different responses. He wanted to remove his dizzy carcass to a dark shelf where the exact nature of every separate feeling could be analyzed. There was no *tristesse*, but there rarely was; after sex he knew the freedom of a good flight. He was airborne. Yet, within, deep within, his most private self had not been moved to participate.

No mystical sensation of loving fingers smoothing the wrinkles from my soul?

He had freely surrendered his parts; it was no one's fault if they tallied to a different whole. Physically, he felt grand. His

[218]

body was obviously delighted with the transaction.

Do I feel guilty? No. Not a jot. Disappointed. I'm not guilty? Perhaps. I'm disappointed about something god-damnit!

"Are you always like that?" Rudd asked shyly.

Should I lie and prettily say he brings out the animal in me, big boy, hot meat?

"I love sex, Rudd. Always have."

"Was I as good as you?"

Jesus! My angel is insecure! Chris is right. Stand 'em on their heads and all men are alike.

"Babe, if you were any better, I would not be alive to talk."

Rudd Rooney relaxed and grunted. His honor was intact. "Is More good in bed?"

Am I ready for this? Give them your inches. . . .

"Yes."

"He's the best-looking dude I ever saw. You leave him because of his drinking?

"Yes and no."

The wife is always the last to know.

"Does he ever get in touch with his anger?"

"He doesn't drink because he's angry. You read that in *Time* magazine?" Lowering his voice, he mocked: "Turning his anger inward, he drank himself into oblivion."

"You seeing anyone now?"

Seeing anyone?

Thoughts of Morgan Connelly skidded across his steadying mind. At one point during the lovemaking, Morgan's presence had forcefully intruded and had been summarily evicted with a not-now-maybe-later interior glance.

"Yes and no," he repeated, turning to face his nosy partner, intending a kiss to undercut his curt one-liners.

The telephone rang. It was Morgan Connelly.

"Always right on cue, Morgan!" Terence laughed.

"Why? What's happening now?"

"I was just thinking about you. What's up?"

The infelicitous phrase provoked the idle Rudd into playing with his sumptuous self. Terence frowned, then grinned lewdly, turning his back for privacy. Rudd, mistaking the action for an invitation, promptly resumed his mating dance.

"I want to end this confusion about Andrew once and for all."

"Now?"

"You busy?"

"Yip . . . I am. Can I call you back?"

"I just want to say that I made a *stupid* mistake. He jumped me in the office and I was sick with loneliness. That's no excuse, but. . ."

"Morgan, you don't have to justify what you do."

"I know. That's why I want to clarify things. I know casual sex is difficult for you . . ."

"You'd be surprised. Don't worry about it."

"It only happened *twice.*"

"Morgan, hold on a minute."

Covering the receiver, he whispered, "Stop a second. It hurts! I'll help you if you hold your horse!"

Rudd giggled and tightly squeezed him: "That Morgan *Connelly?*'

"Yes."

"You sure have nice friends."

"Thanks."

"Morgan, listen, you needn't. . ."

"I know. You sounded so hurt before."

"I was. It confused me."

"I'm sorry."

"Don't be. It wasn't *your* fault. It was my own crazies. Come for dinner. Tonight?"

"I'd like that. Yes. How was the interview?"

"Still in progress."

"Oh, God! I'm sorry! Is it awful, Toddy?"

"No. It's very interesting."

After hanging up, Terence turned his attentions to Rudd. The first success made him secure and comfortable with his playmate; he knew what to expect from the magnificent flesh he grappled with, and now he wanted something more. Rudd expected it slow and easy but Terence, artfully stroked, rose full tilt and carried

Rudd along the track until they fell, gasping and snorting, back to the jumbled sheets, soaked with sweat, delivered and profoundly satisfied with each other and themselves.

"Wow!" Rudd sputtered. "You do that all the time?"

"Whenever I want. It's nothing special."

"I love it, man. It *really* is *hot!* Not too many dudes will do it for you."

"It's an erotic zone like all the others."

"Not on most dudes' fare cards."

Terence laughed, snuggling close to Rudd, stroking the hard-core muscled of his rump. There had been no *gestalt,* only another riotous orgasm.

Only?

"Ter? This *really* the first time?"

"Why? Can you tell? Want your money back?"

Rudd squeezed him and tenderly kissed his cheek. "You sorry?" he whispered in his ear.

"No. It was wonderful. Thank you, Rudd. You're much better than your picture."

Rudd laughed and pulled him over on top of himself.

"You ever think of modeling, Tarzan?"

"No. I'm a lousy salesman. How did you start writing?" When Terence revealed his pseudonymous beginnings, Rudd wriggled out from under him and thudded to the floor.

"Are you shitting me?"

Terence shook his head and laughed, delighted by the dramatic carryings-on. Again he thought of Morgan Connelly.

"You are *her?'*

Terence nodded repeatedly: "Yes!" He studied the honed, naked, pacing animal exquisitely dappled with shadings of fine black fur.

I love men. I love the way they stand, the way they move, the way they smell, the way they. . .

"Rudd, how much time do you devote to your body? You think I'm too old to start lifting weights? I've always wanted muscles in all the right places."

"You've got a great body. Does everybody know about you

and her but me?"

"Not too many know. I don't think it's ever appeared in print."

"Can we run it?"

"Sure."

Sure? Sure!

"Holy shit! Can I use your phone?"

The romantic patch was over. Rudd galloped down the stairs to get his notebook. Terence stretched his full length in the bed and produced a sound between a sigh and a moan of pleasure. One of his harbored fears about recreational sex was that once added to the shopping list it could not be done without. It was a fear tantamount to the fear people at meetings often expressed regarding anger: "If I ever let it out, it would run amok. It would bring down the heavens."

Not true. This is fine. I can manage it beautifully. Welcome to the human race.

He could hear Rudd shouting into the telephone. Rolling over, Terence pressed his side into a tiny puddle of semen. *Already cold. Another leftover from life. Hit the showers!*

William More sat in his study writing checks for Christopher's miscellaneous hospital expenses. The telephone bill was quite astounding; telegrams were expensive.

Lucky the city paid for the rest.

Reaching for his glass, he discovered it empty. Rising, he walked unsteadily to the kitchen for more red wine. Dominic stood at the kitchen sink washing dinner dishes.

"I'm going to need another job to pay for my son's care."

"If you left him alone maybe he'd get a job and pay for his own."

"You don't know what you're talking about, *fool!*"

What had once been a term of endearment was now a weapon inflicting immeasurable pain. Dominic hated the tears collecting in his eyes. Looking at William weaving in place, he started to shout.

"You can't go on a vacation with me but you can pay *his* bills!"

"You think I want to?"

"Yes."

"You're crazy. I don't know how I've put up with you all these years. You're too stupid to live."

"You're killing me! Keep this up and I'll soon be dead."

"Not soon enough, fool."

"God, how I *hate* you!"

"You're not the only one."

"But I'm the one who has to live with you."

"I'm not asking you to."

"Where could I go?"

"Go back to your mother. Who else would have you? Better still," he smiled mordantly, "go to hell!"

"God, how I hate you."

Crying openly, Dominic groped for the dish towel. William poured himself another glass of wine and wended his way back to his study. Unable to follow, Dominic slumped over the sink and wept uncontrollably.

How long can this go on?

Christopher crossed his long legs, the right one over the left. He lit a Pall Mall while tightly eyeing Terence scrutinizing him across the coffee table. Both sensed soaring ambivalences. The cat purred in Terence's lap.

Christopher had requested the meeting. Newly released from Saint Vincent's, he telephoned to explain that he wanted a safe, healthy place to visit, far away from "trouble." Terence had consented, pulling only the briefest of pauses; Christopher correctly inferred the inner struggle. He now rehashed that momentary pause to still the anxiety he felt at Terence's seemingly unfrizzable tranquillity. Christopher could not fathom why calm should be so disconcerting.

"You look wonderful," Terence said sincerely. "I wish I could have such a dramatic recovery."

"You weren't sick."

"Uh-huh."

[223]

I wasn't ill? Is he crazy? Leave it a-lone.
"You've lost weight, T."
"Yes. I'm eating well and sleeping well."
Anxiety fucks up your metabolism.
"You *are* sleeping? Taking vitamins? Exercising?"
"Yes, dear. All of the above."
"Then *you're* OK."

Terence smiled, amused by his friend's arrogantly confident Dr. Spock routine. No denying, he looked the part. His peaceful grin was surprisingly disconcerting.

Drugged?

Christopher leaned forward to pick up a cup of tea. His dark blond hair, worn long and heavily streaked with gray, fell over his eyes. A gesture with the fingers of his right hand raked it back while he raised the steaming cup to his parted lips with his left. Terence took in everything: the perfect crease in the gray wool trousers, the high shine on the Italian black leather boots, the tapered fit of the blue velour shirt unbuttoned at the neck, the spread of the shoulders ("There are fields of him!"); the very weight of his virility impaled attention, as it always had done.

One hot dude!

Terence noticed that Christopher's hands were not shaking, his wrists were not bloated, his skin was clear, and there were no dark circles smudged beneath his clear eyes. The bruises were nearly invisible.

The vitamin E cream I brought the second visit? I love him.

"I haven't had a drink in ten days," he said, washing away droplets of tea by pushing the voluptuous lower lip over the thin, wavy upper.

Terence nodded. What was he supposed to say? "You were locked in a fucking hospital ward, sport!" sailed in from some dark inner region. He clenched his jaw. Silently, he nodded again.

"More tea, Chris?"

"A friend brought me a fifth of Jameson's but I threw it out. Yes, thanks. It's good! Not too weak," he smiled wickedly. "I miss your pishy tea."

Terence laughed, relieved that he had not been mean (and,

parenthetically, *wrong*).

"I've been pretty crazy lately, T."

Visions of Christopher hanging out of opera boxes; leaping onto stages; singing along loudly with famous recitalists; talking back to performing actors; groping strange men on supermarket check-out lines, on buses, on subways, in elevators, wherever they stood still long enough; throwing olives at unresponsive waiters; kissing policemen on the mouth when they gave pleasant answers to unintelligible drunken questions, all these memories queued for a hot one-liner. His tongue swelled.

"I'm sorry you've been so ill;" he said gently, sincerely. There was a long, comfortable pause. The sun brightened the room behind Terence. Winter light formed an aureole around his auburn hair, immersing him in shimmering glow, like the best of Hollywood backlighting in the thirties. He wore a pearl-white cashmere turtleneck, heightening the effect by softening the reflected glare.

"*He and the cat make quite a movie still*," Christopher noted. "*I love him.*"

The heat half closed Terence's eyes and separated his full, moist lips.

"Andrew tells me you're quite chummy with Connelly."

"Yes. I have been. He's a wonderful man."

"Eve, dear, this is Addison. Is it true or does Miss Desmond exaggerate?"

"I don't know! And what does it matter?" Terence laughed, raising his slender hands.

"Come here."

"Why?"

"Don't you want to?"

"I don't know."

"Sure you do. You always want to come."

Christopher smiled his gentle, vulnerable, lascivious best. Extending his arms, stretching his fingers, he opened his firm, round thighs.

"Come here, Terence. You did say you still love. . .."

"I do," he whispered, lightheaded, expanding with desire.

"Come to me, then. I've been good."

"It isn't a question of good or bad, Christo! You know that. Illness is a condition. . . ."

"You love me?"

"Yes. I love you."

"Come to me, *please!*"

Terence stood. The pain in Christopher's voice no longer confused him. For a decade, he had thought if he checked the word *pain* in a dictionary, it would be followed by Christopher's name. Pain had been the principle of everything until at a meeting he was reminded that all people experience pain but all do not drink. He drank because he was an alcoholic, not because he was in pain. Now, suddenly, Terence realized that his love was no longer burdened by fruitlessly tending to a suffering spirit; it concerned itself only with accessible delights.

"I've missed you, Christo."

"I've missed you, too. Peel off those spiffy duds."

Terence went to get some lubricant; it was needed for what he wanted from his lover. Then he straddled Christopher's lap. They clung to each other, locked together; slowly, they rocked back and forth. Terence raised and lowered himself, all the while ecstatically kissing Christopher and resting his head on the comforting shoulder. Even after their orgasms, Terence remained tightly holding the physical connection for as long as they both could manage.

He had had his revelation. With Rudd he had abandoned himself, forgotten everything but the body. With Christopher he had been recalled and carried beyond memory to where they shared dream images.

"I'll stop drinking for you," Christopher whispered, hugging him hard.

"No, no!" Terence sobbed. "You must stop for yourself."

Christopher remained three days. They had a lot to discuss.

When he had decided to approach Terence about the visit, he thought he had changed his mind and was ready to talk. Arriving at the house, he realized he was not yet able. He could not reveal that he was taking Antabus. He felt deeply hurt, still believing himself abandoned, and was made guilty to the point of suffocation by a mere hint to his drinking. He could not understand why suddenly he was expected to earn money; the insane word "enabler" that Terence freely used to describe himself was not very enlightening and thrust him, Christopher, into more paralyzing guilt for having allowed it, for needing such a thing. And worst of all, he did not care about any of it *really*. His brain seemed unable to draw conclusions or even to gather evidence.

He was certain that Terence did not want to hear of his confusion. He felt awkward and clumsy and fat. Seeing Terence self-contained, literally aglow with health, he knew where he wanted to be. If he had to stop drinking completely to share this radiant peace, then so be it. For Terence, he would stop drinking. Suddenly he wanted to do nothing but hold and be held.

"I love you," he whispered in Terence's ear, thrusting deeply.

Terence welcomed him. There was no scolding, no berating, no blaming. There was only overwhelmingly accepting love. He was safe. He wrapped his arms around the sobbing Terence, who said his name as if it were the only word he knew.

"I love you, Christo. I love you."

Then so be it.

During lunch, Terence snapped on the radio for the weather report. An unnamed chanteuse belted some ballad that made Terence sit up straighter.

"*. . . you are my way of life,*" she wailed over the violins. "Can you stand it?" Terence heatedly asked. "Who the fuck wants to be somebody's way of life?"

"*. . . don't ever leave me,*" she continued, undaunted.

"If you leave me," he responded outraged, "you'll take my way of life *with you!*"

"I'd probably hock it," Christopher said softly.

Terence guffawed. He rose from his chair and went to kiss Christopher, who laughed loudly and took every bit of affection he had coming. He blushed happily and kissed greedily in return.

After eating, Christopher went to their bedroom for a nap. He slept for the rest of the day and did not awaken until the following morning, when he opened his eyes in a flaming panic of terror and anxiety. He wanted a drink. He remembered the Antabus. Recognizing the room, he experienced an intense rush of comfort that forced tears. He called for Terence.

"What time is it?" he asked as Terence entered with a teapot and two cups and the cat trailing in his wake. Whiting took his place at Christopher's side.

"Ten-thirty."

"Ten-thirty?" he echoed, bewildered by the sunlight.

"In the morning. You zizzed around the clock."

"Oh, my God! Bad dreams! I've had a bumpy passage."

Convulsed by guilt, he muttered more apologies as he bolted out of bed, startling the cat and spilling the tea.

Terence soothed, said he must have needed the sleep, and would feel even better after a hot tub. Did he fancy some oatmeal?

"I was exhausted."

"I believe you."

"I'm a mess."

"So am I."

You are, *Kukla. Admit it. Good. Notice,* no *contradictions!*

"Come into bed with me."

"Have some tea."

"No. Later. I want *you.*"

"You look flushed."

He quoted Nietzsche: " 'How would I keep from burning when I run after the blazing sun?' "

"Buy Bain de Soleil, toots. This is the twentieth century."

Morgan Connelly forced himself to work. He was held to a tight schedule with the daily strip and he was determined to maintain order in his professional life. He agreed with Terence that people are not compartmentalized, that one aspect of a personality influences another. He knew that a quiet, ordered corner offered not only a respite but also a starting point. His famous characters continued whimsically debating the values of loving.

[228]

Dear Toddy,

This is a note, and unlike some people I never try to pass notes *off* as letters. I would send a telegram if I could afford it but I can't so a dozen lines will have to do you, dear. Last night Davey and I went to a meeting together. It was a neat experience for me, but more of that some other time. We went because the latest man in Davey's life, Mick, the brute with the big paws, beat the shit out of him *again* and I said if he did not do something about it I would never look in his blackened eyes again. He said he would go. On one condition. Me, too. I said what the hell and *off* we went. I loved it! I think he did, too. I can't really tell because he would tell me he did at this point just to keep talking to someone. I'll find out soon enough. As you say, now he knows where to go. It's enough to make me scour the bars for someone who will make me qualify! Seriously, I was very moved by it. Lots of brave, strong, intelligent people rebuilding their lives after a holocaust. Come visit soon so we can talk. I am struggling against putting a leash around Davey's neck and leading him to the next meeting. I know! I know! He has to do it himself. This morning when he called me at the office he laughed (!) and said he felt "better," not too depressed. We all join hands and dance in a circle.

Yours in serenity
Bobbi

—

After dropping Christopher at the train, Terence high-tailed it to a meeting. Overall, their visit had gone extraordinarily well for him: lots of good loving, good food, no skirmishes, lots of belly laughs. He felt remarkably healthy and knew these clearheaded times were the best of times and frequently the most dangerous.

"Happiness seemed as impossible for me as sobriety seems for him. But now I'm happy! He said several times how alone he is. I'm in his arms, and he's telling me he's all alone. He's denying my existence but *no longer for me.*" Christopher slept the first day. The second he read Rimbaud's *Illuminations,* pausing only to eat and make love. The third, he read Robert Herrick for a piece he planned to write soon. Terence was so preoccupied with their not "communicating" that he did nothing for the first day but wait for the kissing to stop and the talking to start.

"My self-esteem started to plummet. Guilt erased my whole mind. The next thing I knew, I was blaming myself for the silence. I assumed it was my fault. I *knew* it wasn't true, but the old undertow caught me and suddenly I was *grateful* he was staying with boring, little-ole me. I even watched a soap opera, bitching how stupid it was, hinting he should turn it off and talk to me. Why wasn't I working? I was shelving my day!"

"Did you ask him to talk?" Racelle A. asked. "Did you tell him how you felt?"

"Of course not! I fell into the trap of: If you *really* loved me you'd dance to the rhythms of my inner life. You'd *know.* You'd read my absent mind. I tumbled into romantic psychosis. I *know* love does not make us omniscient. Love is a state of being. 'Love does not do things.' Then I called a program friend because I was getting snarly with myself and my thoughts were getting smarmy and my alarm bells were jangling. The crazies were arriving by taxi. After the call, I was *fine.*"

"What happened?" Racelle pressed, eager to understand.

"In the hospital, Chris had told me he wanted isolation. He *told me* he wanted to be all alone. He told me and I didn't believe him. He had clearly stated in English that he was not ready to talk, in fact did not want to talk, and I didn't believe him. I persist in thinking that I know better than he, that *I* know what he really wants. After all, since he won't stop drinking when it's obviously such a problem, what the hell could he know? He wanted a safe and healthy place to keep away from trouble. He never mentioned 'communication.' He broke no blood oaths. He hadn't made any! I was expecting him to do what *I* wanted him to do: Once I gave up what we *should* be doing, I loved what we *were* doing! Can you imagine a sane person waiting for the kissing to stop? Once I donned my right mind, I had a wonderful time."

"Also," Racelle added, "once you stopped expecting him to do what he could not do, you were fine. He's just out of the hospital. Let him *think* before he tries to talk. You stopped focusing on him and started doing what *you* wanted to do, which was be with him."

At home, settled in bed, he read aloud to the cat from Nietzsche:

"Sexual love betrays itself most clearly as a lust for possession: The lover desires unconditional and sole possession of the person for whom he longs; he desires equally unconditional power over the soul and over the body of the beloved; he alone wants to be loved and desires to live and rule in the other soul as supreme and supremely desirable. If one considers that this means nothing less than *excluding* the whole world from a precious good, from happiness and enjoyment; if one considers that the lover aims at the impoverishment and deprivation of all competitors and would like to become the dragon guarding his golden hoard as the most inconsiderate and selfish of all 'conquerors' and exploiters; if one considers, finally, that to the lover himself the whole rest of the world appears indifferent, pale, and worthless, and he is prepared to make any sacrifice, to disturb any order, to subordinate all other interests—then one comes to feel genuine amazement that this wild avarice and injustice of sexual love has been glorified and deified so much in all ages—indeed, that this love has furnished the concept of love as the opposite of egoism while it actually may be the most ingenuous expression of egoism."

You said a mouthful there, Fritz. Obsessional *attachment. Combine that with alcoholism and you've got some smart cocktail. Christo wasn't my lover; he was my hostage. And I never bothered to tell him the rules at the camp. Some camp! What is "communication" to me anyhow, but telling Christo what's wrong with him?*

"Our pleasure in ourselves tries to maintain itself by again and again changing something *into ourselves;* that is what possession means."

Uh-huh. Yet there are *ways, Friedrich. The heart can be pummeled into line. It isn't easy, but if it's easy it isn't alcoholism. It isn't true loving, either. Love is a simple thing. Love is a many-splendored thing. Love is.*

TEN

Judith Gunning's day was undeniably abominable. Voyager Press was in the process of moving. The move was rumored for two years, planned for one. Alterations at the high-powered new address were now nearing completion. The employees were given a final date four days away, and the arduous packing had begun in earnest.

For forty years, Voyager was a house divided. The editorial and production staff occupied five floors of an old ramshackle brownstone on Fifth Avenue with spacious offices, cobalt-blue carpeting, high beamed ceilings, a casual but elegant walnut-dado style, and huge windows that opened easily; simultaneously, the less temperamental invisible sales and accounting staffs occupied three floors of a brother building four blocks farther east with cramped offices, pea-green tiling, low plaster ceilings, a sweat shop style, and windows that opened only with great effort.

When the international conglomerate absorbed them, the rumor of a move to solidify management in order to simplify operating costs and procedures was successfully floated. It made good business sense, certainly, to bring everyone under a common roof, but the thought of actually doing it sent shudders down the Voyager decks. It was not known where this sheltering manse would be; since the parent company owned a fifty-story glass and steel box on the Avenue of the Americas, it was nervously assumed by one and all that they would eventually be prowling the block-long corridors of that monument to itself. One and all had been correct.

Terence Strange meandered down chaotic narrow passages from the reception area to Judith's office. Since he knew the way, he had been trusted to go it alone when, after waiting fifteen minutes for Mrs. Gunning, her lines were still busy and he could not be collected by Andrew. Movers, burly men of all sizes, ages and colors, wearing black sweatshirts proudly sporting "Easy Move, Inc.," marched in straggly lines carrying cardboard boxes boldly marked with letters and numbers that corresponded to the symbols assigned each person in the company and to his or her space in the new quarters. Others wearing black ties with the name proportionately smaller, carried huge white paper scrolls: The Plans; this crew rushed around reassuring the anxious employees that only minor problems remained. Several familiar faces lurked in corners clutching wilted plants distractedly, seemingly on the verge of tears.

Cartons were everywhere. Most of the myriad bookshelves had been cleared. Walls were stripped of personal memorabilia. Floors were littered with what looked like the remains of a ticker-tape parade. Dying plants had been discarded, some unpotted on abandoned chairs. Garbage bins overflowed. Yet, amidst the chaos, telephones rang, typewriters sounded, editors stood in doorways conversing proposals and authors, copyeditors sought people for answers to pink-slipped questions, mail was being distributed, and a young man shyly approached Terence with two copies of the new book for inscription: "One for me, and one for my friend Robert. We've been together two years. It's his birthday."

Andrew sat behind a desk piled high with papers loose and bound. Calmly, he smoked a cigarette while talking into two telephones at once as if nothing unusual were happening around him. He smiled at Terence, rolled his eyes, then tilted his head toward a muscular long-haired blond youth pulling a dollied cabinet into the hall.

"Heaven, Terry! It's been *heaven!* They all look as if they come from Central Casting. One is more sensational than the next! I don't know where to start! Beware of La Lupa in there," he said, shifting gears and pointing his chin in the general direction of his boss. "She's got her tits in an uproar."

Terence smiled as he headed briskly into Judith's open office, stepping over piles of papers and hundreds of books scattered like remnants of an exploded patio. The woman stood paralyzed behind a great maw of an empty box slated to take the contents of her desk. Her eyes bulged from staring into the untouched opened drawers.

"It's Armageddon," she said in her little-girl voice, "and I've nothing suitable to wear! If my integration isn't shattered, Terence, *darling*, I know I'll be a better person for it."

"Everything seems to be under control."

"Aren't you *sweet!* Actually, we're all doing our mouseketeer best not to frighten the guests with displays of naked terror. Now, darling, I can't locate Ruschemi's manuscript! Do I unpack *everything* or just blame it on the Bossa Nova?"

"Do you like your new office?"

"Don't ask."

"She hates it," interrupted Andrew, entering to drop a manuscript marked *Ruschemi* on her desk. "She's upset because Emmaline has a couch and *she* has only a brown canvas chair with a tacky matching footrest."

"That is *not* true!"

"It's what you said last night."

"It was but *one* of the things I mentioned. *A deux,* I may add, creep. Do you have a cigarette? I lost mine in here two days ago."

Andrew groaned and tossed his pack over the desk. She deftly caught it, extracted several, then tossed it back. "When can I see the new offices, Judith?"

"Want to go now?" she asked, exhaling an arm's-length streak of smoke. "We'll work on your talk there."

"Be careful, sister!" Andrew warned, right hand raised in front of Terence's face like a traffic warden. Terence winced. He hated Andrew's constant use of campy patter.

It sounded to him like a playback from ancient pre-Stonewall days. Andrew, inspired by something, intoned: "You may be the High Priest but *she* is our High Priestess; and once Cobra Woman makes it to her new temple, she never wants to return. If I were you, Miss Montez, I'd buy two Java offerings at Fredi's takeout and hold that pow-wow on her rug with one eye on the clock. You can do me a favor and drop a wet turd on Emmaline's couch."

Judith hooted with glee. Terence smiled.

"This little private sec," Andrew cracked, "had better straighten her head dress and hop on her vibrating IBM. Young men, young women, *all* must go!"

Judith and Terence obediently bought two coffees before walking over to the new quarters. The day was a satiny one, mid-winter spring, and they both sauntered in silence. Their side of the street was crowded with people enjoying the sun, strolling on lunch hours with no destination but into the warmth.

"The light in New York," Judith sighed, "is like no place else on the planet."

"We're the first to see such light. It's the air pollutants, I read recently—especially the spectacular sunsets."

"That's fabulous to know, darling! The race is making a hasty exit but the lighting effects are lovely."

At the ice-skating rink in Rockefeller Center, they joined a crowd peering over the railings into the sunken arena where a small yellow truck produced overlapping ribbons of smooth surface for skaters to cut with clumsy or show-off-fancy footwork.

"I've always wanted to skate down there," she said wistfully.

"Me, too. Ever since *The Catcher in the Rye*. I should really use it one day. There's something very romantic about it."

"Yeah. If you're sixteen and having a nervous breakdown."

They walked to Fifty-first Street, crossed the avenue, and signed into the new building after Judith showed her identification to the security guard at the elevator bank.

"Judith! When did you get those cards?"

"Yesterday. High-type protection from now on. It's *necessary* they tell us. Are you ready for any of this? It's like visiting a banana republic."

Inside the elevator, a gray cloth shell had been hung to prevent damage by the movers; but Judith insisted, as she defiantly smoked a cigarette, that it was a padded cell for her and her cohorts. The thirtieth floor reminded Terence of the backstage area in a large theater. Painters, carpenters, electricians, rows of movers bearing cartons were doing their jobs. The cacophony was thrilling.

Change can be exciting. . . .

The two interlopers, a mimeographed map between them, scurried through a partially-mirrored foyer. Great pieces of the glass, angled, waiting to be hung, caught bits of their reflections, adding a sense of carnival funhouse for Terence as he careened left, pursuing Judith into a vast, echoing, blood-red corridor. She stopped. Gravely consulting the map, she tried to relate its coded messages to the numbered tags taped to the walls. She hoped aloud to discover where they were standing in relation to where they were going.

Terence thought of his mother who spent much of her professional life as an interior designer in similarly disrupted environments. It never ceased to intrigue him that she chose to control interior spaces. She freely admitted fear of the outside world, anxieties that had climaxed six months after his birth in agoraphobia. It made neat, comforting, textbook sense. He dared not draw too many potted conclusions as to how it had influenced his life.

"I'm A47, darling. Believe it or not, I have visited before."

"A for achievement?"

"More like A for autistic. I think I've got this map up-side-down. You realize if this were happening in someone's manuscript, I'd have no trouble finding my way?"

"Shall we explore?"

"Lordy, no! This place is a rabbit warren. We might never be heard from again. Oh! Here we are. I had the mother sideways. Follow me!"

They walked half-way down the corridor then turned right. Judith counted the doors.

"B13. All righty! This is Jerry's office. See: JL.B13. Thank Christ! Now, if I'm understanding this *carte* correctly, mine should be through *here* from—" She tried the door opposite. It would not open. "Oh, my God! It's locked!"

"Can't we go down to the end and turn right?"

"What *beast* locked this door?" she wailed. "It was *open* the last time I was here!"

"Judith, we can *shlep* around. *Du calme.*"

"No we can't, darling. The architect created a veritable maze.

The corridor joins another at the end there but it doesn't connect with my side of the building."

"It looks like it does."

"It's all done with mirrors. There's one down there producing the effect of infinite space. It's a sweet idea but the corridor's still a dead end for us in editorial."

"Why do such a thing?"

"To win awards. It will be gorgeous when it's finished. Critics will love it. I *think* we can go this way," she said, doggedly studying the map while imperturbably tracing a route with a ringed finger.

She swirled around, resuming command. They retraced their steps until once again they stood fragmented in the mirrors. Instead of left, they shuffled right, smashing into clear glass panels masquerading as doors. Terence laughed, stunned. Judith was not amused.

"Those *schmucks* are going to put the company prow on this glass. I hope there's something here soon besides employees' blood. Let's go. Follow me."

"Uh-huh."

Cautiously, they toured through the unfinished reception area where an angelic youth squatted to install a yellow telephone, then under a huge canvas-draped ladder that held a man wallpapering the ceiling, and into a dimly lit, purple corridor crammed with uncrated desks arranged like oblong sarcophagi. Turning right, Judith opened a gray metal door; both entered a leaf-green hallway. Pointing at a sign, she snorted in triumph. A train of movers like a giant caterpillar wriggled by. She glared at the map.

"OK, darling. Here's C6. The A track runs parallel. We've got to get to it. Try that door there, please. If it's locked, I *know* I'll wet myself."

He turned a brass knob. The fabric-covered door opened. He peered into yet another hallway not as vast but done in a coordinated shade of mossy veld.

"Walk straight ahead, darling. What does the teeny sign say, please?"

"A47."

"Thank Christ! We're home! Not exactly *vaut le voyage,* is it?"

Her new office was smaller than the old, but it had a window ("All editors have windows, darling."), and a thick carpet ("Everyone but Sales has plush."), and a nearby place in a long line of cubicles for Andrew ("Notice, his autographed Rock Hudson picture is in place already.").

"He's outside my door *directly.* Ruth, Emmaline's assistant, is not as close to her which compensates somewhat for the couch."

"Everything's made of plastic. All the cabinets and the shelving—"

"Formica, darling. It's *rude* to say plastic."

The view was astonishing. While Terence peered down and about into the city, Judith explained how each editor had jockeyed for each office, wanting to be closest to the seat of power, the editor-in-chief Edmund Bolger ("our courageous leader").

"We used an alphabetical system, sort of. That order was superseded by rank. I'm a vice president and had *four* best sellers last season so I—"

Terence semi-listened to the plots and counterplots. Down below, the populace went about its rapacious business like insects among tall blades of grass. A Berenice Abbott photo of a similar Wall Street view appeared in his mind. Judith laughed at something she herself said. He smiled. He thought to take notes for a novel with a barracuda editor, a paranoid schizophrenic in regression, as a protagonist; he quickly dismissed the notion as too boring and of interest only to the participants. Working high in the sky obviously did not lift people's instincts out of the trees; like monkeys, they spent their days foraging for food. He decided that capitalism succeeded so completely because it was based on primal behavioral patterns that— "How is he?"'

Judith had not only stopped talking, but she expected him to answer some question. He frowned, embarrassed, feeling like a schoolboy not up on his homework.

"Sorry, Judith. I was thinking about your best sellers."

"Liar."

"I'm sorry."

"This is all pretty boring, darling. *I* should apologize to you. I am *consumed* by this horseshit. I asked about Christopher. How is he?"

Speaking of obsessions, Judith.

"He's fine, I think."

"You staying with him tonight?"

"No. I'm to a meeting then back on the ten-twenty."

"He's really not drinking?"

"So he says. We don't talk about it."

I don't want to discuss this, Judith.

"I don't want to discuss this, Judith."

"It's all *your* doing."

"Judith! Pull yourself together!"

He walked to her brown canvas chair, the only legitimate seat in the office, and sprawled into it, not using the footrest for fear of soiling it.

"It's true, darling. Now that he *sees* you're serious about leaving him, he's stopped."

"Wrong! His not drinking has *nothing* to do with me. He can't stop *for me.*"

Little to do with me.

"No, darling. I don't agree."

"My leaving *may* have forced him into making a decision. He could have chosen not to fight the compulsion. His sobriety has *nothing* to do with me!"

Little to do with me. Keep saying it, Terence. Believe it. If you take the credit, you must take the blame. You didn't cause it. You can't control it. You can't cure it.

"What are you going to do now, darling?"

"Mind my own business. Stay out of it. Decide what *I* want whether or not he's drinking. We've both got to do this on our own."

"Can you leave him alone?"

"I *must!* I couldn't before because I was a dynamic of the disease. Now I can because I'm not and I'm getting better so I can do otherwise. I can make choices again. I was the disease's victim, not Christopher's."

[239]

"Darling, I hope your prose is clearer than your dialogue."

He laughed, spilling coffee on her chair. She screamed and bounded to his side.

"You were supposed to *schmutz* Emmaline's couch, you klutz, not *my* pitiful possessions."

After the mess was cleaned up, they retired to Emmaline's office to read his speech for the luncheon.

<hr />

Christopher left the meeting after the break. He had given it another try for Terence's sake; but as he crossed Fifth Avenue at Seventy-ninth Street, he concluded he would have to find sobriety on his own.

> *Narrow minds I cannot abide;*
> *There's almost no good or evil inside.*

The speaker, a woman in her late forties, had made him want to douse her with hot coffee. Impeccably turned out, she not only looked uncannily like but even affected the mannerisms of Joan Crawford, whom he found unspeakable (except for *Mildred Pierce, Humoresque, Daisy Kenyon,* and *Johnny Guitar*). This dame, one Julie G., played at being Joan for most of her "before" qualification, which covered her life as a classy boozerette, a high-powered career-type lush immersed in public relations and chilled vodka martinis.

Why not be Barbara Stanwyck?

Julie G. drank all the time, had lots of meaningless affairs with no-good bums, inherited money, and shot the whole fortune on the sauce. When she started talking about her recovery, the "after" part, the official line, she dropped Joan and became Loretta Young for a time before emerging as a dumb, silly, uninteresting woman—*he* thought, although the rest of the house, the faithful, the converted, liked the preachy bits best. Christopher detested the hard sell.

If they want to band together in church basements and pray for sobriety, let them. They seem like nice, complacent dullards infected with well-being. Not this fella's sort at all. Must say I liked the story of her carrying her dead cat around for a week in a Godiva shopping bag.

He wandered aimlessly for several blocks before deciding to taxi to the tubs. He berated himself for not having made alternate plans, like a movie, but he had honestly wanted the meeting to do the trick, to make him well for Terence. It was not his fault if things went "cafluey."

Hailing a cab, he wondered how many of Joan's shoes had been picked up at the auction and bronzed.

"You are my way of life," Terence sang softly in Grand Central Station while he waited for the ten-twenty to be announced. There had been no speaker for the meeting and he had volunteered. He had not led a meeting in months. It brought several breakthroughs for him, and now he stood musing on his sense of liberation, aware there was more to come.

Because I surrendered my life once, subordinated myself once, does not mean I will ever do it again. That's a spoke in this wheel. That damn fear is no longer appropriate. Keep saying it. Know it, Kukla. It's true.

A warning tremor guided his thoughts. There were different kinds of surrendering. He was learning the difference between good and bad, right and wrong. Being good no longer meant making people happy.

> *"Who once wore chains, will always think.*
> *That he is followed by their clink."*

Not always. Until proven otherwise. Takes time. Takes time God, help me.

He thought of his present life. He thought of his current work. It seemed much easier being the power behind the throne. For one thing, you never got hit with the spitballs. Christopher never asked him to do any of it. It could be done only willingly. He had handed his life over.

Too difficult living another's life. Tariffs are unbearable

The train appeared on the board. That morning, he had

telephoned Morgan to tell him of his plans to attend a meeting. He had thought to cab to and from the station, but his friend insisted on dropping him off and picking him up later. Sitting in the Jeep, waiting for the train to carry him to the city, Terence had a surge of affection for the older man. Now, as Terence settled himself in the train, it gave pleasure to know that Morgan would be waiting at the end of the ride. He studied his reflection in the window.

My face looks like shit. Always look tired. Some find that sexy. I don't. Wish I did. Wish he did.

His new expensive haircut, purchased after he left Judith, was daring for him. Very layered, it made him appear nattily younger ("Not Natalie Wood?"). He smiled at his very own pleasing face feeling giddy and silly.

He puckered his lips. If the conductor had not interrupted to take his ticket, Terence Strange would have leaned into himself and kissed his image. After the conductor passed down the car, Terence shot a conspiratorial smirk at his smug self, then settled back to read a book on the dilemma of the alcoholic marriage that he had bought at the meeting.

Morgan Connelly was delighted to see him. Terence could tell by the way the reticent man waved unselfconsciously from the platform, by the way the strong arms hugged a greeting as though the two had been apart for months, by the way the blanket was tacked around his legs in the Jeep, and by the way smiles never lessened even after lips were straightened to form words. Happiness was reflected in Morgan's face as clearly as sunshine glazing a lake.

Terence related the events of his day, playing them for laughs, ending with a serious projection: "I think Judith will be leaving Gerald soon."

"What makes you say that, Toddy?"

"She's miserable. He's miserable. Misery is losing its magic. He hates the job. She hates him. She's having an affair with an Italian translator that's become: 'I dig your act/I love *you*.' I feel sorry for them all."

"I like your haircut."

[242]

When the Jeep stopped, Terence was surprised to find himself in front of Morgan's home instead of his own. Terence stuck his head out of the window and spoke to Morgan, who was already halfway up the stairs.

"It's awfully *late*, Morgan. You don't usually stay up. . ."

"Aren't you hungry?"

"Am I? Yes, I guess I am. I forgot about it."

"I haven't."

In the kitchen, the table was set for two. The kettle was switched on, and prepared sandwiches were taken from the fridge. They were splendid: Italian-bread heros packed with Genoa salami and provolone cheese and fresh tomatoes and heaped with mayo—his favorite.

"You know how Virginia Mayo got her name?" Terence asked in mock seriousness. Morgan shook his head. *"Well,"* Terence began, adoring mythology, "she was sitting in a greasy spoon with her agent who had just arranged for a screen test and she needed a spiffy new name for the moguls. They were both eating grilled cheese and sipping steaming java when the waitress yelled out to the cook: 'Two ham on rye, *Virginia,* and hold the *mayo!*" Morgan laughed. Terence concluded: "It's true, you know."

"She told you?"

"Christopher told me. It's practically the same thing. He's like Homer: knows all the secrets of the gods and goddesses."

'Did you see him?"

"No. I spoke with him. He said he was going to a meeting. He'll be fine. He's always been stronger than I. I used to think *I* was the rock, the sturdy character. After all, *I* didn't drink. It's so crazy. Everything gets reduced to that. I think he'll be just as happy never to see me again." Morgan's heart clambered against his ribs. He busied himself with the teapot. "I don't believe it, Toddy."

"I don't believe it either, Morgan. I want to know what he's up to is all."

"Are you jealous?"

"No. What and whom he does when he's drinking has nothing to do with me. He doesn't even know what's going on, so how

[243]

can I be angry? I just wish I knew what he's thinking."

"Did you ask him?"

Terence glanced admiringly at Morgan for posing such an intelligent question. "He says it's none of my business. He's right! I still want 1 and 1 to make 1. I *know* better. It gives me grief to give that received notion up, but I know it doesn't work that way. I'm learning."

After eating, they moved into the comfortable parlor, where Morgan lit a small fire, adding several pinecones for their pungent sweetness. They sipped dry sherry from Victorian heirlooms and talked quietly together. Terence told him about the meeting. When the clocks rang two, Terence laughed and said he wanted to stay where he was forever. Morgan offered the guest room.

After Terence decided puss could manage one night on his own even though he had not been given warning, they walked upstairs to turn down the bed. Terence asked if he could shower. Morgan fetched a large white towel and led him to the room's adjoining bath. Announcing the bed was in need of fresher linen, the fastidious host excused himself and descended to the laundry room off the kitchen. Terence stripped, slid open the glass shower door, stepped into the immaculate tub, and closed himself into the cubicle.

Slowly, he turned the hot-water tap. An unexpected freezing spray walloped his chest and shoulders. Leaping backward with a grunt, he yanked the spigot from the wall. Staring, aghast, the knob in his hand, he felt the water running to warm then rapidly to scalding. He shot a few tentative jabs to reconnect the tap with its bared screw, but the thickening clouds of hot vapor blocked his goal and the water stung his arm like the prongs of a stabbing fork. Clumsily, he dropped the spigot. With a loud crash, it bounced on the rim of the tub and ricocheted, diving for his left ankle. The spikey pain thrust him sideways under the steaming shower. Awkwardly pivoting, he stepped on the pointed tap, lost his balance, and thudded against the tiled wall. The water burned his feet and legs. Frightened, he shouted for help. Panicked, he groped for the sliding door. A gust of cold air parted the heavy steam and showed him to Morgan, whose large hands guided him out of the tub.

"Are you all right?"

"Yes! The fucking tap . . ."

Morgan shut the shower door, hastily covered Terence with the white towel and sat him on the toilet, then reopened the glass section nearest the taps. Quickly, he turned the cold water to its fullest force. The sound of the downpour heightened; the vapor rushed to the ceiling. Bending into the tub, he retrieved the hot-water spigot and screwed it tightly into place, ending the flood.

"Good lord!" Terence groaned.

"Toddy! Are you hurt?"

"I'm OK. I panicked. Stupid thing to do. That's why sixty-five percent of home accidents occur in the tub!"

He stood. His legs were wobbly. Morgan, sopping wet, snapped open a large green towel and tossed it over Terence's head, pulling him into his arms. For a brief moment, Terence verged on tearful explanations and apologies but, instead, he collapsed and leaned against the comforting, sweet-smelling savior who was whispering consolation while briskly rubbing him dry with firm, gentle hands.

Worth it. Nice.

They retreated downstairs to sit in front of the soothing embers. Terence, wrapped in the white towel as if wearing a cape, watched the dripping Morgan throw a hefty log on the fire, then scurry into the kitchen to brew chamomile tea and pour brandy. He was soaked to the skin but too distressed about Terence to dry himself. Terence caught his hand as he served the brandy.

"Sit with me, please. Where's the other towel?"

Morgan shrugged and sat in the opposite corner of the couch.

"I'll bet you've been meaning for years to have that tap fixed."

"No. I never knew it was loose. That was Louis's room. I never use that bathroom."

Distractedly, shamefacedly, he pushed his left hand through his hair, causing rivulets to run like tears down his flushed cheeks and scatter into his beard.

"You should take those wet clothes off before you catch a blue-funk cold. Here, use this."

Unwrapping himself, he pulled his legs up to shield his nakedness, then handed over the towel. Morgan accepted with the palest of smiles. Thanking him, he began to dry his head. Kicking his wet slippers toward the hearth, he tugged off his socks. Standing, he unbuttoned his shirt then quickly rolled off his undershirt, revealing sloping, thick shoulders matted with shiny black hair.

One hot dude. Lovely. Don't stare.

Quicker still, he lowered his blue corduroy trousers, kicked them toward his slippers, and tied the towel around himself at chest level.

"Aren't your briefs wet?"

"No!"

Terence grinned, then consciously straightened his face.

I'm making him nervous. Ask for a robe. Modest.

Reaching for a pillow to hug or tuck between his legs or rest on his lap, he opened his mouth to request something larger to hide behind. Morgan spoke softly; he could barely be heard over the crackling of the fire: *"Don't!* Let me look at you."

"You didn't have to trap me in a scalding shower to get my clothes off, Morgan."

"What need I have done?"

"Ask! I speak English, some French, some Italian menu, some sign language. . . ."

Morgan smiled, daring eye contact. Throwing his pillow aside, Terence slid across the tense divide into Morgan's rising laughter.

William More tossed in agitation. It was two in the morning. The thundering clock was set for six-thirty. He had hit the bed right after the eleven-o'clock news but once he managed to settle himself underneath the covers, he knew he would be awake the night. The television was still playing. He could hear the low voices down the hall. Dominic was watching the movie Chris said he planned to watch. His son had sounded well on the phone. That was a pleasant something in his sorry life.

His son had talked briefly about sobriety. The two enjoyed a laugh over the impossibility of those people and their Holy-Roller fellowship. Hours later, when William slouched in the living room pretending to be reading, submerged in the familiar numbing depression, he regretted for a moment that the fellowship was not for him, that he was too smart, too far gone, too unique, too brimmed with pain that nothing could alleviate. This hopelessness was always with him: a dank river flowing on the edge of his conscious mind, too frequently rising to drown him in frigid blackness.

He stretched his body flat. Each joint swelled with an ache taprooted into its marrow. He wanted another drink. To end passing out every night before ten, he had limited himself to a fifth of gin after dinner instead of his usual quart. Now he urgently felt the shortage. It was pointless. He felt good only when he drank, or at least had the opportunity of feeling good only when he drank. Except for the horrors he faced each morning, his days were bearable most of the time. Others might be troubled by his eternally fogged-in mind; he had adjusted, had even come to accept the limitations imposed on his life by the drinking. He could not *not* drink. He knew that. But it could be worse, he reasoned. He could have been a foul-mouthed, falling-down drunk. William More could always stand up. What precautions could he have taken to protect his son?

The expiatory depression was a problem. And the impotence. He missed sex. In the old days, after the wake-up gin, he maintained an erection if he didn't empty his bladder. That abetted tumescence was long gone. It was just as well. He was of an age; it was no disgrace. And Dominic's demoniacal animus made conversation impossible, never mind sex. In the past, whenever William gathered the energy to grope him on the couch right after dinner, before they spent tense hours together or before they retreated to their separate corners, Dominic bitterly slipped into the passive role but was accepting of the well-managed favors. It lightened the turbulence for a few days. Recently, his galvanic outbursts of rage sapped William's courage; the paralysis was maddening, compounding the guilts arising from Dominic's frenzied discontents.

Damned if I try, damned if I don't. Not worth it, though I never cease to want him.

Work was ever the same. William would never be given more responsibility in the department, had in fact recently been cruelly passed over in the search for a new chairman.

He could not deny his drinking held him back there. Nor had he published the erudite, footnoted, indexed tomes outlined in his head for thirty years. The new batch of students, the open-admissions crowd, the barely literate, certainly did not care that no book titles fattened his blurb in the school catalog. At quiet times, rare moments in the middle of the night, moments solitary, he admitted to himself that he cared.

"I wasted time, and now doth time waste me. . . ."

Reaching behind the poetry books in the case by his bed, he pulled out a half pint of vodka. Waiting a beat to make certain no one was approaching, he unscrewed the top and gulped three fingers' worth. The alcohol sliced the serrated edge off anxiety, flattening it into purgative depression, making it more pervasive but less threatening.

One of his earliest memories was of his father sprawled in a bed doing the same malific deed. When William asked what he was drinking, his father gave him a swig. Rye. It had been rye. Rye was his poor dad's poison.

What's your poison, boyo?

Rye. Gin. Bourbon. Vodka. Being Irish. Born of a father gone on drink, soon gone West in search of freedom, freedom to die in peace; and of a mother gone on the merciful Christ, the nine First Fridays, Miraculous Medal Novenas, and holy martyrdom. A classic story but not any easier to live with or to survive. It was a miracle he was walking around standing up at all. And at his Confirmation, she compelled him to take the temperance oath. His two serious pleasures, boozing and jerking off—neatly Holy Mother Church and Mother More corseted both in the petrifying bondage of sin and guilt.

The television down the hall clicked off. Inadvertently, a groan of self-pity gurgled from his throat as Dominic appeared in the bedroom doorway. William thrashed about, pretending to be awakening from a bad dream.

"Sorry I woke you."

"That's OK. What time is it?"

"Late. Go back to sleep."

"Did you like the movie?"

"I've seen it before."

Dominic turned out the hall light and, in the dark, quietly crossed to his side of the bed. Hastily undressing, he pulled back the covers and gracefully slid naked under them. William could sense the heated tension emanating from his lover and could smell the musky French cologne that was liberally splashed on after bathing. He longed to stroke tenderly that wonderful smooth flesh, perfectly ripened by fruitful visits to the gym. At one time, Dominic shamelessly paraded to show it off, to tempt him, but lately he displayed nothing but loathing.

"Are you all right, Dom?" he ventured meekly.

"Sure! I'm just *great!*"

The inflection made it clear he was reaching for irony. The bellicose tone was high-pitched by anger. William was nauseated by the contractions of his own heart. Why could he not stop? Slowly sending his right hand as an emissary of peace, he slid it under the covers until it rested against his lover's side. Dominic turned his back. Undaunted, William stroked the coarsely haired hard buttocks for several seconds before slipping two knowing fingers into the deep crevice, provocatively searching the dense feathery tufts for the sensitive moist circular smoothness.

"Leave me alone!" Dominic snarled. "I'm tired. It's late."

Tossing himself about ferociously, Dominic rested on his back. William waited. Darting his hand over the hip, he gently seized the beloved genitals, deftly cupping them and laughing from the thrill they always gave him. Dominic grabbed his arm and flung it from himself.

"Leave me *alone!*" he hissed savagely.

"I love you," William whined, intending hurt.

"You're drunk."

"Just a little."

[249]

"You're always drunk. You reek of the shit. I don't want you to touch me. You're disgusting."

Even in the darkness, William could see Dominic's muscled frame hanging violently over his own helpless self. He felt sobering terror.

"You're *disgusting!*" Dominic repeated in fury. "I hate you!"

"Don't call me disgusting, please. My mother always whipped my father with that one. I can't bear it."

William held his breath. His voice sounded arrogantly calm. He wondered if Dominic was ready to kill him. He realized a shiver of pleasure at the thought, then a sadness more piercing than he ever would have imagined.

Leaping off the bed, Dominic rushed from the room, thunderously slamming the door. William contended with physical sickness. He doubted he could reach the toilet; his body was shaking uncontrollably. He had gone too far. Suddenly he was strangely calm. Reaching for the vodka bottle, he had an overwhelming awareness of his own power and a crushing guilt from the elevated joy it gave. He was perversely happy. Comfortably propping himself with Dominic's pillows, he sucked the bottle dry. Climbing up inside, he cartwheeled to the center of the matrix before losing his grip. As he tumbled upward, he called it sleep.

He died of a Tuesday, boyo, of shortness of breath, of diabetes of the bunghole, by accident, because he could not help it. I'm too old to die young. I won't die. Not me, boyo. Hell is full right now. . . .

Naked in the darkness, Dominic sobbed at the kitchen table. His heart was shredded in his breast. The searing hatred forced him to raise his hands and press the open palms against his eyes. This turmoil was like nothing he knew; he had no name for it. How could William do this to him? Drunk all the time, William ruined their lives. Dominic wanted only love. Why William did not stop and love him was a mystery like why Dominic did not leave. Why would William not *see* what was happening to them?

Succumbing to despair, Dominic rested his head on the cold wooden surface and wept. Unable to understand beyond his helplessness and his fear that Billy might die, he was trapped and lost. He wanted to die. He wanted William to die.

It's the only thing to free me from this agony.

Judith turned off the television set. Every time the film appeared on the tube, Christopher alerted her. She had seen it three times, and tonight had perused a manuscript while half watching. Pleased to share his excitement, she always obliged, finding new beauties and new delights in the Ophuls masterpiece. The woman's lifelong obsession, her secret love for the romantic pianist climaxing in the loss of *everything,* including life, sent reverberations up Judith's "chocolate tunnel," as she loved to call her own adventurous soul.

Lisa and I are sister driven organisms.

After Christopher, her precious Gerald was on the wire to tell her that Christopher had called him. The marrieds discussed what they recognized as a danger signal: Christopher dialing through his address book meant he was drinking heavily again. You could not tell for certain anymore, they concurred, because he never *sounded* drunk; yet there was a frenzy in his excitement, a hallucinatory quality to his enthusiasm. Terence had explained to her that he was now firmly ensconced in the third stage of his disease; his body required less and processed the chemical differently, with new results. It was all hideously depressing.

"Like Gerald," she sighed in exasperation.

Gerald must hate his job. She knew things were not going well on that front; accounts had been lost and Thom Beacon was disappointed. She met Thom on the train; when discreetly pumped he was eager to deliver the goods. Gerald was now busily reviving the old arrow gambit. He had spent the day in the garage oiling the *thing.* He planned to go into business for himself.

"But no one makes Westerns anymore," she said contentiously.

"There's a huge market out there. It's *the* growing sport."

Grandmama Vera had come across with the money for the pool. They only had to pay for the construction of the studio and the "business" would take care of everything.

Hope, like arrows, is a thing with feathers . . .

She hung up from him to become completely engrossed in the film until Tito Lucca called at midnight precisely from Los Angeles to confirm his visit for the following night. He planned four days with her in New York. He wanted to know if anything had popped into her life to alter their arrangements. He was the first man who knew the difference between hope and expectation. It tended to confuse her, but she was eager to explore what she realized were the beginnings of her long-awaited much-touted consenting-adult relationship.

My ultima *chance.*

Voyager Press published once a year, for the past ten, literate, elegant novels by Luchino Ruschemi. Each was superbly translated by Tito Lucca. When the newest one appeared in galleys, Signor Lucca journeyed from Rome to correct them before continuing on to Los Angeles for a visit with his brother. The happy arrangement nicely facilitated matters, removing any dependence on Italy's frolicsome postal service.

Lucca, forty-seven, was a full professor of Germanic languages at the University of Milan. He was a colleague of Ruschemi and did the European translations of the books as well. At Voyager, Lucca had worked with a male senior editor who had recently retired; Lucca was not disturbed to discover that Judith had inherited the Ruschemi line. The books required minimal work for the house: an administrator to pass them for press and oversee the marketing. Lucca expected only cursory attention to his English prose. He knew scrupulous exertions were unnecessary because Ruschemi eschewed colloquialisms; his own fluid English was flawlessly rhythmical ("You can dance to it, Drew!"), and perfectly aligned with the master's formal style. The books had done surprisingly well in America. One was adapted into a successful Hollywood film which influenced the sales on all the other Ruschemi titles when new jackets brazenly impressed the movie-magic kinship upon the browser. And twice, Lucca was the recipient of a prestigious award for translation, which gave him the power to do as he pleased.

Judith had never met him. When he arrived to keep their

appointment, Andrew announced him with eye-rolling flourish and much raising of brows. He was extremely attractive in a heart-fluttery way. Tall, slim, with thinning black hair and large Pompeian brown eyes, he would be cast in films, she thought, as a dilettantish aristocrat rather than an industrious academic. He had a clear, olive complexion, a husky voice, high cheekbones, and was impeccably groomed, pristinely wrapped in a dark blue pinstriped suit, a freshly starched white shirt, and a peony-pink silk tie pierced by a diamond horseshoe stickpin.

He looked unhappy. She assumed it due to her being a woman with a sharp blue pencil who had jotted several suggested revisions on his galleys. She began apologizing for the editorial shifting and was launched into a speech on his prerogative to select another editor when he smiled, shrugged, and raised both hands to stop her.

"I don't mind. I am content with most of your comments on my work; there are *a few* we can discuss whenever you wish. My unhappiness has nothing to do with you. It's Karl Boehm, Leonie Rysenek, and *Fidelia* at the Metropolitan Opera without *me* that I find disturbing."

He confessed a testiness with himself that he could not abide. He had not had the perspicacity to order tickets in advance of his arrival because he had been horribly busy all semester in Milan; teaching a full schedule and organizing a film society to study American film *noir,* which was very big among European students that year, had been exciting but time-consuming. Now he was in New York, ticketless for sold-out performances.

Judith smiled, relieved. She called Joey, her ticket broker in New Jersey who was a scalper in the great tradition with a 100 percent markup. She blithely charged them to her expense account. Lucca was demonstrably overwhelmed by her power. He insisted she join him for the evening if at all possible.

"Haven't you a friend you would rather take?"

"No one more than you, Mrs. Gunning."

"Judith. Call me Judith, please."

"Giuditta . . . a lovely name."

"Thank you. May I call you Tito?"

[253]

After the opera, she invited him to her apartment for ice cream and coffee. The evening had been an unqualified delight. Giuditta was convinced it had just begun when she lit the flame under the kettle. The operatic performance was perfection. It elevated them both and made them unwilling to separate.

"Will you please turn on the television for a moment?" he called from the living room. "I want to see the soccer scores."

"Soccer? We don't bother much with soccer over here."

"I know. But these are World Cup games."

"Oh. Maybe the World Cup. What's the World Cup?"

"Like your World Series."

He sat on the couch watching the late news, delayed that night by a presidential press conference. After giving him coffee, she sat watching a segment on a mass murderer which Guido announced "enchantingly American," and then she decided to take a bath. He had nodded, unbothered. She loudly ran the hot tub, puttered around the apartment to keep her presence felt, then immersed herself in the steamy scented brew, sighing as the tensions soaked out of her. She knew sex was on the agenda. She fantasized he would become the cliched randy Italian brute shredding her panties in the hall.

During the evening, he had made not one ungentlemanly approach. No heavy breathing. No rolling eyes. No flared nostrils. He had not even smiled provocatively when she dangled a bubble bath in front of him. He was disconcertingly casual about this thing called sex. He did not seem eager or overly interested. Yet she knew he was ready. Somehow he had made that clear to her. He had not treated her differently at a certain point, had not dropped his voice or hands into lower placements, or heightened his attentions, but a palpable intimacy had evolved. They had not talked about personal things; details, yes; confidences, no. Facts, not information. Most men, she brooded while shaving her legs, noticeably shift gears whenever sexuality lurches into the test pattern. Not this Tito Lucca person. He did not telegraph his intentions: He assumed they would both be around when the message arrived.

After bathing, she offered chocolate ice cream. Then she

girlishly curled into the cushioned corner at the opposite end of the small sofa. The sports spot was ending; it was evidently not going to be a red-letter day for soccer fans. Guido gently caressed her foot, never removing his eyes from the television screen. The playful gesture delighted her. It was erotic in an easygoing, comfortable way with a playfulness she adored. He squeezed her toes, not venturing elsewhere. When the weather forecast began, he turned to her as if they were sitting in an outdoor café. "I'll have to buy a paper tomorrow."

"Yes. I can get you the Italian papers if you wish."

"I would like that. May I bathe?"

She offered to open the taps for him. He refused, explaining that he liked it precisely the warm side of tepid. While he bathed, she did the few dishes and turned down the bed. He came to her neatly wrapped in a towel. She could not remember ever having such a satisfying initial sexual encounter. It was free of anxiety and splendid. He was splendid. She was splendid, he insisted, provoking rapturous responses from them both.

"Giuditta," he sighed, at precisely the right moment. They spent three days together. They worked in her apartment. When the galleys were finished, she had taken a sick day to ride with him on the Staten Island ferry, and to bus up to the Cloisters. It had been an "enchanted patch." Now he was returning for seconds before flying home to pasta and the domesticated caresses of a loving wife and two loving kids. She was not certain it was a good idea. During their brief time together, she had grown to regard him with a fondness that verged dangerously on infatuation, which verged dangerously on upsetting the precariously balanced life she had difficulty balancing without him. How would she continue without joy, without rapture when he returned to Milan?

She paced the living room. She smoked cigarettes and fretted. She had never *seriously* considered leaving Gerald. There had been periods of "Let me out!" but she had always quieted down and curled on the Azerbaijan carpet in front of the fire. She had never formulated a plan. Now she considered the possibilities.

Could I work in Milan? Live Back Street *in Milan?*

[255]

ELEVEN

Terence tranquilly lay beside his soundlessly sleeping friend. Gray dawn slowly developed oblong patches into windows on the dark brown bedroom walls. The eerie outside stillness, time without sun or moon, was intact but would not hold.

Amid tender fondlings and exploratory fumblings, they had laughingly tumbled to the blue shaggy rug spread in front of the fire. Morgan exulted, at first quietly with shy, light sighs, then, as both became charged, loudly, using words, shouting in the thrall of his own grasping excitement; Terence, pressed, groaned from the weight of his own.

Now Morgan slept. They had walked upstairs, arms around shoulders and waist, silent with contentment. Once in the bed, they had begun again, stirred by the feel of cool sheets covering accessible nakedness. Morgan had gently taken him and Terence had gone over the edge into flailing frenzy, braying at the extremity of his own lust. Their pantings were not lessened when Terence erupted into full-throated laughter, exulting in his own excess and in the silliness of all sexual transactions which he loved beyond bounds and shamelessly.

Surprised, Morgan clasped his laughing boy to himself and waited for his own senses (and his exultant heart) to stop dancing caracoles. As soon as he could manage, he conjectured that he had never had such complete sex; had never known such a responsive partner; had never felt such deep union or been so blindly aroused. Terence stopped laughing. Crawling on top of Morgan to rub their heated parts together, he returned the kisses, reveling in the body contact and in the black tones coloring the. tired voice.

Then they had grown silent. Morgan slept. Terence tried but could not. This experience bore more relation to Christopher than to Rudd Rooney. It was wonderful, which clarified nothing. It was not—he strained to verbalize—*not* as calming as the connection with Christopher, where comfort was a major ingredient, nor as stressful or provocative of restlessness as with Rudd. There were many similarities—primarily pleasure that made his tongue cleave to the roof of his mouth. Physically, he felt grand: Everything quivered and vibrated deliciously when he took a deep breath.

The lost chord?

He peered at Morgan Connelly, clearly visible now in the dawn light. This peaceful being was the third person with whom he had shared a bed and the fifth he had handled carnally.

Handled? A good graphic word, less vulgar than most.

The first was twelve years old, but he was twelve as well. Tucked in a capacious bush in summery Central Park, yards off a dirt path, their Schwinn bikes propped against a ginkgo tree, their shorts dropped to their skinny ankles, they squeezed and tape-measured every which way. His precocious friend feigned an innocence equal to his own, had shown exciting action pictures borrowed from an older brother's sock-drawer collection, and with a flushed "Let's try this," had taught the combined rudiments of masturbation and fellatio.

Terence remembered, with a quizzical smile, insisting his clever friend smell his breath for telltale signs. Signs of what? Had he been cognizant of semen's existence, or the cause of the mysteriously knockout conclusion to their efforts? Had there *been* a KO, or had they saved that for another time? They fooled around at every hidden opportunity for over a year until Terence discovered at a religious retreat that what they were doing had a name, then several names, and was a weighty black sin. His friend wanted to continue, was willing to trust to the confessional and the power of saving grace, but Terence was frightened of fire and bored with his friend. He efficiently severed all relations.

There was no sex but solitary sex ("Taking myself out on a date") until the dune experience with the family lawyer, who clocked in as No. 2. Then Terence met Christopher

More on a theater stage at a graduate school party. All awareness of his own sexual preference had been avoided, a feat requiring as much psychic energy as he later generated to deny

Christopher's alcoholism. Terence considered himself cold, unable to love, destined by his own crippled emotions never to form a meaningfully satisfying relationship with a woman; men were an undiscovered universe. Enemies had called him a fag; he believed them intolerant of his uniqueness, not clairvoyant.

He was in love twice disastrously before Christopher. The first time was with a pert female beauty named Cookie Conklin. Sixteen, she was a classmate, a cheerleader, a friend who, in her turn, predictably fell for the high school jock, a blond and flawless football divinity with whom she boldly necked and daringly fished in the darkest corners at every party.

If I only knew then *what I know now. . . .*

The second experience was more complex. At Yale he loved an instructor, a male, a Jesuit with special dispensation to teach in the psychology department while completing further research on a government-sponsored project. This brilliant man in his turn fell passionately for a female student for whom he eventually left the Church and the university to set up a private practice in Chicago. It had been agonizingly painful for everyone. The proud chosen woman owned an anemic ego that required support from several close advising friends—Terence being one of the closest. For two whole years he empathized, confusing his own grieving, his unrequited love, with her much-bandied pain arising from her "responsibility" to do the right thing. She had never loved the priest. Terence loved the priest and no one knew, not even Terence. He was so unaware of his own needs that he spent ten months being counseled by the priest for depression and free-floating anxiety.

Then he met Christopher More. Tall, bony, darkly blond, flamboyantly brilliant, and funny, Christopher was extravagantly gorgeous. Christopher More, drinking Manhattans from glasses large enough to hold umbrellas, and making it quite clear that the best love was male love, at which he excelled. The thrilling stories of daring escapades were endless. Terence absorbed them all and was enthralled. He was envious of the mind, the body, the style; jealous of the experience, the sophistication, and the wisdom; he was aroused and terrified. And everything from the very beginning.

They were both majoring in theater arts at New York University. Christopher was there because he wanted to find a lover and because the theater was a lark. Terence was there because in his last year at Yale he discovered that he lacked the stamina to become a therapist; he had the intent and the ability, but he could not detach professionally: He cried a great deal. He often took to his bed after the casework sessions or the visits to the state mental hospitals where the students observed and mingled with the patients. Once he fainted after a demonstration of shock therapy; revived, he lectured the head of the hospital on the uselessness of such barbaric treatment, as selfish a "cure" as doping the patients quiet with stupefying tranquilizers. At another time he nearly suffered cardiac arrest when a rationally conversing patient segued into a psychotic episode without polite apologies or the merest hint of preparation for the leap; before his horrified face, the man withdrew into catatonia. Terence had required sedation.

"People would tell me things they had been withholding from staff doctors for years. While we were playing checkers, one man announced he had found his mother hanging in the bathroom, the same bathroom where he later found his sister. These were major traumas for him. He even showed me their pictures. It was terrifying."

"No doubt," Christopher sympathetically clucked, thinking he could love this sweet person forever.

"I wanted everyone to get well. Everyone doesn't, you know."

Impulsively, Terence decided to use his other interest, the theater, as an excuse to continue school, avoiding the draft and Vietnam. He had always been an excellent actor, worked frequently in dramatics at Yale playing leading roles, taken classes at the graduate school, and had solid technical skills to offer the admissions board in New York City, where he wanted to live. Christopher had offered his outstanding NYU undergrad achievement, an M.A. from Harvard, four plays he had written and directed for the Harvard Theater Club, and a resume that included Richard the Third, Constantine, and L'il Abner.

The two met at a cocktail party given on stage to welcome

the new graduate students. Christopher got wildly drunk and made a centerpiece of himself by singing several mock opera arias accompanied on the piano by another new student who invented Verdian and Straussian chords to the screaming delight of most of the guests. For several weeks, Terence assiduously avoided the overwhelming Christo More until a classroom exercise in improvisation brought them together. They worked superbly as a team.

"You're awfully tense," Christopher gently criticized afterward. "But your timing was *perfect*."

"I'm working on the tension. *You* were great." Christopher smiled, not saying a word. Years later, he confessed to nearly biting off his tongue to avoid a quip passing his lips.

"Why?"

"Because you were so *intense*. You looked as if you were living on a window ledge. *I* didn't want to be the one to push you off. And I was being *nice*. I'd seen you naked after dance class and I wanted you. I couldn't scare you away!" Whenever they were paired for improvisation, the class churned in expectation. There was always a moment, usually in the first two minutes, when one would break from the predictable path of the exercise and recklessly charge into a clearing of hilarious absurd invention, with the other effortlessly following and neatly topping. Juggling for domination, each was willing but not eager to be dominated. Some of these classes were taped and used for years afterward as examples of spontaneous shared creativity, as demonstrations of sophisticated playing. The impeccable timing they displayed, the technical agility they paraded, the compatibility they revealed won serious respect. Terence Strange and Christopher More became casual friends.

At that time, Christopher shared an apartment with another young actor whose name he had found attractive on the housing bulletin board. It had not taken them long to realize they were not well matched. Perceval Yates was small ("All over!"), nervous, efficient, obsessively neat, compulsively clean ("Washes the soap!"), and riddled with allergies ("Including life!"). He did not drink or smoke or keep late hours, and he professed to being contentedly asexual ("Useless as tits on a bull."). They stayed together because

Christopher was out a great deal and too lazy to move his bed or mailing address; and Perceval loved complaining about him: It galvanized everyone's attention.

Terence Strange liked Perceval Yates. They shared a passion for Mahler and Bialies and countless other things. They regularly went to movies or the theater or concerts together and spent lunches or dinners or intermissions discussing Christopher More. One December evening, in a coffee shop near Carnegie Hall, while bitching about Christopher's habits, Perceval paused, leered Terence in the eyes, and whispered: "If *I* were *you*, I wouldn't bend over in *his* presence."

"What does that mean?"

"He's after your ass."

"How do you know?"

Is it possible?

"He told me."

"He just *told* you? When? Between your howling about the dust balls or the burned pots or the piss on the bathroom floor?"

"We talk a lot. He's a good guy when he's not being a shit."

Terence felt a buzz of excitement. He thought Christo never noticed him beyond the cursory exchanges after class or during the intense group conversations at his own apartment—a comfortable meeting place for his classmates, many of whom were more intimate with Christopher than he.

"He *said* that ever since he saw you showering after dance class he decided you're the class treasure."

"Treasure?"

"He said *tesoro,* but that's what that means. He said you've got the prettiest cock he's ever seen. How can one be *prettier* than another?"

Terence laughed, delighted. He promptly bought Christopher a Christmas present: a fountain pen, "For Your Verse" on a card attached. It was a great success but elicited a response that startled: "You are a dangerous man, Terence Strange."

"What do you mean?"

"You play cruel games. I'm afraid of you."

'I don't understand."

"*Yes,* you do! You're a spiritual hooker and I can't figure how to reach you."

I can't be reached. I don't exist. Give me a life. Let me in. I'll make you feel wanted. I'll make you feel needed. Let me in. I'll take care of you. I know what you need. Come in and take it. Let me in. All you must do is love me. Love me. Love me in return for my life. Come in. Give me a life to live. Everyone is welcome. The needier the better. The needy are grateful and easier to control. Like me. I can't be reached. I don't exist

Five months later, after countless nights of conversations lasting until dawn, and glorious days walking in Central Park—two fugitives from boring classrooms talking together on Umpire Rock nestled in the glacial grooves, or floating for hours in a wooden boat on the Lake—they understood each other. Terence and Christopher became passionate friends. Then Christopher was cast as Brutus to Terence's Cassius in the end-of-term production. The daily, grueling rehearsals, the excitement of working together on such a vast project, of being constantly together, forced one into the other. They realistically shared reliable strengths.

One radiant afternoon in early May, a week before opening night, Christopher took Terence to the Park for a ride in a hansom cab drawn by a white horse. They were discussing some new blocking. Having commandeered control of their play from the incompetent student director, they were making many changes. Introducing a *non sequitur,* Christopher confided he was in love.

"Who is he?" Terence asked, honestly thrilled for his friend.

"Guess."

Terence named the favorites, the standard good-looking, the tall, dark, and handsomes, the leading-man numbers Christopher vociferously fancied.

"Nope. Guess again."

"I give up. Who?"

"You!"

Terence was stunned. He could not grasp it.

Lying in bed with Morgan Connelly over a decade later, he relived the paralyzing shock and disbelief. How could Christopher More have loved him? How could anyone have loved him knowing what he was, knowing how he operated? How could anyone love

[262]

a spiritual hooker?

"I love you," Christopher said over and over and over.

They made love for the first time the opening night of their triumphant *Julius Caesar*. At the raucous cast party, Terence drank too much wine and Christopher insisted on steering him safely home. They had spent countless nights in the apartment together; Christopher slept on the couch. That night, after three pots of tea, they went to their separate places. As Terence settled himself, he caught sight of Christopher leaning on the doorframe joyously weeping. Terence opened his arms and took him into his bed.

The delirious euphoria, the lyrical youthful passion, the sonnet sequence Christopher produced in one week finally convinced Terence that he was loved. Christopher More loved *him*. Christopher would teach him what love was; Christopher had experienced love before ("Don't ask!"), for him it was an undeniable reality. He sang to Terence repeatedly:

> *Is it the way you touch with a glove*
> *Is it the gay gods cavorting above*
> *Or is it at long last love?*

Terence responded as best he could. He was flattered to be adored by Christopher More, who did it so well. Terence wanted the love. He enjoyed it, reveling in the sex. He wanted to love in kind, but he believed he could never reciprocate with equal abandonment. He was fond of Christopher. He admired and respected Christopher. But love? He could not. Not anyone. Christopher laughed, narrowing his eyes.

They went to France for the summer. Christopher battered at his defenses. He laid siege: cajoling, caressing, loving in the great histrionic tradition. He suffered the sporadic rejections with ferocious intensity, bewailing Terence's emotional recidivism with mounting fury. At Mont St. Michel, after an argument ostensibly about money, Christopher tore up all the available cash, shouted a drunken tirade against anyone trying to control him ("Nobody manages me!"), then sped alone back to Paris, intending to fly home. He stayed to confront Terence one last time. Terence had been terrified. Crying the entire night, Christopher was comforted by his forgiving friend. They would have idyllic days and passionate nights until Terence withdrew into moody silences and a separate bed.

"You confuse *can't* with *won't!*" Christopher roared one evening as they walked along the Seine. "You're so *stupid,* I could strangle you! I love you madly but I could kill you." Terence moved away from the edge.

"I won't hurt you, Terence! Don't worry. I'd never hurt you. You *must* know that much about me. I can't take this B-picture any longer. I'm going home."

Terence watched Christopher walk away. He knew this exit was the final one. It had been quietly stated: a fact, not a threat. Inside himself there was a violent upheaval, a simple recognition. This man quietly mounting the stone steps, this man still within calling distance, this man tearing free was dropping him back into the void where he, Terence Strange, could hide, forever alone, forever safe again. Safe? But he never felt safer than when he lay in this loving man's arms.

"Christopher!" he shouted.

Christopher stopped.

"Chris! Wait! Please wait!"

Christopher turned, scowling.

"Chris! Christopher! Don't leave me!"

I love you. I love you.

Across the distance, each waited for the other to move. Christopher's face blanked; he tensed his body, uncertain of his next move. He intended to leave. He was checking out. He was ending his Lotte-Lehmann retirement routine. He was not interested in another momentary relapse brought on by some childish fear of being abandoned on foreign soil. Until the very moment Terence turned away to sit by the river's edge, Christopher remained unconvinced. Then he discovered Terence was crying. Warily, he descended to the quai. Affecting indifference, he strolled the few yards separating them.

Terence looked up. His revealed face was tear-soaked. His mouth opened in an attempt to speak. No words sounded. Slowly rising, he stretched out his arms. Christopher spoke his name. Terence moved toward him. The two embraced. Held safely, Terence cried with such relief, gasping and choking, that Christopher made him sit, the better to cradle him in his arms. Ignoring the curious passersby on the embankment, Terence wept until he could confess the accepted truth: "I love you, Christo."

"I know, my darling, I know. We each have to come out in our own way."

"But you would have left me."

"I don't give up so easily, Pet. I would have cornered you in New York. . . ."

Morgan Connelly stirred.

Terence halted the rapid self-colloquy, then continued traveling in the dawn's increasing light. Christopher More was the only true friend he had ever known. The perspicacious poet *had* cornered him in New York.

Nonsense! I was ready.

He had misread Christopher's intentions because he could not yet read. He thought himself judged rather than observed because *he* could not see, would not see. After all these years, had he forgiven Christopher for loving him?

Where does that leave me? At the beginning. Where I am right now.

He thought of his friends in the program. Their smiling faces came to him with the urgent sounds of the birds singing outside the windows. His friends loved him.

I know *I am lovable now. I'm not a monster. Not even the most adept spiritual hooker in the universe can* make *somebody love him.*

He studied Morgan Connelly. He had not tried to make Morgan love him, he was certain. Besides, the man never *said* he loved him. What was important at this moment was how *he* felt about Morgan Connelly. A love sonnet, the first gift from Christopher, turned his heart:

> For this pale fraction of the time of day
> When one must lie in sleep, and one in wait,
> A gallant peace dictates the direct way
> Beyond our frail dimension to the strait
> Where we dream love, identity, blue waves

That carry us to shore—sundown; we now,
Becoming as a day does from its halves
One light and shadow residue, see how
One may sleep and be still no moment far
From one's love than the afternoon dares be
From morning, noon, or night, than any star
Can be from those eyes love lets that star see
One wakes quite suddenly, occurs again,
Becomes oneself, says: "Self, he dreamt the rain. "

Morgan Connelly awoke. Rolling on his side, he moved himself into a crouched position close to Terence. "Are you all right?" he whispered, kissing Terence's cheek and covering his chest with his left arm.

"Yes."

"Are you sure?"

"Yes. Of course I'm sure."

"I love you."

Christopher was dreaming. He sat in an oblong windowless classroom. He was warm and comfortable, although the wooden seats were too small and the crowded space was fogbound with cigarette smoke. He faced a blackboard the size of a conventional movie screen. On it twelve sentences were ornately sculpted in coffee-colored neon. His mother's amplified voice was suddenly heard. She urgently demanded to know what people did to stop. Christopher raised his trembling hand. The cultivated voice of a BBC announcer called upon him to answer.

"You stop drinking," Christopher recited, "by not drinking. It's very hard because it's normal for an alcoholic to be drinking. Alcoholics recover by going against their natures. It takes great strength to continue drinking when you're so sick all the time. You can use that same strength not to drink once you want to get well."

"That's a fine contribution, Christopher M."

"I know. Thank you. And good luck."

His mother hummed the opening bars of Jerome Kern's "Bill"

as an introduction to the Hammerstein lyrics, which she crooned in her choir-contralto voice:

> *But along came Bill*
> *Who's not the type at all,*
> *You'd meet him on the street and never notice him;*
> *His form and face,*
> *His manly grace*
> *Are not the kind that you would find in a statue*
> *And I can't explain. . .*

He craned proudly around the room at the nodding, smiling faces. He remembered that Terence was in another room, a similar room, somewhere in this vast hive of rooms and had missed his performance, was missing his mother's song, unless they were tuned to the same station. In a corner, Whiting was balanced on his hind legs and waltzed to the music with Josie.

He awoke peacefully.

"A cartoon dream," he snarled angrily, willing it gone. "Jesus, I need a drink!" Glancing at the clock, he knew the shop was open for business. He dialed and was waiting for the nice man to answer when the incomparable voice of Helen Morgan broke through his concentration:

> *. . . I love him*
> *Because he's I don't know,*
> *Because he's just my Bill.*

He had passed into sleep without shutting off the radio. His mother's favorite lullaby, second in nightly hits to "Danny Boy," was nearing its "swoon-making" first-verse conclusion. He hung up to listen.

His mother's singing for him remained as indelible a sense memory as the cool of summer mornings by the Jersey shore and the first taste of Terence's most private love. Her overly hasty death occurred early in his life, obliterating residual discord. There remained lodged at his center a sphere of purified feeling as lambent as an evening star, everlastingly risen on the horizon of his childhood, it was visible to him only when conditions favored his receiving anything through the static of anxiety or the anesthetic of alcohol.

He sighed, straining to isolate pleasure from pain. His entire body swelled with a love for her that washed his closed eyes with quick tears. By dint of habit, he wrestled to contain the emotion; with a thrust, he released his grip and surrendered to its penetrating embrace, lavishly weeping. The sardonic observer in himself, inhabiting the bandstand at the back of his brain, warily watched the proceedings and avidly recorded the highlights for the Dr. Reynall archive.

> . . . *It's surely not his brain*
> *That makes me thrill*
> *I love him*
> *Because he's I don't know,*
> *Because he's just my Bill . . .*

Christopher reached for the phone. He requested the components of a Manhattan to burn out the scourge of cheap sentiment before it swamped the revelations. His mother's death revisited activated a centripetal force that sucked in the loss of Terence, the inability to work, the inevitable wet brain of his father, and the urgencies drowning himself.

And what about me? Tawdry. More d.o.a. Won't do. Thanks, no. Reshoot the last reel. Cast someone else. I'm wanted on another set. Too old to play ingenues. Can't do 'em anymore . . . unless their smooth, endless legs are wrapped scarf-tight 'round me neck. The only viable noose.

"The noose of love," he sang while he dialed Dr. Reynall to schedule an emergency "glue together" session for that day.

He jumped out of the bed when the doorbell rang. Pulling on a robe, he galloped for the delivery boy. "Just in time, you got here just in time, before you rang my time was running low," he crooned, feeling the shakes starting to decimate his ability to knit words into phrases. "You Are My Special Angel" was the last song of the morning. He sang it to the two bottles separated by a thin piece of corrugated board inside the paper bag that he clutched to his chest. Once in the kitchen, he was gripped by a demon.

"Mix the potion," he melodramatically ordered his anarchic hands. "Transform this lunatic, insatiable Hyde back to the respectable Jekyll. Mix, man. Keep him at bay for at least the time needed to shave without his slicing your throat."

He drank the cocktail from a dirty milk glass. Leaning against the refrigerator, he waited for the drug to work its magic. Slowly, the twisted features of his face returned to their usual alignment. The demon eased its clawed grip on his terrified heart. The tremors ceased to flit between limb and organ, between brain and balls.

"Exorcised!" he whispered. "Hit the deck! Don't spare the soap, Jekyll. Never know who'll sit beside one in this anteroom to hell. Spic and span, eh what?"

Morgan Connelly thrived on his love for Terence Strange. The sex was consistently memorable. Both would climax wet with each other's tears and too breathless to say anything for several minutes—hearts pounding, minds erased clean, and bodies still stiff with excitement, those particular parts eager for more.

"I'm too old for this!"

"Horseshit!"

Between Terence's house, where they went to take care of the cat, and Morgan's house, where the dogs needed feeding and walking, there were endless possibilities for many different kinds of spontaneous or carefully arranged couplings. There were twenty-one rooms in which anything could happen. They restricted themselves to nine, but were flexible enough to be comfortable in eleven.

"He said he loves me."

"Oh? What did you say, Toddy?" Waiting for a reply, Bobbi exhaled smoke into the mouthpiece. It sounded as if a train had just rushed through her office.

"I kissed him."

"And then what?"

"We made love again."

"What did you do after?"

"I don't remember."

"Oh, for shit's sake! Do you love him?"

"Yes . . . yes, Bobbi, I love him."

I really love him.

"What are you going to do about it?"

"What is there to do about it? We're doing all we can."

"What about Chris? Are you going to tell him?"

"Bobbi, I feel very strongly about absolute truth. *I'm against it* If he finds out. . ."

"How could he?"

"I haven't a clue. How do people usually?"

"Well, in your last book . . ."

"Don't remind me."

"How's the new one?"

"It's not. I've been preoccupied lately. Morgan can always work. He's amazing. I love his self-discipline."

"I like the sound of *that!*"

"Bobbi, this is all very confusing. I do nothing but sit here and wait for Morgan to call."

"I don't like the sound of that."

"Uh-huh."

Call Thomas S., Flowerpot.

Judith stood weeping at the airport. She had waved in the general direction of the plane until her arm hurt; then, feeling bereft, she started to cry.

I hate good-byes. Have trouble taking out the garbage.

She wept as if her life were over; she was convinced it was. She knew she was being melodramatic, but she felt entitled to this public display. She wanted Tito Lucca. He made her feel good. He made her forget her problems.

Was that not what men were put on this planet to do? she

brooded. She thought of Gerald and groaned. Of all the men she could have married, *why* had she picked him? Why had she not married that lawyer? What was his name? Hanley. MacDonald Hanley. He was rich. He had *really* loved her. It was a pity he was so short. And so boring: tax law. *He* never would have allowed things to get in such disrepair.

My life is a mess. *Oh, not all of it.* Most *of it. The best part. Sex made me marry Gerald. He forced my hand.*

She wondered if Hanley ever married. She turned and faced the crowds. They all looked so *happy.* What did they know that she did not? Maybe she would bump into Hanley and they could spin the bottle again? But no Tito Lucca. He was gone. Her last chance for true happiness had just zipped into the blue, out of her clumsy grasp.

On her way out of the airport, she stuffed several travel brochures into her large purse. They colorfully-spelled out the joys of Italy. She already knew about the joys of Italy. As she hailed a cab, she fought back more tears bravely.

"The most sickening thing of all," she thought as the cab sat stalled in traffic, "the most disturbing thing is that I have been here before."

Too long ago, when she had decided to leave her first husband, she experienced the loathing that she now poured on Gerald. If she seriously examined each side by side, they were the same man, those two.

"Not the same man *exactly,* darling," she said to Andrew that night over drinks. "Stuart was a total shit, a self-centered bastard."

"So is Gerald, dear."

"Not really. He's self-centered, yes. A bastard, yes. But of a different sort. It's hard to explain without oversimplifying to death."

"Men are beasts."

"Oh, Drew. You are the comfort of my middle age." *How could I have married the same turkey twice?*

Terence worked at his desk. He sat directly in the late-morning sun as though encased in a yellow Lucite box, so clearly defined were the solar rays. The cat dozed on the other side of the room.

The doorbell bonged twice its Big Ben carillon before Terence begrudgingly rose. Once standing, he hurried toward the front door. He did not want Mr. Hunion, the postman, to wait in the cold gusts that pummeled the stoop.

Who else but Hunion at this hour?

He remembered receiving a gift from Christopher a few days after moving to the country: three live lobsters tagged Faith, Hope, and Charity. It had not seemed funny at the time but now it made him smile.

Who else without calling first? Morgan? Maybe Morgan!

It was Gerald Gunning. He looked frantic, about to burst, and tightly wrapped against the cold. In his right hand he waved a packet of letters removed from the mailbox at the end of the short drive. His eyes held the glaze of the crazed. Draped over his bared teeth, sneering lips pushed hard to form an unconvincing smile. In the gusts of wind, the bottom halves of his coat flapped against his legs like miniature wings maniacally attempting to take him elsewhere.

They're revving down from carrying him here.

Terence looked over Gerald's shoulder for the Jeep. It was parked across the highway. He had walked up the drive, which was why the approach had not been heard. A sneak attack?

Gerald did not want to intrude or interrupt or interfere. He would have called, but his phone was not working and everyone knew the public one at the shopping center had been dead for a decade. He had no particular reason for being there. He had suddenly remembered that Terence took a break at eleven, and since they had not seen one another in a decade, and since it was eleven in a little while give or take an hour, it seemed like a wonderful opportunity since he just happened to be passing by and why not? Did Terence mind? No? Yes, he would *love* a cup of hot tea. How nice!

What is *the matter* ?

"How are you, Gerald?"

"Great! Absolutely tops!"

Tops? He's abbaz!

"You look upset, Gerald."

"Me? No! I'm great!"

"Good, Gerald, good for you."

OK. I believe your words. Smile and nod, Terence.

"Terry! You're right. I can't ever fool you. And why kid myself?"

"What's wrong, Gerald?"

You asked for it, Peachpit.

"I'm in love."

"What's wrong with that?"

They stood in the hallway at the foot of the stairs. Gerald still held the mail, still had his hat pulled down to his brows and his coat buttoned up to his throat. He never wore a scarf. He never caught a cold. Prayer, he said, was the answer to the chill, the answer to all illness.

"Take off your coat, Gerald. Go sit down. I'll put on the kettle."

And go for a walk.

Gerald Gunning was in love with a woman named Cynthia Liveright, who was the wife of one of the chief mucky-mucks in his agency. The whole thing had just "happened," was out-of-this-world "cosmic," exploding instantaneously, all in one breath, and "at first sight," he concluded, marveling at life's miraculous contingencies. It sounded from his description like atomic fusion in the heart's vena cava.

It all came about over lunch at Lutéce. She was in the city from Sharon—yes, they were neighbors, had nodded at one another for years at the club. She joined her husband, Nick Liveright, who was lunching with Gerald, to advise him on his liaising and discuss his failure to conquer all but Isabel Glinn and Hubbard, Inc. Why should he mind if Cynthia joined them? He felt tremendous relief. Nick would never scold him in front of Cynthia.

Cynthia and Gerald knew from the moment they collided that it was beyond their control. It was bigger than both of them; it took in all of Lutéce. They had all they could do to keep their fingers from galloping across the tablecloth. They warred against it, were defeated by it, of course, by the stampeding forces of Fate.

"Terence, it was like something from the movies. Or from one of your books!"

"Uh-huh. Have you . . . ?"

"Yes. Just now. I lied. My phone isn't out of order."

"How did it go?"

"Awful! Just God-awful! Can you recommend a therapist? Mine's dead."

Terence suggested a Gestalt type he knew positive things about. He was listing the eclectic man's values when Gerald interrupted, rising to depart.

"Thanks, but I think I've found my man."

"Who?"

"Dr. Ackroyd. Primal therapy. Nick says he's great."

"Nick who?"

"Nick Liveright."

"Well! Happy screaming."

"Nick says you don't scream that much."

Gerald hastily digressed. The job was hateful, dried up his creative juices. He hated commuting. He was afraid to ask Judith if he could stay overnight with her. What if she refused? He hated not working because Judith resented him. Maybe Judith hated him? *He* had not asked her to go back to work. They could have managed, but she would do without nothing. She was very spoiled. It was unfortunate. Judith lacked vision. She resembled his first wife in that respect. How could she devote her life to producing so many lousy books? He had to go. He was having trouble finding mauve feathers. Was Judith having an affair? "Ask Judith."

"What if she says yes?"

"Don't you trust her?"

"No."

He left promising eternal gratitude. He took the mail with him.

"I come today
Because I feel that way,"
Thinks everyone who comes to stay
Forever. And he gives no weight
To what the world may say:
"You're rather early! You are late!"

Christopher stood stiffly framed in the front window cradling the cat when Morgan and Terence drove up to the door. The two had picnicked at Morgan's pond. Christopher was sipping whiskey. He crossed to the sofa and waited. They entered in silence, having spotted him lurking among the leaves.

"I've been calling for *days*," Christopher explained loudly. "*Where* have you been, T.?"

"Here and at Morgan's."

Why *are you sitting there? Watch it, Kukla.*

Christopher rose to shake hands: "Good to see you again, Morgan. I've been thinking about you lately."

"I've been thinking about you, too."

"Many of the same thoughts, I'm sure," he smiled wickedly. Pulling back, he added: "*So!* What have you been up to, T.?"

"Working . . . reading . . . the usual things."

Christopher nodded and awkwardly sat down.

Terence watched gimlet-eyed from across the room. *Sad. Sad watching someone you love die. Or sad not able to make him stop?*

You've been drinking was what he thought to say. With pleasure he realized he was not about to say it.

He knows. He knows. He knows.

"I thought you died on me," Christopher lurched ahead, looking uneasy. "Then I decided you had the phone unplugged. He pulls the phone out of the wall, Morgan. It always makes me upset."

Terence smiled. Unable to form any sentence suitable for exporting, he nodded and recited, "I'm sorry you feel that way." Morgan sat, perplexed and obviously concerned.

Should I leave? This is between them. See what happens. Perhaps I can help him. . . them. So clearly them.

"I called Gerald," Christopher laughed, "and *he* met me at the station. Your car was here in the garage. He said he saw you this morning. He looked insane. He gave me our mail. Why did Gerald have *our* mail?"

"He took it by mistake," Terence flatly reported, ignoring the plural pronoun. "I've been with Morgan, Chris. The weather was suddenly glorious."

"Yes, it is." Christopher smiled like an understanding parent.

I'll bet *you've been with Morgan!*

"So! T., what have you two been up to?"

Barely got that out, bub. Not a glance between them. Guilty as hell Knowing T., it's love. Always all or nothing. Got to marry him to hold his nuts . . . to see the rest of him. . . .

"Terence, I think you and Christopher should be alone."

"Don't leave, Morgan!" Christopher pleaded, louder than he intended. He was uncertain of what he wanted to happen, and he was frightened; that he did not want. The three whiskies on the train confused rather than clarified; they increased the panic that propelled him to Grand Central when Terence did not answer the phone. Although the panic was justified, he regretted the drinks. He wanted to deny them. He wanted to lie. He wanted the glass on the table to disappear. He wanted their confession but feared posing the leading question. *He* wanted to make a confession, then felt righteous. Big deal, it was true. Booze made things worse. He should have stuck at one. The last thing he wanted was to goad anyone into an argument without understanding how.

". . . keep the tension high enough to warrant the next drink," that Crawford clone drawled from her podium inside his head. She had said something about tension at the meeting he left after Act One.

"Please, don't leave, Morgan," he repeated, bewildered by his own thoughts. How that female flushed into his brainpan was beyond his ken, and undeniably the most disturbing element in this sordid mess. "Terry, please, Terry, make some *strong* coffee."

Terence quickly moved into the kitchen. He had not said a word, but he wondered if black smoke was pouring from his ears. He was angry at Christopher, drunk or sober, for disrupting the day. And the damned sadness was gouging deeper by the second.

Plowing my heart. Enough! Like I've abandoned a wounded sparrow in a thicket Oy! *Avoid cheap metaphor, please?*

"Terence, you did real *good,* kid!" he whispered to himself. "Terence, are you there?"

Poor Chris. Nothing I can do for you, Chris That *is what's sad! OK to feel sad, Kukla. Life is sad sometimes. But watch it!*

At the window, he spread his hands in a stage gesture of helplessness. Across the footlights, he watched himself in the costume of a medieval chatelain from a mystery play performed at Yale. He scattered keys that for him had no locks. He then waved good-bye.

Everybody, go home, will ya? Let yourselves out. Self-deception? Nope. I feel air all around me. I'm free. I set myself free. On with my life. Take people as they are .Say good night Danvers.

"How's the coffee coming?" Christopher called.

"Nearly ready!" he lied, hastily lighting the kettle. "You taking sugar these days?"

"Four lumps, giant ones."

Four lumps, giant ones? *Sugar is poison! He is out of his gourd. Sugar* is—Christ! *Terence, shut up! Mind your own goddamn business.*

"Make teatime," he instructed himself aloud, reciting:

"'Under certain circumstances there are few hours in life more agreeable than the hour: dedicated to the ceremony known as afternoon tea.'"

When he delivered the coffee, he was calm and ostensibly relaxed. Morgan and Christopher were discussing snow. To avoid a relapse, Terence busied himself with the cups and the napkins and the cookies and the spoons, carrying each from the kitchen separately to keep the show traveling. Morgan and Christopher switched the subject to cats. Terence methodically sorted the mail. There was a letter from Bobbi and one from Rudd Rooney.

My three men . . . together again . . .

Christopher grabbed his hands. "You're so funny when you're angry, T. Please don't be angry with me. I'm sorry for busting in here like this. I really want to get well."

Well, *notice, as in sick.*

Terence dared look in his eyes. He found confusion and remorse and fear in great quantity. He compared the expressions to schools of fish darting around in the depths of a pool; he didn't know one fish from another. How could he tell *what* Christopher was feeling beyond the obvious unhappiness? Terence could not read the man's mind. All he was certain of was nothing he said or did could punish Christopher as much as he was now punishing himself. Terence glanced at Morgan. Morgan was occupied with Whiting.

"I'm not angry with you, Christo. I love you."

"Good! I love you, too. And, I'm angry enough at myself for all three of us." The three laughed. Christopher squeezed Terence's hands, then hastily raised them to his lips.

Tell me it's not too late.

"You're too good to me, T. Everyone says so."

"Don't believe what those people tell you. Most of 'em are five-cent jawbreakers."

Morgan stroked the cat and registered how long it was before the younger men unclasped hands. He recorded every nuance, not missing a pulsebeat, not heeding his aching heartbeat.

Them. Truly. The room is charged. They are.

The three drank the weak coffee, ate the cookies, and spoke of innocuous things. Each assiduously avoided particular corners, knowing the others were smart enough to play the room.

I want you both. Impossible.

Got to marry him to tickle his cooze. . . to sniff his wuss.

Them.

HAPPYBIRTHDAYTOOUHAPPYBIRTHDAY
A BIRTHDAY NOTETTE FOR DEARONE:
C. is with me. We send our best wishes. Morgan says hullo.

C. arrived unannounced and uninvited 3 days ago. Morgan and I skipped back here and found a lit C. perched on the couch. Now that I've stepped out of his mirror, I think maybe he's beginning to see what's going on. Who knows? I don't have a clue what he's going through so how can I make it better? M. stayed for din. We had a neat-o time. (Can you stand all this birthday cheer?) C. asked me if I thought we 3 should get into a bed. I said no. The idea titillates but I said no. I'm afraid. Yup, afraid. God only knows what would happen afterward. What would we do for an encore? Meanwhile, I'm a one-man person one at a time. One man is a sky full of stars! C. loves to see me shocked. He saw me shocked.

We're getting along fabulously. Everything's changed. We've

been talking. He's now taking Antabus. We talk about guilt, the way we both employ it. We talk about manipulation. If he continues to drink, and he may, things can never be the same as they were. I'm fascinated to see how dependent I'm becoming on M. for all kinds of things. I'm having trouble ordering from a menu again! I don't like it.

I love them both.

I forget how much C. makes me laugh. I'm sure one reason our titanic relationship has kept afloat in its sea of ice cubes is the humor. How can you not love someone with whom you laugh a lot?

I'm not sneaking out to meet M. in the tick-infested woodshed.

C. and M. like each other. I think. He hasn't asked. I haven't told. I keep waiting (hoping?) for the Confrontation Scene. I miss the drama of the drinking sometimes. I see me in between, holding them apart *or* C. holding his drooped head while M. weeps, crazed. Something tells me it ain't gonna be, pal, because I don't want it anymore. Not what I say, what I do. I honestly don't try to know what is going to happen. I play things one day at a time. Life is like Parcheesi. . . .

Judith and G. have invited us three male friends to din tomorrow. We all said yes. We're a model nuclear family. Who will win custody of Le Strange?

Happy Birthday. I've sent you a large breakable package but the pieces won't be there on the day.

What else is new?

xxxxtoddyxxxx

P.S. Lest you think me stronger than I am, mucho meetings and many calls help. I feel serene about everything . . . he said. There really is a Power greater than myself. My Others guide me.

TWELVE

Saturday, the spring rains began to fall.

Terence and Christopher settled in front of a wood and peat fire talking. For three hours after lunch, Terence napped while Christopher read Virginia Woolf's letters.

As if hypnotized, Whiting crouched for six hours in front of the refrigerator waiting for a cornered vole to make a run for it.

Morgan allowed himself to sleep late. At noon he called Terence to confirm their evening plans. He was to pick them up at seven. He spoke quickly, never alluding by word or inflection to the pained confusion that kept him stirred through the sleepless night. The intimacy created by Terence's softly modulated voice gave him hope. He could not bear to be discarded.

After hanging up the phone, he fantasized a *ménage à trois*. Realizing neither he nor Terence could sustain such a complex arrangement—he could not speak for Christopher—Morgan rejected the plan and returned to his original objective of separate yet integral. In the four hours after lunch, he blocked out a month's Sunday strips, a task that usually took days.

Judith and Gerald made love before descending for breakfast, though they heard the children carousing outside the bedroom door impatient for admittance. Gerald had promised a drive to the library while Judith did some produce shopping in the village. Husband and wife were thoughtful and considerate of one another all morning. They delegated the more unpleasant dinner-party tasks to the cook hired for the occasion. They held hands in the village. They kissed twice on Main Street.

At the day's finish, the children reeled from the strain of the unceasing amicability. Each had tensely waited for the ridiculing phrase or the upturned eyes; they were drained silly by their expectations. They ate their dinners in dejected silence. Hurrying to their separate rooms, they were eager to discuss this confusing detente that any moment could blow up in their faces. They met in Deirdre's quarters. Both scented danger. What they had witnessed was forced and unnatural and too damn polite. Who was placating whom?

What is *coming down*?

———

Dominic scraped the kitchen floor with a dull steak knife. He planned to spend the day cleaning; the kitchen seemed the most sensible place to begin. It and the bathroom were the filthiest rooms, the rooms most abused by William. Dominic worked to lift a noodle ground into the linoleum. It was a remnant of his tuna casserole prepared for the previous night's dinner, the dinner William refused to eat at 8 P.M., then found irresistible at 1 A.M.

Walking into the kitchen this morning, Dominic found the oven heated to 350 degrees, the gouged-out casserole trailed across the top of the stove, splattered over the walls, the window, the floor, and stuffing up the drain in the sink. He found bits of grated cheese like a snowfall in every corner, as well as stuck to the thorns of his flowering cactus. Wine droplets like acid tears ate into the varnish on the table. A broken glass glinted in the trash alongside two good forks, a silver serving spoon, and the remaining quarter-pound chunk of provolone.

He cried. He cried for the mess he had to face every morning. He cried for the hours he had to spend cleaning; *and for what?* So he could live in a stinking pigsty with a man who made everything disgusting? And *that* was only the beginning! The bathroom floor around the toilet bowl was clotted with piss and vomit and diarrhea. The clothes in the hamper stank from the shit stains, and the gin sweated out through William's pores. The tub was grimed by flaking skin and falling hair. And the living room! Just the thought of his beautiful furniture ruined beyond repair, burned and cut, reeking of cigarettes and gunge and dropped food and overturned gallons of wine, gin, Manhattans, vodka martinis—*years* of spilled drinks pouring their miserable lives away. Just the thought made more tears splash onto the floor. He had to stop crying. Tears blurred the wax's sheen.

There were so many hurts. Not all the scratches and nicks and burns and stains in their home could come close to the total. Dominic performed a detailed litany in his head. Throughout the day, while he washed and polished, he recalled as many injuries as he could, fueling his anger to propel himself through the loneliness until William awoke and they could be together on this, their favorite day of the week.

———

Bobbi whistled while she worked. Baking pies demanded intense concentration, and the old times were the best tunes. The gang was converging to celebrate one of the guys' birthdays. The official cake was a six-pack of beer covered with chocolate frosting, but the special treat was Edelston's apple pie. There would be no telephone calls or unannounced visits this morning. Word had spread that she was peeling and cutting and magically seasoning; not a soul dared interrupt.

Kneading, she paused. Had she pinched enough salt? These were full-dress maneuvers! Not only was there a major reputation to uphold, but also Michele was expected, and in the past few encounters every initial impression had been confirmed in spades.

Be still my heart!

Besides, last night Davey had stopped by after his meeting to talk to her about this and that and he said Howard had told him that *she* adored apple pie and made a mean one herself, being a farm girl from Idaho. Bobbi added a pffffft more salt. She whistled a whippoorwill call, then resumed an uptempo "The Way You Look Tonight." Challenges were fun.

Gerald pressed his point: "One drink can't hurt you, Chris. You've got to learn to drink in moderation, like everyone else. Nothing can hurt you if you do it in moderation," he advised, grinning broadly, offering an iced martini for the third time.

"No, thank you, Gerald. I'm fine with the tamarind."

"But. . ."

"Gerald, darling," Judith called from across the room. "He said *no*."

Tito, where are you when I need you?

"But Judy, I only want. . ."

Sissies *all*.

"We *know* what you want, Gerald," Terence quipped, losing his patience but reclaiming it and maneuvering from his original intent. "We won't think you a rotten host if none of us is *plotzed* when we sit down to dinner."

Everyone laughed. Morgan smiled approvingly at him for not slamming yet managing to make a strong statement. Christopher zoomed in on that affirmative glance; he flushed with annoyance. This furry chap, this home wrecker, this *homme fatal* was most definitely a threat, a serious menace to his established position. Now that he, Christopher More, was over the shock of Terence's involvement with another man, it was time for action swift and deadly. He must remain sober to keep his eyes bright, focused, sharp, peeled for funny business, monkey business, hanky-panky, kibitzing, whatever.

A fuck is a fuck, right? Wrong! He loves him.

He had said nothing *yet* because there seemed no point to belaboring the obscenely obvious. *Not to mention monogamy* (and he *would* mention it, since he was being brutally honest about all this nonsense). *He* had never pretended to kneel in that pew. It was Terence who plucked the harp on that altar since old Caspar was a pup. What was happening to all the old virtues?

I have to do something. What? I'll think of something, something mean, lowdown, and dirty.

Conversation was erratic. Everyone was preoccupied.

My life is L'Avventura *on American Express.*
She promises she loves archery.
Six months with each?
Castration would be convenient.
Them.

The party rose to go into dinner. Terence and Morgan, discussing the magnetic pull of marigolds on butterflies, gracefully fell in behind Judith and Gerald. Christopher roughly clasped Terence's arm and yanked him from Morgan's side.

"May I have this dance, T.?"

Startled, Terence stiffened. Linking his free arm with Morgan's, be glowered at Christopher, then loudly informed him that his dance card was filled.

"Shall we *all* do the continental, you gay *divorcé?*" Christopher curtsied, chastised, but he narrowed his eyes with matching theatrical ferocity.

"Yes!" Terence smirked, hissing the final consonant. "What a *clever* idea. Is it OK with you, Morgan? Chris More is the foxiest trotter I know."

"I don't know if I can keep up with you two," Morgan smiled.

"Do try, Mr. C.," Christopher sweetly encouraged. "Let's all start off on our left foot. And let's not bend our knees when we kick out. That way Toddy will feel more at home."

"Please don't *skip*, Chris!"

"Lions and tigers and bears, *oh, my!*"

Inside the dining room, Judith and Gerald stared dumbly at the flowered oval table. They ignored the fracas caused by three grown men, arms tightly knit, squeezing through the narrow passage. The costumed maid meekly apologized for the sixth place inadvertently set. The five voted not to undo it: an invitation to the uninvited, whom Christopher fervently hoped would be Savonarola. The empty seat separated Gerald from Judith. They held hands across the breach.

While the maid cleared the soup bowls, Judith told the men that Gerald planned to convert Gerald, Jr.'s, fortress into a studio. She also mentioned that her much-needed vacation was ready to roll. Italy for three weeks: Milan.

"Will you be going, Gerald?" Christopher asked, to make conversation, not trouble.

"No," Gerald cheerfully responded, adeptly pronging a prime rib.

Freud was right. Women are less moral than men. She's going with her lover. Nothing I can do.

"She's going with some friends. I can't get away just now."

"Anyone *we* know?" Morgan quickly asked, noticing Gerald's preoccupation with the carving knife.

Silly cow! Only a fool would start something at our age. We're too old for all this grief.

"Someone from the office?"

"No!" Judith smiled, gaining an eyelock and holding without flinching.

You of all people must understand.

"Some friends in the industry."

"I *love* Italy!" Terence interjected, grinning at the roast potatoes, wishing he were anywhere else.

Wonder what he looks like?

"I hope it doesn't rain."

"Judith, you'll have a *great* time!" Christopher shouted, convivially touching her hand.

Fuck like bunnies, you will. Rain and shine Hoopla! Hi-jinks! Like these two. Shit! Will one glass of goddamn Burgundy really make that much difference?

"Here's to us!" he shouted, raising his Perrier.

I hope you all get the clap!

Monday morning, Judith and Christopher returned to Manhattan. Gerald drove them to the station. Terence waved good-bye from the begonia-filled bay window.

Alone, he wandered from room to room, picking up towels and scattered clothing, hoping to gather enough for a colored load. Bored, he settled for sheets and pillowcases; a wash would get the day off to a rousing start. He was riddled by separation anxiety. For ten minutes, he chased the cat around the house playing hide-and-seek.

Take small steps.

He wanted to call Morgan. Terence knew that would make him feel better. Morgan always made him feel better. He rephrased the thought, taking responsibility for his own feelings. He resolved to call Thomas. He had to solve these problems, not ask someone to take them away. At five past nine, the phone rang. It was Bobbi.

"Well?" she asked without a greeting.

"Well, what?"

"Don't get smart."

He related all the gossip. "I have never seen them so flashy with their affection. They actually *kissed* between courses! She sat *in his lap* during the coffee-in-the-music-room scene."

"You think they'll sell the house?"

"Never. He'll remarry and stay. Mater would not swing for a third."

"Did you see Morgan yesterday?"

"No. He never called."

"He wouldn't."

"No. I suppose not."

"Seeing him today?"

"I don't know."

"Want to?"

"Yes."

He'd better call.

"What's with Chris?"

"Everything. I don't know what's going to happen."

"Did I ask?"

"Isn't that why you called?"

"No. *That* is not why I called."

There was a long pause.

"OK. Why'd you call?"

"I *called* to invite you to our justly famous and much loved Cherry Blossom Festival."

"I don't believe this."

Bobbi laughed. "Why not? I'm being serious. You've never seen the blossoms."

"Here I am . . ."

"It would do you good to get away."

". . . my heart in the washer with the sheets . . ."

"If it doesn't *snow* like it did last year, it'll be fun."

". . . at a major crossroad . . ."

"Oh, brother!"

"I'll think about it. Actually, it's not a bad idea."

"Thanks."

"When is it?"

"Two weeks."

It was not a bad idea, he mused, two hours later, staring from his desk into the back garden. A fresh page of yellow legal-size paper was on top of a neat pile. On the bottom line of the piece underneath it was the last sentence he had finished Friday afternoon. Geoff was writing a letter confessing an infidelity and asking Hildy for advice.

Never give advice, Hildy. Share strengths and hope.

He pressed down with his lead pencil, intending to stop after the letter; it neatly segued into an amusing (and pivotal) confrontation he had planned for later in the narrative but found more natural now. It all cleaved together nicely. Three hours gone, a chapter ended. Exhilarated, he reread the work, making minor adjustments.

Not bad. First draft nearly completed. Don't know if it works. Find out later. Why can't I manage my life this smoothly? Why don't you try, lover?

Dominic Perrugio shuffled the papers on his desk, looking for the union's schedule of contract negotiations. He was sick from exhaustion and could barely sit up in the leather chair. Leaning forward, he pressed his arms on the neat piles of paper, loose and stapled, before closing his eyes in exasperation.

The weekend had been unspeakably awful. William, drunk the entire two days, had not allowed him to sleep. Every time Dominic dozed, his disturbed friend turned on lights, shouted in pretended nightmare horror, slammed him with an elbow, pulled the covers away, or—the worst—dumped a glass of water on him when he dared move to the couch.

"Why are you doing this?" Dominic had raged.

William drunkenly shrugged and mumbled that he did not know and could not sleep himself and wanted company.

At three that very morning, Dominic punched William in the face, knocking him unconscious. Dominic had spent the rest of the night weeping in the dark kitchen awaiting the cold dawn.

Rage eroded his mind. After such a weekend, to have to call William's school and make excuses—the flu this time—had been the end. Hearing himself lying for the thousandth time spun him into a vortex *of* self-loathing. Why did he stay with the man? Why did he not leave? He got nothing from William. Why hang around hoping for a miracle? William would never stop drinking. He denied he had a problem. Why stay to be shit upon? Was he a masochist? It was his home. He loved his home. But they fought constantly. What kind of a home was that? They never went out. They had no friends left. Every conversation revolved around the drinking. William barely ate. Why did he bother to cook? William sat. He just sat in his reclining chair in the living room drinking away his evenings, *their* evenings, boozing away his life, *their* only life.

"Dear God," Dominic prayed, "how much longer?"

He began to cry. Sitting at his desk, facing the emptiness of his life, he wept. He was trapped. William was deliberately destroying him, destroying them. There was but one way out. At some breaking point during the endless night, he had plotted to murder William. Fleetingly, he thought of it now. William's swollen body was constantly damp, slimy from the excess alcohol discharged through the epidermis. If a wet limb touched a live wire, perhaps just *brushed* against one, could the jolt cause death? Dominic knew enough about electricity to construct a detailed set. With lethal wires dangling like slender silver cobwebs from lamps and cabinets, tied to metal doorknobs, or tucked between the toaster's lips, William would prepare his last midnight snack. By means of one tiny wire, Dominic could be free.

Easy. I want him dead. Before he kills me.

He crumpled a piece of paper. Opening his eyes, he recognized the missing schedule. If he hoped to be prepared for the meeting, he had to begin immediately. Wiping his eyes, he blew his nose and rang for his secretary. She seemed to buy his story about a bad cold. She had heard that Mr. Perrugio lived with another man, a schoolteacher, a college professor who drank too much. Her father was an alcoholic. She sympathized with her boss. She knew what bastards drunkards could be.

Morgan Connelly gazed out the window from his drawing board. He was oversensitive to the first signs of spring. The colors were lighter; the sun looked closer. It was Louis's favorite season. For the first time, he missed him with a sorrow devoid of pain. He closed his eyes and sat with Louis on the bench by the pond.

"I don't love you less."

"I know."

"I feel good when I think of you."

"I'm glad. That's how it's supposed to be. Stop grieving and love me again."

"Yes. I love again."

"Good-bye, Morgan."

"Good-bye, Louis. I love you."

"I know."

He opened his eyes and smiled. His heart felt lighter, roomier; he pictured a large field filled with goldenrod. Glancing at the clock, he sighed. One o'clock. Rereading the storyboard, he scrutinised his own work, then resumed studying the variations in hue on the oak bark outside. Stratis the gardener, returning from lunch, appeared on the path from amid the birch trees.

Punctual as always.

Since the beginnings of his professional career, Morgan followed a daily routine from which he rarely deviated: Three hours a day, from ten in the morning to one, were allocated for work. He allowed nothing else during these hours. If the projects were going well, the three became the twelve he usually spent sitting at his drawing board; if the work moved haltingly, the rule compelled him to give as much attention as he could manage. He discovered while at Princeton how he detested wasting time. Faced with three full hours, he compulsively imposed order and usually did productive work.

Today was a perfect example. He had no desire after breakfast to do anything but call Terence. He had not kissed his boy in what seemed a month. He knew Christopher had returned to New York City with Judith: The arrangements had been finalized over dinner. He, Morgan, identified the lonely stillness in his own house as the one Terence must be experiencing in his own. Yet Morgan would not break that silence by telephoning.

Nothing as unattractive as desperation. Not that I'm desperate. Nowhere near.

Sunday he had expected to be a miserable day, yet he had awakened with a small idea that he parlayed into a new series for the daily strip, putting himself a full month ahead of schedule. He surged with energy while he drew. He recognized the feeling as happiness, and had been cognizant of a tremendous sense of freedom. It was not the first time states of mind were revealed over the drawing board. The work was good.

He knew that no matter what occurred between him and Terence, the pleasure of loving was worth any upset. He was no longer alone. He would never be alone again. If Terence could not sustain the sexuality in their intimacy, he would still remain a beloved, trusted friend. Could Morgan doubt it after the firmness with which Terence hugged his arm on Saturday night, or after the sweet way they kissed good night (on the brow) while Christopher pouted on the doorstep? These had not been acts of defiance. They were assertions of their right to a discrete relationship.

Now, however, there was a dangerous ache in Morgan's chest. It was always difficult not to have one's life on one's own terms. It was asinine to underestimate the tyranny of love. He was aware that Terence was fighting a battle to reconstruct his boundaries. Morgan would not call. He would not trespass. He would not attempt to influence the outcome. Terence had to decide for himself what he wanted. He had to ask; only then would he be able to receive.

Lifting a pencil, Morgan jammed it into the electric sharpener. Then, quickly, he sketched a fair likeness of Terence's face. Without pausing, he continued stroking downward, drawing the narrow neck and the shoulders, stretching the slender arms open but curving them like pinned wings. Lovingly, he circled the nipples, flicking the lead to create the fine hairs on the hard chest. The curve of the right rib cage descended into the slightly rounded pelvic area—its hollow navel a balancing circle to the two directly above—then rose to the hilly muscles of the right thigh. He extended the thin line over the ridge of the knee to the slim ankle, ending it at the high instep after carefully detailing five short, straight toes. Completing the right leg with one sinuous stroke, he skipped the genitals to slope down the arcs of the inner left leg, then up again with symmetrical precision to connect hip, waist, and left side to the poised waiting arm. The legs strained against the paper's edges.

He studied the figure. It could be leaping into the air. It could be sprawled in the sun on a beach. It could be sleeping. It could be. . . .

He dropped the pencil. Staring at the drawing, he made a fist of his left hand and tapped the board.

Christopher More, poet, home through the day, recumbent in bed and propped by six pillows, tracked a word's derivation in his *Concise OED*. After locating its correct usage, he squeezed a notation into the margin of the bound galleys, then diligently resumed reading. He had received the novel to review two weeks earlier, the very day he returned from visiting Terence.

His piece of drek had been sent by messenger from a prestigious literary magazine to which, in more reliable days, he was a frequent contributor. Gladdon Frye, editor and college chum, had been discovered at a recent meeting. (When asked to lead the Lord's Prayer, Christopher had declined the honor, saying truthfully that he disremembered the lyrics, to no one's amusement but Gladdon's.) The note enclosed with the set of galleys made no reference to their collision but seemed freighted with hidden messages. The "hope you are well" seemed particularly ominous.

Christopher loathed the novel but was uncertain whether to be bitchy or kind because he could not remember why he loathed it. All the scrupulous notes did not help him retain the basics of the plot; they did not even help him to keep the characters straight. His memory was obviously fading fast, an unsettling fact he could not deny as each word of the book in his trembling hands vanished into a black hole in his mind's inner space. He could not remember the last book he had been able to finish.

They occupy the hand not holding the drink.

He tried to convince himself that Gladdon wanted a nasty review. Was Christopher More not famous for his karate mouth? He wanted to call Gladdon to ask for an extension but he hesitated. Had the editor not mentioned in his note that this was a print week: He was frightfully busy; lunch next week? Besides, the thought of speaking to Gladdon made him rubescent from top to toe with rebarbative guilt and confusion. He had not attended a meeting since bumping into him haloed in salvation and cigarette smoke. Christopher had said he was not a true believer ("Just looking. Window shopping."). It was not as though he had lied to lasso the scruffy assignment. Gladdon had nodded sagely, smugly, hatefully, as if he had just signed Jesus to do a piece on Transubstantiation.

Always was a prissy shit.

Christopher was tippling for the past two weeks—steadily, but "stylishly," as a precaution against the mean reds which lately were savage. The month of Perrier or seltzer with tamarind, and only the occasional nip ("no deep potation") had worked miracles. He had no intentions of revisiting the Eumenides whose crag he had inhabited for aeons. He suspected he could control his bibbing once he got a healthy grip on it. He had been inebriate only twice; neither bout had been his doing.

Lunch with his father to pick up the monthly stipend and the rent check had ended badly. He took the subway up to Bill's and was appalled at the unkempt state of the man: He looked eighty.

The blood vessels in his cheeks had burst, giving him a whorish, raddled look; his rheumy eyes bulged in the puffy face under the drastically thinning, filthy hair. Their meeting was for noon. By two, both were besotted on the couch. His father's deterioration haunted him for days.

The second bacchanalia was with friends. He had talked animatedly and lost count of the refills because he was trying to keep track of the number of sniffs he had of coke. That night there had been no mind left. Usually four drinks were his limit. It was the fifth that knocked him over the top into the blue ruin; the fifth forced the sixth; the fifth was the killer. (Julie G. had insisted it was the first that was to blame. Evidently, he and Julie G. had different metabolisms.)

He tossed the galleys across the room. "I don't care if that gesture went out with Mrs. Fiske!" he shouted, climbing out of bed. "It makes me feel good and that is the primary function of life on this orb!"

It was five o'clock. He filled the tub and lifted the phone off its hook so as not to be interrupted during his aulic ablutions. On his way back to the bathroom, he fixed himself a cocktail, which was billed the first drink of the day. He didn't rate the swig upon awakening at noon—that was medicinal, "to quiet me nerves and get me activated." While he soaked in the bubble bath, he sipped and dreamed of his new friend, Matthew, due at six. He knew to expect a deliciously heavy date which would demand especial care with the stiff brush and the washcloth. They planned a pizza and the Oscars on TV.

Two nights before, or was it three?, he had gone to a new lavender bar in the east Sixties for just-one smart infiusion to help him unwind ("I require the company of serious Uptown Women."); and for a giggle at the ritzy divas trying to be "chick" while crammed into a perfumed space the size of a service elevator decorated with clusters of blue amorini; *and* to get out of the house where he was edging toward antsy. He had spent an hour reworking those "booze-soaked" poems; he felt virtuous ("I always feel strong when I write."), not up to consenting-adult adventures, yet hungry for a pretty face or a few kind words or a morale-boosting flirtation. He had heard Committee Room was not like the other bars; for him it was: Too loud, too frantic, not the kind of place you could take your mother if you had one.

Matthew approached at the bar and smoothly began the chit-chat. Tall and slim with gigantic jet velvet eyes the color of his skin, he had a smile that draped plump sensuous lips over perfect white teeth "to make you cream." (Christopher was enchanted by strong, straight white "keyboards." Sporting a crooked lower grouping and mostly uneven uppers, he dreamed M-G-M caps when he became less frightened of pain.) Teeth and eyes were what he noticed first in a man; Matthew got full marks. And when those buffed ivories were parted, a deep luscious baritone was heard; Christopher tightened the grip on his glass. Matthew ordered refills, leaving the change from the twenty on the bar. He gulped his drink and called for another. He looked a peer, but one could never be certain: The masterful lighting burned soft pinks, and warm golds to shoo away time's relentless claw, encouraging dreamtime. As he spoke above the din, he revealed an attractive intelligence, and Christopher recognized an empathic personality. Matthew was employed in Manhattan's Civil Service. He lived but two short blocks away.

"Everyone is paranoid in the Service," he explained after the introductory patter, having flattered Christopher by a respectable knowledge of his work, a knowledge deeper than "Knightgiggle."

"All the day, every day, we interview angry people. So what the fuck do you expect, baby? My lover couldn't hack it. He split after four years. I'd come home most nights too down to do anything but drink. Told me to quit. Both the booze and the job. I transferred into what I thought would be a better office, Professional Services, but it's only more of the same. I've been in nearly fourteen years and I'm practically ready to retire. I'd be a lunatic to quit with all that time behind me. Now we're all afraid of being beaten or shot at our desks. We represent The Man. It's not pleasant, baby, believe me. Want another?"

"I never *see* the lower orders," Christopher mused.

"Well, you are one lucky guy," Matthew whispered drunkenly. "Let me buy you another."

Since the mugging, Christopher rarely went to bars with more than ten dollars in his pocket. It was a practical way of limiting his intake. He graciously accepted Matt's offer to buy, then decided he would take care of the last round, the nightcap. (He thought of his father: "Nightcap" was a word his father often used.) The two men moved from the bar into a quieter corner. They spoke for another half hour before Matthew invited him to his apartment. Christopher accepted without hesitation. He did not spend the night. They fumbled on the couch until Matthew was finished, then Christopher inscribed some books and walked home.

Tonight, bobbing in his tub, he ruminated with growing pleasure on Matthew's company. The swell man had called that afternoon to ask if the poet would sign copies of his new book for friends. He had not minded that Christopher did not remember who he was. The deep, warm laughter awakened sense memories, or so Christopher swore. Sex was on his mind. He hoped he could function. Lately, he was not always reliable: The alcohol worked as a stimulant *and* as a depressant—it was very confusing.

The music on the radio swamped him. Mozart's piano concerto number twenty had been in progress all the while; the second movement took his attention. He drifted in the water like a long white reed, aching for Terence to scoop him up. Wherever this music was, he saw them naked together, entwined in front of the fireplace, lazily loving in their warm country house with a Currier & Ives winter-day backdrop, while Rosina Lhevinne's recording played over and over. After a third spin of the second movement, Terence had decreed: "The Messiah has come. Now it's our turn."

"The things one remembers," Christopher mumbled, draining the tumbler. "Heigh-ho! Imagine that! Just like in the movies!"

Wrapped snugly in a huge emerald-green towel, he snapped off the radio by switching on the record player. He selected Welitsch's *Salome* which seemed more appropriate to his darkening mood, and set it for continual replay. His profound love for Terence shot steely spears of jealousy that cut him deeply. The whole thing was infuriating. His love fused with anger and rattled through him. It was strongest now that he stood perilously close to losing it. Life without Terence would be crack-your-cheeks cold *for* a very long time, perhaps—dare he say it?—for eternity. He was startled by the violence of his rage at Terence for this emotional involvement with the barbate Connelly. He was hurt, badly traduced, and would moderate the sauce to end it—bloodily, if necessary. Rearing his head, he bellowed: "I'm so *bored* with Judea!"

But not tonight. Tonight he would forget his troubled soul and get riotously happy real fast. One of their friends was nominated for Best Actress and was a sure bet according to everyone in the know. Christopher phrased his congratulatory telegram to Joan Barbara. Pausing as he distractedly rooted around his closet in search of his trousers, he decided he would stay relatively sober: "The better to call T. when Joanie wins, my dears," he sang, extending the final sibilance to harmonize with Salome and the intercom's buzz. He was in very good voice. Suddenly, his tops were back.

It was Matthew. He rang his guest up and fixed himself another tumbler.

"You're early, toots."

"Sorry, baby. I called to ask if it was OK but your line was busy. Am I *too* early? I walked as slow as I could. This neighborhood is help-me *fabulous!* No lower orders crawling 'round here! Why is the park locked? Christ! Is that a genuine Pollock? I've never seen so many books outside a public library!"

The living room, overlooking Gramercy Park, contained several thousand volumes in floor-to-ceiling oak cases that were constructed around a large drip painting by Jackson Pollock. (Terence had bought the work with the first book's paperback money. Christopher had understood the seriousness of the situation on the home front when Terence packed his bags and separated himself from their beloved painting.) Additional books were piled on and under the tables and the Barcelona chairs; mounds were crammed into corners; one heap was a pedestal for an empty shot glass; dozens lay scattered on the blue and alizarin orange carpet like lounging friends; and slim ones were lodged between the thriving plants on the wide sills of the immense front windows.

"The Pollock is authentic. My fellow Irishman's saintly light blesses our home sweet home. He was, you know, a real McCoy on his father's side crossed with a good McClure. The Pollocks adopted his daddy. And now we've adopted him! Ain't life amazing?"

"Sure is, baby." Matthew chuckled. He was glad he'd stopped for a few drinks before coming up; Christopher was obviously a few paces into the party. The painting was awesome. The whole set-up intimidated him. The poet was clearly monied. He wasn't surprised. Christopher More was a classy guy.

Who's the "we," I wonder?

"We read a lot, Matt. The park's locked against the populace. It's the only key park left in this town."

"You must spend a fortune on books," Matthew exclaimed.

"No . . . not really. We know dozens of people in the industry. We do buy *some,*" he gestured grandly as he crossed toward the bedroom, detouring to lower the music a jot and to drop the phone back into its cradle. "I'll get dressed."

"What's your hurry, baby?" Matthew asked, approaching.

"Aren't you hungry?"

"Yup. For this," he whispered, patting Christopher's butt.

The phone rang.

"Don't answer it, baby." Matthew produced a quart of Jameson's from a pocket before removing his pea coat. The two friends swigged while waiting for the phone to die. "I remembered you like the Irish, so I brought a little to get us started."

"Started on what? Ending civilization as we know it?"

"You kill me, Christopher."

"I might say the same of you, toots, but *I* know better."

"What's that mean, baby?"

"Skip it. Drop your drawers, Kong."

Half a bottle later, interlocked on the couch, both halted salubrious movements when the intercom buzzed.

"Don't answer it, baby."

"I can't, big boy, unless you carry me."

They laughed as quietly as they could drunkenly manage.

The intercom buzzed again.

"You expecting anybody, baby?"

"Only you, sailor."

They laughed again, louder this time, returning their attentions to the parts in hand.

The doorbell rang. Within seconds, the locks on the door were turned. It swung open to admit Terence, who paused in the hall to free his key.

"Oh, my God!" Christopher gasped, shutting his bleary eyes, unable to move anything else.

Terence noticed the music first. It made him angry. The lights Christopher always left blazing—the brighter the better; usually he was sensible enough to shut off the records. *"Ich habe deine mut gekusst,"* indeed! Where was the party tonight? To his right, something shifted slightly. Evening shadows? He sighted the hunched forms on the couch; they looked like a giant eggplant. Instantly, his anger vanished when he comprehended what he was interrupting. He stood immobile. Stupefied, he opened his mouth to howl. "Sorry," he gurgled, exiting with a sideways shuffle, closing the door with a bang and turning both locks before leaping down the stairs three at a time to run, coat flapping, into the street.

"Who was *he?*" Matthew cautiously whispered.

"My husband, baby."

"Uh-oh! Help *me!* I was afraid of that."

"I need a stiff drink."

Terence flagged a cruising cab and ordered Grand Central. After bumming a cigarette, he realized, to his annoyance, that he was preparing to cry. Stubbing out the "puffer," he had a second thought. Suddenly, he roared with laughter.

The old trouble; things won't fit.

At midnight, moments after Christopher sent Joan the cheering telegram, Matthew headed for home alone. He found his host's rowdy, drunken enthusiasm too much to handle. Fifteen minutes later, "jumping over the wall," Christopher hailed a cab and headed for Brooklyn.

At 12:30 A.M., Dominic dialed the Gramercy Park apartment. He let the phone ring two dozen times before admitting defeat. He would wait until the morning. It was time enough to break the news that Christopher's father was dead.

THIRTEEN

At sunrise on William More's deathday, Terence had half awakened. Bobbi's invitation was accepted. He would take the train from Penn Station at seven that night, arriving in Union Station at ten. Leaving home at three in the afternoon allowed two hours in Manhattan. He needed three books from the apartment, a certain yellow sweater suitable for blossom viewing, and, of course, he hoped to see Christopher.

Morgan had departed for New York on movie business at the beginning of the week; he was scheduled to return during the day—perhaps before his own departure? Terence doted on his friend. He regretted not having taken his Manhattan phone number. The last few times, their meetings had been colored with a pale sorrow, as if Morgan recognized something Terence had not revealed to himself. Was their inevitable end speeding in? Why inevitable? Both concurred, without verbalizing, that a small separation was desired.

The only commitment Terence Strange made was to love Morgan Connelly. They never discussed Christopher More. Terence originally assumed the two men evoked discrete emotions; now he was not cold certain. He knew himself deeply attached to both.

Emotionally, I'm wallpaper. I've just peeled myself off Christopher and now I'm adhering to Morgan. I know the signs.

He deeply loved the older man. Of that he was most positive. The hot flashes, the giddiness, the lungings of the heart were abating, slowly, evolving into a profound happiness, a mellow sense of well-being. Comfort. Comfort was a key word. Why could he not yet comfort himself?

The four days apart had not been easy. He was sexually eager for the man. His dreams had been sweaty; awakening, he was decidedly aroused. A shard of a dream pricked his mind. Running through Manhattan streets, chased by several hooded men, he was fleeing incarceration in a schoolhouse "for his own good." Running, refusing to surrender, he claimed their demands were killing him. Awake, he pondered why he saw the program in those terms. He knew the dream pertained to Morgan Connelly.

Pus-filled depths not yet drained. All is not *hamburger heaven.*

Stretching, he arched his back, wordlessly debating whether or not to pound away his horny self. Lazily, he opted to hoard; orgasms were stronger after a self-imposed mini deprivation. Besides, and more to the heated point, early mornings were not the best time for him: His nerve ends took at least a half hour before swinging a decent synapse. He remembered a conversation with Dominic on the subject; both Mores had chortled over this "fancied" matutinal incapacitation.

Both Mores confuse quantity with quality. Must call Dom this afternoon.

Getting out of bed, he marched sharply to the bathroom and urinated. The distraction from tumescence gone, he curled beneath the coverlet with a black sock for a sleep mask and hugged the purring cat. He dozed. At nine, he ambled down to start the tea. He telephoned Morgan. As expected, there was no answer. After breakfast, he bathed.

He was nearing completion of the novel and felt agitated. Central characters had done everything required of them, points were neatly made, themes connected, but there was no cataclysm in sight. The form, such as it was, required a catastrophe to climax properly. Where was a novel without a disaster? In his first serious book, one fellow went out carelessly with the Atlantic's tide on a mucky Tuesday's dawn in Amagansett. In his second, a complicating factor conveniently stepped off the rear of the *France* at lavender dusk.

If so easy to confuse life with art. Are you listening?

He called Morgan. No answer.

He chased the cat around the house, trying to decide which character's death would pay the highest dramatic dividends. This last-minute reconnoitering had not happened with the other books. Usually he knew from the start who was going to do what to whom, why, and how the repercussions would whirl them to a fade-out. And if he did not know at the beginning, he certainly knew well before the middle.

Must someone die?

He tried Morgan again. Obviously, the man sold his house and moved away. No matter what happened, he knew Morgan would never be unpleasant. He felt safe.

Not even a tape-recorded message?

He asked himself what he wanted. He did not want any-one to die. There were other ways to solve problems, ways that would suggest the power he was convinced human beings could display over their own lives if they found the courage. He decided to follow Morgan's example and set aside three hours a day to be used exclusively for writing. He would solve the problem by letting it solve itself, by working with the characters until an acceptable climax developed. He knew the outcome, it was getting there that troubled him. He would trust himself to figure it out one step at a time. The answer would come to him. He must not force solutions.

He fed the nudging cat. While he stood in the kitchen watching Whiting eat, the phone rang. He leaped for it. It was Andrew.

"*She* wants you."

"How is Judith?"

"*Un*-believable. I wish I had a silver bullet."

"What's wrong?"

"Ev-ry-thing! This place sucks! The plastic shit—"

"Andrew! Formica, Andrew."

"Not you, too, Delia? Plastic is what this shit is, god-damnit, *and* it shimmies and shakes whenever a girl revs up her typewriter! Did you see that *rave* in the *Times?*'

"What for?"

"For this airless hell-hole, Freida. That troll loved every cranny of this overdressed snakepit. He adored the mirrors we're still crashing into. *Loved* the Formica: 'successfully combines utilitarianism with beauty' end quote. I *mean!* Come off it, Roxie! Has that tea-room queen ever carried his tits into an office to do

[302]

anything but fart? Nothing *works right!*"

"I don't read him. Anyone who considers Radio City Music Hall obsolete is a nerd. He's perfect for the *Times. Gelt uber alles. Jawohl.*"

"*Terence?!?*" Judith's voice boomed over their chatter. "He's all yours, Madame de Sade. See ya, honey."

There was a loud bang, as if the receiver had been lobbed into its cradle from across a room.

"Is he gone?" Judith whispered.

"How should *I* know? Andrew?"

There was silence.

"He's gone!" Judith sighed. "He is driving me insane! I'd throw him out a window if only I could open one. 'Environmentally controlled' means *caged,* as in zoo!"

"What is wrong?"

"Ev-ry-thing! Don't ask! Listen, darling, I called for a reason. *Guy* magazine wants a comment on your revelation. I told them I'd wait to see the movie. I also told them to call Amanda. She was your editor *before;* she'll have something florid to say once they drag her in from off the ledge. She probably keeps a phone out there with her. *She* has a window that opens if not much else."

Judith was deranged. She loped over a dozen subjects, pausing to discourse on some favorites: "The world-view of gays is controlled by straight men, darling, because *they* rule the world! The same applies to the world's view of women, darling. And cats! Cats are perceived as *feminine:* aloof, independent, cold. *Dogs* are a man's best friend! Those so-called *men* would shrivel up if they accepted that we all share the same hopes, needs, fears, and desires. Why am I telling *you* this, darling. You told me! You know Gerald's in therapy again?"

"Uh-huh. He told me. When did he start?"

"Eight days ago. He's been seven times in eight days. Doctor Primal says he's facing his mid-life crisis totally unprepared. He promises heavy screaming in store. What about me? *I* am not prepared!"

"I hear they don't scream all that much," Terence said softly, noting how she thrived on the drama of the crazies. He noted further that he had done the same in spades. He squelched his impatience.

"Don't you believe it! One of the editors here has a neighbor who screams all the time, darling. They used to call the gendarmes until they found out she was only doing her homework. He says he's been living with it for two years now and it still startles him, not to mention the dinner guests!" she laughed maniacally. "Gerald's drawing plans for a cork-lined room. I *really* don't care. What am I going to do?"

"You'll think of something."

"Yes, I know I will. I'm workin' on it. Thank you, darling. I have to go now. Andrew is crying. He probably broke a nail. Talk about wanting to sca-ream!"

Sitting on the train to New York City, Terence welcomed a lovely sense of relief. He had received a postcard that morning from Morgan with a traditional electric night view of Manhattan. A message in chancery script blamed hectic conferences for the longer stay and wished him a riotous blossom viewing. Squeezed up the side, obviously an afterthought: "I miss you."

He had never readied Christopher. When he called the apartment at one, the phone was unhooked to avoid interference during the holy hour of soapdom. He should, of course, have dialed earlier. He would call from Grand Central. If Christopher did not want him, he would manage without the books, the sweater, and the visit. He recently noticed he was no longer as rigid as he once was about plans. It was a major accomplishment, this flexibility. He was learning. Perhaps the change had worked into a deeper channel?

Isn't being gay learning to accept alternate routes? I have a head start.

Glancing up the aisle, he snarkily acknowledged his mistake in not settling certain matters before leaving home. The steady vibrations of the heated train had instigated an erection; it happened on buses, too. The disturbing sight of a beauteous young conductor rapidly approaching sent a frisson of sexual longing jerking up the length of his tightly bound carcass. Dizzily unsettled, he shyly glanced into the blond man's hooded violet eyes with their heavy fretting of beige lashes. The man smiled, softly requested the ticket, and absently rested a large suntanned hand with inordinately long fingers and artfully pared nails on the back of the vacant seat opposite. Terence observed the light hairs above the knuckles. Handing over the ticket, he stripped the visitor of the coordinated blue ensemble, then spread him diagonally across that broad, empty beach of a seat. Effortlessly, he lapped among those eternally desirable limbs. Boldly, he hummed:

> *I love the look of you, the lure of you,*
> *I want to take a tour of you. . . .*

A woman spoke. She was somewhere above and behind him and far too close. "Excuse us. Is this seat taken?"

Both young men politely said no. Terence slid closer to the window, allowing her space on the aisle; the sweetheart of a conductor stepped out of his purview. Terence frowned, scolding himself for unseemly behavior in a narrow public place. The extraordinary hand flashed like a golden butterfly in his peripheral vision to snap up the woman's ticket. Terence stared straight ahead.

A disgrace. Can't take me anywhere. Wonder if there's anything wrong with me? Drag him into the toilet! Don't have to act on every impulse. Enjoy the buzz. Bring it home to Morgan. Make it work for you. Rah, team! I love men. . .

The woman carried a small bundle. Carefully adjusting it on her lap, she loosened the wrappings, releasing the disarrayed head of a white Persian cat similar to Terence's but recognizably different. The cat blinked and looked worried. Terence smiled, distracted from his lust by the animal's distress. The woman, in her sixties, was elegantly turned out. She straightened her black fur hat and unfolded the blanket. The cat's right hind leg was strapped to its full extension in a bright red elastic bandage.

"What happened?" Terence asked with honest concern.

"He broke his fibula."

After identifying himself as a fellow-Persian owner, Terence asked several technical questions. The woman explained about cat's paws and fibulas. When he returned to the accident, digging for specifics, she was delighted. Lowering her voice, she graphically detailed the incident, adding the colorful bits eliminated first time around: the height of the cabinet, the carpet, the claw getting snagged, the precise location and the quality of the break.

Terence was enthralled. From the moment he grasped the cat's predicament, he worked himself out of his own. The cat in his book, also a white Persian, was practically a central character. It belonged to the pair of lovers who had temporarily split. To have the animal break its leg was a perfect catastrophe to close the emotional chasm that had opened between its owners. There was something slightly, even perversely farcical about the accident; it would nicely sustain the positive current he wanted in their basically healthy relationship.

When the rewrapped Sam disembarked, Terence dug out his notebook. He outlined the final three chapters, making minor adjustments in the rest to incorporate the new material. His heart dilated with satisfaction. He had his ending. It had come as soon as he released it. It was exactly what he prayed for: no overwhelming *tristesse,* no aching sense of loss, no downpour of brutal reality to scour away delusions; no death, no destruction, and no disillusionment. Time would not be the enemy. There would be sufficient remaining for change. New routes would be prescribed. Happiness would be offered.

Of course Marcel Proust was right. But not today. I don't want it that way this time. Control the things I can.

At five, when he reached Grand Central, he felt elated. It was a mystery the way things connected. As he strolled the thronged main concourse surrounded by racing commuters, he knew he led a blessed existence. Many pages of the new book were devoted to that cat. While writing the dozens of episodes in which the animal played a prominent part, he had been amused and challenged to avoid anthropomorphic "terminal cutes." He knew many of the incidents would be cut, yet he had continued producing them because—and this was the hardest thing to explain—they had made some inner sense. He had intuited their value to the whole.

Only surrender. Things occur, adding to the whole. Everything participates when allowed. Let go. Go with the flow. Go with this flow and you'll end up in New Jersey!

He fought his way to a telephone row. Christopher's line was busy. In the passing crowd, a tall, nicely trimmed man held his eyes. Having been removed from this barrage of humanity, he savored the buzz at the limitless possibilities he had no desire to pursue. He loved the city. He thought of summer with the unveiled, swaying limbs, with the conspicuously sinuous curvings.

Too easy. Too much buffet meat. Ptomaine of the soul. Summer in New York is death. Cut the crap.

A paperback ministore displayed Titania Allgood's titles in their newest uniform reprint ("Could the covers be more tits and a wink vulgar?"). He hunted the rows for his other works with their "sensitive" soft-focus shots of clasped male hands. He wondered which approach to book selling he hated most. He found the books. He stared at his name in print. The pleasure today was exquisite and immense. Opening the first one, he peeked at random. The prose pleased him. The dialogue sounded true to his ears. He searched for a remembered scene. It read well, as well as he hoped. He browsed deeper. A dapper middle-aged man in a black suit and bowler hat reached around him to pluck one copy of each from the rack. Terence turned, thrilled.

"You familiar with them?" the man asked, flapping the two books.

Terence nodded, overcome by shyness.

"I hear they're *very* well done," the man announced with confidence. "I read about them in *Time.* "

Terence nodded again. The man looked away.

"I want to read them. My son is gay."

"Think they'll help you understand?"

"I want to understand," he said intensely, blushing but frankly relieved to be talking about it. "The wife is taking it pretty well. I'm glad he told us. I just want him to be happy."

"If he's capable of happiness, he'll be happy. I'm gay. I'm very happy."

The man nodded curtly and thanked him. Pleased, Terence waited for him to leave before returning to the phone. The line was still busy.

He embraced a walk downtown. It was a beautiful day. There was plenty of time. He would stop at corner telephones along the way. Secreting his bag in a locker, he struggled against the stampeding horde, trying to be polite yet aggressively forceful with the same push. The quickenings he felt altered his route. Instead of going down Park Avenue, where the crowd would thin by Fortieth Street, he enthusiastically turned right and proceeded at a clip along Forty-second Street to Fifth Avenue.

By the time he reached Fifth, he was ready for the bins. There were far too many attractive people in shameless haste homeward. He projected their matching up with welcoming, adoring mates to form blissful cutout couples, holding hands and hugging a great deal, sitting down to fresh asparagus in magazine-spiffy plant-filled settings with a platoon of purring white Persians, tails erect and twitching at the joyous familial reunion. He hated them all for their smug, comfortable lives.

Crossing downtown against the light, he was shouted at by an angry cab driver. Frightened, he hastily maneuvered through the stalled honking traffic, nearing the curb as the light turned green and a cluster of obedient citizens sprang at him. He shrank back. He felt small, in great danger, like a tot lost in Macy's at Christmas. Spinning around, helped by the impetus of the dividing crowd, he searched for a taxi. He was crumbling, disintegrating from the rub of the throng.

One little yellow bus coming up, puh-lease!

He smiled, relaxing, loving Christopher's euphemism. A little yellow bus, indeed! For phrases like that one fell in love for a lifetime, he thought, stepping on feet and flailing out to regain the sidewalk. It was easy to make his way once he got a grip on himself. Was he not a city boy? He could deal. It was a skill one never lost, like riding a bike.

A stocky Italian man with a prominent nose hurried by, swiveled, turned back, and grabbed Terence by the arm. The man was shorter and wore a pea coat with a long red wool scarf that had a matching ball-top cap. "Terence!" he called happily. "What a surprise! How *are* you?"

"Joseph! I am fine. How are *you?*"

"Fine, *fine!* Haven't seen you in months. We've missed you. The meetings aren't the same without you. How are you doing?"

"OK. Some days are great."

"How's Chris?"

"I don't know. He says he's stopped drinking but I don't know. I'm on my way to see him now, I think."

"You're not living with him?"

"No."

"For today?"

"Right! For today."

"It's hard, I know. No one ever said it would be easy. If he's quit, great; if not, there's nothing you can do about it. Working hard on a new book for us?"

"Yes. It should be finished soon."

"I can't wait! Listen, Terence, I gotta run. I'm meeting Tony and I'm late already."

"How is he?"

"Great! It's his first anniversary tonight. We're having dinner with some friends to celebrate, then we're all going to Lenox Hill together. Can you join us?"

"Can't. I'm on my way to D.C."

"To visit Bobbi?"

"Yes. What a memory you've got!"

"When I care, I remember."

Joseph grabbed him. He kissed him on both cheeks. Terence was so moved he could not speak.

"Be good to yourself, Terence. And come back to us. We all miss you. We quote you all the time."

With a wave, he was gone. Terence stood astonished by the love he felt for the man. He had been going to meetings regularly upstate, once a week, sometimes twice. There was little anxiety or fear about Christopher but he had not eased up on his pursuit of sanity. He went for himself, to heal himself from the traumas of alcoholism, and to recover himself. He planned to go for the rest of his life. There were no graduates. He knew that when things were going well, it was the time to use the program's strength, the program's power; it was when he was calm and rational that revelations sparked growth, when courage was husbanded against the stressful times, husbanded against attacks of the crazies.

Terence dialed Christopher from a box in front of the' library. The phone rang but it was not answered. He landed a cab.

Tony's sober a year already.

He was delighted for him. So many of his friends had lovers or husbands or wives or parents or siblings who were now in recovery, dry *and* sober, in the program. He had witnessed their tears of joy when they shared the news. He had cried with many of them. He had watched them struggle with the new complications brought by sobriety. When the drinking stopped, all problems had not disappeared. Joseph had worked the program with a religious fervor and the results were evident from week to week. He knew his own health was the reward. Hope caressed him. He saw that projected army of contented couples, problem-free, as an insidious trap, a deadly game fostered by the crazies.

No one is problem-free, Kukla. Love does not work miracles. Love is not life's anodyne.

He wanted to resume living with Christopher. But Terence was not ready to live with anyone. He had gone away to live on his own, to prove to himself that he could live on his own. He had frittered away the last weeks fantasizing a life *à deux,* a life coupled with Morgan Connelly. Terence wanted to be serene. Not waiting, not watching, not expecting, but *happy.*

His heart spasmed as he sped downtown in an overheated taxi. He had no way of knowing what was going to develop. He could never fathom what was playing in Christopher's mind. It was accepting his own inability to understand what Christopher experienced in his alcoholism that helped Terence accept that he could not cure it.

I can't understand his disease. He can't understand mine. "You weren't sick," he said. He can't understand mine! *He doesn't know!*

How could he know? I always told him he *was the sick one. When they come into our meetings they don't know about their co-alcoholic responses. It's a difference in personality. Another part of the forest.*

The recognition shot its light into dark distances. Christopher could not fully understand him; Christopher could not make him whole.

It works both ways. Why do I need a deity for a lover? Because deity-lovers have access to the soul and guarantee omniscient nurturance, Kukla.

He had just learned he could not bestow saving grace, yet he still expected the gift from Christopher. No one had such power.

No human one. Welcome to the human race? You've got to do this for yourself.

Floating free, surrounded by choices, he was chilled by fear. Joseph's kisses warmed his cheeks.

You are not alone, Kukla. You are never alone.

He was a single, encased being, but like a leaf on a tree he was connected to others and a part of a greater whole. One's lover offered certain comforts; one's others offered the rest. To be whole, one must be separate. Separateness was not loneliness, as detachment was not indifference. It was a central fact of life.

Welcome to the human race!

Jumping out of the cab, he looked up at the lit windows. Rushing up the steep stone steps, he hoped Christopher was in.

Morgan Connelly glanced at his watch: seven on the dot. The Metroliner would be pulling out of Penn Station with Terence aboard. His own train was leaving Grand Central in ten minutes.

The week in the city had been productive. He approved the final cut of the Easter television special, hired a new young woman to augment his staff, agreed to be a guest lecturer at Cooper Union one day a week starting in the fall, and confirmed a trip to the Coast to conclude a deed for another feature film. He also had an enjoyable lunch with Judith; they discussed a new idea for a book. She had been extraordinarily perceptive and sensitive. She understood his need for absorbing work.

He had few doubts that his time with Terence was limited. The young man had resolved some major issues; one did not have to be telepathic. He was in passage when they met. They had moved together for a time; now Terence was edging away. A life was evolving that did not include Morgan Connelly, a life that perhaps excluded, for now, Christopher More as well.

Morgan was prepared. He was as ready as he ever would be. However, there was one thing that needed to be settled. He wanted a private, extended moment in which to say good-bye. Weeks before, Terence had suggested they share a few days in East Hampton. As soon as possible, Morgan intended to insist, perhaps demand, that they go there *now*. It was a talismanic gesture basic to his nature: Being Irish, he knew the value of ritual farewells.

———

At nineteen minutes to ten on the night of his death, William More's bottles ran dry.

The dragon wing of night o'er spreads the earth. . . .

He searched the holes where emergency supplies were stashed: inside the air conditioners, behind the bedside table's books, in the decorative salt and pepper shakers, in his antique Underwood, in his fancy leather briefcase, on the ledge up the flue, in his summer shoes, in the animals' traveling box, in the fridge's motorcase, but he had been careless, had not remembered emptying the bottles that if collected would fill a Christmas shopping bag.

Dominic was sequestered in the television room with the door tightly closed, engrossed—thank Christ!—in the Oscar telecast. He had met a nominee at one of Christopher's Halloween parties; now, waiting for the envelope, he could not have been more excited if she were his own sister. There was something wrenchingly beautiful about Dominic's simple, faithful nature. As William tiptoed past the door, having just checked the toilet tank, he knew he could not interrupt to ask for this particular favor. If he wanted something to help him sleep, he would have to get it himself.

The liquor store was gated at ten. He glanced at his watch: nine minutes to ten. The thought of no booze propelled him out of his panic and into the closet, where he stealthily slipped into a coat before silently sneaking out of the house.

The cold surprised him. It squeezed the breath from his lungs, made him lightheaded, and froze his lethargic senses; it made him unable to discern right from left. He slowly reckoned the store was left by the bright lights at the end of the block. His feet succumbed to frigid numbness. He looked down at the pavement. He assumed he stood ankle-deep in a puddle, but saw instead he had neglected to put on shoes. His green argyle socks gave no protection from the ice. He dared not risk going back into the house. There was no time to spare.

Lurching to the right, he stumbled a few yards. At the sound of the bank's clock marking the hour, he twisted himself around and, losing his balance, slipped to his knees in slush. He stared at his watch. He could not see the numbers. The residential street was deserted. He needed help. Why had he not telephoned for a delivery? He could have waited on the warm porch to catch the boy before the bell was rung.

Moaning, he clumsily raised himself. He straightened and stiffly shuffled toward the main avenue, flailing his arms in terror of the darkness as a hot stream of urine sluiced down his legs. Weeping, he prayed aloud that the liquor store would be open for him. Sometimes Mike was busy with the last loquacious customers. Sometimes he never noticed the time. Sometimes. . . .

He squinted at the shop across the avenue. It was still open! He could see glistening bottles displayed, aligned, waiting in the sun-bright windows, shimmering like molten light. He was blessed. His heart pounded with exultation. The quarts seemed afloat in exquisitely serene enchantment. He laughed, dazzled, spellbound by their epiphanous beauty.

He did not notice the red "Don't Walk" flashing on the opposite corner. He did not see the oncoming Riverdale bus. Arms outstretched, stumbling into the street like a gleeful toddler into the welcoming surf, William More felt slammed hard then violently sucked into the hollow of the wave. He gasped for

Dominic. The wheel beneath the driver's seat swiftly rolled over his head.

After the twentieth ring, Dominic set down the receiver. He had telephoned Terence immediately after trying Christopher but, again, there had been no answer. Maybe they were together someplace nice? Desperate and alone, he tried to claim a modicum of calm.

The two policemen who came to tell him were gentle and kind. Cards in William's wallet were their source of identification. Dominic had run into the bedroom to look for his friend. He had not heard him go out. He had assumed him in bed when at eleven he left the television to go to the bathroom and had not seen Billy asleep in his chair.

The two policemen waited patiently in the living room. They respectfully requested that he, or another friend, identify the body in the morning. They gave him a telephone number to call. Could it have been suicide? They could not find his shoes. Suicide would complicate things. Suicide was against the law.

"No . . . not suicide. Drunk. He was always drunk lately. He was going to Mike's for more. . . ."

How could he do this to me?

Yes, the bus driver had seen him weaving but thought he had stopped at the corner. It all added up, made sense, came together as death by misadventure. Sorry, but they had to ask.

Suicide? Should he tell them William had that week been forcibly retired? It was to take effect at the end of the term. Suicide? Would he commit suicide? Drunk. He was drunk. It was an accident. He was always drunk. Dominic warned him, but he refused to listen.

How could he do this to me?

When the police left, he wandered aimlessly around the house. It could not be true. He looked in the bedroom again. It had to be true. The police would never lie to him. He felt a flickering sense of relief, then a jolt of terror that caused him to tremble and moan out loud. Guilt and horror paralyzed him. What was he to do?

[314]

He called Father Jerome at the parish house. They had not spoken since their terrible altercation in the confessional. Citing the latest papal bull on homosexuality, Jerome had ordered Dominic to leave William, to end his life of sin or remain outside the Church's loving embrace. For twenty years, the priest had severely lectured him, citing William's shameful drunken behavior as proof of God's refusal to sanction the unnatural union; yet, for twenty years, he begrudgingly administered absolution because he had baptized Dominic and because he believed in the efficacy of grace. Then, suddenly, he could no longer in good conscience continue to do so.

When told of William's death, Father Jerome spoke at length of God's wrathful vengeance, adding that he was not surprised to hear of William's violent end. He conjectured suicide. He flatly refused to allow a Requiem Mass at Saint Mary Magdalen's. William had never been seen in the church; he was not a member of the parish; he had never supported the parish in any way. William was no better in the eyes of God than the drunken bums on the street, *worse* because he knew better, had a fine education, while they bore not the stain of disgusting perversion. The priest could not be blamed. He had warned them both by denying Dominic absolution. Many a prayer was offered for the salvation of their souls, in the hope that they would open themselves to God's forgiving love.

"Because William must burn in hell for all eternity does not mean, my son, that you must suffer the same fate."

"No matter where he is, Father, I want to be by his side."

"You people are beyond redemption," he sighed wearily.

Before ending the conversation, Father Jerome suggested Dominic call Defazzio's Funeral Home. He recommended the simplest possible casket and service; they would take care of everything. Dominic knew Saint Mary Magdalen's received a 10 percent commission on every referred customer. He wanted to ask if that constituted financial support for the parish but hung up in the middle of the priest's sales pitch.

Distraught, Dominic dialed his mother in California. Instantly recognizing his voice, she joyfully shouted his name, then wailed in disbelief as he stammered his message. Bounding into sorrow, she consoled him with melodic Italian phrases. His oldest brother joined the conversation on an extension and immediately wept, all the while shouting to his wife the reason for the call. Dominic heard his sister-in-law blaspheme in shock, then demand to know how it happened. Another extension was lifted. His nephew called his name.

Raising his free hand in supplication, Dominic begged them to help. He sobbed for William, clutching the telephone to his chest. The distant keening vibrated against his rib cage and echoed amid the devastation. He tumbled headlong into his loss.

"Goddamn you, William!" he screamed. "I loved you, Billy! *How could you do this to me?"*

His brother promised to take the next plane. If he, Dom, could get through the night, he would not be alone in the morning.

He hung up the phone. He called Christopher. Then he called Terence. He walked into the living room and sat on the floor next to William's chair. They had never spent a night apart since he moved in—how many years ago? What was he to do? How would he survive? Where was Billy now? Where had the police hidden his body? He picked up a slipper of William's and hugged it. Curling himself into a ball, he lay on his right side and cried himself to sleep.

"So? What did you do, Toddy?" Bobbi asked, concerned.

"I said 'sorry' and left."

"Sorry?"

Terence sipped hot tea as the clock struck midnight. The ride on the Metroliner had been a comfortable one physically; emotionally it was full of happy surprises. Things did fit. Opening his notebook, he found:

What complex blunderers we all are: how we're struck blind sometimes, and mad sometimes—and then, when our sight and our senses come back, how we have to set to work, and build up, little by little, bit by bit, the precious tilings we'd smashed to atoms without knowing it. Life's just a perpetual piecing together of broken bits.

The Reef, p. 313

We learn we cannot go on functioning as we have been, impulsively and automatically, if we hope to improve our lives.

ODAT, p. 155

For today he would continue to live alone. How would he do it? One day at a time. With the tools of the program. At meetings, he often talked about projecting disaster. Now he listened to himself: "For years I bought theater tickets for Christopher and me, then projected every possible misery: Would he get drunk and cut up rough? Would he disgrace me? Would we be eighty-sixed? I'd be sick with anxiety and fear and anger-in-advance: That *he* should be putting me through all of this madness! That *he* should be doing this to me! By the time our fun night arrived, I was demented. I couldn't wait for it to be over. Then, I would quickly forget the horror and start planning our next lovey-dovey outing. I'd buy theater tickets for Christopher and me. Talk about a sick merry-go-round! I did this year after year, until I learned at our meetings how the disease was setting me up. I stopped denying the illness. I stopped expecting him to do what he could not do: be sober after sundown. I learned *how* I got into trouble. I started going to the theater with friends, or alone. What did I want? Pretend Chris and I were the ideal couple, or live my life without anger and fear?"

I know what I want. I know how to do it. I want to be calm. I want to be serene. Then I can love wisely and well. When did this become so clear? Now, fella. Just broke through the surface. Taproots abound. Afraid. Natch. I'm a traveler who shouldn't be traveling. Fear is natural. Human. I'm human, remember? Nothing human is alien to me. Nothing wrong with feeling fear; it's being fear I'm to be wary of. It will come to me if I believe it will come to me.

"You said 'sorry' and left?" Bobbi repeated.

"What was I supposed to do? Help out in small ways?"

"Who was it?"

"One of Christopher's two or three hundred intimate friends. How should I know? It's all part of the illness."

"What do people usually do?"

"Say sorry and leave. Or go crazy and engage in the illness. I don't want to be demented with nubby gnashed teeth and bleeding gums. He's not doing anything to *me*. He's doing it to himself. Or, in this case, to someone else. . . ."

Bobbi snorted.

"I really believe," Terence continued, "that he's alcoholically insane. This has nothing to do with me. He's never sober anymore. If he's not shrieking into the telephone, he's looking for some stranger to rub up against. One drink and he leaps into the whirlwind."

"What will happen to him, Toddy?"

"I don't know! I pray he'll hit his bottom and go for help. I pray a lot for us both. I have hope. I love him. Sometimes, I just pray for hope. *I love him.* Sometimes, it's real hard. But as my friend Thomas says: 'If it isn't hard, it's not alcoholism.' "

"Want some of this?"

She offered a lit joint. He shook his head. For him, grass was not conducive to thought. It made him want to shed his clothes and boogey around the room; but, he enjoyed watching Bobbi get stoned. For her, it was only a sometime thing. She grew very intense and talked exclusively of Michele.

"Oh, my God!" Bobbi groaned, trying not to exhale. "He said 'sorry' and left!"

It rained torrentially the entire weekend. They sat huddled together on the couch talking over recent history for hours, listening to country and western music, and playing Scrabble.

"You're going back?"

"I love him. I want him."

"When?"

"I don't know yet. Not today."

"What if he . . . ?"

[318]

"Don't know. If he is, he is."

"You'll be OK?"

"I know what I want. I want to live with him. I love him. When I go back, I can no longer blame him for my being there. I see where he ends and where I begin. I'll work hard. I know how to do it now."

"Lots of meetings?"

"Uh-huh. Lots of talking it out and keeping a perspective on things. How are you doing?"

"I think it's the real thing."

"What about the pain, of breaking up? You always say you live alone because you couldn't face another crash."

"I did say that, didn't I? Dumb to live life that way. Davey and I talk a lot about projection."

Saturday, they lunched with her new friend, Michele. They talked together until Davey and Terence went to a meeting. Bobbi and Michele prepared dinner for the gang. At midnight, a group was formed to go dancing. Bobbi refused the offer, but everyone else, including an excited Terence, sped off to the disco floor. His place was mobbed, the music nearly too loud to be heard, and the dancing frenzied. For an hour, Terence was delighted, but the inability to talk and be heard, the crush of glazed-looking types, the posing, the hungry stares, the base narcissism and manic energy to score that kept everyone locked into a fantasizing self, filled him with a sense of displacement.

This is what I thought I was missing? Christo was cheating me out of this? Oy!

"Want to go home?" Michele signed.

"Uh-huh."

She had driven her own car for just such an emergency; Bobbi had asked her to keep an eye on him. When they reached home, Bobbi had a fresh pot of tea waiting for them and a mound of warm tollhouse cookies.

"Right on time!" she quipped as they walked in the door.

"Can't hear a thing. I'm deaf."

"It wears off. Nice, huh?"

"His face changed as he got crankier and crankier. You should have seen it!"

"I've seen it. Many times."

"I hated it."

"Your face *changed!*"

"Like Jekyll and Hyde, I know."

"Oh, *those* girls!" Bobbi laughed, causing Michele to pound the wall with glee. "Were they there, too?"

"It wasn't what I wanted. I expected everyone to be together, having *fun!*"

"In a *bar?* Toddy! The senior prom it is *not!*"

"If I stayed much longer, I would have killed myself."

"Probably you would have killed someone else. The crankier he got, the more the mean ones started hanging around."

"The place is too crowded. You couldn't dance!"

"That's the way they like it, dear. It's all they know. For many, it's all they want. Remember live and let live? Shut up and drink your tea," she commanded, sitting by him on the couch. Michele sat on his other side. Bobbi kissed his cheek. The two women smiled at one another, then laughed in secret harmony.

Sunday afternoon, the three friends toured the National Gallery of Art and the National Portrait Gallery and the Freer. After dinner, on the way to the train, they detoured so Terence could wave good-bye to the cherry blossoms.

William More's funeral was a quiet affair. There was no wake. A simple Low Mass was arranged by the college in the chapel. Over the closed casket, the chairman of the English Department spoke a short, moving eulogy, stressing William's loving nature and his generous gifts as an educator. His colleagues attended as well as several hundred students. Dominic sat in the front pew between his brother and sister-in-law. When the draped casket was carried from the altar to the hearse a city block away across the quadrangle, there were enough mourners to line both sides of the gravel path. Fourteen automobiles were listed to form the cortege.

Terence stood at the far end of the path. The image of Bill

lying inside the passing box sent him into tears. He sobbed aloud and sagged. Morgan touched his elbow. The two had sat at the rear of the chapel. Each time Terence twisted around to see if Christopher had entered, Morgan anxiously studied his face. The two had spent Monday and early Tuesday trying to locate Christopher. They had followed every lead in his much-tracked address book. Christopher had vanished.

Standing erect, not watching the casket slide into the hearse, Terence scanned the area. Fleetingly, he saw Christopher charging through the crowd bellowing for his father. Recognizing the re-enacted sequence from *Imitation of Life*, stripped of its umbrellas, horse-drawn hearse, and restraining cordon of police, Terence blinked it away.

My life is coming attractions. Can I function without a Moviola and film clips for a mind?

He invoked Christopher walking with dignity, riding beside and standing beside Dominic as William More, lover and father and friend, was buried. At the same moment, he wanted someone—still Christopher!—to bellow and blast the stillness. When would the world understand the ravages of alcoholism? How many more had to die? A scream spiraled up from deep inside his bowels. He was thrown off balance by his rage. Morgan took his arm and led him away.

"Are you all right?"

Terence nodded, then shook his head.

"You look like you're going to faint, Toddy."

From rage, Morgan, at our stupidity.

"I can't go to the grave."

"OK. Shall we go home?"

"I don't want to go home."

"Let's go to East Hampton for a few days."

"Morgan, I love you."

Morgan smiled. He put his arm around Terence's shoulders, pulling him against his side. The younger man leaned gratefully. They moved slowly through the dispersing crowd. No longer fused by the act of mourning, the crowd split into clusters, then divided again into chatting couples or single people on their way

[321]

to class. Morgan and Terence walked to the car, each intensely aware of his finite self. They clung to one another, drawing solace from every shared step.

Goodbye, pater. Rest in peace.

"My name is Christopher"—he paused before summing up, with a profound sense of relief—"and I'm an alcoholic." Taking a deep breath, he plunged. The men and women in the small church basement listened quietly. When he started to tell about missing his father's funeral that morning, tears choked him. He gasped, astonished by his weeping in front of these strangers. The tears would not stop. Chester, on his left, gripped his hand. Christopher tried to stop speaking, apologized, but continued, compelled to explain how it had happened without his meaning it to happen, how so many things had happened that way in the past few years. How many years? Years lost, years gone. Years over and done. Years not to be repeated.

Chester says no remorse. Remorse leads to the next drink.

He spoke to Chester in short, simple sentences until the entire story was clearly in front of himself. He heard his excuses, his rationales, his lies; he saw how they fell back upon themselves to nourish each other and suck away his life. He missed his father's funeral because he was holed up in a bed in a brownstone in Brooklyn with a millionaire friend who kept an endless supply flowing and had no one else to drink it with. There was no sex. Not even conversation. For three days and four nights they drank themselves into oblivion. He didn't remember any of it. He missed his father's funeral. And that was only the curtain raiser. . . .

"It's the end," he moaned. "I give up. I can't do any more of this. I feel so *sick.*"

There were no more words. Slumping forward, he groaned and pounded his head on the back of the empty seat. Chester clasped his shoulder and pulled him up. The woman to his right grasped his forearm and said, "You'll be OK now. You've come to the right place. Next step is a doctor, hon, to head off the DTs."

Another male voice, from behind, said gently, "I know what

you're going through, Christopher. I didn't know my mother was dead until a month after they buried her. It's small consolation but it could be worse. *You* could be dead."

"I wish I *were!*" he shouted.

"I don't believe you, Christopher. If you wanted to be dead, you wouldn't have come here. You'll see a lot of things at these meetings, but no corpses."

Everyone laughed. Christopher smiled.

He had found a note from Terence by the telephone in the empty apartment. It was too late to do anything but sit and stare out the window. Immediately, he'd opened the full-quart bottle borrowed from Brooklyn. In fifteen minutes he polished it off and fell asleep on the floor. Five hours later, conscious in the dusk, he was too wrecked to move. Overcome by bald terror, he crawled to the phone. He could think of no one to call after Terence did not answer. His telephone book was gone. The death of his father harrowed him. He vomited great silvery slugs of mucus all over himself. The trembles were building momentum. Trying to reach the bathroom, he blacked out, then snapped to with such violence that his neck muscles cramped, blocking his breathing.

Hysterical, he dialed 911. No one answered. In a fury, he dialed Operator and ordered her to connect him with these people. They would understand what was happening to him. They would know what he should do. They would get him help before the books started cutting up rough in his hallucinations.

Cracking up. Dying. . . dying . . dying. . . .

They sent Chester, who was a big man with a deep, soft voice, a pointed Adam's apple, and enormous hands and Mike, a smaller version. They offered chocolate bars, helped him wash, fed him coffee thick with sugar, and brought him to the meeting. Chester assured him these people would tell him what to do. By then he knew what he had to do.

He listened to the others. He understood what they were saying. He was comfortable and at peace with them. He had never believed he belonged in their midst. He always thought he was not like others. He had blotted out too many years warring to be unlike others, assiduously denying all affinities. Now, because he could not take one more step alone, he accepted a fraternal bond. How could he not? Everything they said clearly had his name on it!

He started to weep silently. The friends on both sides held him tightly. The comfort he found with them was overwhelming. These people did not drink any longer because they could not, not because they wanted to be good *or* wanted to be holy or even wanted to be loved, but because they could not continue to live and drink at the same time. They could not drink. *They would not drink.* One day at a time. It was over for them. One day at a time. They had stopped as he had to stop. It was over for him. He did not want to stop drinking. But he could no longer bear the havoc, the pillage, the annihilation. He had no control over himself. He had no control over his life. He had to stop. The only choice left was to stop. It was not a question of the fourth drink or the fifth. It was a question of survival.

My name is Christopher and I'm an *alcoholic.*

It was done. It was over. He had to live without it because he could not live with it. And he wanted to live. Why else was he here? Why else had he come home?

My name is Christopher and I'm an alcoholic.

Why had it taken him so long to understand? He had said it because it was true. Now it felt true because he had said it. With his very own breath, he had given it life and it had granted him freedom.

———

"The Ice Age ended in Mineola."

Terence spoke vaguely, in reverie, staring out at the Long Island Expressway from the passenger seat of Morgan's Mercedes. Morgan quizzically glanced at him: "What did you say?"

"The Ice Age. It ended in Mineola. . .not too far south of here."

"Was there a big bash?"

"A party?" Terence looked startled.

"Sure! A closing-night party. To strike the Ice-Age set and celebrate!"

They both laughed. The early spring day was beautiful. There was little traffic on the road. They were comfortable together. Laughter was easy.

"I *mean* part of the glacier stopped here, Morgan, up there somewhere. Which is why the north shore is hilly and rocky while my portion of the south fork is flat and smooth, although the terminal moraine struck about five miles from my house on the way to Sag Harbor. It's true, you know."

Change comes hard. More cheap metaphor, fella. They kept the conversation light until their first walk on the empty beach three hours later. The large wooden house was built on Further Lane with winter in mind, and was still surrounded by potato fields leased to local farmers. The two turned up the heat, built a fire, brewed a potful of tea and made fierce love, then, encased in bulky fishermen sweaters and blue stocking caps, headed for the shore. The sea was rough. It seemed in a desperate hurry, tumbling, rolling over, and shredding itself to reach the shore where they walked.

"I've always wanted a place here," Terence said, staring out to the horizon, a bold gray line against the heaving blue. "Chris says he can't work here. The sea separates consciousness from personality, he says; it eradicates the I. He's right. For me, that's why it's so calming. It's like eternity, and the surf is my allotment. I crave it. I think the Garden of Eden was the ocean and *that's* why I can't go home again! I can always use the big house."

"It's not the same as your own."

"No. It's not. I think I'll buy a house for me alone. And for Chris."

I've said it!

"That's a wonderful idea, Toddy."

Hurts less than I imagined. Because he's at my side?

"Morgan."

"I know, Toddy. I know. You don't have to explain."

"I love you *both*. And I've learned what I cannot do. But I still have a tendency to self-destruct. To *meld!* To become absorbed like this surf into the sand. But I'm getting better. I will be well."

"I know, Toddy. I understand."

The two stopped walking and embraced. They resumed

strolling arm in arm; the one had arrived at the sea's end, the other stood at the beginning of land. They moved together toward Amagansett, zigzagging to outline with their footprints the ocean's ragged, lacy hem. The detonating sound of the furling waves was an accompanying familiar.

"I wanted this time with you," Morgan confessed without shame. "It feels wonderful here. I'm glad we came."

Terence pulled free to sit on a piece of driftwood. Three yards back, he had not expected to cry. Suddenly a trembling seized his heart.

"Morgan, I love you. You know I love you. I love him. He and I had eleven years of loving as best we knew how. I want to try starting all over with him. Trying the new way. Dumping the past. I see my crazies so clearly now. They have nothing to do with him. I knew but now I *know.* I want to try again. I love him. I don't know what's going to happen. I have to trust myself. I'm not doing it alone; I have all the help I need. I have to trust him to find his way as I've had to find mine. He's as much a child of God as I am, Morgan. I will do it. I will live my own life with him *as he is.* I can't change him but I sure as hell can stop tormenting us both. I want to make a life with him. Things don't have to be the same. I'm not the same person I was. We'll have to discover each other all over again. He may not like the person I'm becoming . . . the person I *am.* "

"He'll love you. How could he not?"

"I love you, Morgan."

They sat until the sun began to set behind the dunes. The chilling dusk was deathly gray and blew a wispy, sliding mist eerily groping for them on the beach. They wended their way back to the house. Silently, they walked with arms linked.

They made love tirelessly throughout the night. While Terence slept, Morgan walked the beach awaiting the sun. The dawn looked like frigid gray water submerging the stars; the sea resembled undulating burial mounds. He trudged, defeated and ravaged by sorrow. Elaborately, the sun's swelling rim surfaced, changing the tremulous air from a dull, neutral element to animated, tawny iridescence, and the sea from ebony to coruscating silver. Alerted, the day awoke and fervidly embraced *him.* He saw plovers ride the high wind. He ached to join them.

He had done it. He had loved again. He had never thought it would happen, yet it had happened. Could it not happen again? There was no longer any reason to deny himself life. He had triumphed over death.

"*Morgan,*" he whispered aloud, possessing the light.

There's nothing left, kids, but to believe in reincarnation and carry on!'

Eating salami and sipping Earl Grey laced with clover honey, Christopher did not answer the phone. He sat immersed in Scott Fitzgerald, Mozart, and afternoon sun. Glancing up at the Pollock, he drew in sustenance from its spiritual beauty. He was feeling extremely fragile. The recent call from Chester to confirm their plans for dinner before the evening meeting had fortified and comforted him ("It's good to get calls."), but he did not want to talk with anyone else right now. It was cocktail time. He craved a smart Manhattan. He craved *anything* potent. Earl Grey tea, no matter how dark, no matter how sweet, tasted nothing like a Manhattan. He added another tablespoon of honey. He ate one straight.

They're right. Wonderful stuff. Like a hit.

The recommended doctor had prescribed five days of Ativan. Each day, Christopher reported for a vitamin B shot and careful monitoring of blood pressure and body temperature. The doctor suggested Antabus. Christopher hesitated—perhaps for added support when he started feeling stronger? When he started feeling he could handle a drink? Right now, he still recognized he could not drink. He sipped tea and attended to the explosion of emotions released by the absence of anesthetizing alcohol. His friends had warned him.

Don't panic. Twenty years of feelings. Uncorked geysers. Easy does it. You drink in response to feelings not because of them. OK.

Besides the three evening meetings that week, he had attended two afternoon ("matinees"), and was planning a two-a-day marathon for the next month, one day at a time. There was no denying the meetings helped. The compulsion to drink was still there, but it seemed like something outside himself—held at bay by the meetings. It was the people, really; the people were terrific. They told him that the program would eventually inform his life. He had serious doubts the simplistic jargon would ever be of value when this crisis passed. Chester warned that "smart" people were often the stupidest when confronted with basic truths; everything had to be complicated or was deemed worthless. Smart people had the most defenses to overcome, the most lives to shed. The simplest things were often the most difficult to grasp. In any case, it was the people for now. Christopher loved the people; they seemed to love him. And he could make them laugh.

The hardest thing is giving up the stories.

To his left, within easy reach, was a new address book in which he kept the meeting schedule, as well as the collected telephone numbers of the program people with whom he felt *simpatico,* the people with whom he most identified, and the people he found particularly attractive in one enviable way or another. A few were to be reckoned with; they were the ones with whom he could talk and be understood..

> *Since I grew tired of the chase*
> *And search; I learned to find;*
> *And since the wind blows in my face,*
> *I sail with every wind.*

———

Terence darling,

I have been sitting here at my desk thinking about you and Christopher and about Gerald and me. Something you said months ago has been haunting me. You said: "People don't save other people, Judith." I said I agreed with you, and who knows, darling, perhaps at that moment I did agree with you; but I find at *this* moment I am disagreeing with you so vehemently that I am writing you because I can't reach you by telephone and I must tell you or burst open. Christopher has stopped drinking and I am in love. I have finally met the man who is capable of saving me, darling, of making me feel secure and whole. I never *really* loved Gerald, Terence. That's why I was unable to effect any change in his life. Just knowing how much Tito loves me (and I him!!!) has given me the courage to admit to myself that I cannot continue living with Gerald. Tito has saved me from drowning in a sea of loveless despair. He is the "we" of me. (I can't resist using that because it is too apt, darling.) Tito understands me, Terence. As you understood Christopher once. All that is good in him you held in your hands. You *have* saved his art, Terence, and his life. Perhaps you deny the influence you once had because you feel guilty about no longer loving him? It's easy to give away what you no longer need. I know you care for him but do you *love* him? *In love,* as they say in Regency Romances? Love *does* make one of two halves. It heals all wounds. It's a primal force. It blesses us with true sight. Through Tito's eyes I see myself as I am. I *see* what must be done—to free myself. For him, I can do *anything.* He is my strength, my courage, and my reason for living. I don't know how we are going to manage to be together but we will do it somehow. Love will save us because we believe in its power. Like God, it only exists if you believe. Like fairies, too, but we *know* they exist, darling. Try and believe and it will help you to continue to help Christopher. Or maybe it will help you give Morgan the happiness he deserves. All this talk about Self worries me. It's 1982, darling. The me decade is closed. *Finito!* What good is a self without someone to give it to, to have and to hold, to cherish, etc? I'm a silly old woman, I know, but for the first time in my life I am in love (that sounds familiar too). I think we're only unique in our *love,* Terence. Love *is* health. Love is the only reason for staying alive. Love can make people well. Look at me!! I've never felt or looked better in my entire *vie.* I think this program of yours has you all turned around. I don't think we really exist until someone loves us. We aren't powerless over other people if we love them. *El amor brujo,* you know? Listen to the Latin soul. The French invented romantic love. The Americans invented est. You were the wise Titania Allgood *first,* darling. It's time to give love a try *again.* It is the answer to all of life's vicissitudes. What is life but a *carte de tendre?* Now that we've settled that, I'm going to use this to roll a joint and go back to work. Why did I ever throw away the key to my diary?

Terence buzzed the intercom. When there was no response, he let himself in and quickly climbed the stairs. He would pick up the things he wanted and leave. He would write a short note inviting Christopher to the country.

Terence and Morgan had returned from Long Island after lunch. Morgan went directly home; Terence went to visit Dominic. The visit was not a success. Dominic planned a move to California. Enraged and despondent, he had refused to consider joining Terence at a meeting; William was dead, there was no longer any need. Terence tried to explain that 85 percent of the people who lose their alcoholics hook up with another, that many people join the program after their mate dies: It was the place for Dominic to take his grief and his torment; it was the place where he would learn to forgive William who, though terminally ill, had tried to give what was left of himself; it was the place where he would learn to forgive himself for what he believed himself to be. Dominic was adamant. His fury at William for dying and ruining his life consumed him. It left Terence deeply shaken.

Yesterday I hated you, Christopher. Today I understand.

He could hear *The Marriage of Figaro* through their door. Panic grappled for his mind. He turned from it and reasoned: *I called before, he did not answer. He could be asleep. He could have popped out. He could be otherwise engaged. He could be in a bottle. He could be in the tub. Ring the bell. If he doesn't answer, you can decide what to do then. One minute at a time, please.* He rang the bell. When there was no response, he rang again. *If you use your key, you must take the*

[330]

responsibility for what you find, Kukla. Is it worth it? You won't know what's going on in there until you open the door, so don't go getting yourself in a state trying to figure it out. You can handle whatever it is. You can always say "sorry" and leave. Don't project. Discover. Is it worth it? You can leave. What do you want? I want to be calm. It isn't worth it. It's his home. I'll go have a bagel on Third Avenue. I can call later if I want.

"Come in!" Christopher shouted.

Nervously, Terence opened the door. The voice of Victoria de los Angeles filled the hallway as completely as sunlight filled the room. He stood straighter and smiled. "Chris?" he called hesitantly.

"Over here."

Terence saw the long body draped in a white caftan aglow with dazzling light. He smiled more broadly. He relaxed. Pleasurably, he took in his friend's bright, sober beauty.

"Are you alone?"

Christopher chuckled. "Why? You want to kiss me but you're afraid I just washed my hair? Or you afraid someone else might be hiding in this dress? Close the door."

The music, suddenly a presence again, united them. Both were eager to touch, to move together. Mozart defied disharmony.

"I was hoping we could have dinner together and talk, Chris. Do you want. . . ?"

"I can't tonight."

"Uh-huh."

Christopher grinned wickedly. "I have a date with Chester."

"Uh-huh."

Hmmmnn. I asked for it. Too bad. His loss.

Terence turned away. He noticed how ordered the room was. Surfaces were cleared and polished (*"You could powder your nose in that table!"*); the rug looked freshly vacuumed. Did Chester do windows? He was absorbed in detection. He missed what Christopher softly said. The words circled his head like dancing butterflies; they caught his attention despite himself. He looked in his friend's happy face.

"I've been going all week with Chester."

[331]

"Going all week?"

"That's what I said, bub. With Chester. For Christopher More."

Terence felt his surroundings lift like a stage set. He raised his eyebrows to mask his inchoate condition. He worked to arrange his face. He frowned as joy seared him.

"Are you going to cry, T.?"

Terence nodded. Christopher rose and bridged the void, swooping him into strong arms. Terence wept.

No Mahler. No Messianic choir. No Panavision 360 revolve. And I wasn't here! That makes sense. . . .

"Everything is going to be different from now on," Christopher reassured.

"Yes. Yes. I know. You will get well."

"It takes a long time. They say at least ninety-one days from start to beginning. I've been very ill. I'll make it."

"Yes. You will."

Ill. Not wicked. Thank you, God.

"It won't be easy. I've got a lot of work to do."

"Yes."

Me too.

"I think I know I can do it."

"Yes. You will."

Both can. Must leave him alone. Must do this on his own. He has his own recovery. I have mine. Can't make him well. Wait till I tell Thomas and Joseph and Rose Mary and Racelle . . .

"Then stop crying, *tesoro.*"

"Yes. I love you, Christo."

"I love you, too."

The floating world dimmed as the sun began to set. The two kissed. They turned to the windows to watch the light-show. Terence was flushed with gratitude. Christopher gossiped, not unkindly: Gerald and Judith were divorcing; Gerald planned to wed Cynthia Liveright's sister, Eleana.

"I've never even heard of her!" Terenee puzzled.

"She has, according to Andrew, the biggest tits and the tiniest brain in Fairfield County."

"How's Judith?"

"In great shape! In love! When she called to offer her condolences, I told her my *good* news. All she said was, Terence will be so pleased! She didn't ask how it was for me."

"What did you say?"

"I said, you and I will *both* be very happy, thank you very much."

Will we both *be very happy? Later. Not now. Yes!*

They laughed, holding one another tightly. Terence again began to weep. It was a miracle. He did not understand any of it. He overflowed with gratitude. Christopher lovingly scolded, then squeezed with all his strength.

"I've been afraid to ask anyone. I've been waiting for you to come home. How were pater's obsequies?"

Terence briefly described the service, answering the few questions. Christopher did not want details. In time, he promised, they would come back to it. Terence gave an outline of Dominic's plans, then fell silent.

"Are you staying with me tonight, T.?"

"No."

No? No, you are not! *meeting and country, Kukla.*

"Why not?"

"I have to be alone for a while."

"I need you now."

"Uh-huh."

I know. I can feel it No! *What you feel is your own need for him. Watch it! Get out of his head!*

"I feel so alone, T."

"But I'm here with you,"

"That's true. I guess I'm projecting."

"You got it, stranger."

They laughed.

"What about Morgan?"

"I love him. I did with him what I did with you: *attach* with need. I want time alone to think and finish my book. Then I'm coming home."

Christopher hugged him, kissed him, and laughed loudly. "When? How long?"

"At least three months."

Ninety-one days from start to beginning. One way to stay out of it, nosy.

"Will you be in the country?"

"No. I'm moving to East Hampton until I finish the book. I think I'll go to England."

"You hate traveling alone."

"How do you know? How do I know? I've never done it! I feel comfortable about England. England's an old friend. It's important for me to move around on my own. I want to do it but keep it as simple as possible. Maybe you can join me there and we can revisit Tintagel. Who knows? We'll see. When I finish my book, you can take me out to dinner *someplace nice*. We'll talk."

"I *might!* I will take you out to dinner. I've been on the horn begging for piecework. I've called them all. It's amazing how many don't want to know me. I can't think about it. I will pay the rent. I will feed myself. I owe Bernice plane fare. I owe Angelo a decent book. I will feed that cat of ours when you drop him here. *And* I just opened the phone bill! It almost made me drink. I want to write them and explain I've been ill: suffering from the black cord disease!"

They laughed and kissed seriously. An hour later, when Terence rounded the corner, he glanced back up at the apartment. Christopher stood in the tall center window. He blew Terence a kiss. Terence waved and smiled. He strode a distance, then slackened his pace as the old abyss dropped open with the precision of that stage trap door. He stalled, ostensibly captured by daffodils queerly resembling silent-movie telephones. His fear was no alien bloom. Pulling a deep breath, he seized the courage to charge. Closing his eyes, he dropped to the rim of the black hole, the source of the rising flood of anxiety. Bravely but warily he peered over the scraggly edge. His mind focused, clearing sensory static. Zooming in, he sighted his awed self, his captive self, magnificently small, a compact parcel of sentient clay collected for an instant to blindly ride earth's epicycle. Terence Strange, startled visitor, orbiting a lucent yellow star, lacking invitations to go elsewhere just yet. It had to be and be it would, nicely. If he tumbled ass overtop into the taunting abyss, he would be welcomed by his own loving *self* and guided back up to this extended twilight, to this one luminous moment of spring's eternal nascency. Was it ever so? Of course.

Home is where the self is, friend. Call yourself. You're always in. Listen and learn.

A sonnet of Christopher's steadied his feet.

> *Sir, in my heart there was a kind of fighting*
> *That would not let me sleep—till night came day*
> *Till morning turned me you, the grey time lighting*
> *Passages the like and length away*
> *From me myself alone I never knew*
> *The measure of no less the time to go.*
> *And now the long and likely seem past due*
> *And in my heart a kind of truce I know*
> *The reason for, the place and time to be,*
> *The company to keep the shore to land,*
> *The one to follow and to lead, to see*
> *To and to find by ear, by sight and hand .*
> *I must to England you know that, and why;*
> *For morning turned me you when you were I.*

Terence filled his lungs with the warming air. Malachite trees glistened behind the spiked black-iron fence; stirred by a breeze, a purple flowering limb performed benedictions and shooed him away. He turned and quickened his pace again. He would not fall. Not he. Not Terence Strange. He would not fall now. He would leap. He would bound up into the dark. He would fly higher and higher until swept into infinity by the flow of the solar winds.

This is it. My one, my only life. No perpetuity. Flame I am assuredly. *A sunspot. A wave. So much to learn. So much to give. To take.* Now! *Tune in today, Terence now, and tomorrow and tomorrow, one comfortable day at a time until fade-out. Until burnout. Until. . . yes!* I will!

AFTERWORD

"Memory is the basis of individual personality...."
                    –Miguel de Unamuno, Tragic Sense of Life

You thought that it would be a piece
of cake, but it turned out to be a slice
of life....
                    –Tim Dlugos, Rego Park, Entre Nous

Memory will lay its hand
And you will understand
My hatred.
                    –Gwendolyn Bennett, Hatred (1926)

"Don't ever tell anybody anything. If you do, you start
missing everybody."
                    –J. D. Salinger, The Catcher in the Rye

I have never been able to talk about, never mind write publicly about, what happened to me after the publication of this book in 1982. A few years ago, I did a podcast with Sarah MacLean, a bestselling romance novelist and a keen advocate of my *Gaywyck* (1980), as the book, a classic to her, that proved genres have no gender. When I began to recount why it took me so long to publish *Vadriel Vail* (2001)—the second volume of my proposed *Gaywyck* trilogy (now a quartet)—I choked up and could not continue without a pause in the recording; then I glided over my having gone off on a tangent after being silenced and incapacitated by my not unusual experience with AIDS.

In 2023, the ground-breaking gay editor Michael Denneny read from his autobiography at Politics and Prose in Washington, D.C; he choked up when he reached the Eighties; and paused before he could continue. I choked up with him. I decided that my memories would have to remain stashed away in my diaries safely stowed in the Yale Beinecke Archive with all the rest of my papers, a space I share with my life-companion James McCourt, with whom I also share a 60th anniversary this year, 2025.

Revisiting this book after four decades, I am happily surprised by how funny it is; by how the narrative zips along very engagingly; and by how profoundly moving it is—complete with bursts of tears as the main character, Terence Strange, comes to terms with what the disease of alcoholism has done to his life, he being the "other victim" of the family disease, so called because a "disease" is simply something with symptoms. (Nothing complicated or metaphysical about that medical fact.) It is his beloved Christopher More whose compulsive drinking has made their lives unmanageable until Terence is graced with the courage to change. I had many, "Who wrote this?" moments!

In their emotionally charged Introduction to this edition, Eileen Myles lovingly describes 1982, when the novel is set, as "a moment just before everything happened and I'm thinking of AIDS and a lot of technology that's invisible now…." Encountering that mention of AIDS, my PTSD, my trauma, walloped me; but five years of intense analysis calmed me enough to rationally consider writing a detached—ho, ho, ho!--Afterword to this edition in which the terrifying acronym does not rear it historical head despite its having been a part of my life since 1980 and the publication of *Gaywyck*.

Gaywyck, my first published novel, was a big hit, in part because of Amistad Maupin's very funny, very appropriate review of my serious parody of the classic romances: novels, movies, songs, poems, honoring the Gothic novel's form but giving it a happy ending, and stealing famous lines from everywhere, lines spoken by women; his last line was "Read the sonofabitch, you'll love it!" Well, many people obeyed. And many people loved it, indeed; and many people wrote me from everywhere, and one boy called in the middle of the night from Out There in America's Heartless Land to tell me from a phone booth that he had discovered the book in his local A&P because many book vendors did not look closely at the brilliant cover, which is a standard Gothic Romance image but with two men! He had looked at what he saw. I was in the phone book: He wanted to know if it is true that two men could love each other and make a life with each other because he was in love with his gym teacher and was planning suicide until he found *Gaywyck*.

(Years later, I was at a party given by the celebrated poet James Merrill (1926-1995)—he died of AIDS but kept it under wraps even from his autobiography—when he smiled at me and mumbled with a chagrinned look the theme song of many hefty poets admitting a dirty secret, "iloveyourbook." His creative work and life partner David Jackson was standing beside him; he announced very loudly, "Your great book saved my nephew's life!" It was another version of my night caller's tale of salvation via the enduring love of Robert & Donough Gaylord. During the rest of the evening, others fessed up.)

After Maupin, a call came from The Advocate asking me to do a phone interview. I said I was going to California and would love to come to San Francisco where swell people put flowers in their hair. A date and time were set. I was told it would be short because the interviewer was eager but unwell. Turned out, he was one of the first diagnosed with what was then "the gay cancer." We talked until he was forced to leave for a hospice by the friends who were packing up his home around us. Then in L.A, Jimmy and I stayed with a friend who had been with us at Yale Grad School of Drama; Joanie had three gay male roomies. One Saturday night, they were raucously preparing for a night out in gay bars bantering for bathroom time to douche. During the next few years, all three died of AIDS.

My treasured friend Susan Sontag's "time's relentless melt" comes into play here. My memory is kaleidoscopic, fragmented, lacking historical reckoning. I've a visual memory; I had a major publishing career because of my ability to "store" images—that and my common sense! —while Jimmy has a stunning verbal memory = my go to for salvaging the "when" in our co-joined lives.

I have nothing but a heartbreaking muddle surrounding me and AIDS. I confessed this to my editor for this current edition with a reprint press, Tom Cardamone; he advised me to "name names," because I was writing about our queer history and my experience was as fragile as memory and as short lived. Names brought memories attached to them. I decided not to add dates unless they were available on Google because they had a public persona in our community. It was a start. It defanged my memory police.

In the summer of 2023, I received an email via my Authors Guild website from Anya and Friends in Moscow. Its header is: Our letter of Gratitude for '*Gaywyck.*' Naturally, I responded to their emotional outpouring of love for my book and for *Vadriel Vail*. My response increased the group to over 800 "queers"— as they identify themselves—from Russia to Armenia, Serbia, Thailand, Georgia, Kazakhstan, Poland Ukraine Germany, Belarus and the UK.

They regularly send me long emails and wonderful art works based on the books with entries from many, many people who are in every profession and range from 17 to 78. Our Zoom calls will have over 80 participants. We talk about everything, including their lives as "terrorists not yet punishable by death," and one called these meetings a "group therapy session" while another christened me the founder of gay liberation in Russia, etc. They have taken the last words from *Gaywyck* as their motto: "our love endures."

It was during the most recent Zoom call that I talked about my struggling with this Afterword. I spoke openly, tearlessly fluid, naming names; their fascination with the epidemic and their basic questions about the disease—it's the same here—assured me it was time for me to do the work as it is meant to be done or shut up forever—to paraphrase Martha Graham.

Well, it was never and obviously never will be "a piece of cake." Tim Dlugos (1950 – 1990) had my number when he gave me an inscribed copy of his *Entre Nous* in 1982, the year he thrust a copy of this newly published book into the arms of our mutual friend Tom Carey and demanded he read it immediately. Tim was another one of those, "iloveyourbook" poets: he called me over in an inexpensive, loved Ukrainian restaurant on Second Avenue in the East Village and mumbled his congrats and sincere blessings.

I look at his dates and stop cold.

I know there is no safe cartographic passage through my mishuganah memory's minefields. Pick a subject. Any subject. Growing up gay in the Fifties on Long Island? Sexual molestation during my 8th grade physical for Catholic school. The Catholic Church provoking a nervous breakdown in my Eighth Grade spirit for engaging in a love affair with a fellow male student. HUAC. AIDS and Reagan/Thatcher. It was the poem by Gwendolyn Bennet that gave me the apposite word: Hatred. Indeed, I have worked hard to liberate myself from it. (I cling to the words of the Roman playwright Terence, "I am human; therefore, I am indifferent to nothing done by humans." Fuck!)

I want to try to enter the AIDS memory realm indirectly: at the beginning before it entered my life directly. It's 1964 in New Haven. Jimmy, my brilliant, flamboyant classmate, is having a party to introduce us to one of his best friends, Richard "Dixie" Mahar—the nickname was an unmistakable clarion call; he brought a giant kielbasa in his suitcase and with it came hysterical adolescent ad-libs about his fortunate traveling companion.

Remember, this is 1964, please, and the past has a future we never expect. It is conservative Yale with no political demonstrations yet. I have not been to a gay bar, and most of my classmates are equally naïve = when Dixie shows us snaps of himself in Callas Tosca drag, Joanie—a fellow New Yorker— drags me into an abandoned bedroom confused to tears as to why men would want to dress as women. Yes, youngsters, Hartley's "The past is a foreign country; they do things differently there," is damn true; just like the idea of two men building a life together was outa' sight in 1982.

Dixie's roommate, Stephen Pearlman, had a particular musical genius. He mixed live performances by great classical artists to produce perfect discs for the major classical labels. He once created a diva's voice that none of the demented opera queens, including Jimmy, gathered in his music room in Brooklyn could identify because he fashioned his own whistling into a human voice! Years later, at another Dixie-Stephen gathering, he sat opposite me. He winked at me and reported in a loud whisper how the previous night he had been fucked by 11 men at the Baths, had the most sublime night of his life, and wanted me to join him asap. Intrigued by the visual images suddenly in my soup bowl, I leaned forward for more dirt. Suddenly, I was lifted from my seat by my collar, and shuffled out the door by Jimmy, no stranger to those Baths, saying loudly, "Say goodnight, Gracie!" Several years after Dixie died of a lung disease, Stephen and his new wealthy partner died of AIDS, despite a blood transfusion machine installed in their Connecticut country home.

That same '64 Yale Yule, Jimmy took me to a NYC party at his longtime friend, Richard Greene's vast apartment, which he had sublet via his broker dad who could not sell it at the time. Vast. Like 15 rooms. On a tour with Jimmy, we discovered in an empty room a naked young man hoisted onto an ironing board being noisily blown by an older, fully clothed man. A group was cooking dinner for a good-sized crowd. I gave my new Yaley friend an Xmas gift: a Zippo lighter that I had engraved in Tiffany's with nary a blink there: JIM / YALE YULE / '64 / VIN. (I'm holding it now. For our 25th anniversary, he gave me a Tiffany silver salver: VIN / YALE 25 YULE / JIM, now on my laptop.)

Richard Greene became one my staunchest friends and allies in a gay world riven with gossip and envy. When J and I were living in "Swinging London," from 1965 to 1972 with a two-year NYC intermission, he was working there as a solicitor; when we returned to NYC, we were homeless yet spent only one night on his couch in an upper west side brownstone because he brought home a trick and, naked, they walked through the living room to reach the bathroom for their many "golden showers." After years shared with him and other friends at musical events, the last time I saw him--meeting him AIDS-ridden often—J & I were on the #1 uptown subway going to the NYCB and there he was literally clinging to a pole, an emaciated, facially scarred with purple blotches, barely recognizable man with a cane. He detrained before we could greet him. That image of him haunts my NYC subway. There are others who, with Richard, traverse my place-memory with the grace of light, in the way Proust's famous madeleine regains lost time for him.

In 1975, I was fired by The New York Review of Books where I was the typesetter. It was where I met Susan Sontag, a major player in our lives. The official cause for my being axed was theft of petty cash. (I still love it: I was fired for whistleblowing, the first of 2x I achieved that honor.) Unemployment = the East End of Long Island for over 2 decades of summers and one decade of winters. After the first one in Shinnecock Hills, East Hampton became our home during what I call "B.C., before computers," when the livin' was easy and being buck naked on the empty beach Monday to Friday was bliss. I began *Gaywyck* the summer of '75 when J's Mawrdew Czgowchwz—of which Sontag is godmother—brought him a fan letter from the genuine Maria Callas!

Another summer in East Hampton, we were invited to a dinner party where we met David McIntosh. The Gay Center, as it was then known, was established in 1983 and David, a fellow writer, was working on the garden there. He was young and vibrant and so very lovely. After dinner, he went into the living room and fell asleep on the couch in front of a wood fire. Slowly and quietly, we joined him in front of the fire where we all sat in communal silence. I was told he was ill with AIDS. His sleeping peacefully, trustingly on the couch is an image that surfaces every time I visit "his" garden.

I love to dance. Every Thursday in East Hampton for a decade, I danced with my pal Mary Ings at the Attic. Tom Carey once described my disco doings as "Snoopy's Dance of Life." Well, J does not dance. "Mawrdew," as his myriad "girlfriends" called him—when we left for London, one gave him an overnight bag with a short, red, frilly "nightie"—would go to dish the dirt and drink. On a dance night at the Palladium, one of his most brilliant schoolmates and a producer of Holly Woodlawn, a pal of ours, in *Broken Goddess*, Bill "Geeze" Corley told him in his exaggerated, campy New York accent: "One daren't kiss one's dearest sister these days not knowing where her mouth has just been!" The joy of rimming had become a horror scenario with amoebic dysentery savaging weakened immune systems; the powerful antibiotics used to treat the ravaging invaders was equally dangerous and did not help Geeze in his battle with AIDS. Years later, J had coffee with Geeze's cousin in an uptown diner with their mutual friend sharing the table in his urn.

A NYT journalist wanted to meet Jimmy. He asked Edmund White to give a dinner party and introduce them. That dinner party introduced us to John Purcell, with whom Ed was living at the time. John was a classic beauty, an art student who had studied in Florence, and a brilliant young man in need of a job. I was a freelance picture editor, the only one in NY publishing, who researched, edited, designed, and captioned photo inserts in nonfiction trade books. My mentor, Michael Korda, editor-in-chief of Simon & Schuster, gave me an office in the editorial department. I had lots of work in 1983. (Eventually 163 books for all the major NY publishing houses.)

From the get-go, I knew John was special. Turned out, he had a great eye, and I could trust him to help me research; editors bought my eye and everyone else with whom I tried working did not succeed. He was also a rip. He would smile at men in the building's revolving door, and they would miss their exit; he would smile at drivers as we crossed the street, and they would miss their light. One night, he went to some fashion extravaganza and the next day he called me from an island off the coast of North Carolina to tell me he was staying in a house called "Gaywyck" and would I talk to the guy who had flown him there in his private jet to confirm he really knew me?

Jimmy and I treasured him. When he fell ill with AIDS, we lost touch with him. He went to Paris with Ed. Years later, on a holiday there, we saw him approaching us on the sidewalk. I promptly began to faint at the sight of his ravaged beauty. Luckily, we were in front of a café. I plopped myself in a chair and bent over to get the blood to my head pretending to be tying my shoelace. I regrouped because I love him and wanted to be with him for what I knew would be the last time.

Enter "The Fainting." My analyst told me I was having the correct response: people were being devoured by a bodysnatching, deforming retrovirus. (Left over from ancient infections, some millions of years old before humans existed, they jump around our genome. Some remain alive, like the bubonic plague virus and can cause diseases our immune system can fail to detect!) Being a loving witness was beyond me no matter how hard I tried even after full analysis for five years, a grueling exploration of my traumas: The imprint of my mother's agoraphobia is incalculable. AIDS made the world unsafe for me.

This book, as well as *Gaywyck*, led to a barrage of requests from readers, many in recovery programs to sign books for their loved ones—lovers, sons, fathers, brothers, cousins, uncles, colleagues, neighbors, friends. Wanting to be of service and supportive any way I could, I began visiting hospitals along with J: he was on a mission to give succor; he always stayed until death arrived in hospitals or on "flight decks," as we called the mental wards. (His great AIDS novel, *Time Remaining* (1993), is reprinted by this imprint now.)

One of my many recovery program meetings was a men's gay group. We met every Friday evening at St. Vincent's. (I preferred mixed meetings, but a close friend, Joe, was regular at this one and I became very established there, too. We queers were something else!) There were 14 of us regulars. Each week, 10 would go for pizza before the Everhard Baths. Joe and I went to a local bar to have a beer to remind ourselves that we did not have a drinking problem! Over the years, 9 our friends who happily cavorted at the Baths, died of AIDS.

From my first hospital visit, I realized it was not the piece of cake I expected since I'm a natural care giver. On one early visit, the dying young man was a dancer with NYCB, a company I revere. (It is said: "Beauty is the only form of spirit that our eyes can see.") The room was full of "Apollo's Angels"—Jennifer Homans' name for dancers; the contrast between them and their shriveled dying colleague full of tubes shattered me for days. I could not leave the house. For me, reality is a hard task master.

Only Joseph Conrad's, "The horror! The horror!" at the climax of his novella *Heart of Darkness*, with all its dramatic force, sums it up for us survivors.

(When I was an undergraduate, I wanted to be a psychiatrist.

My studies led me to visiting a mental hospital and after each dramatic interaction with a patient, which happened to me always, I would come down with conjunctivitis or "pink eye." I would bitch to my supervisor about my penchant for "cheap metaphor." With AIDS, I graduated with more direct methods of self-communication: Instead of blurring my vision, I totally erased it.)

The second time J discovered me on a gurney in a hallway put paid to my Ms. Nightengale performance. I had devised a method of not dropping on top of the patient in his bed: I would go into the room's toilet and lower my head to the bowel's cold porcelain rim, regroup my weak forces, then skedaddle after hasty kisses all 'round. I would normally be able to sit in the closest stairwell with my head lowered with deep breaths until I could walk home or cab it.

I tried attending wakes; seeing the decimated, heavily made-up remains in an open casket sent me reeling home. Memorial services filled our calendars. Yes, their emotional wallop enervated me. So, I was walloped. Big deal! I was alive and living happily with the man I loved more profoundly than ever blessed with Gratitude, with a capital "G."

I marched in the NYC streets to ease my Hatred for the world at large. I was invited by Larry Kramer to attend the founding meetings of the GMHC. I wanted us to talk about what alcoholism was doing to our communal health and our ability to practice "safe sex," but Larry had the focus of the possessed and rightly was not interested in anything that would divert from the central message: Silence = Death.

I withdrew into my joyous publishing career; and, for snatched weeks in East Hampton I was lost for a decade in a LONG heavily researched historical novel about a great 19th-century straight actress with a very gay colleague in Ireland then the USA—and the Civil War like Fannie Kemble—which our devoted agent Elaine Markson, who after receiving 33 rejections for *Gaywyck* because no one wanted a gay romance, especially gay people, or wouldn't there be a line of them? She submitted Theatricals to a friend at Knopf, who had rejected this gay novel = "Tell Vincent that most people are not as interested in the theater as he is!" I withdrew the book. Fortuitously, I fell in love with The Princess de Cleves. *Vadriel Vail* was born, along with the other *Gaywyck* books, which took many more years with my five drafts of everything. For me, their world in Gramercy Park was a safe, nurturing place.

There are too many dark memories. After weeks of working on this short essay, I declared "BASTA!" Then today, we saw octopus salad. Voila! Enter a light-hearted memory. Though always the villain in movies, the wonder of them grabbed me after a Godzilla-sized one attacks a submarine 20,000 Leagues down under in the movies. I was gob-smacked by its accepting such a challenge! No one could invent such a warrior! Then, there was a spate of bestselling books + a great Netflix, Oscar winning, documentary, My Octopus Teacher = I learned a lot more about this brilliant eight-limbed mollusk.

Did you know they have a brain in each arm, all operating separately but able to work in concert; they can shape-shift, change color, and use camouflage to make themselves invisible? I once joked with Jimmy that we gay people have a great deal in common with them. He laughed, yet did agree when I added after Stonewall—where he was! And after AIDS brought us all together, our diverse, unique gay community worked in concert, too. Silly? Yup, but it delights me for the mollusks, too, live lives of calculation and endeavor and learning and watching and remembering and trying new ways to solve old problems.

Alcoholism kills a sense of humor. Living with death kills its last abstraction. AIDS defeated me, as had alcoholism. With AIDS, however, the only help was my analyst, Jack Burlison. I accepted my powerlessness over AIDS, then a disease with no recovery. Unlike alcoholism, there was no Hope. (Despite successful meds, for millions today, there is still no Hope.) As Emily Dickinson imagined: Hope is the thing with feathers. With those fluffed feathers, those of us blessed with serenity and courage, both states of grace, can learn to fly to a safe place where health can be restored, recovered co-joined love can prosper and profoundly endure one precious, irreplaceable day at a time....

VINCENT VIRGA is the author of the first gay gothic romance, *Gaywyck* 1980) with a happy ending, as well as *A Comfortable Corner* (1982) and *Vadriel Vail* (2001). Virga is the only person in NYC publishing who researches, edits, designs, & captions picture inserts for nonfiction books; he has done 163 books. He also spent over two decades working with the Curators at the Library of Congress on 29 books. He is experiencing a renaissance with all his fiction returning to print, including two unpublished *Gaywyck* books completing the *Gaywyck Quartet*. His life-companion since 1964 is the fellow writer James McCourt. Their papers are held at Yale's Beinecke Rare Book & Manuscript Library. Virga also co-founded a museum in Co. Mayo, Ireland. They live in Manhattan and Enniscoe House in Mayo.

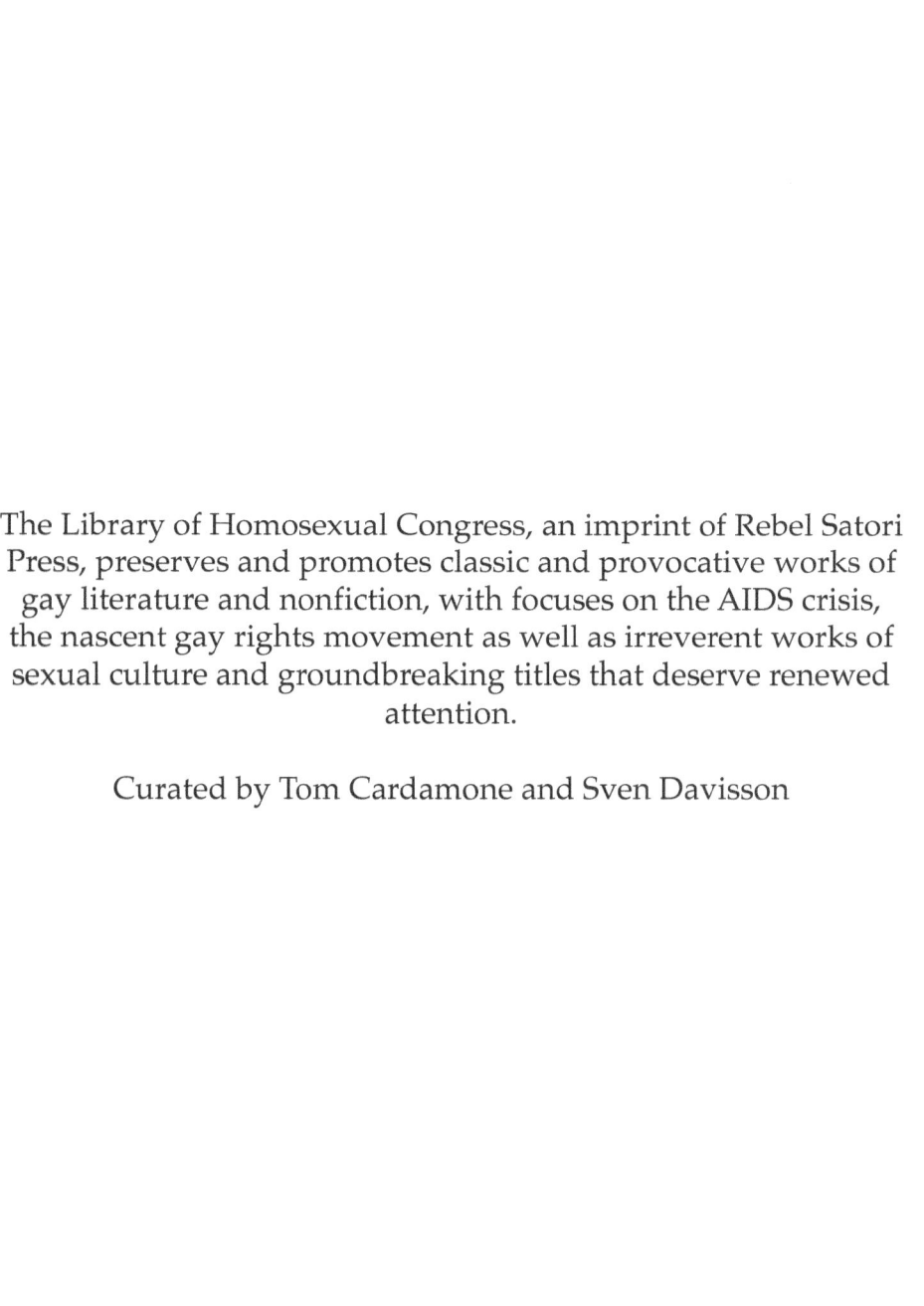

The Library of Homosexual Congress, an imprint of Rebel Satori Press, preserves and promotes classic and provocative works of gay literature and nonfiction, with focuses on the AIDS crisis, the nascent gay rights movement as well as irreverent works of sexual culture and groundbreaking titles that deserve renewed attention.

Curated by Tom Cardamone and Sven Davisson

www.ingramcontent.com/pod-product-compliance
Lightning Source LLC
Chambersburg PA
CBHW020421030726
47495CB00006B/1616